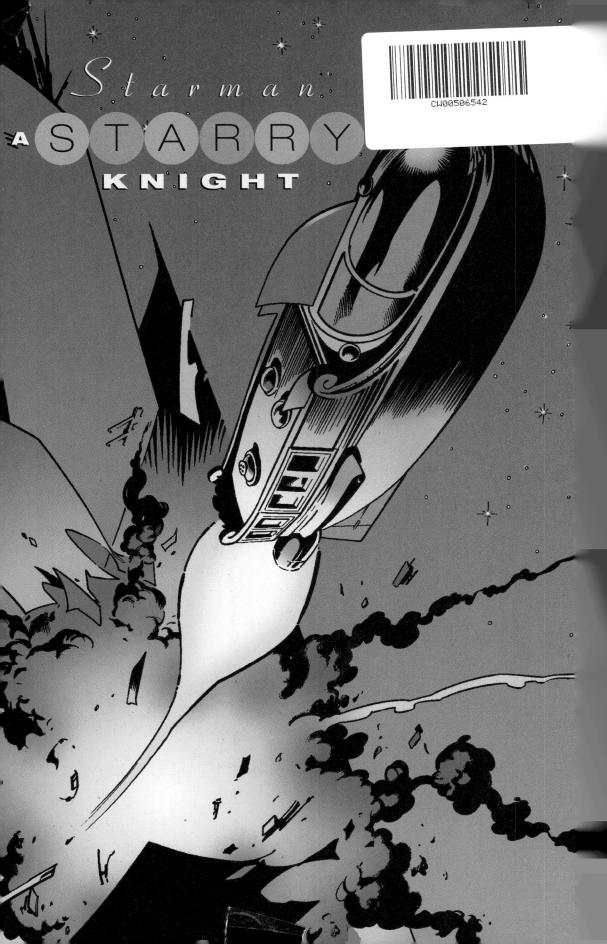

Starman

A STARRY

KNIGHT

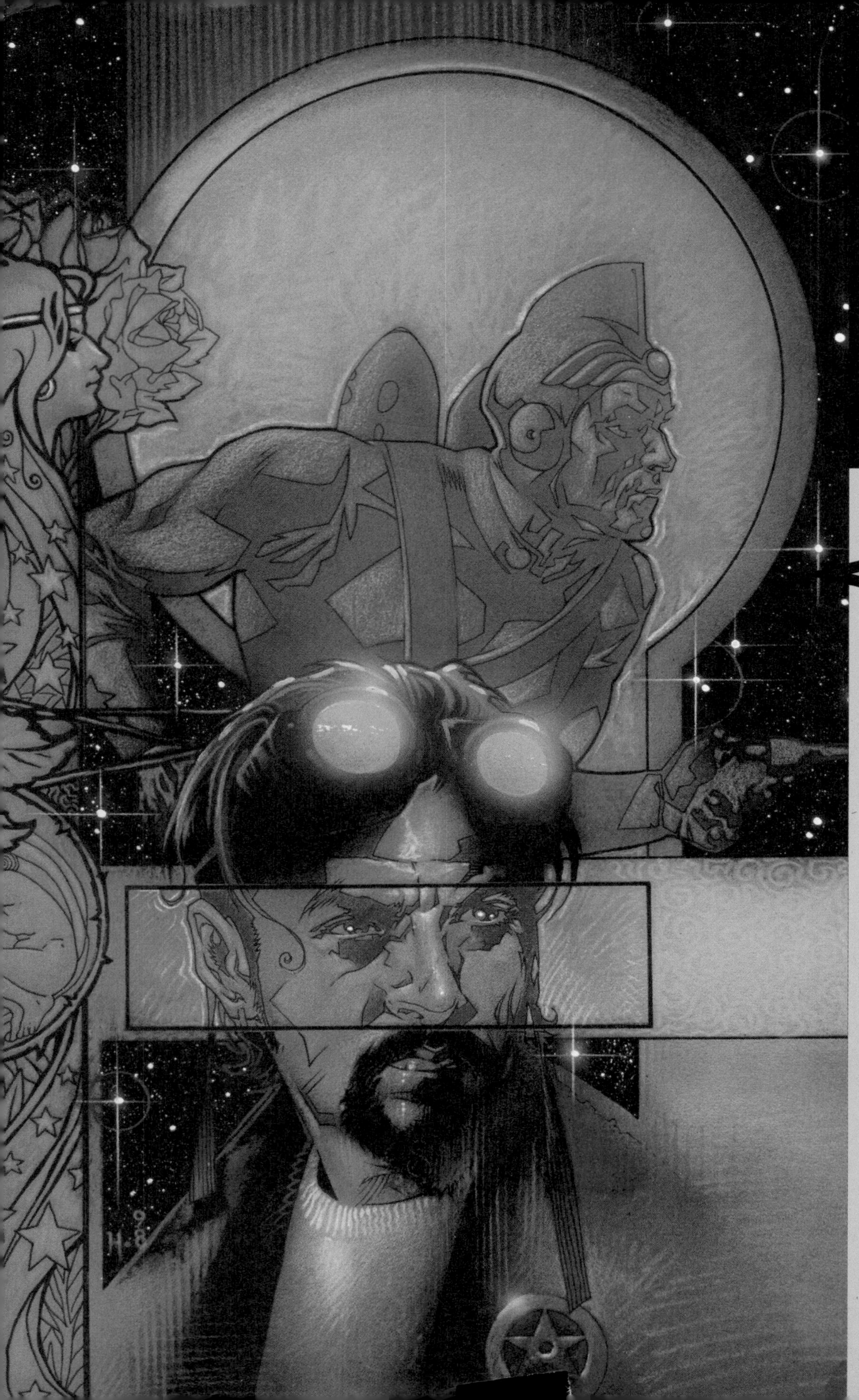

Starman

A STARRY KNIGHT

James Robinson
David Goyer
Writers

Peter Snejbjerg
Steve Yeowell
Pencillers

Wade von Grawbadger
Keith Champagne
Steve Yeowell
Inkers

Gregory Wright
John Kalisz
Colorists

Bill Oakley
Letterer

Tony Harris
Original Covers

Jack Knight created by
James Robinson
& Tony Harris

STARMAN: A STARRY KNIGHT

Published by DC Comics.
Cover, introduction and compilation
copyright © 2002 DC Comics.
All Rights Reserved.

Originally published in single magazine
form as STARMAN 47-53.
Copyright © 1998, 1999 DC Comics.
All Rights Reserved.
All characters, their distinctive likenesses
and related indicia featured in this
publication are trademarks
of DC Comics.
The stories, characters, and incidents
featured in this publication are
entirely fictional.

DC Comics, 1700 Broadway,
New York, NY 10019
A division of Warner Bros. –
An AOL Time Warner Company
Printed in Canada. First Printing.
ISBN: 1-56389-797-0
Cover illustration by Tony Harris.

Everyone has a favorite hero.

We find a human element we can relate to, acts of heroism we aspire to, and amazing powers and abilities we wish we possessed.

Jack Knight has these in spades.

And we have James Robinson and a slew of brilliant artists to thank for that.

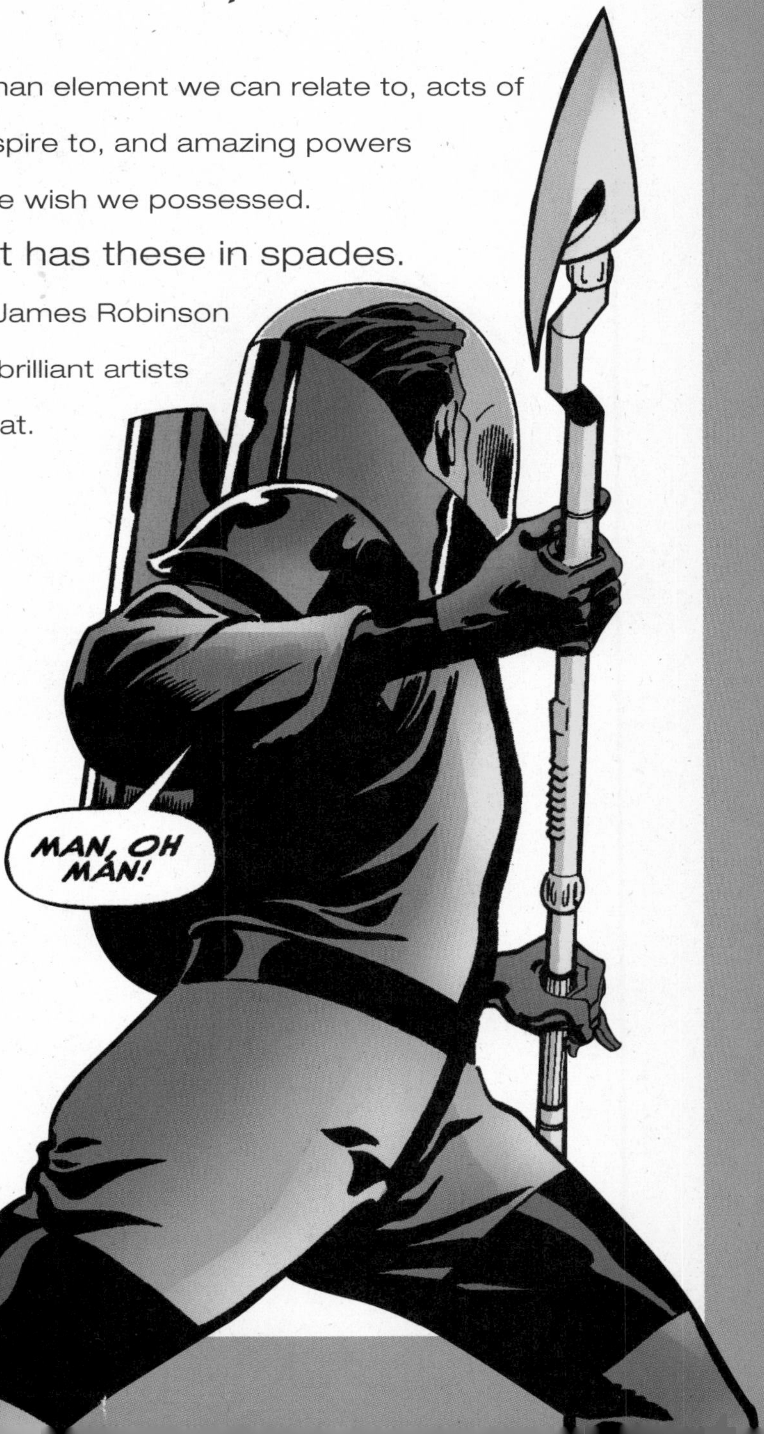
MAN, OH MAN!

In fact, anyone who's a fan of the classic Golden Age heroes owes James a lot. Without him, I have no doubt that the JSA would still be battling it out in limbo, kept hidden from today's comics audience.

During the mid '90s, at the height of revamping and reintroducing past heroes (since everything, and unfortunately anything, was selling), STARMAN hit the stands. Among all the knives and guns, shoulder pads and line-filled art, Jack Knight looked somewhat out of place. There were no "Bad Girl" pinups or brutal vigilantism. Just a regular guy flying around in his jacket and sneakers. A guy who would rather see a screening of Browning's *Freaks* than put on a cape and stop crime.

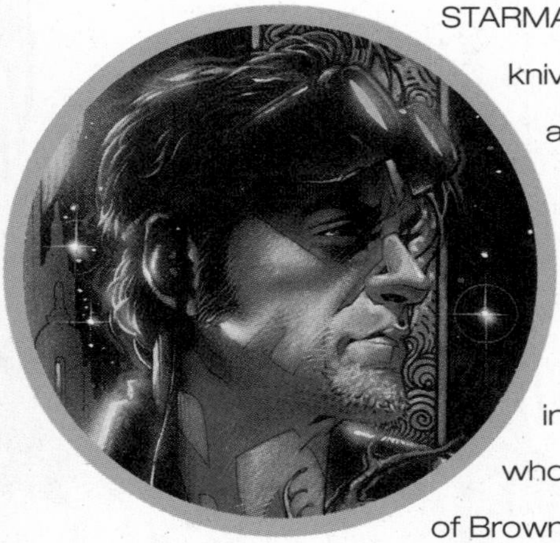

But it worked. It totally worked. While most of the gun-toting anti-heroes and bad girls faded away, Jack Knight had become an instant classic.

And to a lot of readers, Starman had become "the" favorite hero.

So what about this book was different from the slew of others that quickly disappeared? Why has Jack Knight not only survived, but also attracted a legion of fans and garnered endless critical acclaim?

Simple. James Robinson knows how to make a hero. And he knows how to make characters.

James has the special ability to reach into an older concept and find the diamond in the rough. Without throwing away what's gone before, James takes that diamond in the rough and polishes it, adding his own intricate, faceted design work along the way, adding levels of humanity, joy and sorrow.

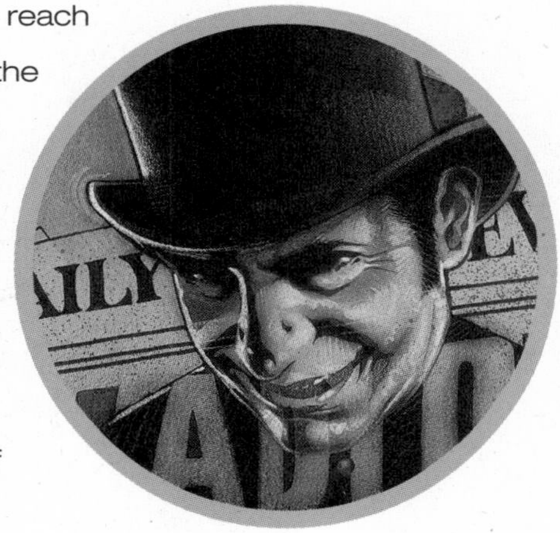

And although STARMAN is very respectful of the past, it isn't locked in stasis by it. Opal City was created and populated by James. And he makes it look so easy, damn him. Yet, how many writers could transform those rare and obscure heroes and villains, like Mikaal and the Shade, into such complex and engaging characters? It comes from his instinctive storytelling ability and his passion for comic-book heroes.

Within the first half of A STARRY KNIGHT, we're treated to a fantastic journey through time and space. Mikaal, Star Boy, the Shade, Adam Strange, Jor-El (yep, Superman's dad), Will Payton and a killer named Solomon Grundy all get a chance to shine.

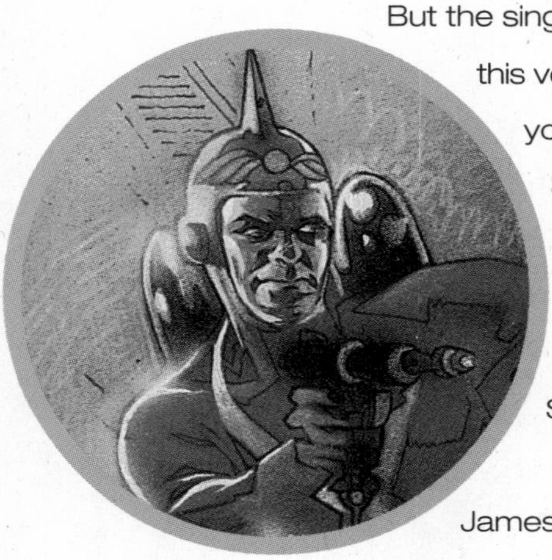

But the single best element you'll find in this volume? The one that just shows you how original and human Starman is... Jack's motivation for heading into space... which you'll find out soon enough.

So who's *my* favorite hero?

James Robinson, of course.

Geoff Johns

July 2001

Geoff currently writes *The Flash, JSA* and *Hawkman* (with James Robinson) for DC Comics. He also writes and produces in Hollywood, where he's lived for the last five years... but he still misses Detroit.

Starman
A STARRY
KNIGHT

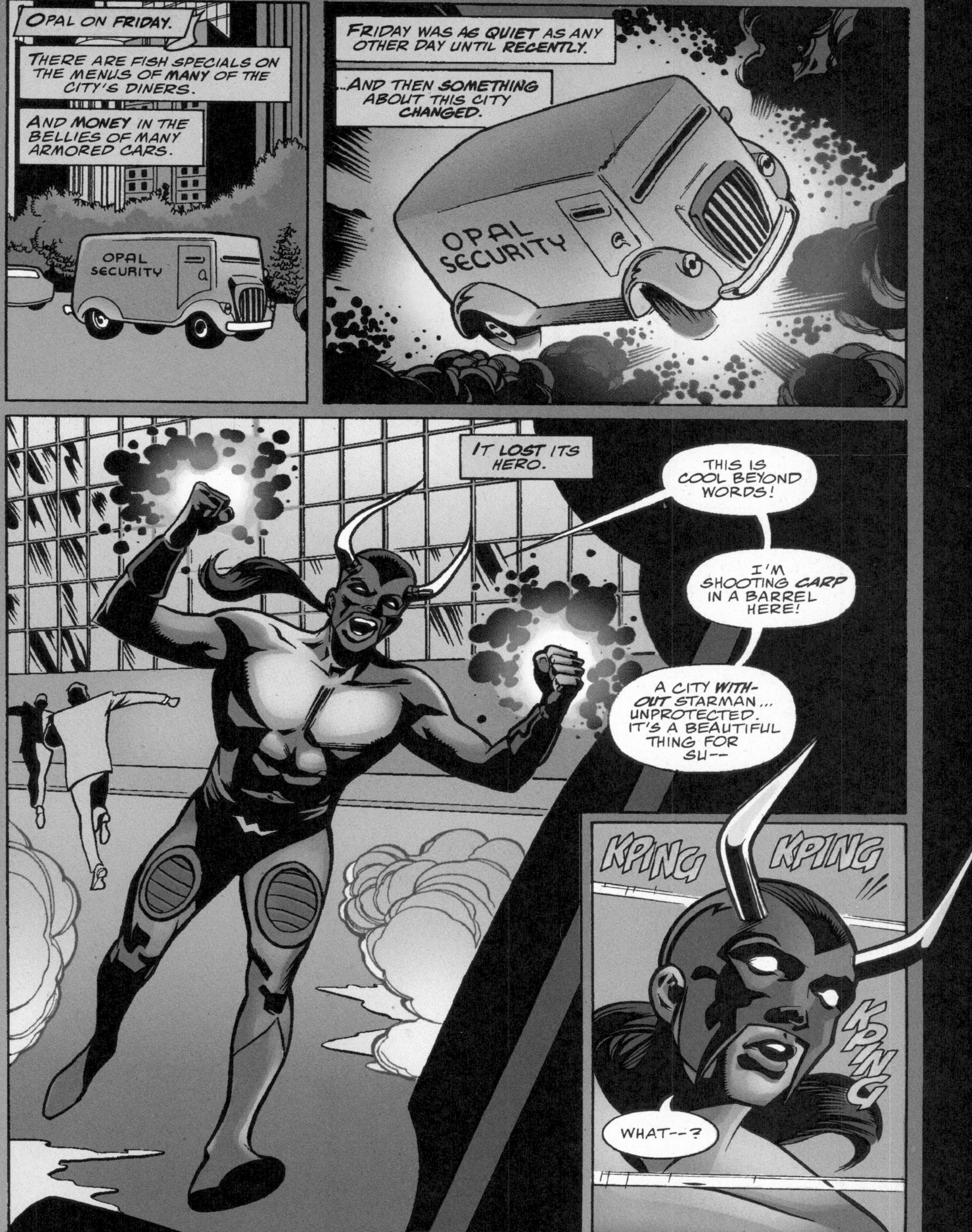
OPAL ON FRIDAY.
THERE ARE FISH SPECIALS ON THE MENUS OF MANY OF THE CITY'S DINERS.
AND MONEY IN THE BELLIES OF MANY ARMORED CARS.
OPAL SECURITY
FRIDAY WAS AS QUIET AS ANY OTHER DAY UNTIL RECENTLY.
...AND THEN SOMETHING ABOUT THIS CITY CHANGED.
OPAL SECURITY
IT LOST ITS HERO.
THIS IS COOL BEYOND WORDS!
I'M SHOOTING CARP IN A BARREL HERE!
A CITY WITH-OUT STARMAN... UNPROTECTED. IT'S A BEAUTIFUL THING FOR SU--
KPING
KPING
KPING
WHAT--?

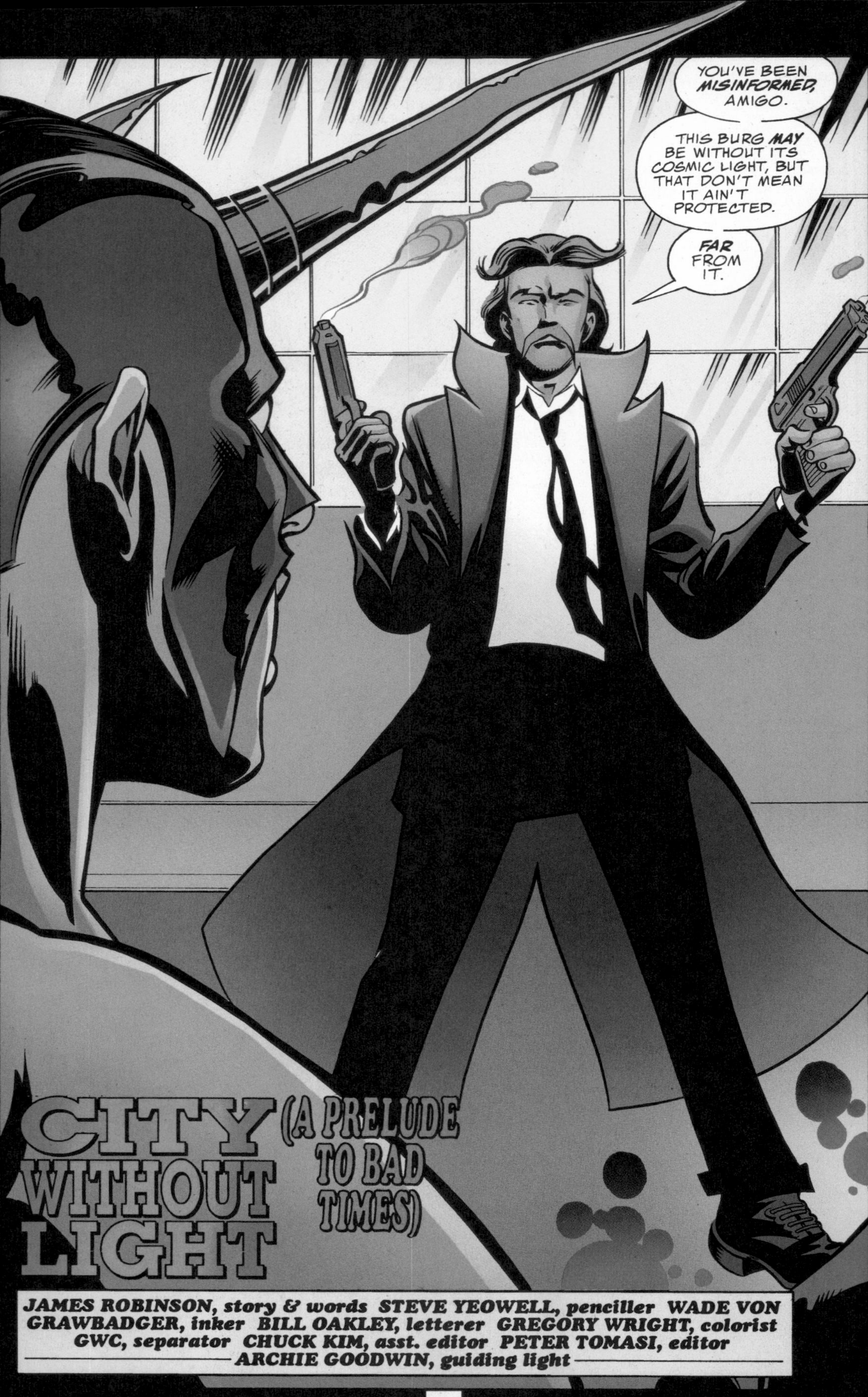
YOU'VE BEEN MISINFORMED, AMIGO.
THIS BURG MAY BE WITHOUT ITS COSMIC LIGHT, BUT THAT DON'T MEAN IT AIN'T PROTECTED.
FAR FROM IT.
CITY WITHOUT LIGHT (A PRELUDE TO BAD TIMES)
JAMES ROBINSON, story & words STEVE YEOWELL, penciller WADE VON GRAWBADGER, inker BILL OAKLEY, letterer GREGORY WRIGHT, colorist GWC, separator CHUCK KIM, asst. editor PETER TOMASI, editor
ARCHIE GOODWIN, guiding light

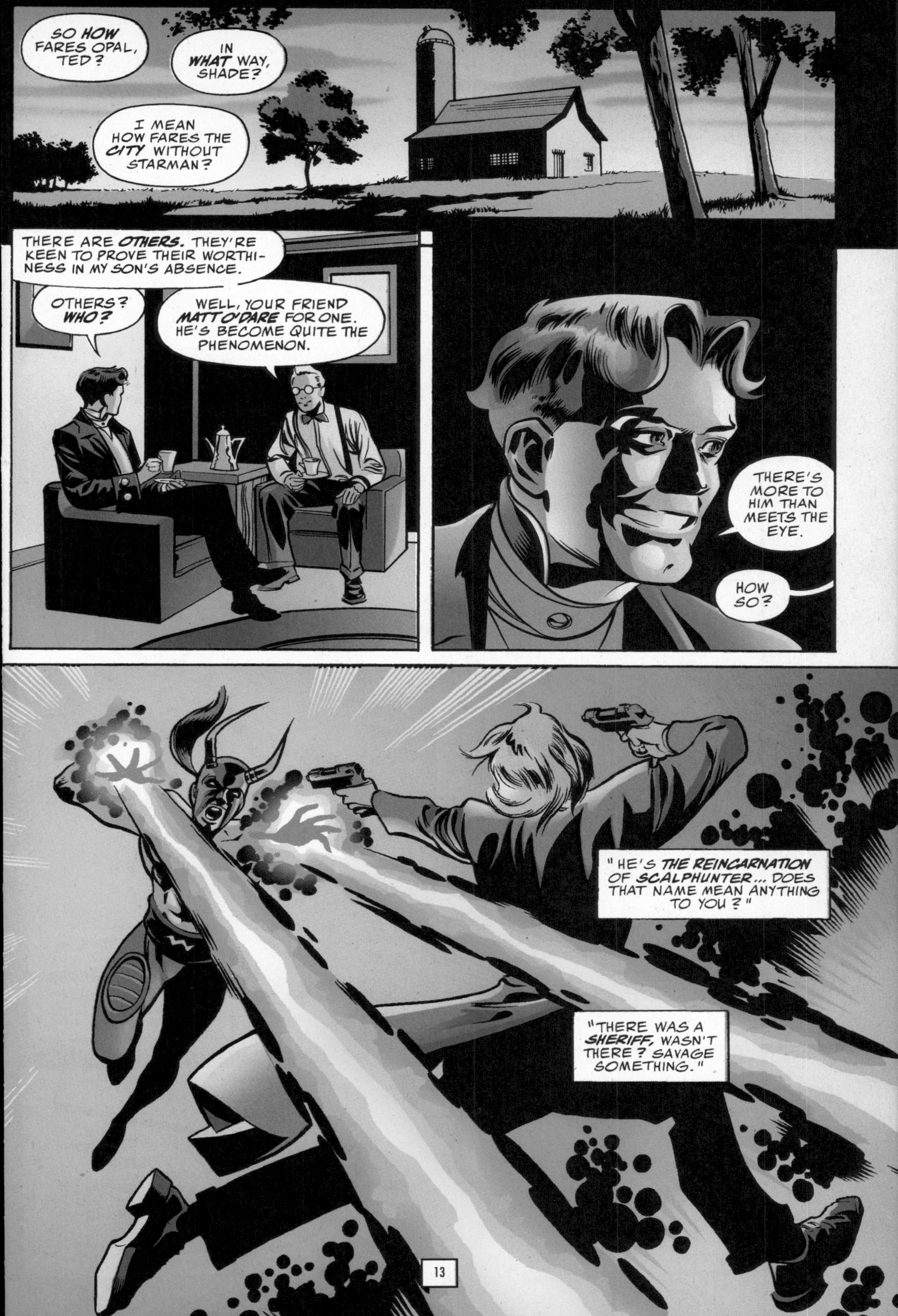
SO HOW FARES OPAL, TED?
IN WHAT WAY, SHADE?
I MEAN HOW FARES THE CITY WITHOUT STARMAN?
THERE ARE OTHERS. THEY'RE KEEN TO PROVE THEIR WORTHINESS IN MY SON'S ABSENCE.
OTHERS? WHO?
WELL, YOUR FRIEND MATT O'DARE FOR ONE. HE'S BECOME QUITE THE PHENOMENON.
THERE'S MORE TO HIM THAN MEETS THE EYE.
HOW SO?
"HE'S THE REINCARNATION OF SCALPHUNTER... DOES THAT NAME MEAN ANYTHING TO YOU?"
"THERE WAS A SHERIFF, WASN'T THERE? SAVAGE SOMETHING."

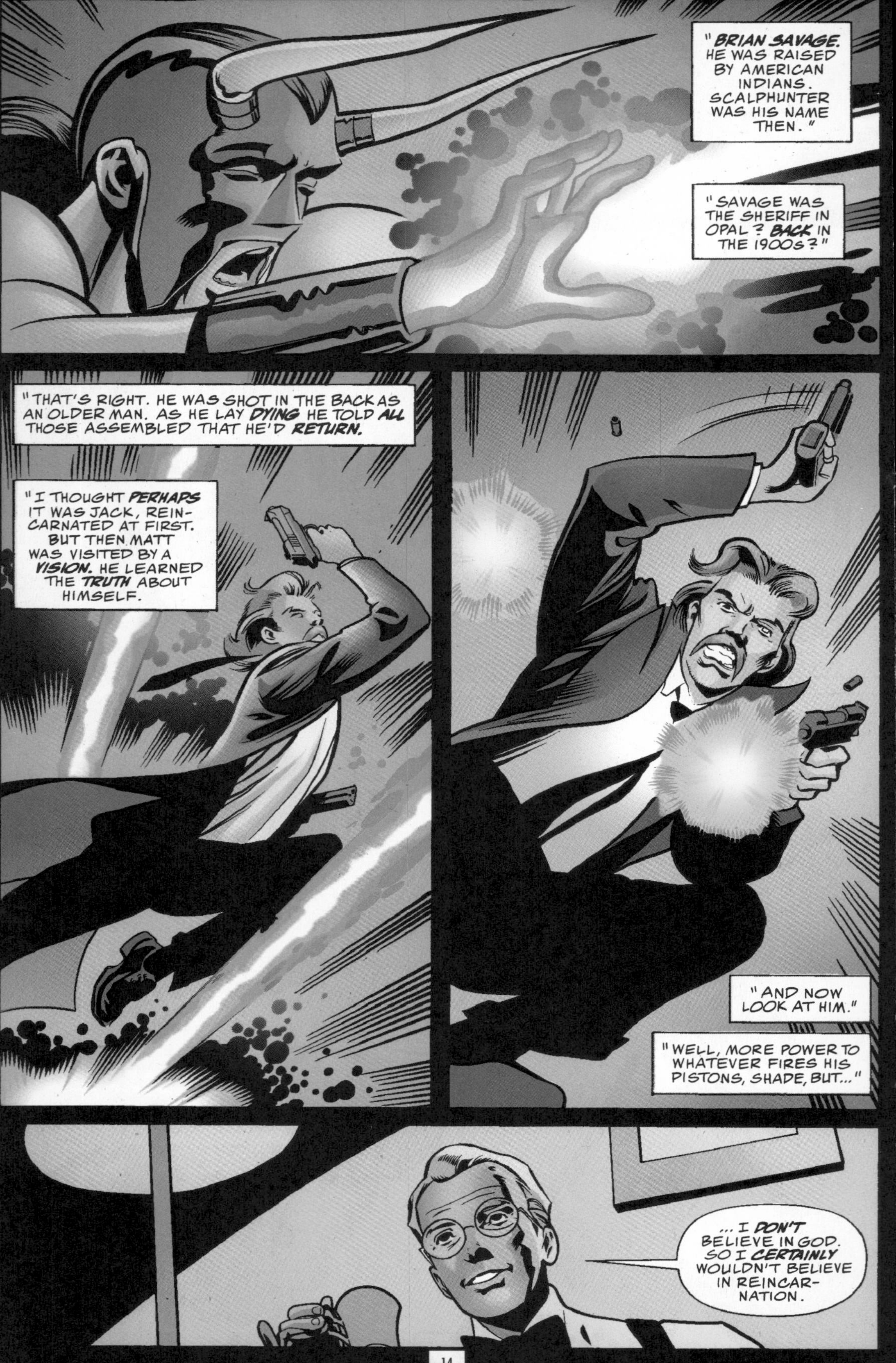
"BRIAN SAVAGE. HE WAS RAISED BY AMERICAN INDIANS. SCALPHUNTER WAS HIS NAME THEN."
"SAVAGE WAS THE SHERIFF IN OPAL? BACK IN THE 1900s?"
"THAT'S RIGHT. HE WAS SHOT IN THE BACK AS AN OLDER MAN. AS HE LAY DYING HE TOLD ALL THOSE ASSEMBLED THAT HE'D RETURN.
"I THOUGHT PERHAPS IT WAS JACK, REINCARNATED AT FIRST. BUT THEN MATT WAS VISITED BY A VISION. HE LEARNED THE TRUTH ABOUT HIMSELF.
"AND NOW LOOK AT HIM."
"WELL, MORE POWER TO WHATEVER FIRES HIS PISTONS, SHADE, BUT..."
...I DON'T BELIEVE IN GOD. SO I CERTAINLY WOULDN'T BELIEVE IN REINCARNATION.

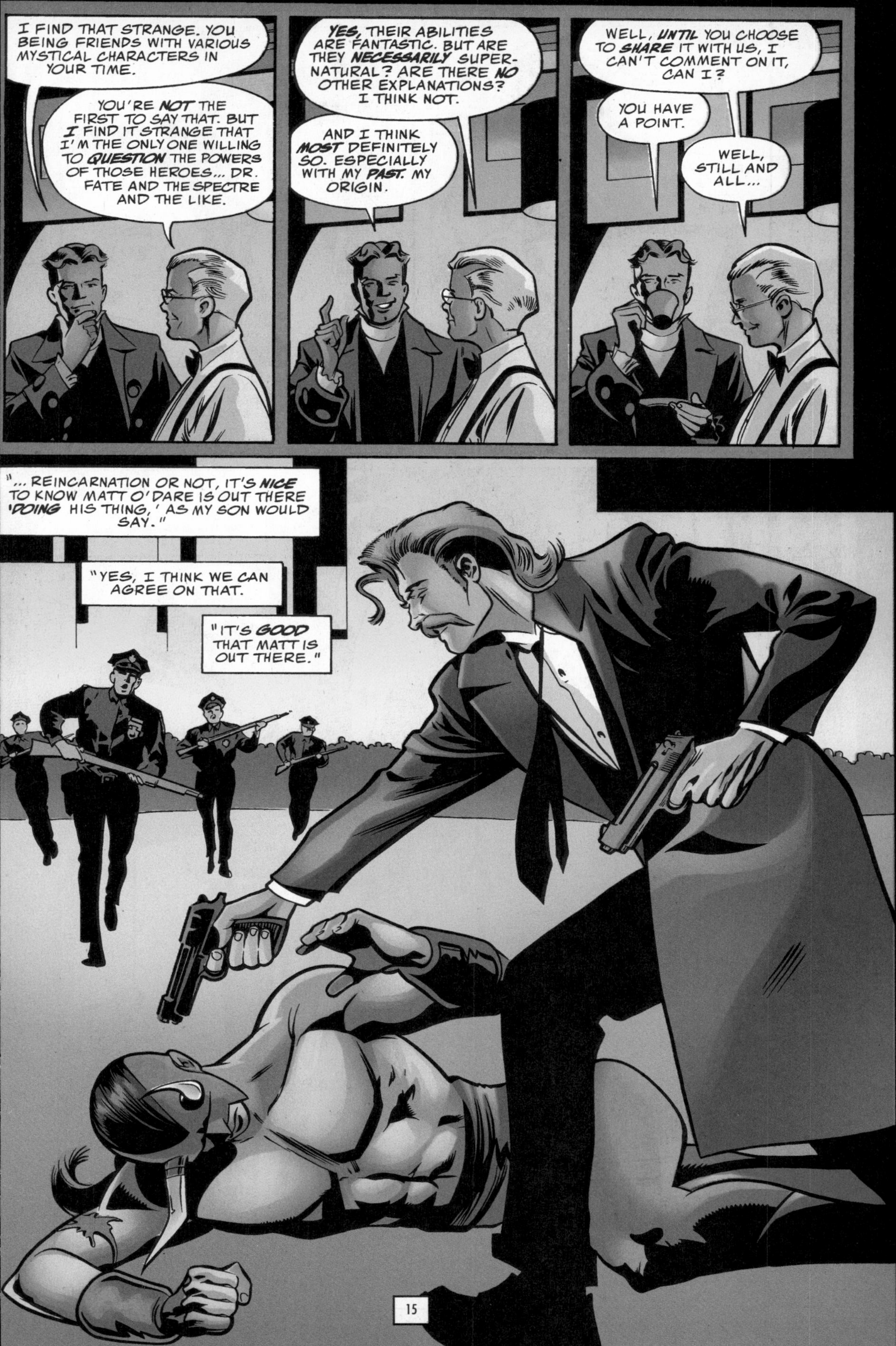
I FIND THAT STRANGE. YOU BEING FRIENDS WITH VARIOUS MYSTICAL CHARACTERS IN YOUR TIME.
YOU'RE NOT THE FIRST TO SAY THAT. BUT I FIND IT STRANGE THAT I'M THE ONLY ONE WILLING TO QUESTION THE POWERS OF THOSE HEROES... DR. FATE AND THE SPECTRE AND THE LIKE.
YES, THEIR ABILITIES ARE FANTASTIC. BUT ARE THEY NECESSARILY SUPER-NATURAL? ARE THERE NO OTHER EXPLANATIONS? I THINK NOT.
AND I THINK MOST DEFINITELY SO. ESPECIALLY WITH MY PAST. MY ORIGIN.
WELL, UNTIL YOU CHOOSE TO SHARE IT WITH US, I CAN'T COMMENT ON IT, CAN I?
YOU HAVE A POINT.
WELL, STILL AND ALL...
"... REINCARNATION OR NOT, IT'S NICE TO KNOW MATT O'DARE IS OUT THERE 'DOING HIS THING,' AS MY SON WOULD SAY."
"YES, I THINK WE CAN AGREE ON THAT.
"IT'S GOOD THAT MATT IS OUT THERE."

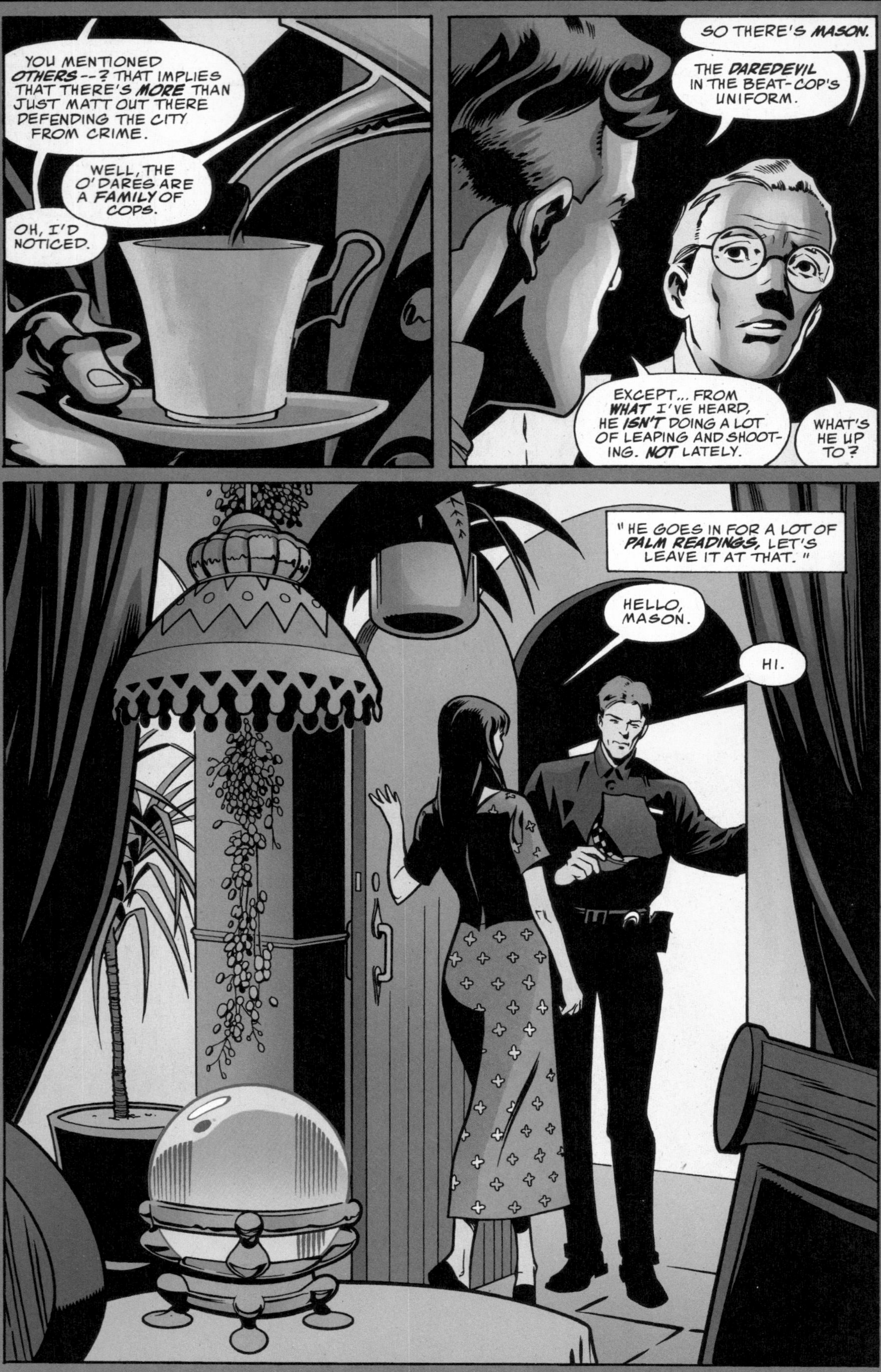
YOU MENTIONED OTHERS--? THAT IMPLIES THAT THERE'S MORE THAN JUST MATT OUT THERE DEFENDING THE CITY FROM CRIME.
WELL, THE O'DARES ARE A FAMILY OF COPS.
OH, I'D NOTICED.
SO THERE'S MASON.
THE DAREDEVIL IN THE BEAT-COP'S UNIFORM.
EXCEPT... FROM WHAT I'VE HEARD, HE ISN'T DOING A LOT OF LEAPING AND SHOOTING. NOT LATELY.
WHAT'S HE UP TO?
"HE GOES IN FOR A LOT OF PALM READINGS, LET'S LEAVE IT AT THAT."
HELLO, MASON.
HI.

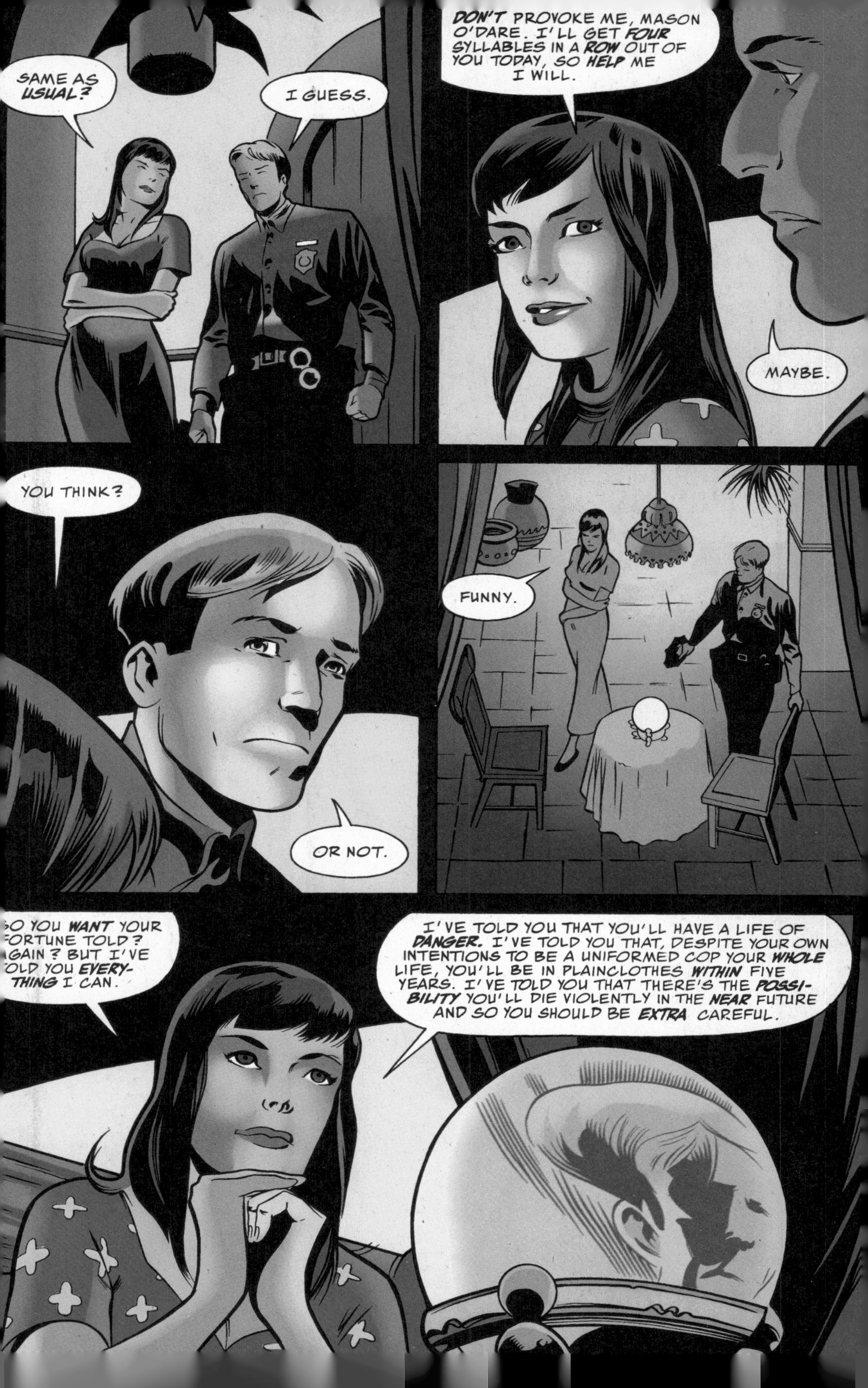
SAME AS USUAL?
I GUESS.
DON'T PROVOKE ME, MASON O'DARE. I'LL GET FOUR SYLLABLES IN A ROW OUT OF YOU TODAY, SO HELP ME I WILL.
MAYBE.
YOU THINK?
OR NOT.
FUNNY.
SO YOU WANT YOUR FORTUNE TOLD? AGAIN? BUT I'VE TOLD YOU EVERY-THING I CAN.
I'VE TOLD YOU THAT YOU'LL HAVE A LIFE OF DANGER. I'VE TOLD YOU THAT, DESPITE YOUR OWN INTENTIONS TO BE A UNIFORMED COP YOUR WHOLE LIFE, YOU'LL BE IN PLAINCLOTHES WITHIN FIVE YEARS. I'VE TOLD YOU THAT THERE'S THE POSSI-BILITY YOU'LL DIE VIOLENTLY IN THE NEAR FUTURE AND SO YOU SHOULD BE EXTRA CAREFUL.

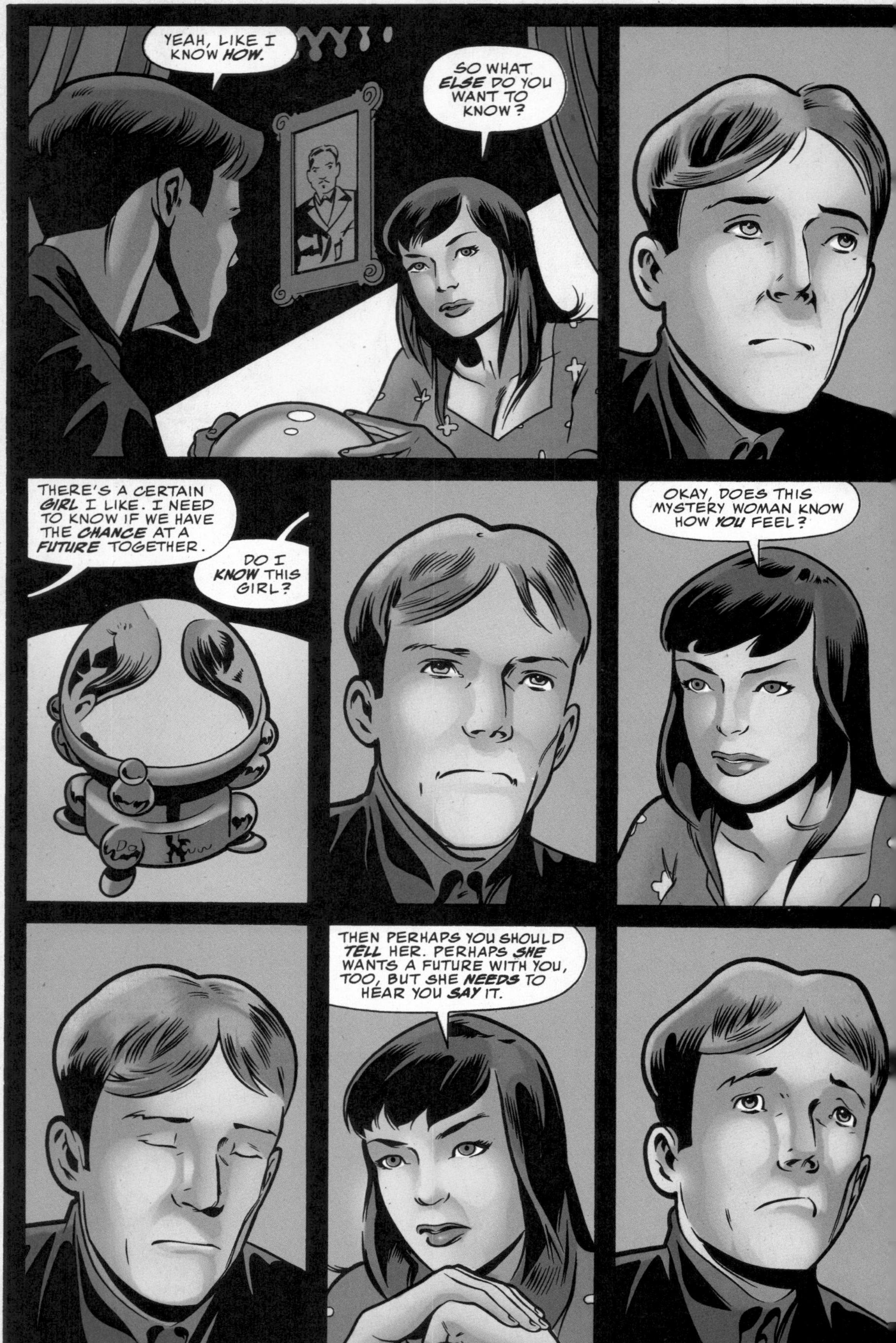
YEAH, LIKE I KNOW HOW.
SO WHAT ELSE DO YOU WANT TO KNOW?
THERE'S A CERTAIN GIRL I LIKE. I NEED TO KNOW IF WE HAVE THE CHANCE AT A FUTURE TOGETHER.
DO I KNOW THIS GIRL?
OKAY, DOES THIS MYSTERY WOMAN KNOW HOW YOU FEEL?
THEN PERHAPS YOU SHOULD TELL HER. PERHAPS SHE WANTS A FUTURE WITH YOU, TOO, BUT SHE NEEDS TO HEAR YOU SAY IT.

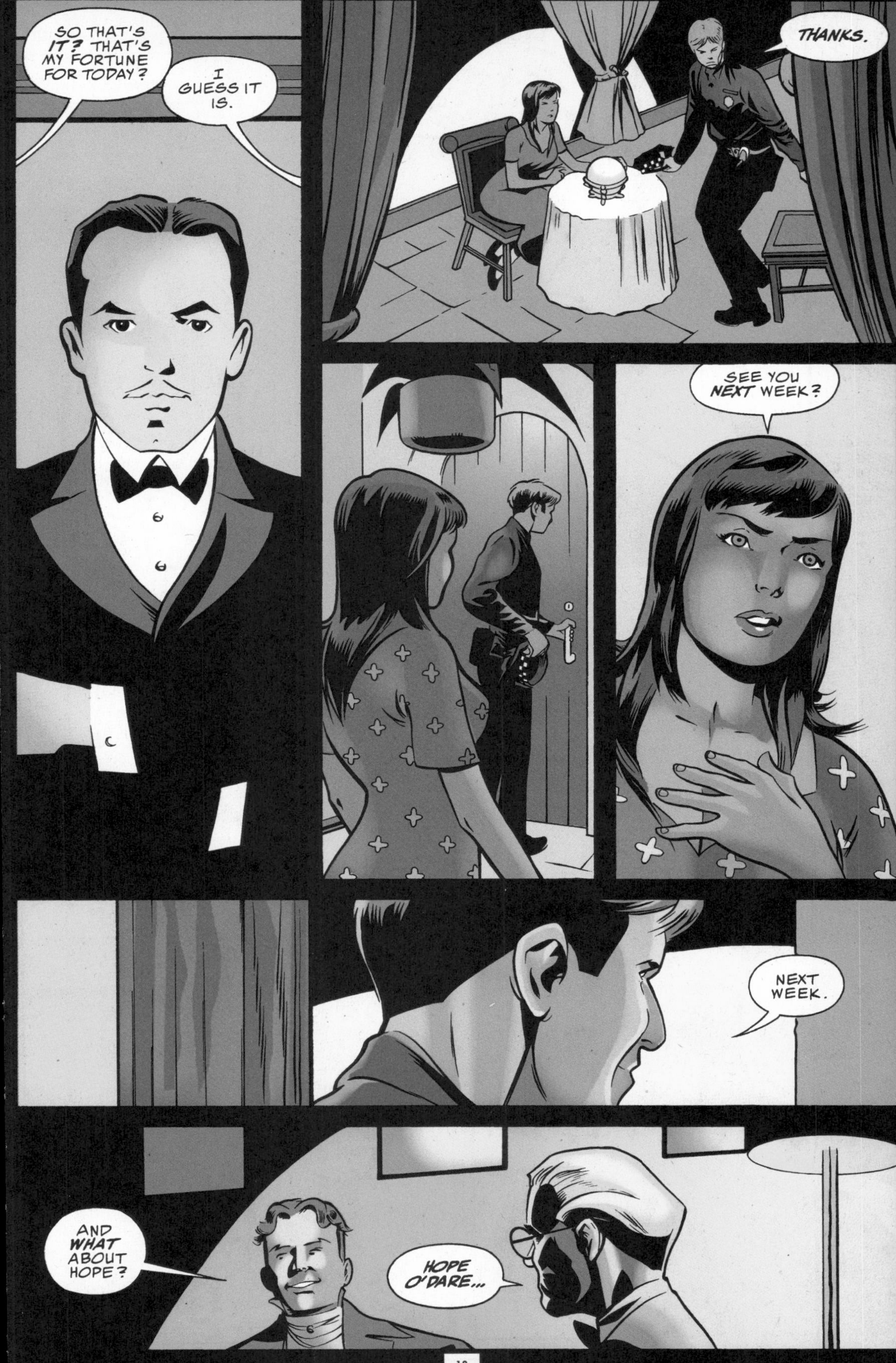
SO THAT'S IT? THAT'S MY FORTUNE FOR TODAY?
I GUESS IT IS.
THANKS.
SEE YOU NEXT WEEK?
NEXT WEEK.
AND WHAT ABOUT HOPE?
HOPE O'DARE...

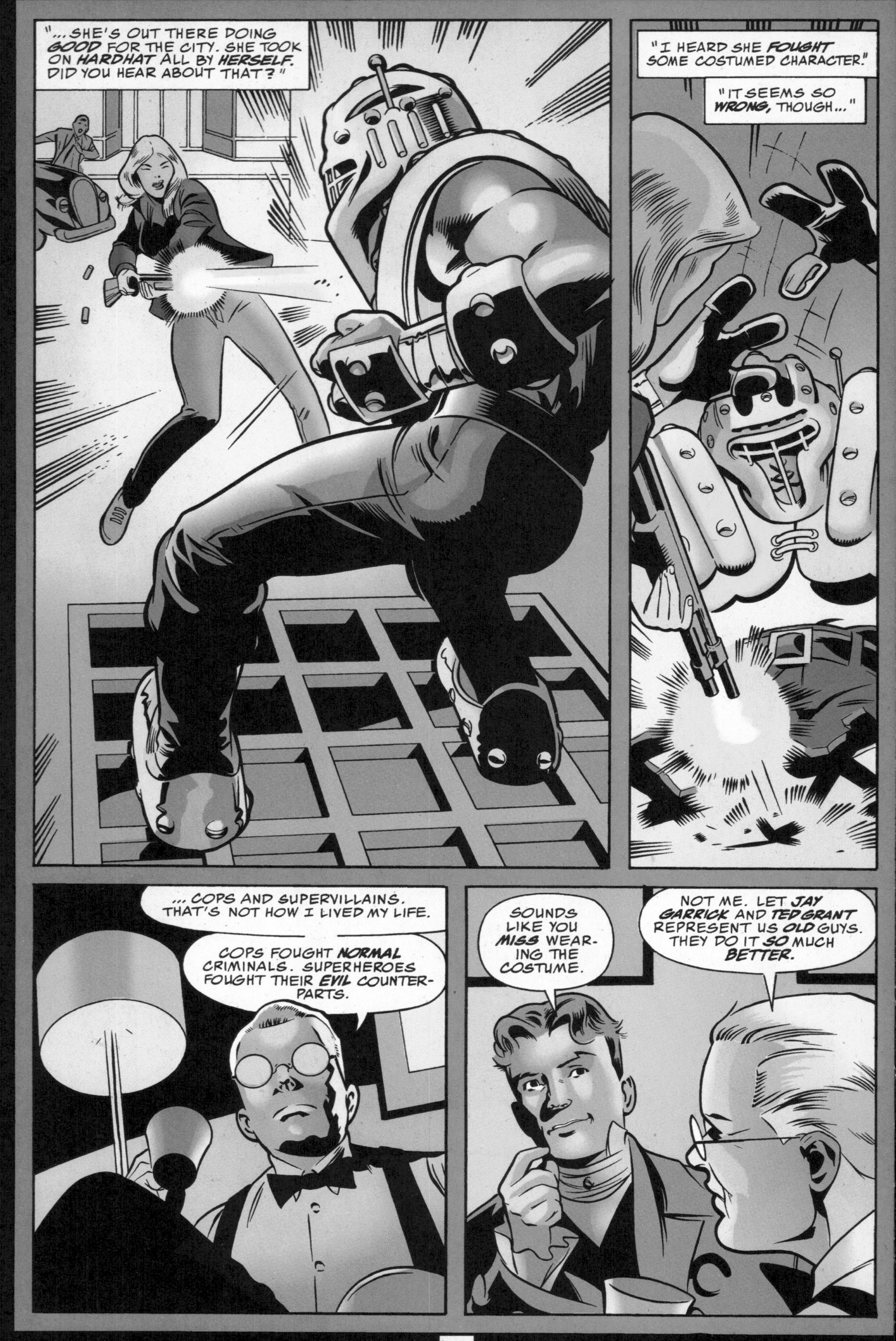
"...SHE'S OUT THERE DOING GOOD FOR THE CITY. SHE TOOK ON HARDHAT ALL BY HERSELF. DID YOU HEAR ABOUT THAT?"
"I HEARD SHE FOUGHT SOME COSTUMED CHARACTER."
"IT SEEMS SO WRONG, THOUGH..."
...COPS AND SUPERVILLAINS. THAT'S NOT HOW I LIVED MY LIFE.
COPS FOUGHT NORMAL CRIMINALS. SUPERHEROES FOUGHT THEIR EVIL COUNTER-PARTS.
SOUNDS LIKE YOU MISS WEAR-ING THE COSTUME.
NOT ME. LET JAY GARRICK AND TED GRANT REPRESENT US OLD GUYS. THEY DO IT SO MUCH BETTER.

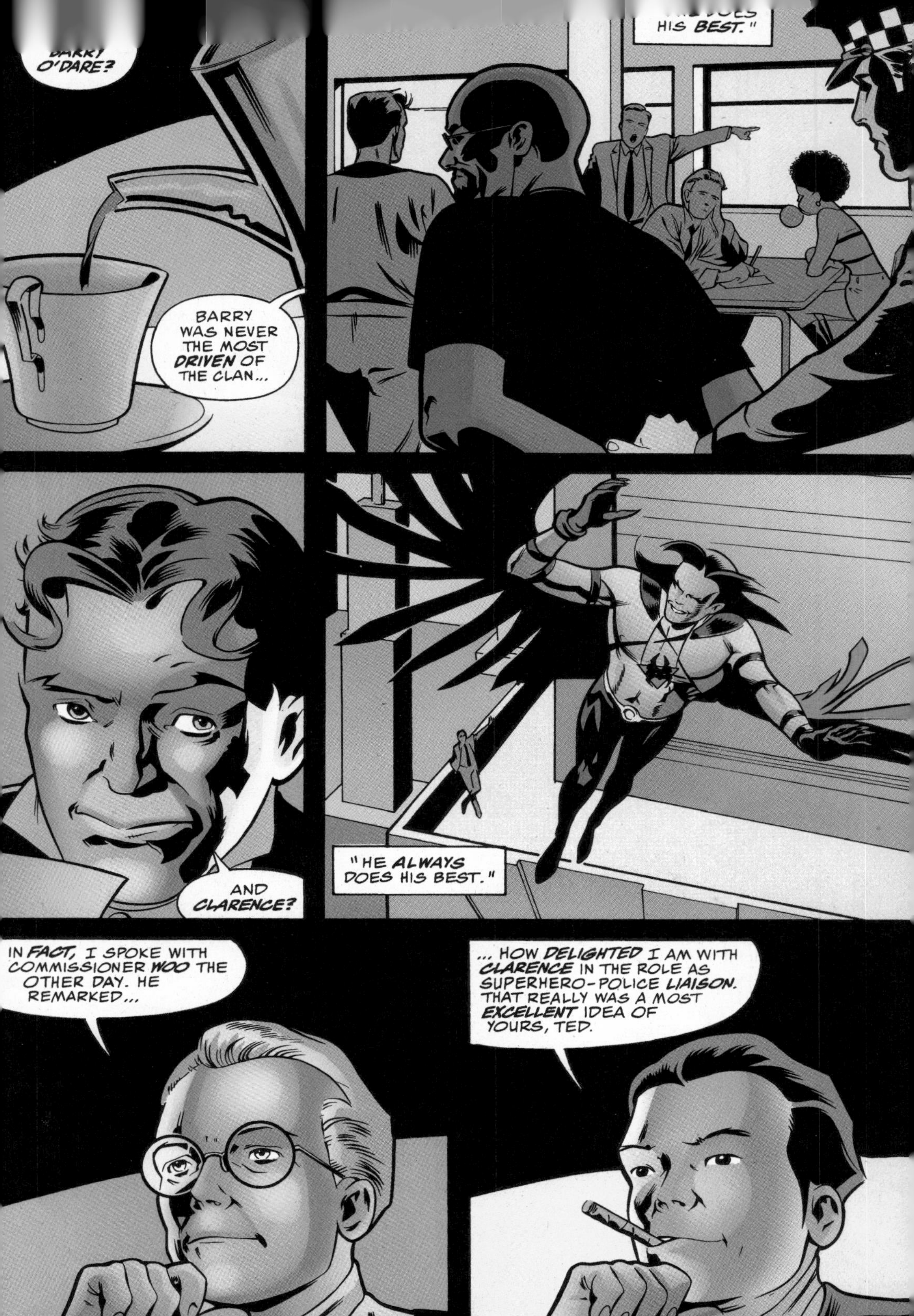
O'DARE?
HIS BEST."
BARRY WAS NEVER THE MOST DRIVEN OF THE CLAN...
AND CLARENCE?
"HE ALWAYS DOES HIS BEST."
IN FACT, I SPOKE WITH COMMISSIONER WOO THE OTHER DAY. HE REMARKED...
... HOW DELIGHTED I AM WITH CLARENCE IN THE ROLE AS SUPERHERO-POLICE LIAISON. THAT REALLY WAS A MOST EXCELLENT IDEA OF YOURS, TED.

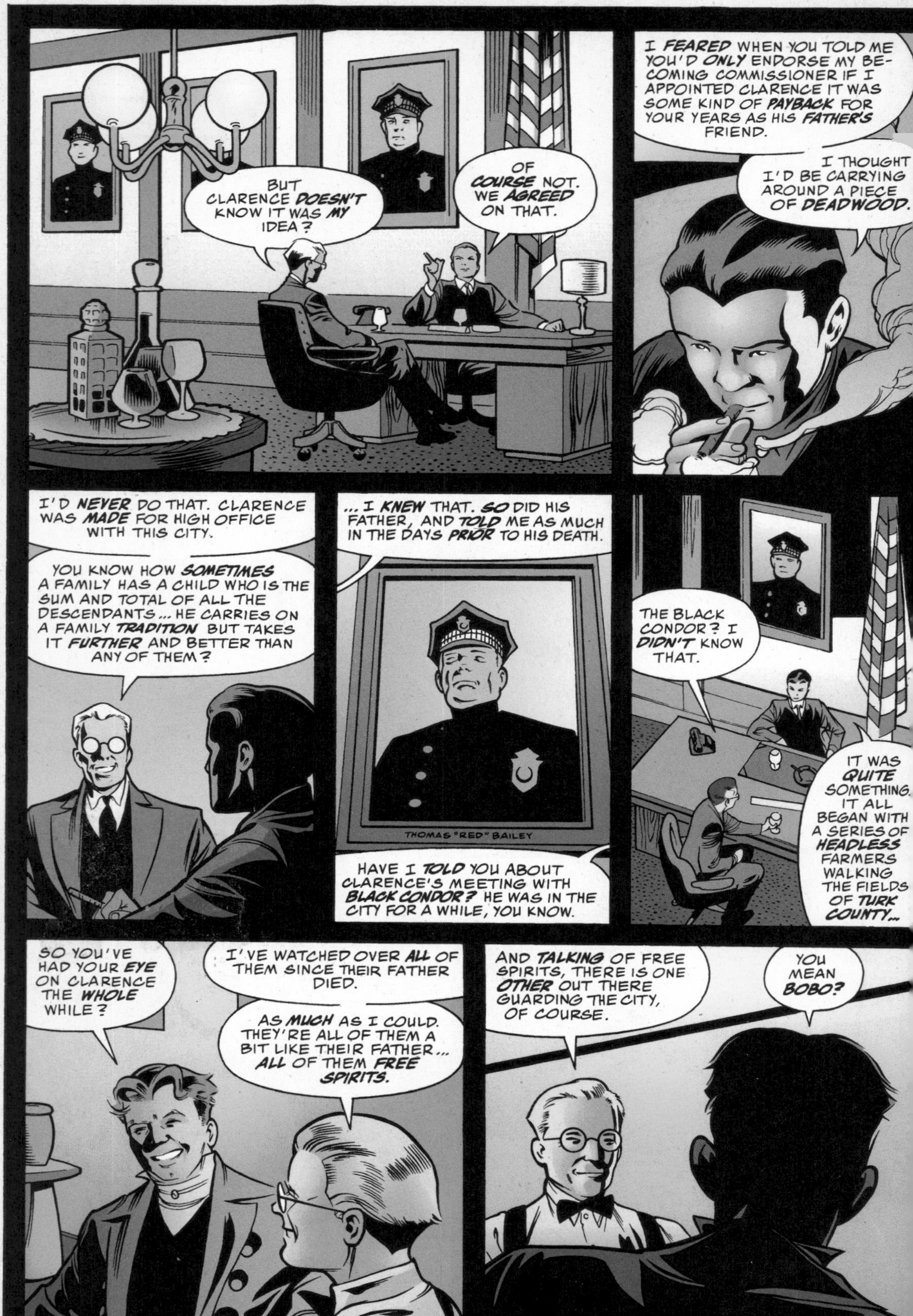
BUT CLARENCE DOESN'T KNOW IT WAS MY IDEA?
OF COURSE NOT. WE AGREED ON THAT.
I FEARED WHEN YOU TOLD ME YOU'D ONLY ENDORSE MY BECOMING COMMISSIONER IF I APPOINTED CLARENCE IT WAS SOME KIND OF PAYBACK FOR YOUR YEARS AS HIS FATHER'S FRIEND.
I THOUGHT I'D BE CARRYING AROUND A PIECE OF DEADWOOD.
I'D NEVER DO THAT. CLARENCE WAS MADE FOR HIGH OFFICE WITH THIS CITY.
YOU KNOW HOW SOMETIMES A FAMILY HAS A CHILD WHO IS THE SUM AND TOTAL OF ALL THE DESCENDANTS... HE CARRIES ON A FAMILY TRADITION BUT TAKES IT FURTHER AND BETTER THAN ANY OF THEM?
...I KNEW THAT. SO DID HIS FATHER, AND TOLD ME AS MUCH IN THE DAYS PRIOR TO HIS DEATH.
THOMAS "RED" BAILEY
HAVE I TOLD YOU ABOUT CLARENCE'S MEETING WITH BLACK CONDOR? HE WAS IN THE CITY FOR A WHILE, YOU KNOW.
THE BLACK CONDOR? I DIDN'T KNOW THAT.
IT WAS QUITE SOMETHING. IT ALL BEGAN WITH A SERIES OF HEADLESS FARMERS WALKING THE FIELDS OF TURK COUNTY...
SO YOU'VE HAD YOUR EYE ON CLARENCE THE WHOLE WHILE?
I'VE WATCHED OVER ALL OF THEM SINCE THEIR FATHER DIED.
AS MUCH AS I COULD. THEY'RE ALL OF THEM A BIT LIKE THEIR FATHER... ALL OF THEM FREE SPIRITS.
AND TALKING OF FREE SPIRITS, THERE IS ONE OTHER OUT THERE GUARDING THE CITY, OF COURSE.
YOU MEAN BOBO?

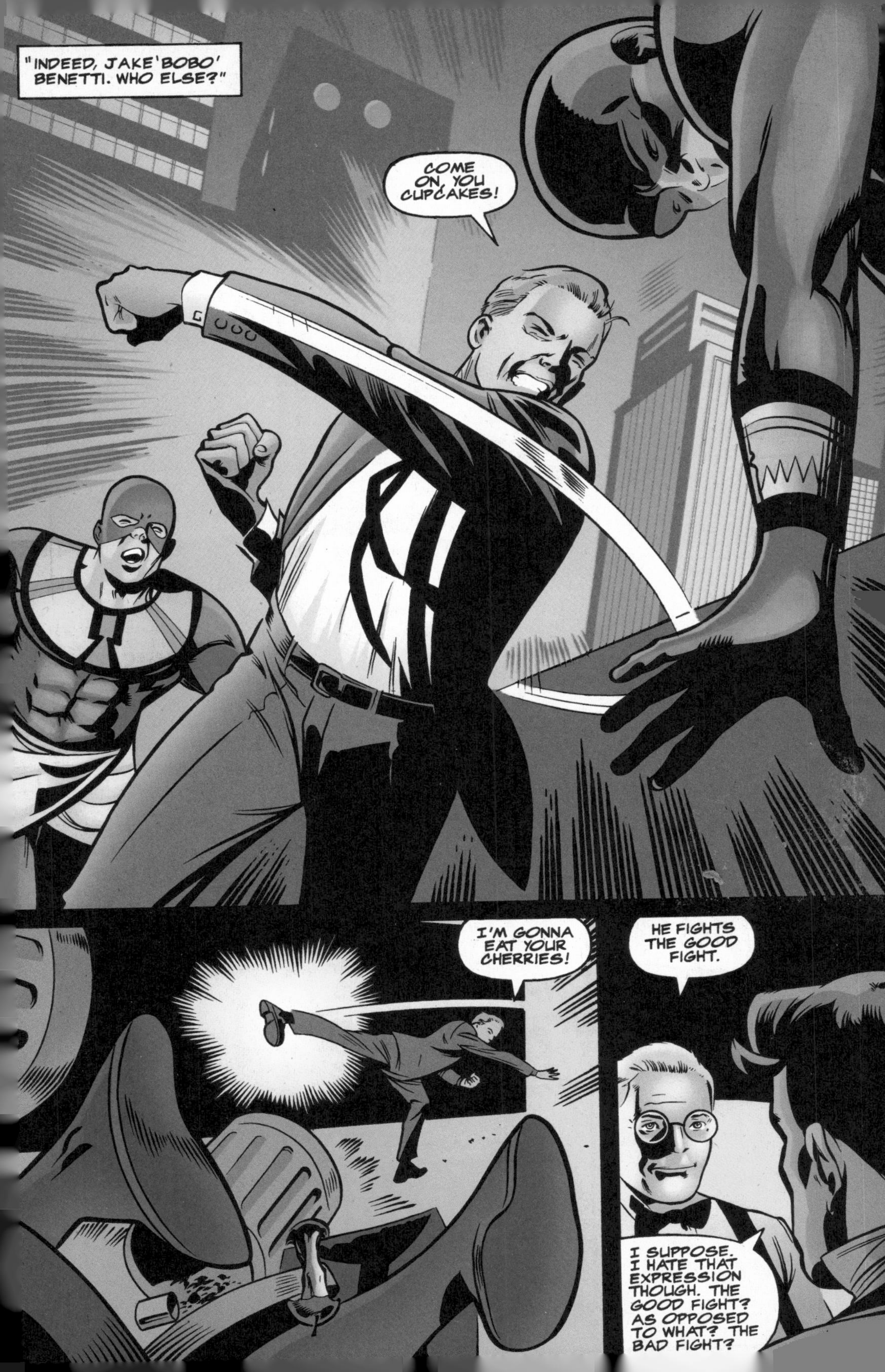
"INDEED, JAKE 'BOBO' BENETTI. WHO ELSE?"
COME ON, YOU CUPCAKES!
I'M GONNA EAT YOUR CHERRIES!
HE FIGHTS THE GOOD FIGHT.
I SUPPOSE. I HATE THAT EXPRESSION THOUGH. THE GOOD FIGHT? AS OPPOSED TO WHAT? THE BAD FIGHT?

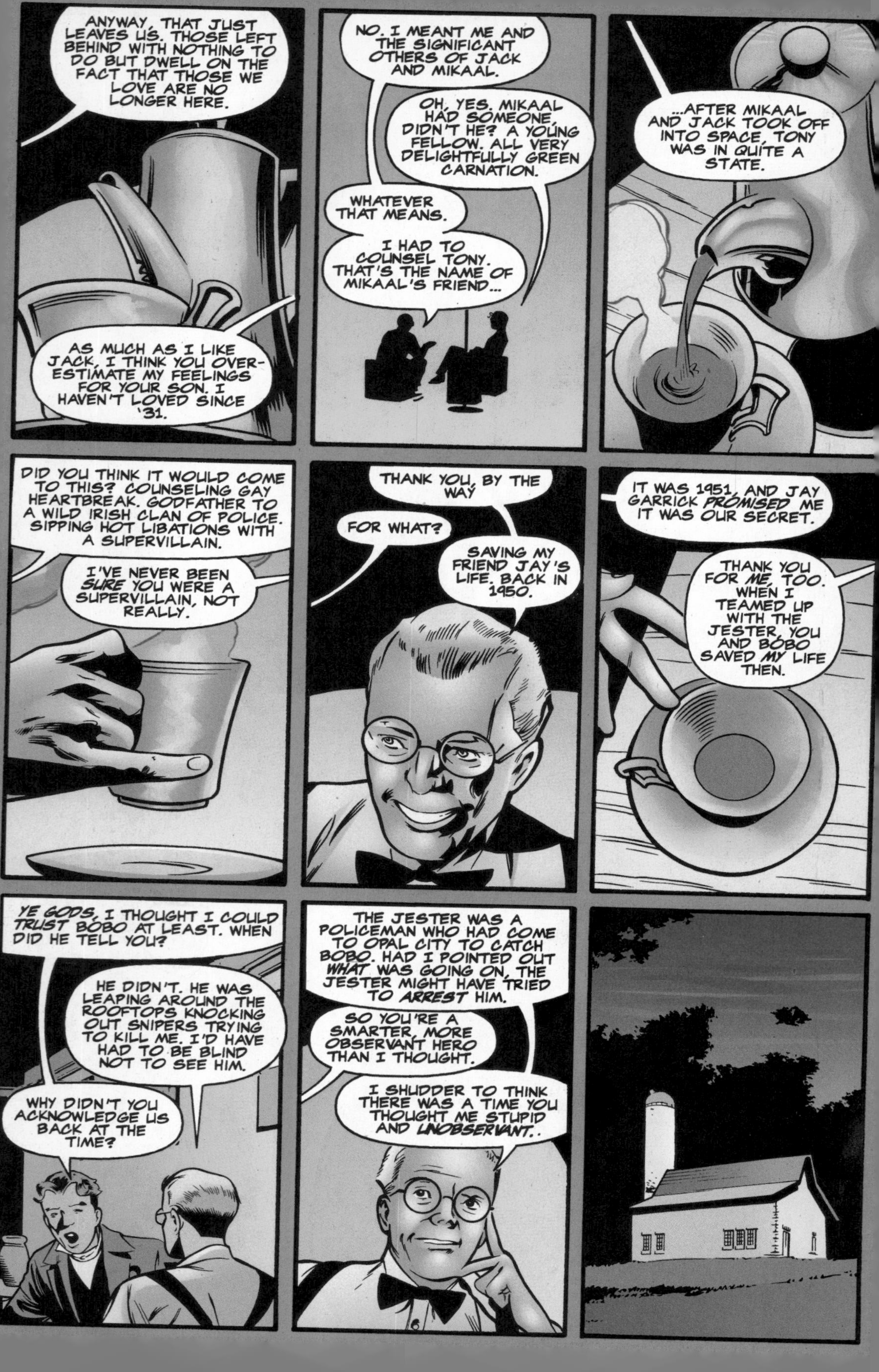
ANYWAY, THAT JUST LEAVES US. THOSE LEFT BEHIND WITH NOTHING TO DO BUT DWELL ON THE FACT THAT THOSE WE LOVE ARE NO LONGER HERE.
AS MUCH AS I LIKE JACK, I THINK YOU OVER-ESTIMATE MY FEELINGS FOR YOUR SON. I HAVEN'T LOVED SINCE '31.
NO. I MEANT ME AND THE SIGNIFICANT OTHERS OF JACK AND MIKAAL.
OH, YES. MIKAAL HAD SOMEONE, DIDN'T HE? A YOUNG FELLOW. ALL VERY DELIGHTFULLY GREEN CARNATION.
WHATEVER THAT MEANS.
I HAD TO COUNSEL TONY. THAT'S THE NAME OF MIKAAL'S FRIEND...
...AFTER MIKAAL AND JACK TOOK OFF INTO SPACE, TONY WAS IN QUITE A STATE.
DID YOU THINK IT WOULD COME TO THIS? COUNSELING GAY HEARTBREAK. GODFATHER TO A WILD IRISH CLAN OF POLICE. SIPPING HOT LIBATIONS WITH A SUPERVILLAIN.
I'VE NEVER BEEN SURE YOU WERE A SUPERVILLAIN, NOT REALLY.
THANK YOU, BY THE WAY
FOR WHAT?
SAVING MY FRIEND JAY'S LIFE. BACK IN 1950.
IT WAS 1951, AND JAY GARRICK PROMISED ME IT WAS OUR SECRET.
THANK YOU FOR ME, TOO. WHEN I TEAMED UP WITH THE JESTER, YOU AND BOBO SAVED MY LIFE THEN.
YE GODS, I THOUGHT I COULD TRUST BOBO AT LEAST. WHEN DID HE TELL YOU?
HE DIDN'T. HE WAS LEAPING AROUND THE ROOFTOPS KNOCKING OUT SNIPERS TRYING TO KILL ME. I'D HAVE HAD TO BE BLIND NOT TO SEE HIM.
WHY DIDN'T YOU ACKNOWLEDGE US BACK AT THE TIME?
THE JESTER WAS A POLICEMAN WHO HAD COME TO OPAL CITY TO CATCH BOBO. HAD I POINTED OUT WHAT WAS GOING ON, THE JESTER MIGHT HAVE TRIED TO ARREST HIM.
SO YOU'RE A SMARTER, MORE OBSERVANT HERO THAN I THOUGHT.
I SHUDDER TO THINK THERE WAS A TIME YOU THOUGHT ME STUPID AND UNOBSERVANT..

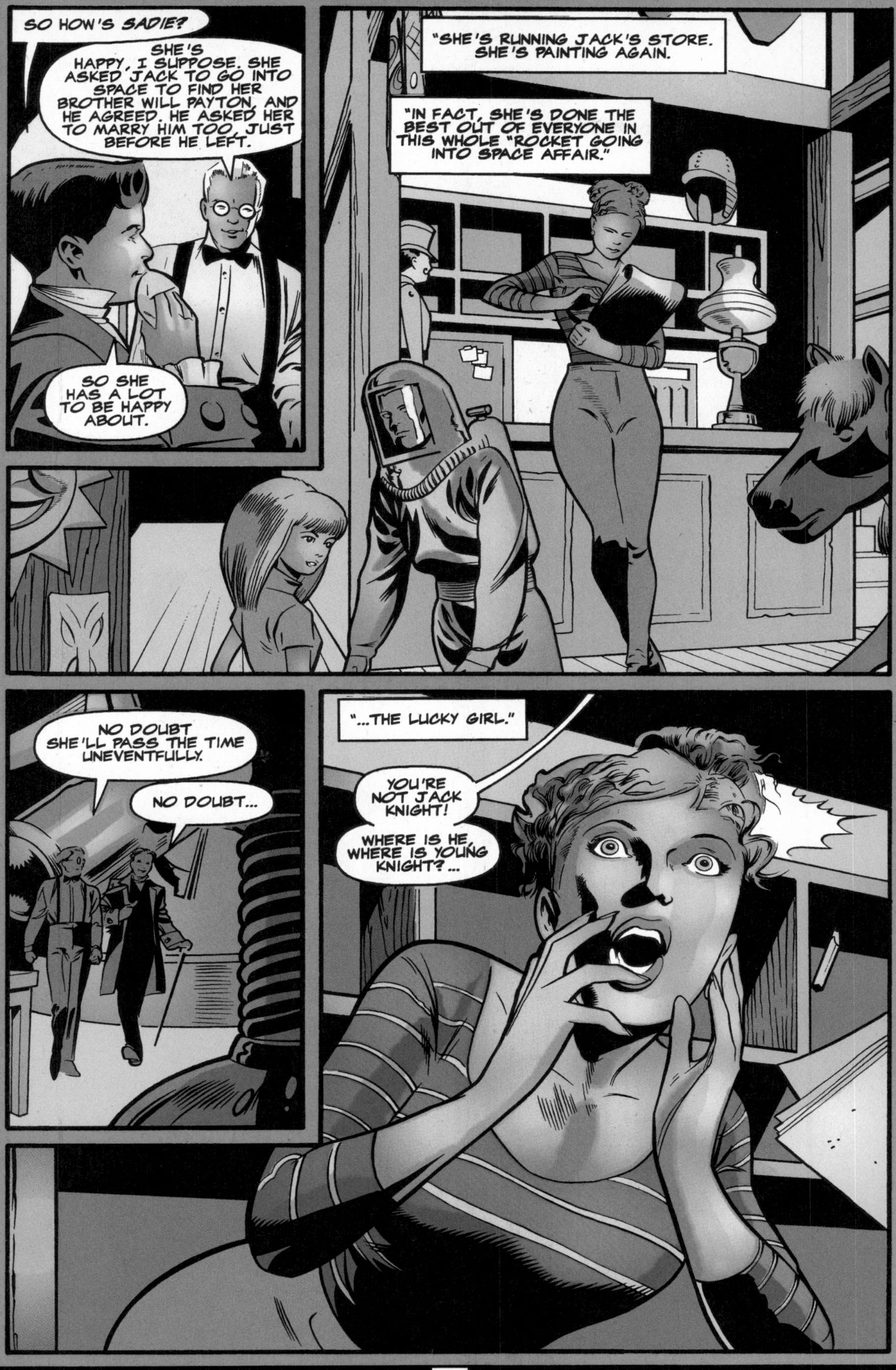

SO HOW'S SADIE?
SHE'S HAPPY, I SUPPOSE. SHE ASKED JACK TO GO INTO SPACE TO FIND HER BROTHER WILL PAYTON, AND HE AGREED. HE ASKED HER TO MARRY HIM TOO, JUST BEFORE HE LEFT.
SO SHE HAS A LOT TO BE HAPPY ABOUT.
"SHE'S RUNNING JACK'S STORE. SHE'S PAINTING AGAIN.
"IN FACT, SHE'S DONE THE BEST OUT OF EVERYONE IN THIS WHOLE "ROCKET GOING INTO SPACE AFFAIR."
NO DOUBT SHE'LL PASS THE TIME UNEVENTFULLY.
NO DOUBT...
"...THE LUCKY GIRL."
YOU'RE NOT JACK KNIGHT!
WHERE IS HE, WHERE IS YOUNG KNIGHT?...

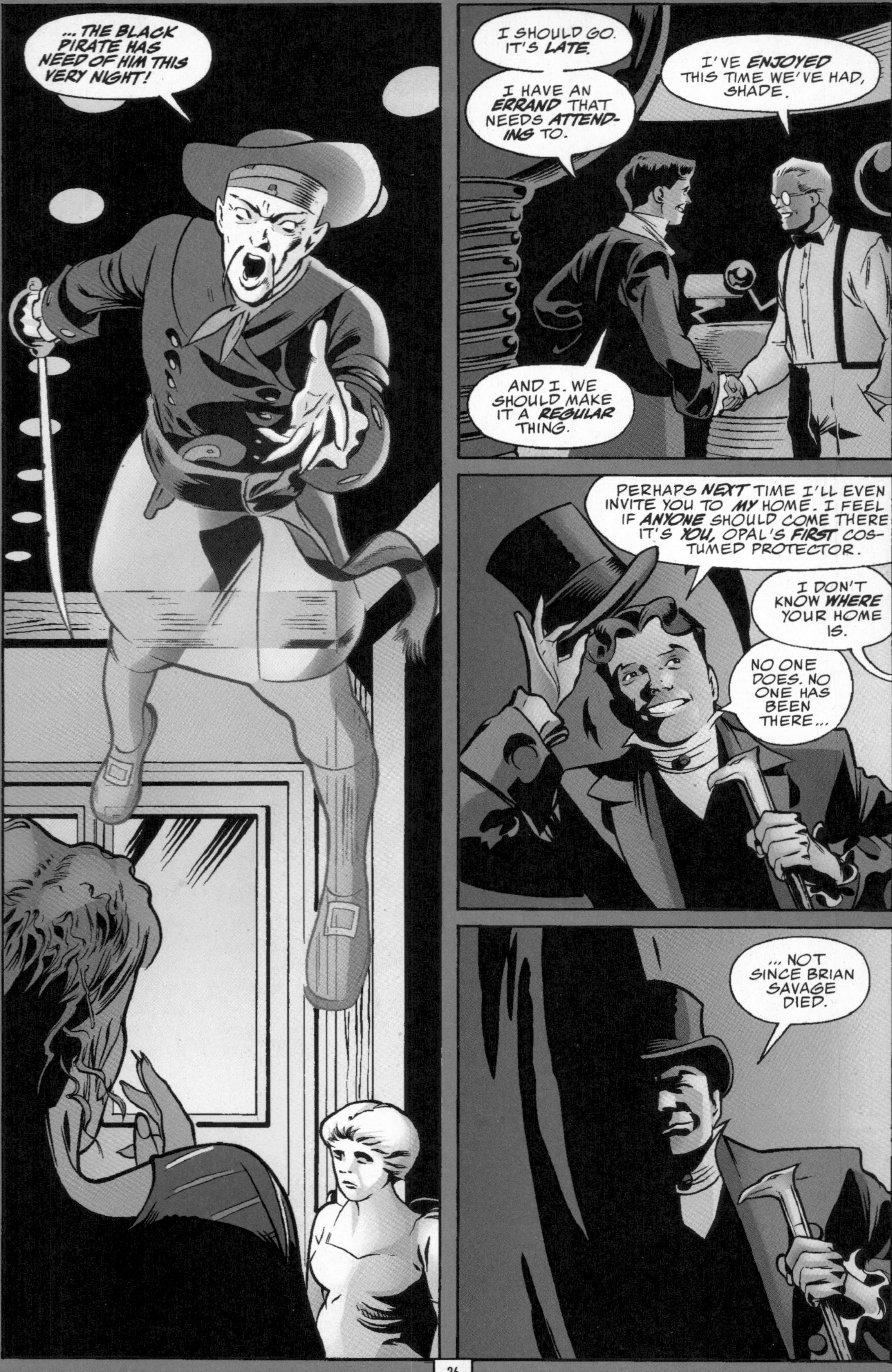
...THE BLACK PIRATE HAS NEED OF HIM THIS VERY NIGHT!
I SHOULD GO. IT'S LATE.
I HAVE AN ERRAND THAT NEEDS ATTENDING TO.
I'VE ENJOYED THIS TIME WE'VE HAD, SHADE.
AND I. WE SHOULD MAKE IT A REGULAR THING.
PERHAPS NEXT TIME I'LL EVEN INVITE YOU TO MY HOME. I FEEL IF ANYONE SHOULD COME THERE IT'S YOU, OPAL'S FIRST COSTUMED PROTECTOR.
I DON'T KNOW WHERE YOUR HOME IS.
NO ONE DOES. NO ONE HAS BEEN THERE...
...NOT SINCE BRIAN SAVAGE DIED.

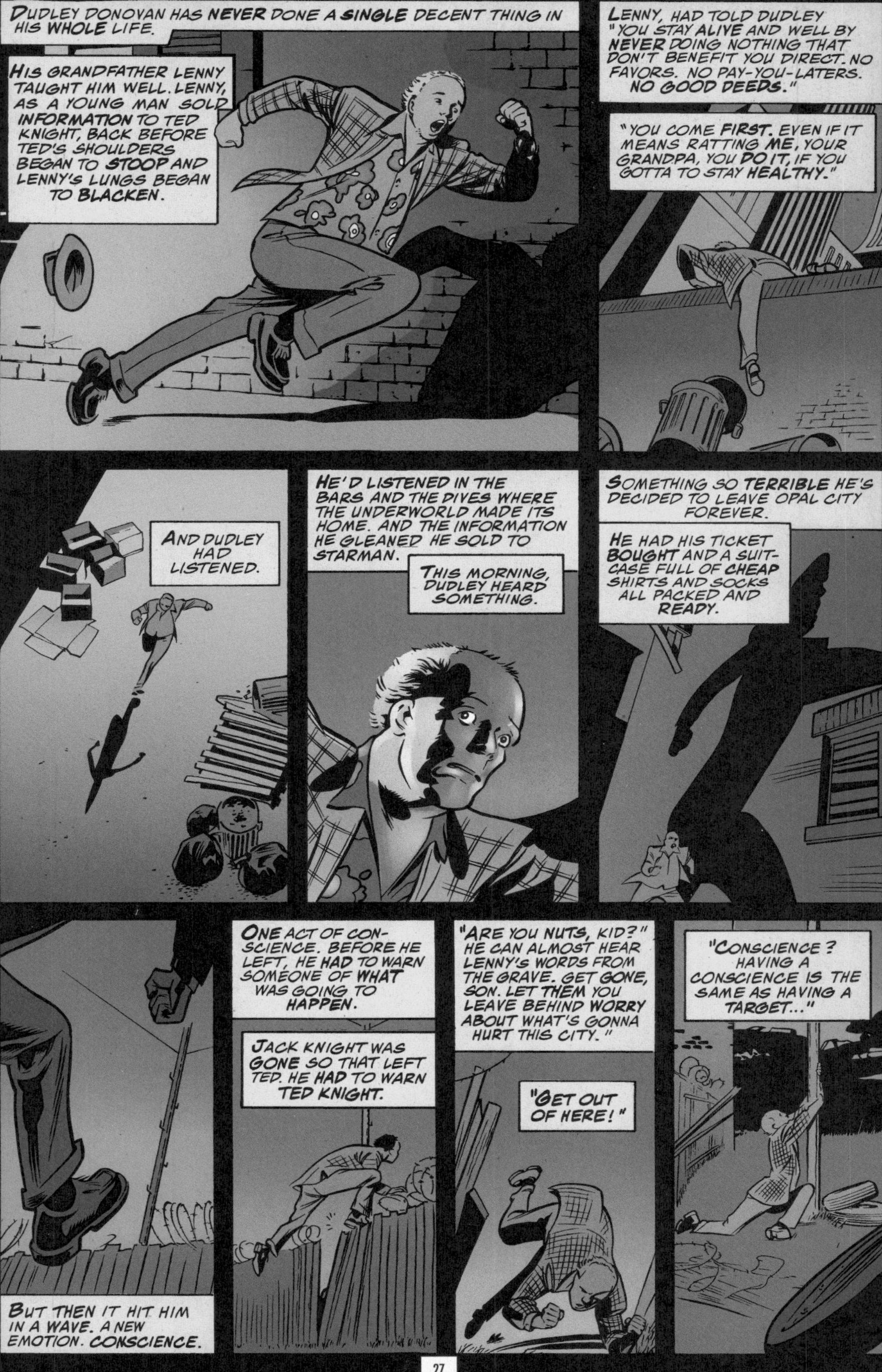
DUDLEY DONOVAN HAS NEVER DONE A SINGLE DECENT THING IN HIS WHOLE LIFE.
HIS GRANDFATHER LENNY TAUGHT HIM WELL. LENNY, AS A YOUNG MAN SOLD INFORMATION TO TED KNIGHT, BACK BEFORE TED'S SHOULDERS BEGAN TO STOOP AND LENNY'S LUNGS BEGAN TO BLACKEN.
LENNY, HAD TOLD DUDLEY "YOU STAY ALIVE AND WELL BY NEVER DOING NOTHING THAT DON'T BENEFIT YOU DIRECT. NO FAVORS. NO PAY-YOU-LATERS. NO GOOD DEEDS."
"YOU COME FIRST. EVEN IF IT MEANS RATTING ME, YOUR GRANDPA, YOU DO IT, IF YOU GOTTA TO STAY HEALTHY."
AND DUDLEY HAD LISTENED.
HE'D LISTENED IN THE BARS AND THE DIVES WHERE THE UNDERWORLD MADE ITS HOME. AND THE INFORMATION HE GLEANED HE SOLD TO STARMAN.
THIS MORNING, DUDLEY HEARD SOMETHING.
SOMETHING SO TERRIBLE HE'S DECIDED TO LEAVE OPAL CITY FOREVER.
HE HAD HIS TICKET BOUGHT AND A SUIT-CASE FULL OF CHEAP SHIRTS AND SOCKS ALL PACKED AND READY.
BUT THEN IT HIT HIM IN A WAVE. A NEW EMOTION. CONSCIENCE.
ONE ACT OF CON-SCIENCE. BEFORE HE LEFT, HE HAD TO WARN SOMEONE OF WHAT WAS GOING TO HAPPEN.
JACK KNIGHT WAS GONE SO THAT LEFT TED. HE HAD TO WARN TED KNIGHT.
"ARE YOU NUTS, KID?" HE CAN ALMOST HEAR LENNY'S WORDS FROM THE GRAVE. GET GONE, SON. LET THEM YOU LEAVE BEHIND WORRY ABOUT WHAT'S GONNA HURT THIS CITY."
"GET OUT OF HERE!"
"CONSCIENCE? HAVING A CONSCIENCE IS THE SAME AS HAVING A TARGET..."

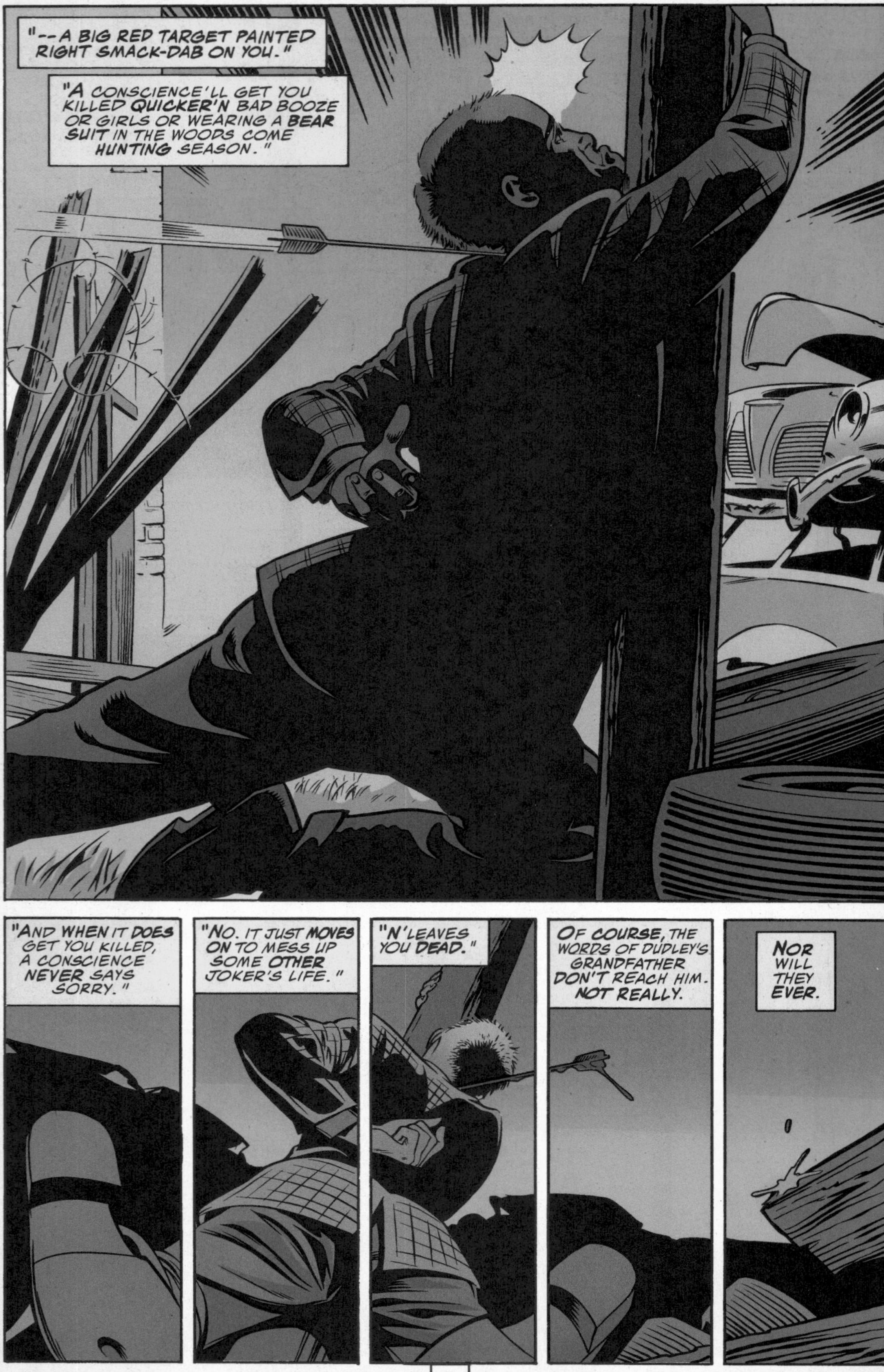
"--A BIG RED TARGET PAINTED RIGHT SMACK-DAB ON YOU."
"A CONSCIENCE'LL GET YOU KILLED QUICKER'N BAD BOOZE OR GIRLS OR WEARING A BEAR SUIT IN THE WOODS COME HUNTING SEASON."
"AND WHEN IT DOES GET YOU KILLED, A CONSCIENCE NEVER SAYS SORRY."
"NO. IT JUST MOVES ON TO MESS UP SOME OTHER JOKER'S LIFE."
"N'LEAVES YOU DEAD."
OF COURSE, THE WORDS OF DUDLEY'S GRANDFATHER DON'T REACH HIM. NOT REALLY.
NOR WILL THEY EVER.

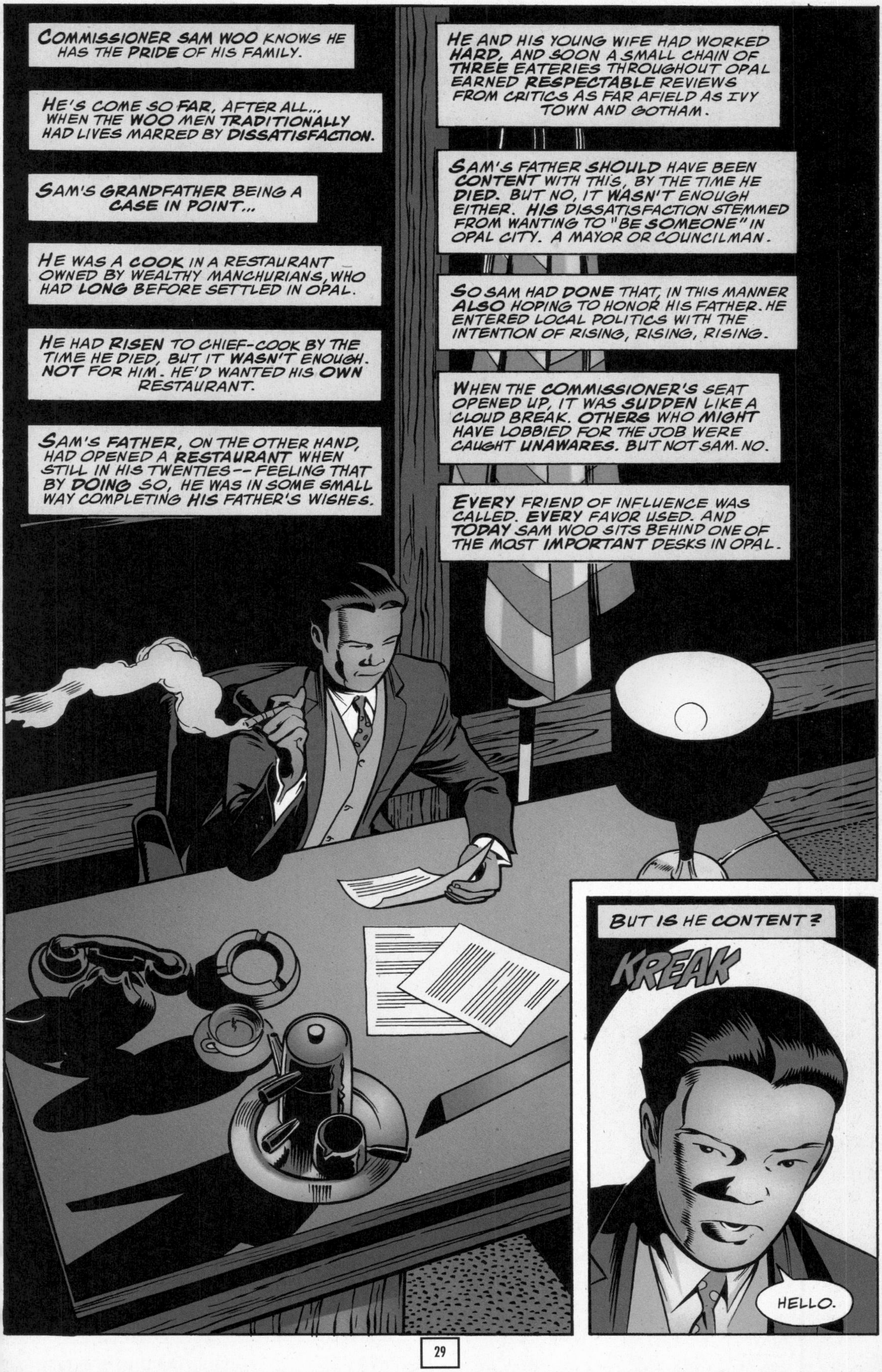
COMMISSIONER SAM WOO KNOWS HE HAS THE PRIDE OF HIS FAMILY.
HE'S COME SO FAR, AFTER ALL... WHEN THE WOO MEN TRADITIONALLY HAD LIVES MARRED BY DISSATISFACTION.
SAM'S GRANDFATHER BEING A CASE IN POINT...
HE WAS A COOK IN A RESTAURANT OWNED BY WEALTHY MANCHURIANS, WHO HAD LONG BEFORE SETTLED IN OPAL.
HE HAD RISEN TO CHIEF-COOK BY THE TIME HE DIED, BUT IT WASN'T ENOUGH. NOT FOR HIM. HE'D WANTED HIS OWN RESTAURANT.
SAM'S FATHER, ON THE OTHER HAND, HAD OPENED A RESTAURANT WHEN STILL IN HIS TWENTIES-- FEELING THAT BY DOING SO, HE WAS IN SOME SMALL WAY COMPLETING HIS FATHER'S WISHES.
HE AND HIS YOUNG WIFE HAD WORKED HARD, AND SOON A SMALL CHAIN OF THREE EATERIES THROUGHOUT OPAL EARNED RESPECTABLE REVIEWS FROM CRITICS AS FAR AFIELD AS IVY TOWN AND GOTHAM.
SAM'S FATHER SHOULD HAVE BEEN CONTENT WITH THIS, BY THE TIME HE DIED. BUT NO, IT WASN'T ENOUGH EITHER. HIS DISSATISFACTION STEMMED FROM WANTING TO "BE SOMEONE" IN OPAL CITY. A MAYOR OR COUNCILMAN.
SO SAM HAD DONE THAT, IN THIS MANNER ALSO HOPING TO HONOR HIS FATHER. HE ENTERED LOCAL POLITICS WITH THE INTENTION OF RISING, RISING, RISING.
WHEN THE COMMISSIONER'S SEAT OPENED UP, IT WAS SUDDEN LIKE A CLOUD BREAK. OTHERS WHO MIGHT HAVE LOBBIED FOR THE JOB WERE CAUGHT UNAWARES. BUT NOT SAM. NO.
EVERY FRIEND OF INFLUENCE WAS CALLED. EVERY FAVOR USED. AND TODAY SAM WOO SITS BEHIND ONE OF THE MOST IMPORTANT DESKS IN OPAL.
BUT IS HE CONTENT?
KREAK
HELLO.

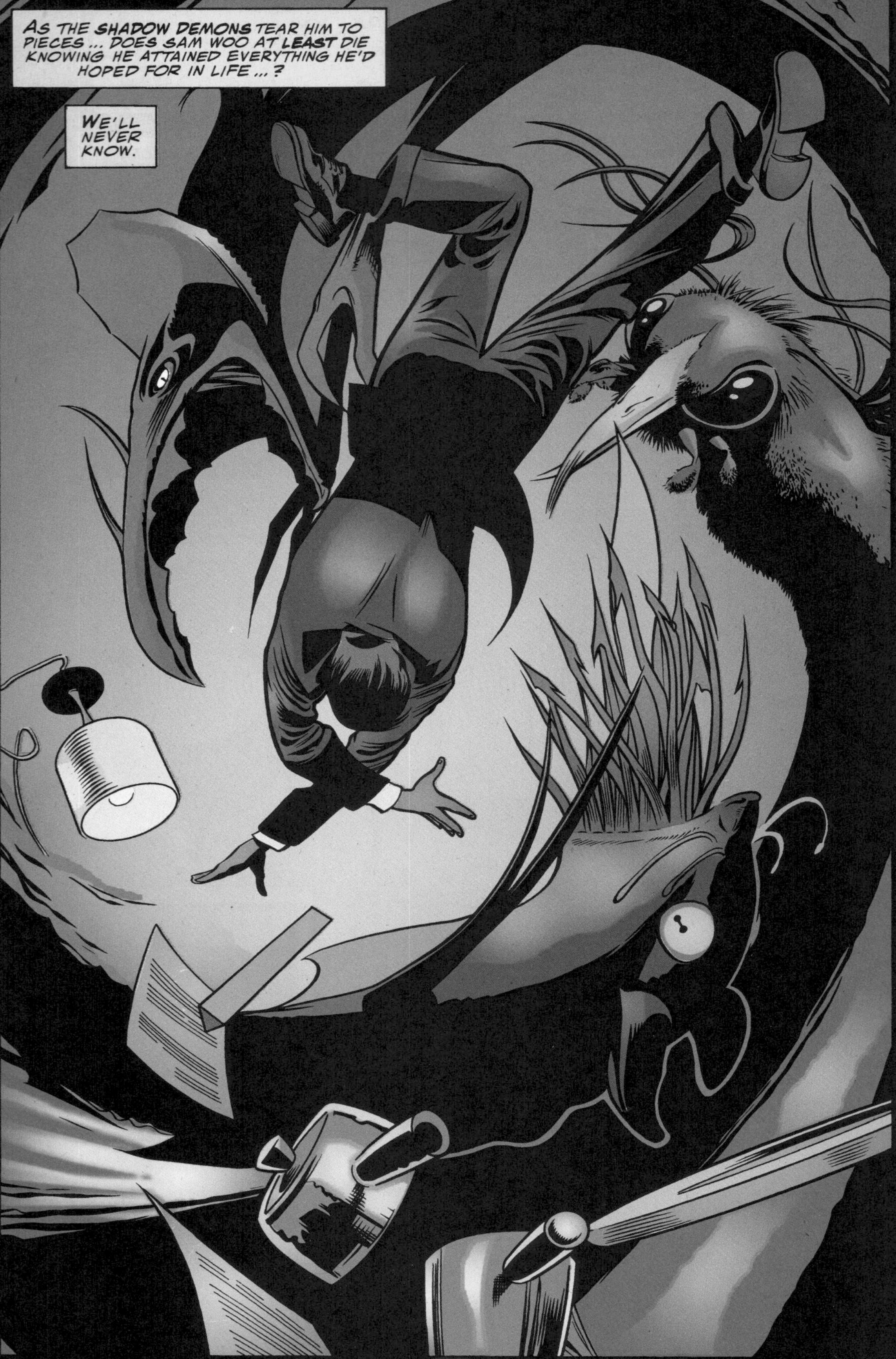
AS THE SHADOW DEMONS TEAR HIM TO PIECES ... DOES SAM WOO AT LEAST DIE KNOWING HE ATTAINED EVERYTHING HE'D HOPED FOR IN LIFE ... ?
WE'LL NEVER KNOW.

OPAL ON FRIDAY.

FRIDAY NIGHT -- NOW TIRED AND OLD. MORE THAN HAPPY FOR YOUNG, SUNNY SATURDAY TO RUN INTO TOWN AN HOUR FROM NOW AND TAKE OVER.

STILL, THOSE AWAKE MIGHT SPEND A MOMENT OR TWO OR THREE OR FOUR TO THINK OF A LOVED ONE ...

... PERHAPS THE LOVED ONE WHO LIES BY THEIR SIDE.

CLARENCE.

FAITH, HONEY, HOW ABOUT A REWARD FOR A LONG, HARD WEEK?

I WAS JUST GOING TO SAY THE SAME THING.

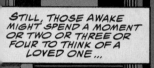

WHILE OTHERS ...

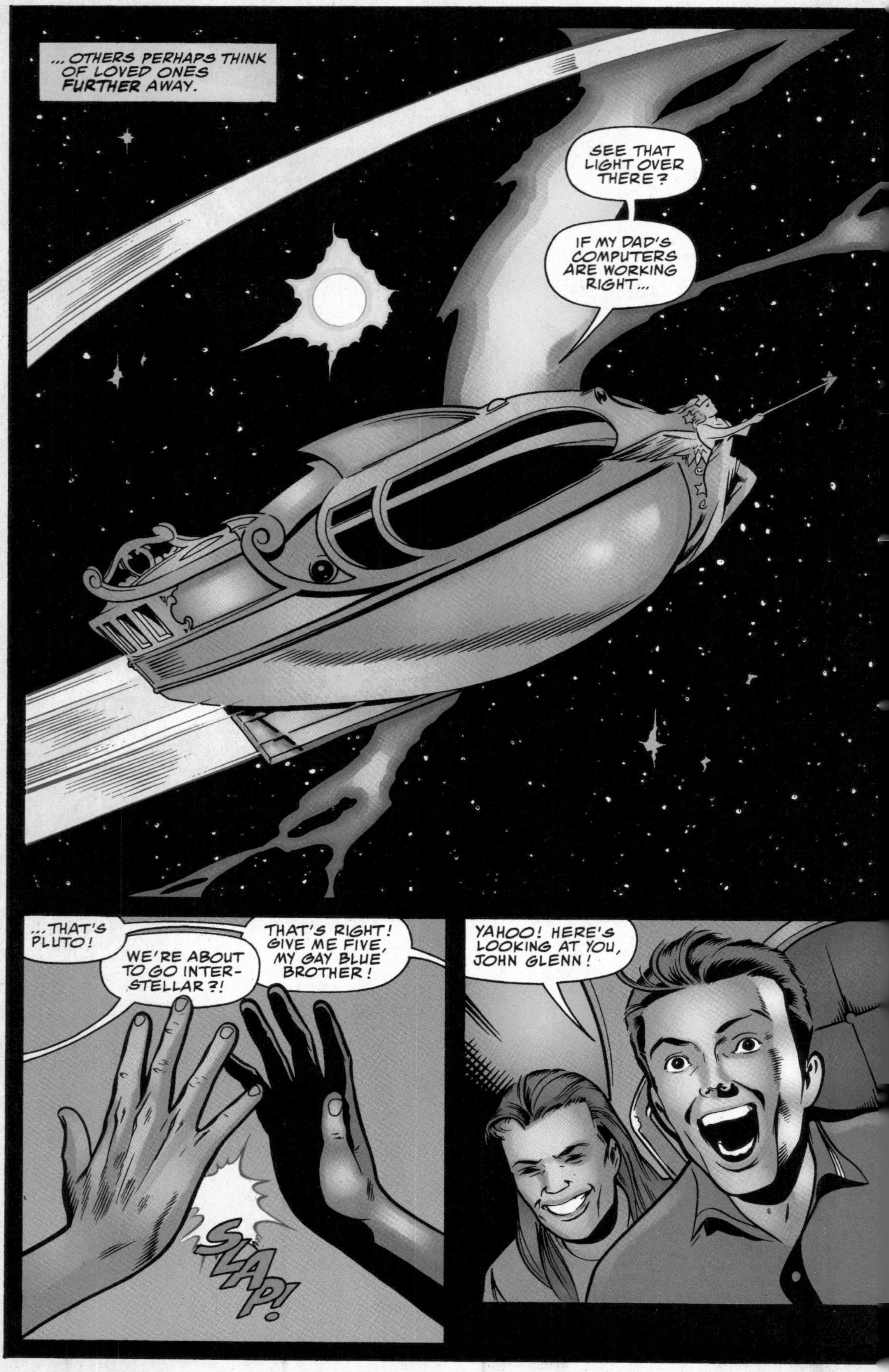
...OTHERS PERHAPS THINK OF LOVED ONES FURTHER AWAY.
SEE THAT LIGHT OVER THERE?
IF MY DAD'S COMPUTERS ARE WORKING RIGHT...
...THAT'S PLUTO!
WE'RE ABOUT TO GO INTER-STELLAR?!
THAT'S RIGHT! GIVE ME FIVE, MY GAY BLUE BROTHER!
SLAP!
YAHOO! HERE'S LOOKING AT YOU, JOHN GLENN!

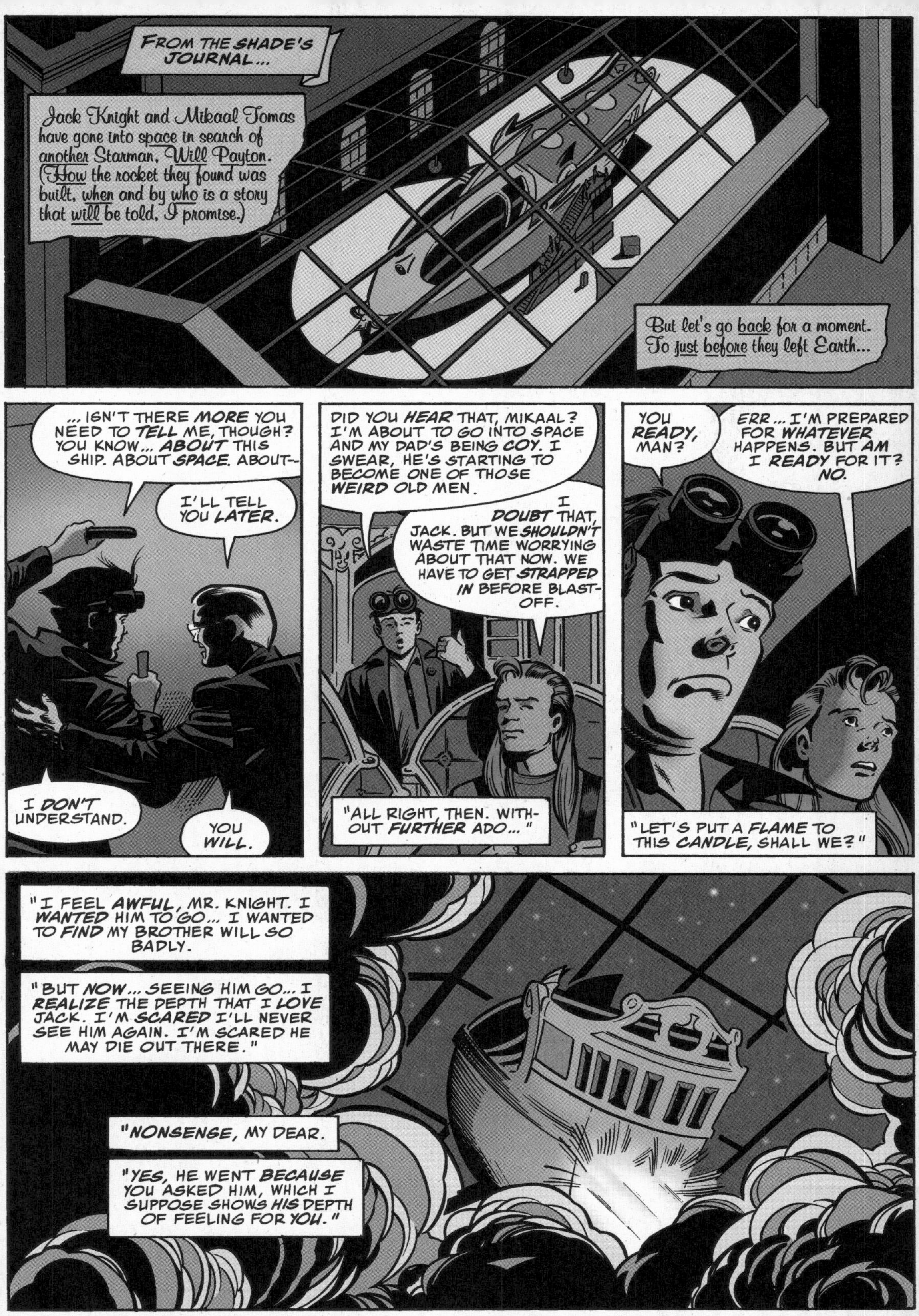

FROM THE SHADE'S JOURNAL...
Jack Knight and Mikaal Tomas have gone into space in search of another Starman, Will Payton. (How the rocket they found was built, when and by who is a story that will be told, I promise.)
But let's go back for a moment. To just before they left Earth...
...ISN'T THERE MORE YOU NEED TO TELL ME, THOUGH? YOU KNOW... ABOUT THIS SHIP. ABOUT SPACE. ABOUT--
I'LL TELL YOU LATER.
I DON'T UNDERSTAND.
YOU WILL.
DID YOU HEAR THAT, MIKAAL? I'M ABOUT TO GO INTO SPACE AND MY DAD'S BEING COY. I SWEAR, HE'S STARTING TO BECOME ONE OF THOSE WEIRD OLD MEN.
I DOUBT THAT, JACK. BUT WE SHOULDN'T WASTE TIME WORRYING ABOUT THAT NOW. WE HAVE TO GET STRAPPED IN BEFORE BLAST-OFF.
"ALL RIGHT, THEN. WITHOUT FURTHER ADO..."
YOU READY, MAN?
ERR... I'M PREPARED FOR WHATEVER HAPPENS. BUT AM I READY FOR IT? NO.
"LET'S PUT A FLAME TO THIS CANDLE, SHALL WE?"
"I FEEL AWFUL, MR. KNIGHT. I WANTED HIM TO GO... I WANTED TO FIND MY BROTHER WILL SO BADLY.
"BUT NOW... SEEING HIM GO... I REALIZE THE DEPTH THAT I LOVE JACK. I'M SCARED I'LL NEVER SEE HIM AGAIN. I'M SCARED HE MAY DIE OUT THERE."
"NONSENSE, MY DEAR.
"YES, HE WENT BECAUSE YOU ASKED HIM, WHICH I SUPPOSE SHOWS HIS DEPTH OF FEELING FOR YOU."

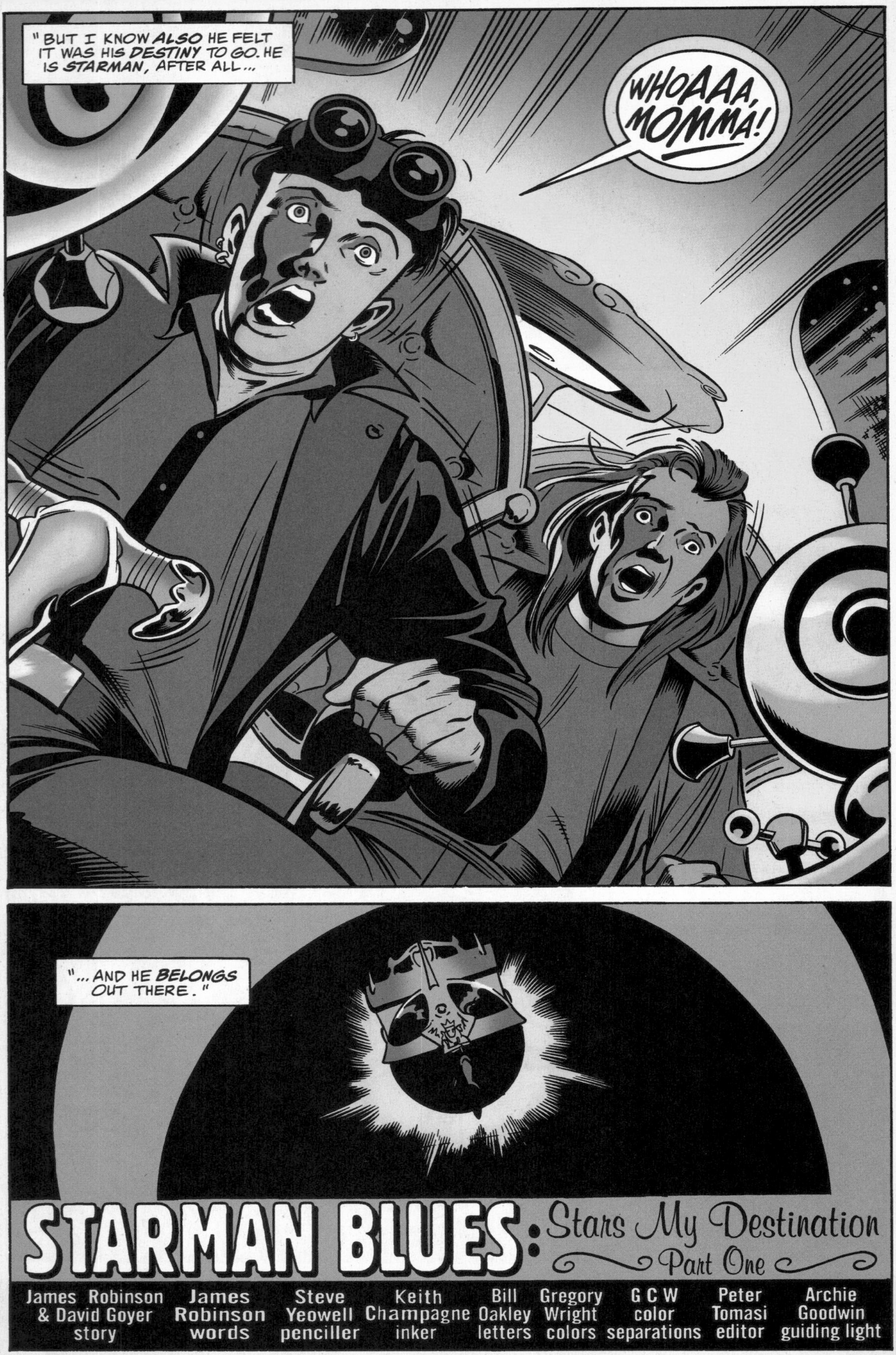
"BUT I KNOW ALSO HE FELT IT WAS HIS DESTINY TO GO. HE IS STARMAN, AFTER ALL...
WHOAAA, MOMMA!
"...AND HE BELONGS OUT THERE."
STARMAN BLUES: Stars My Destination
Part One
James Robinson & David Goyer story
James Robinson words
Steve Yeowell penciller
Keith Champagne inker
Bill Oakley letters
Gregory Wright colors
G C W color separations
Peter Tomasi editor
Archie Goodwin guiding light

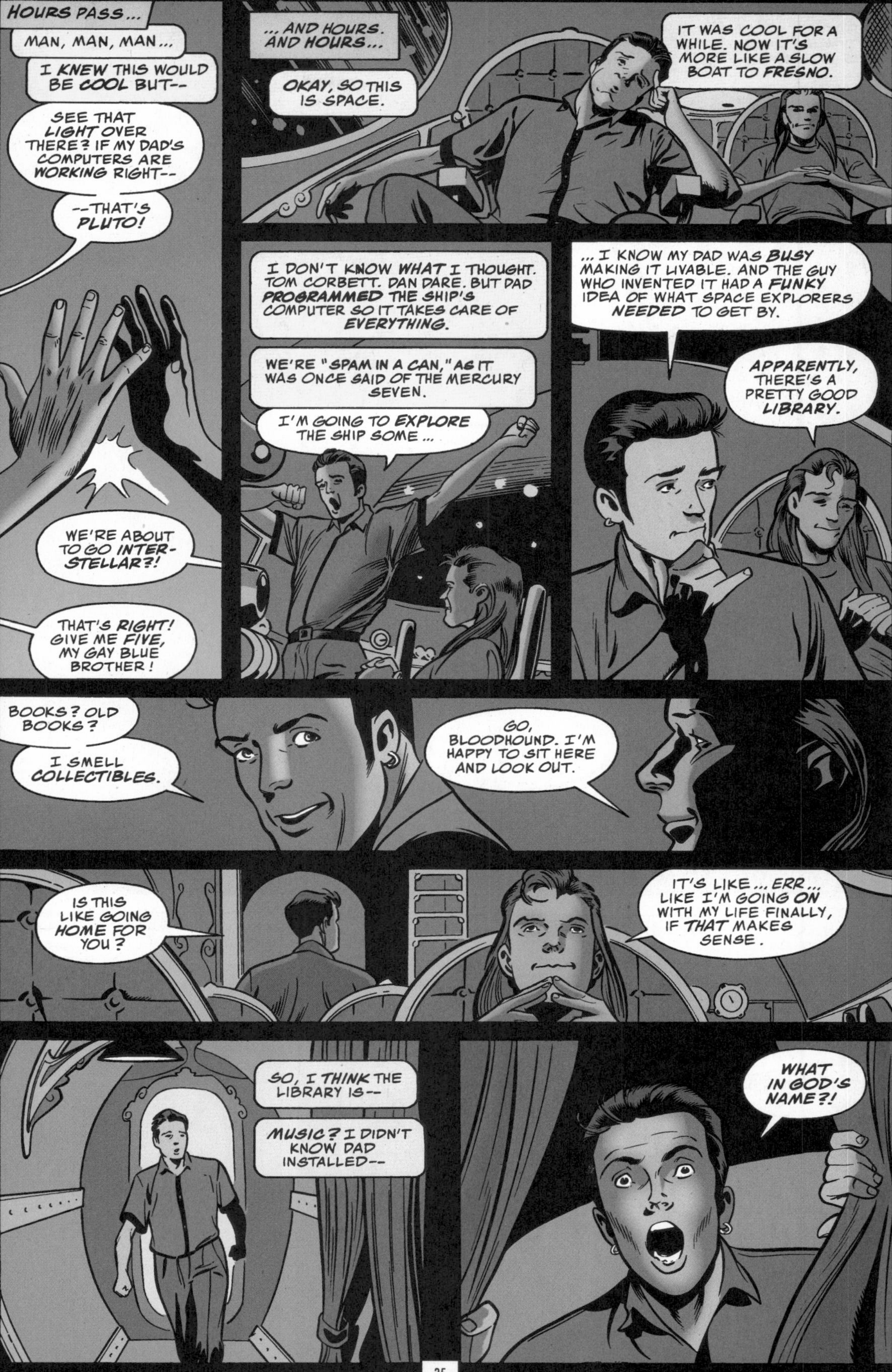
HOURS PASS...
MAN, MAN, MAN...
I KNEW THIS WOULD BE COOL BUT--
SEE THAT LIGHT OVER THERE? IF MY DAD'S COMPUTERS ARE WORKING RIGHT--
--THAT'S PLUTO!
...AND HOURS. AND HOURS...
OKAY, SO THIS IS SPACE.
IT WAS COOL FOR A WHILE. NOW IT'S MORE LIKE A SLOW BOAT TO FRESNO.
WE'RE ABOUT TO GO INTER-STELLAR?!
THAT'S RIGHT! GIVE ME FIVE, MY GAY BLUE BROTHER!
I DON'T KNOW WHAT I THOUGHT. TOM CORBETT. DAN DARE. BUT DAD PROGRAMMED THE SHIP'S COMPUTER SO IT TAKES CARE OF EVERYTHING.
WE'RE "SPAM IN A CAN," AS IT WAS ONCE SAID OF THE MERCURY SEVEN.
I'M GOING TO EXPLORE THE SHIP SOME...
...I KNOW MY DAD WAS BUSY MAKING IT LIVABLE. AND THE GUY WHO INVENTED IT HAD A FUNKY IDEA OF WHAT SPACE EXPLORERS NEEDED TO GET BY.
APPARENTLY, THERE'S A PRETTY GOOD LIBRARY.
BOOKS? OLD BOOKS?
I SMELL COLLECTIBLES.
GO, BLOODHOUND. I'M HAPPY TO SIT HERE AND LOOK OUT.
IS THIS LIKE GOING HOME FOR YOU?
IT'S LIKE... ERR... LIKE I'M GOING ON WITH MY LIFE FINALLY, IF THAT MAKES SENSE.
SO, I THINK THE LIBRARY IS--
MUSIC? I DIDN'T KNOW DAD INSTALLED--
WHAT IN GOD'S NAME?!

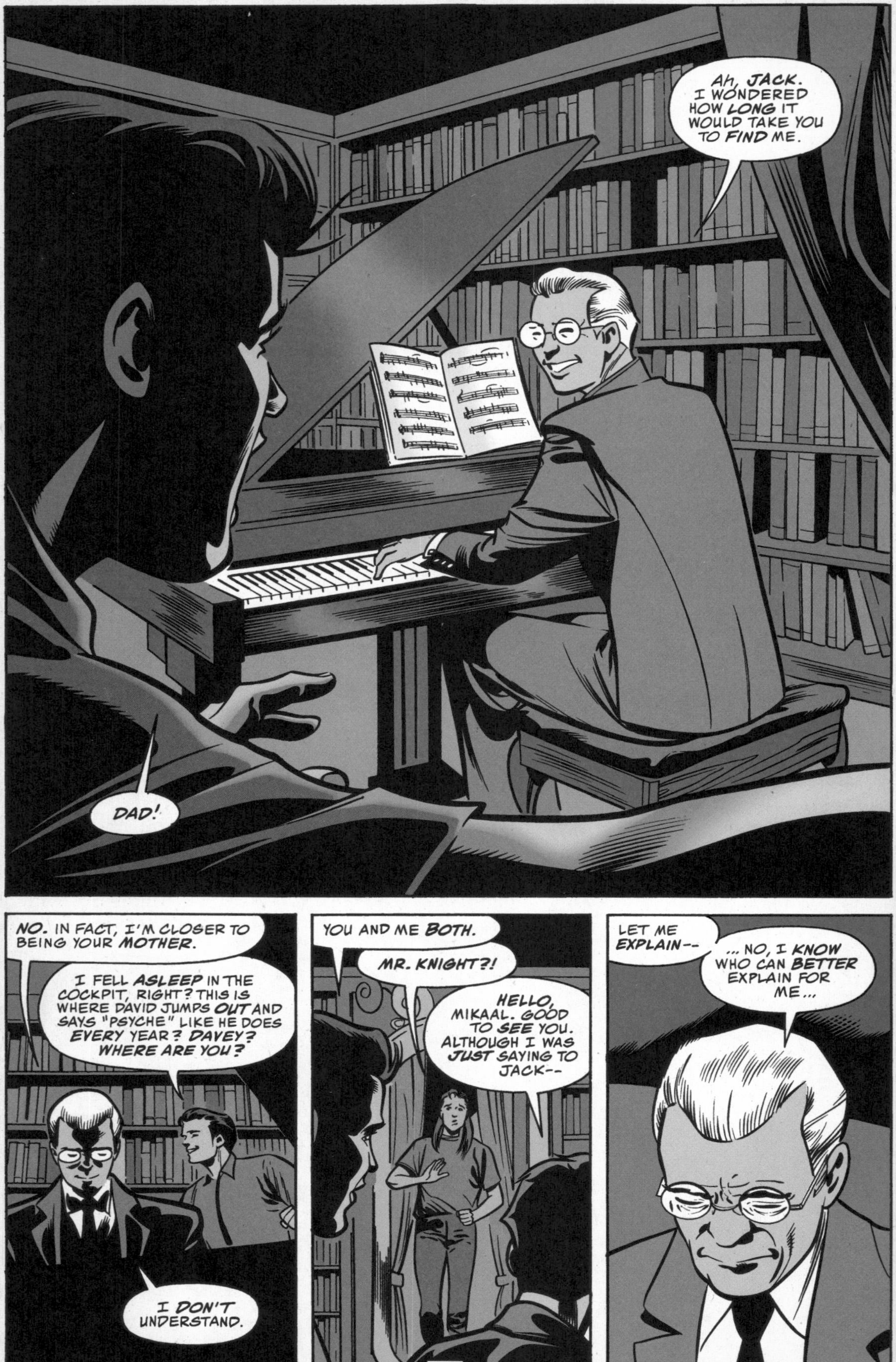
AH, JACK. I WONDERED HOW LONG IT WOULD TAKE YOU TO FIND ME.
DAD!
NO. IN FACT, I'M CLOSER TO BEING YOUR MOTHER.
I FELL ASLEEP IN THE COCKPIT, RIGHT? THIS IS WHERE DAVID JUMPS OUT AND SAYS "PSYCHE" LIKE HE DOES EVERY YEAR? DAVEY? WHERE ARE YOU?
I DON'T UNDERSTAND.
YOU AND ME BOTH.
MR. KNIGHT?!
HELLO, MIKAAL. GOOD TO SEE YOU. ALTHOUGH I WAS JUST SAYING TO JACK--
LET ME EXPLAIN--
...NO, I KNOW WHO CAN BETTER EXPLAIN FOR ME...

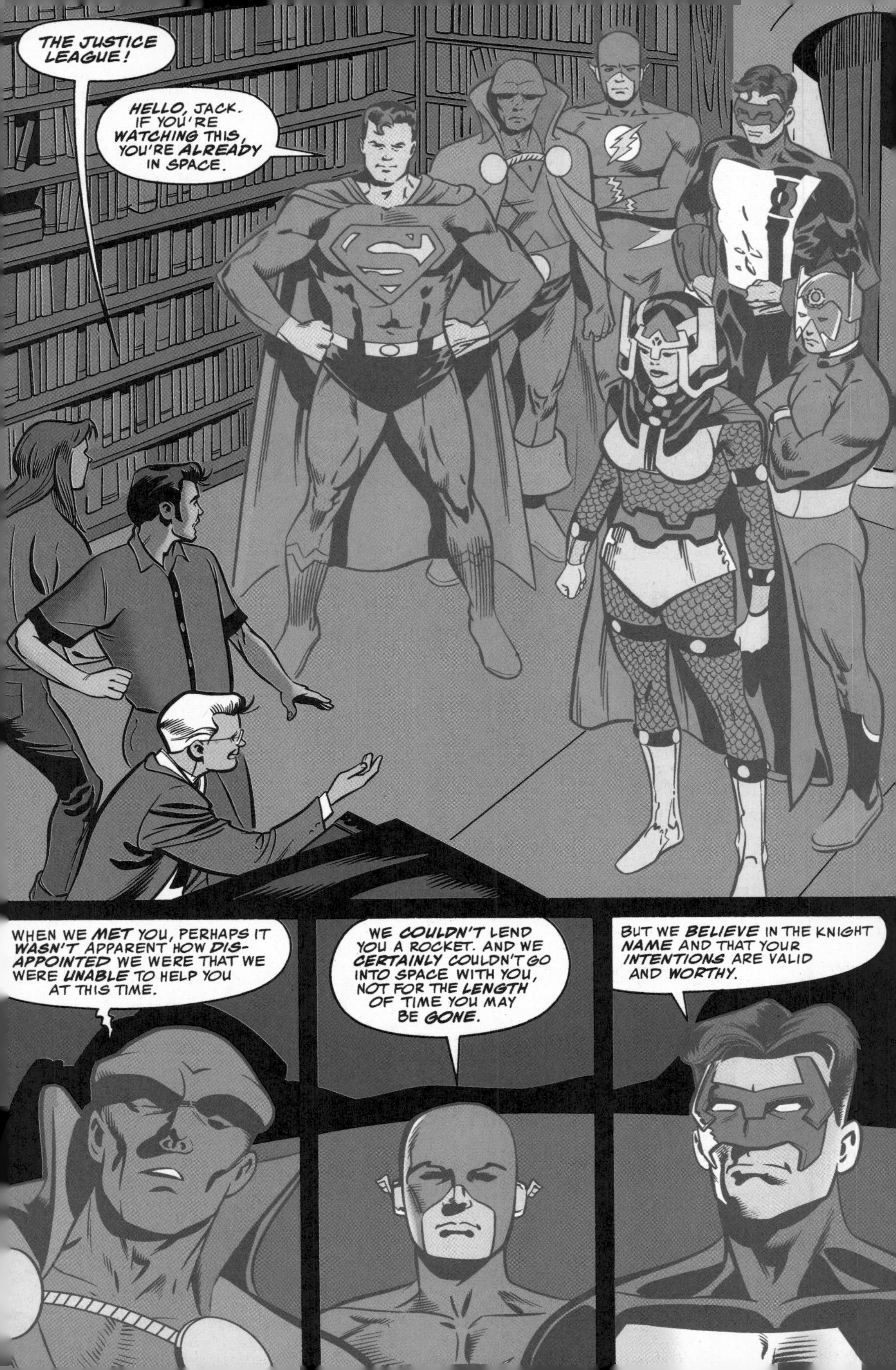
THE JUSTICE LEAGUE!
HELLO, JACK. IF YOU'RE WATCHING THIS, YOU'RE ALREADY IN SPACE.
WHEN WE MET YOU, PERHAPS IT WASN'T APPARENT HOW DIS-APPOINTED WE WERE THAT WE WERE UNABLE TO HELP YOU AT THIS TIME.
WE COULDN'T LEND YOU A ROCKET. AND WE CERTAINLY COULDN'T GO INTO SPACE WITH YOU, NOT FOR THE LENGTH OF TIME YOU MAY BE GONE.
BUT WE BELIEVE IN THE KNIGHT NAME AND THAT YOUR INTENTIONS ARE VALID AND WORTHY.

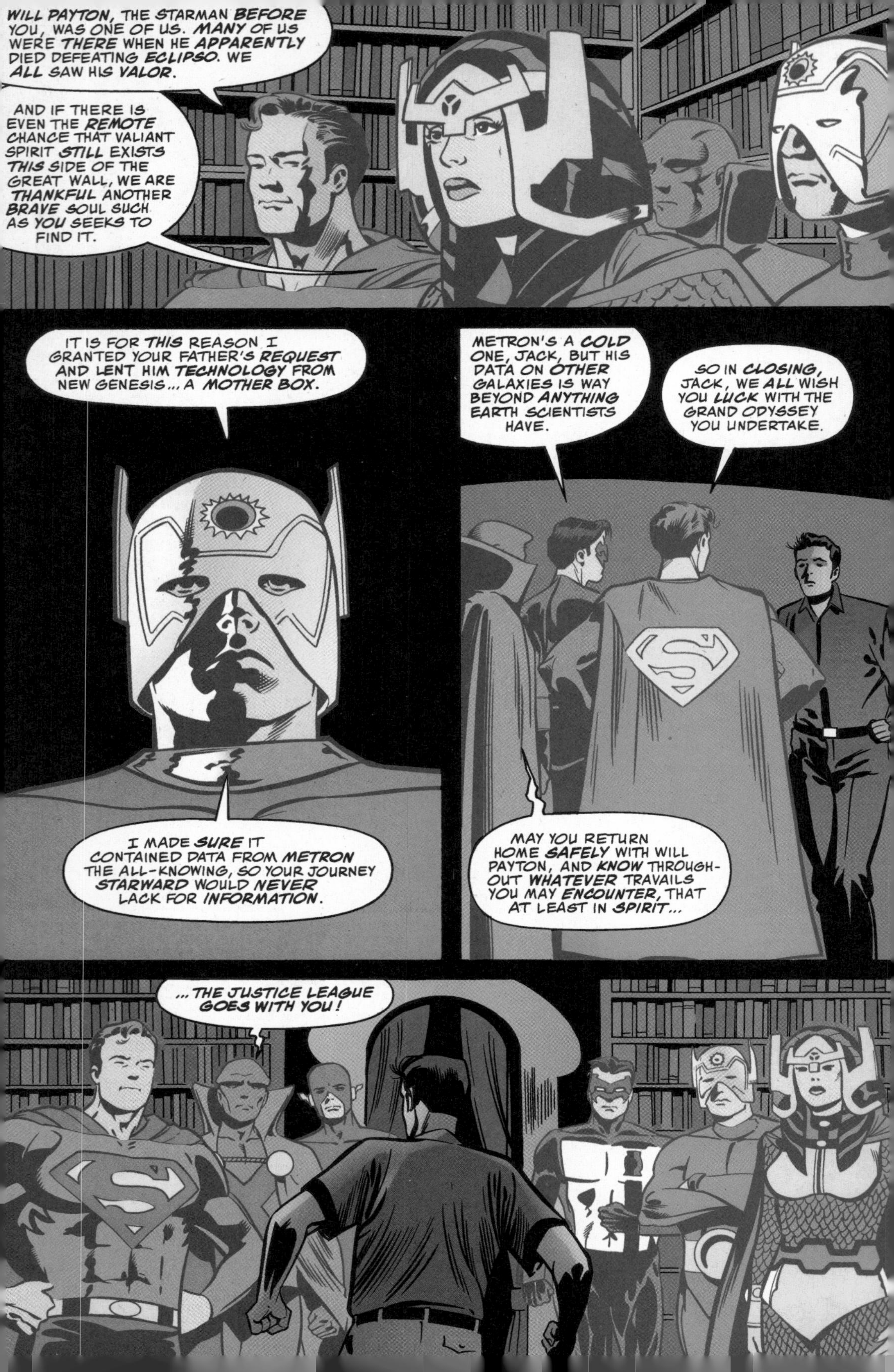
WILL PAYTON, THE STARMAN BEFORE YOU, WAS ONE OF US. MANY OF US WERE THERE WHEN HE APPARENTLY DIED DEFEATING ECLIPSO. WE ALL SAW HIS VALOR.
AND IF THERE IS EVEN THE REMOTE CHANCE THAT VALIANT SPIRIT STILL EXISTS THIS SIDE OF THE GREAT WALL, WE ARE THANKFUL ANOTHER BRAVE SOUL SUCH AS YOU SEEKS TO FIND IT.
IT IS FOR THIS REASON I GRANTED YOUR FATHER'S REQUEST AND LENT HIM TECHNOLOGY FROM NEW GENESIS... A MOTHER BOX.
I MADE SURE IT CONTAINED DATA FROM METRON THE ALL-KNOWING, SO YOUR JOURNEY STARWARD WOULD NEVER LACK FOR INFORMATION.
METRON'S A COLD ONE, JACK, BUT HIS DATA ON OTHER GALAXIES IS WAY BEYOND ANYTHING EARTH SCIENTISTS HAVE.
SO IN CLOSING, JACK, WE ALL WISH YOU LUCK WITH THE GRAND ODYSSEY YOU UNDERTAKE.
MAY YOU RETURN HOME SAFELY WITH WILL PAYTON, AND KNOW THROUGH-OUT WHATEVER TRAVAILS YOU MAY ENCOUNTER, THAT AT LEAST IN SPIRIT...
...THE JUSTICE LEAGUE GOES WITH YOU!

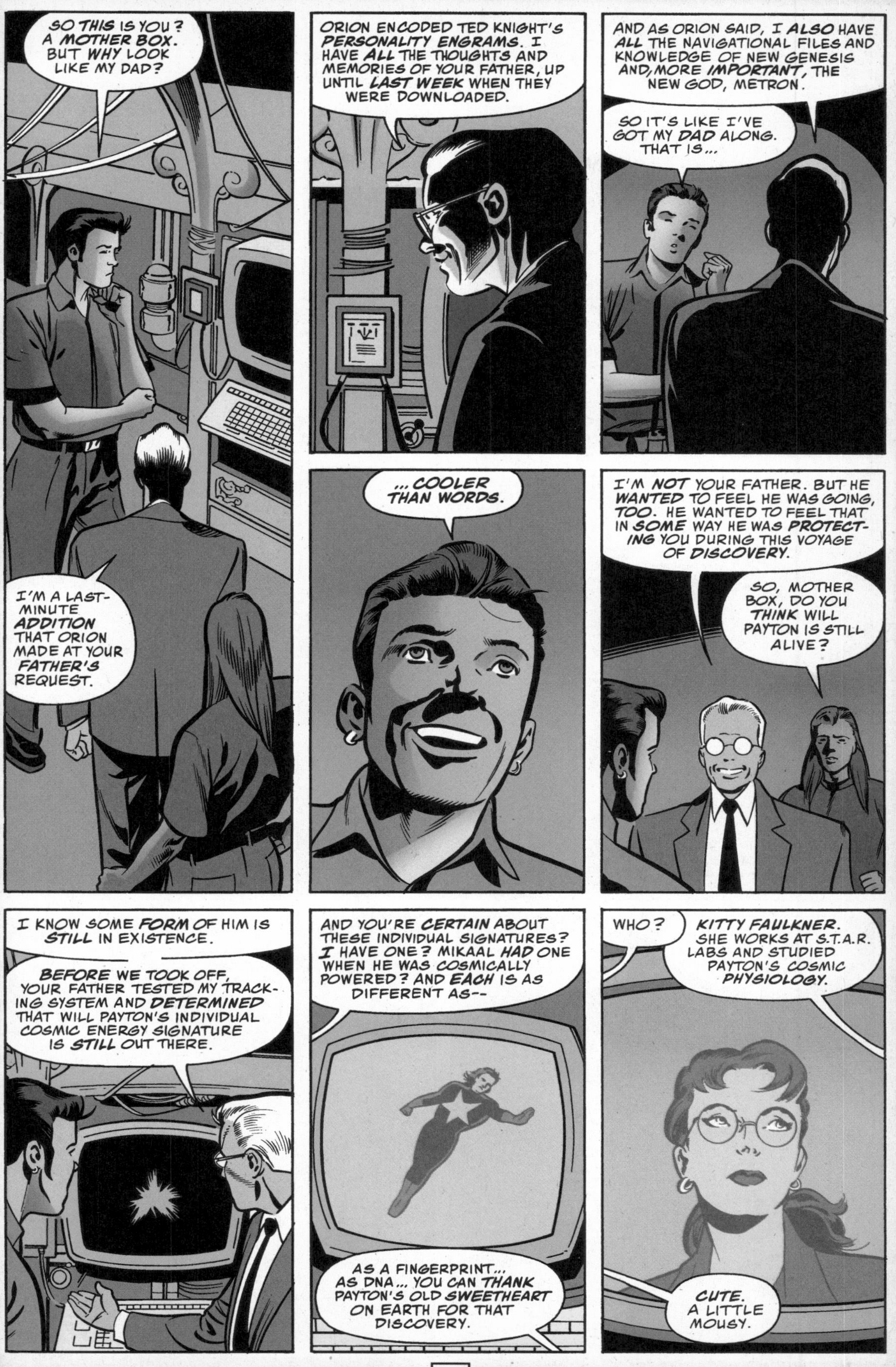
SO THIS IS YOU? A MOTHER BOX. BUT WHY LOOK LIKE MY DAD?
ORION ENCODED TED KNIGHT'S PERSONALITY ENGRAMS. I HAVE ALL THE THOUGHTS AND MEMORIES OF YOUR FATHER, UP UNTIL LAST WEEK WHEN THEY WERE DOWNLOADED.
AND AS ORION SAID, I ALSO HAVE ALL THE NAVIGATIONAL FILES AND KNOWLEDGE OF NEW GENESIS AND, MORE IMPORTANT, THE NEW GOD, METRON.
SO IT'S LIKE I'VE GOT MY DAD ALONG. THAT IS...
I'M A LAST-MINUTE ADDITION THAT ORION MADE AT YOUR FATHER'S REQUEST.
...COOLER THAN WORDS.
I'M NOT YOUR FATHER. BUT HE WANTED TO FEEL HE WAS GOING, TOO. HE WANTED TO FEEL THAT IN SOME WAY HE WAS PROTECTING YOU DURING THIS VOYAGE OF DISCOVERY.
SO, MOTHER BOX, DO YOU THINK WILL PAYTON IS STILL ALIVE?
I KNOW SOME FORM OF HIM IS STILL IN EXISTENCE.
BEFORE WE TOOK OFF, YOUR FATHER TESTED MY TRACKING SYSTEM AND DETERMINED THAT WILL PAYTON'S INDIVIDUAL COSMIC ENERGY SIGNATURE IS STILL OUT THERE.
AND YOU'RE CERTAIN ABOUT THESE INDIVIDUAL SIGNATURES? I HAVE ONE? MIKAAL HAD ONE WHEN HE WAS COSMICALLY POWERED? AND EACH IS AS DIFFERENT AS--
AS A FINGERPRINT... AS DNA... YOU CAN THANK PAYTON'S OLD SWEETHEART ON EARTH FOR THAT DISCOVERY.
WHO?
KITTY FAULKNER. SHE WORKS AT S.T.A.R. LABS AND STUDIED PAYTON'S COSMIC PHYSIOLOGY.
CUTE. A LITTLE MOUSY.

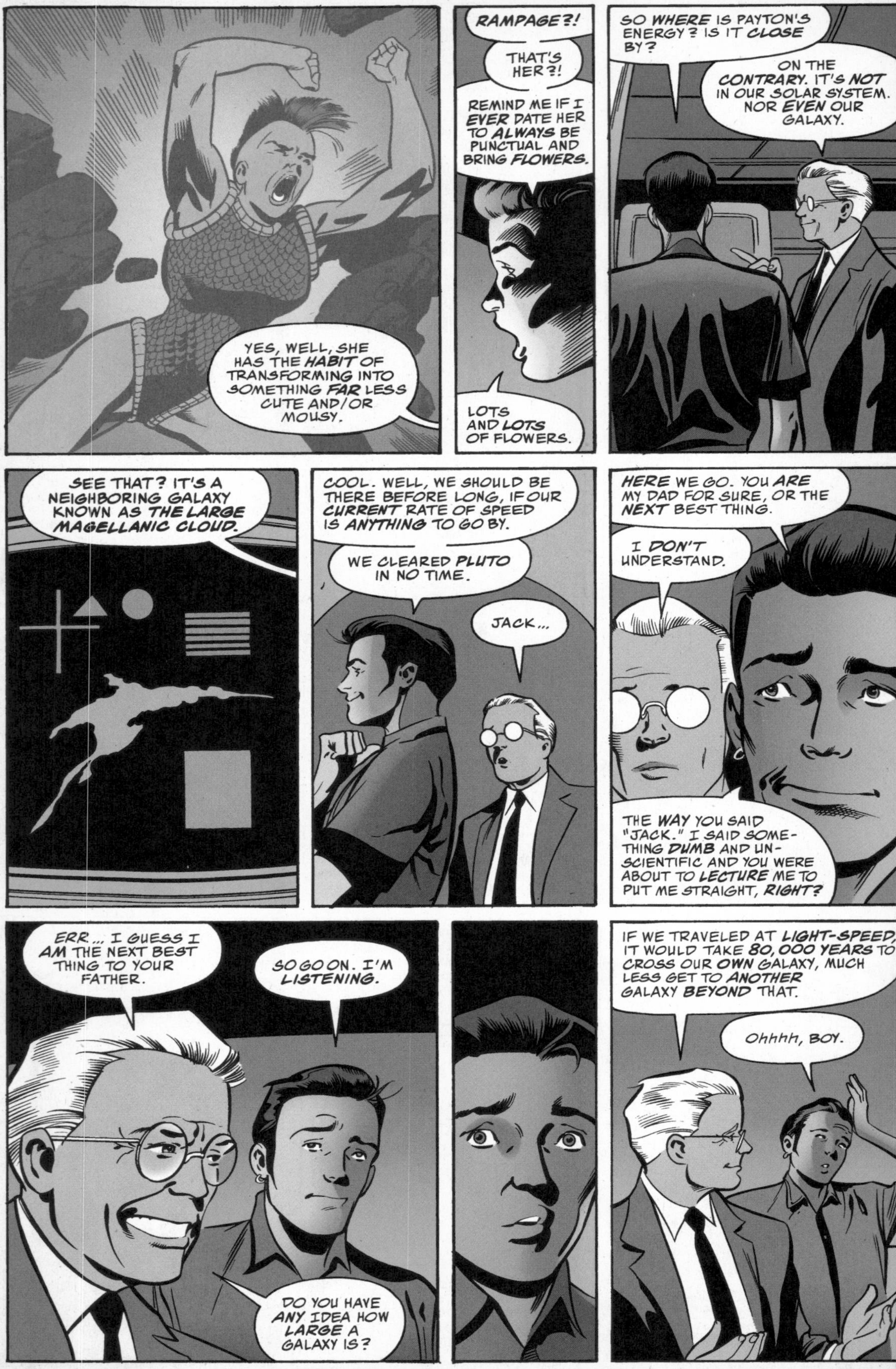

YES, WELL, SHE HAS THE HABIT OF TRANSFORMING INTO SOMETHING FAR LESS CUTE AND/OR MOUSY.
RAMPAGE?!
THAT'S HER?!
REMIND ME IF I EVER DATE HER TO ALWAYS BE PUNCTUAL AND BRING FLOWERS.
LOTS AND LOTS OF FLOWERS.
SO WHERE IS PAYTON'S ENERGY? IS IT CLOSE BY?
ON THE CONTRARY. IT'S NOT IN OUR SOLAR SYSTEM. NOR EVEN OUR GALAXY.
SEE THAT? IT'S A NEIGHBORING GALAXY KNOWN AS THE LARGE MAGELLANIC CLOUD.
COOL. WELL, WE SHOULD BE THERE BEFORE LONG, IF OUR CURRENT RATE OF SPEED IS ANYTHING TO GO BY.
WE CLEARED PLUTO IN NO TIME.
JACK...
HERE WE GO. YOU ARE MY DAD FOR SURE, OR THE NEXT BEST THING.
I DON'T UNDERSTAND.
THE WAY YOU SAID "JACK." I SAID SOME-THING DUMB AND UN-SCIENTIFIC AND YOU WERE ABOUT TO LECTURE ME TO PUT ME STRAIGHT, RIGHT?
ERR... I GUESS I AM THE NEXT BEST THING TO YOUR FATHER.
SO GO ON. I'M LISTENING.
DO YOU HAVE ANY IDEA HOW LARGE A GALAXY IS?
IF WE TRAVELED AT LIGHT-SPEED, IT WOULD TAKE 80,000 YEARS TO CROSS OUR OWN GALAXY, MUCH LESS GET TO ANOTHER GALAXY BEYOND THAT.
Ohhhh, BOY.

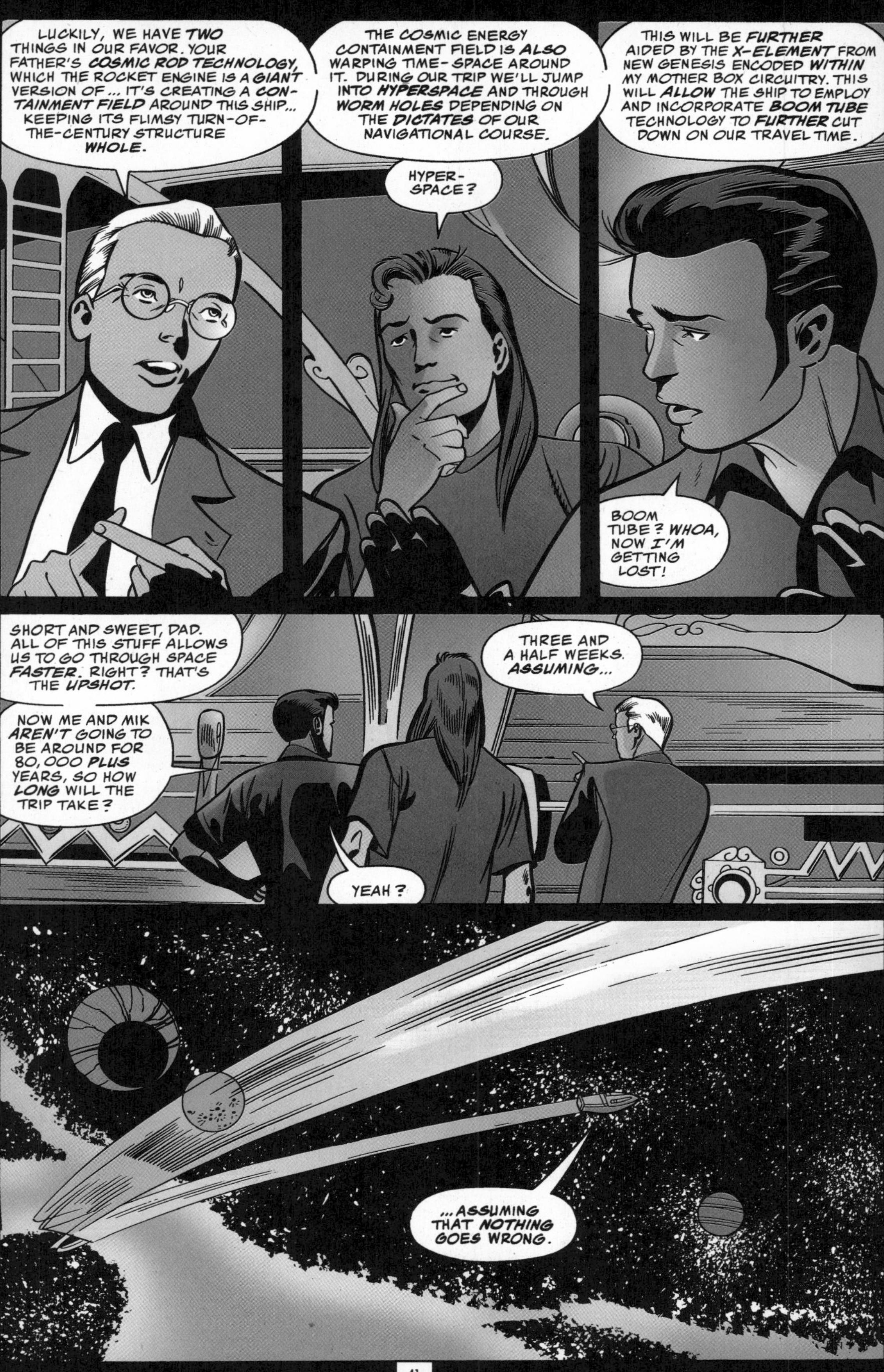
LUCKILY, WE HAVE TWO THINGS IN OUR FAVOR. YOUR FATHER'S COSMIC ROD TECHNOLOGY, WHICH THE ROCKET ENGINE IS A GIANT VERSION OF... IT'S CREATING A CONTAINMENT FIELD AROUND THIS SHIP... KEEPING ITS FLIMSY TURN-OF-THE-CENTURY STRUCTURE WHOLE.
THE COSMIC ENERGY CONTAINMENT FIELD IS ALSO WARPING TIME-SPACE AROUND IT. DURING OUR TRIP WE'LL JUMP INTO HYPERSPACE AND THROUGH WORM HOLES DEPENDING ON THE DICTATES OF OUR NAVIGATIONAL COURSE.
HYPER-SPACE?
THIS WILL BE FURTHER AIDED BY THE X-ELEMENT FROM NEW GENESIS ENCODED WITHIN MY MOTHER BOX CIRCUITRY. THIS WILL ALLOW THE SHIP TO EMPLOY AND INCORPORATE BOOM TUBE TECHNOLOGY TO FURTHER CUT DOWN ON OUR TRAVEL TIME.
BOOM TUBE? WHOA, NOW I'M GETTING LOST!
SHORT AND SWEET, DAD. ALL OF THIS STUFF ALLOWS US TO GO THROUGH SPACE FASTER. RIGHT? THAT'S THE UPSHOT.
NOW ME AND MIK AREN'T GOING TO BE AROUND FOR 80,000 PLUS YEARS, SO HOW LONG WILL THE TRIP TAKE?
THREE AND A HALF WEEKS. ASSUMING...
YEAH?
...ASSUMING THAT NOTHING GOES WRONG.

RISEWAKESHAKE!

R;∀Q!

KOMAK! YOU'RE DEAD!

DARKWENT? CAN YOU ADDLESPITE?

◁;º∠Ṏ∀Ö∴

TURRAN KHA? YOU'RE DEAD, TOO! I KILLED YOU BOTH!

SLIP-GLASS! SAW AND FLIGHT-FAST!

FALLOWFIND THIS PIECE OF SLIGHT. OH, SHE'LL DARKWENT TWO TIME!

LYYSA! YOU MURDERED HER! HOW CAN YOU ALL BE ALIVE?

NOT SHE!

NO! NO!!

I KILLED YOU--

--KILLED YOU ONCE.

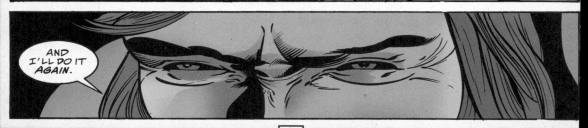

AND I'LL DO IT AGAIN.

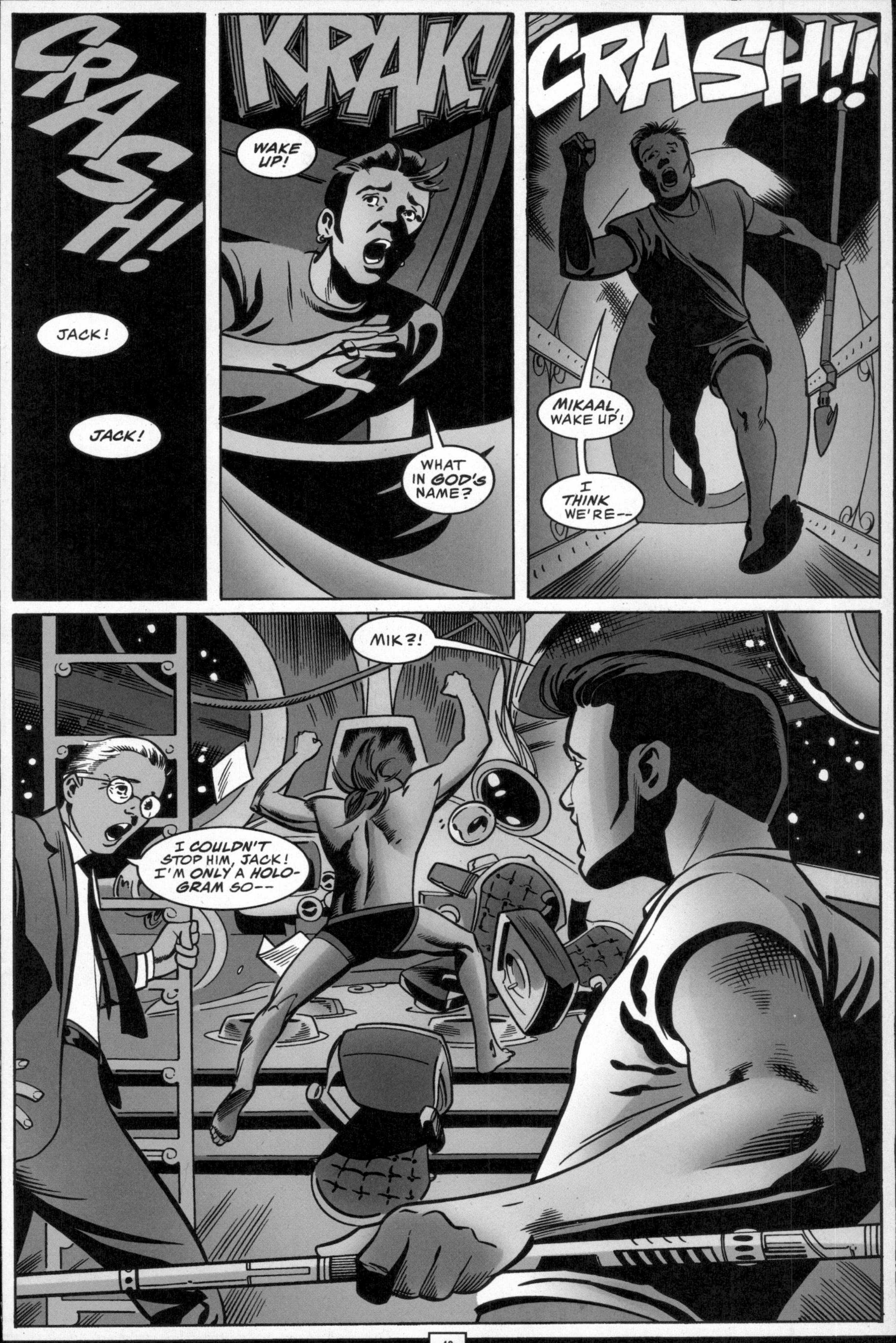
CRASH!
JACK!
JACK!
KRAK!
WAKE UP!
WHAT IN GOD'S NAME?
CRASH!!
MIKAAL, WAKE UP!
I THINK WE'RE--
MIK?!
I COULDN'T STOP HIM, JACK! I'M ONLY A HOLOGRAM SO--

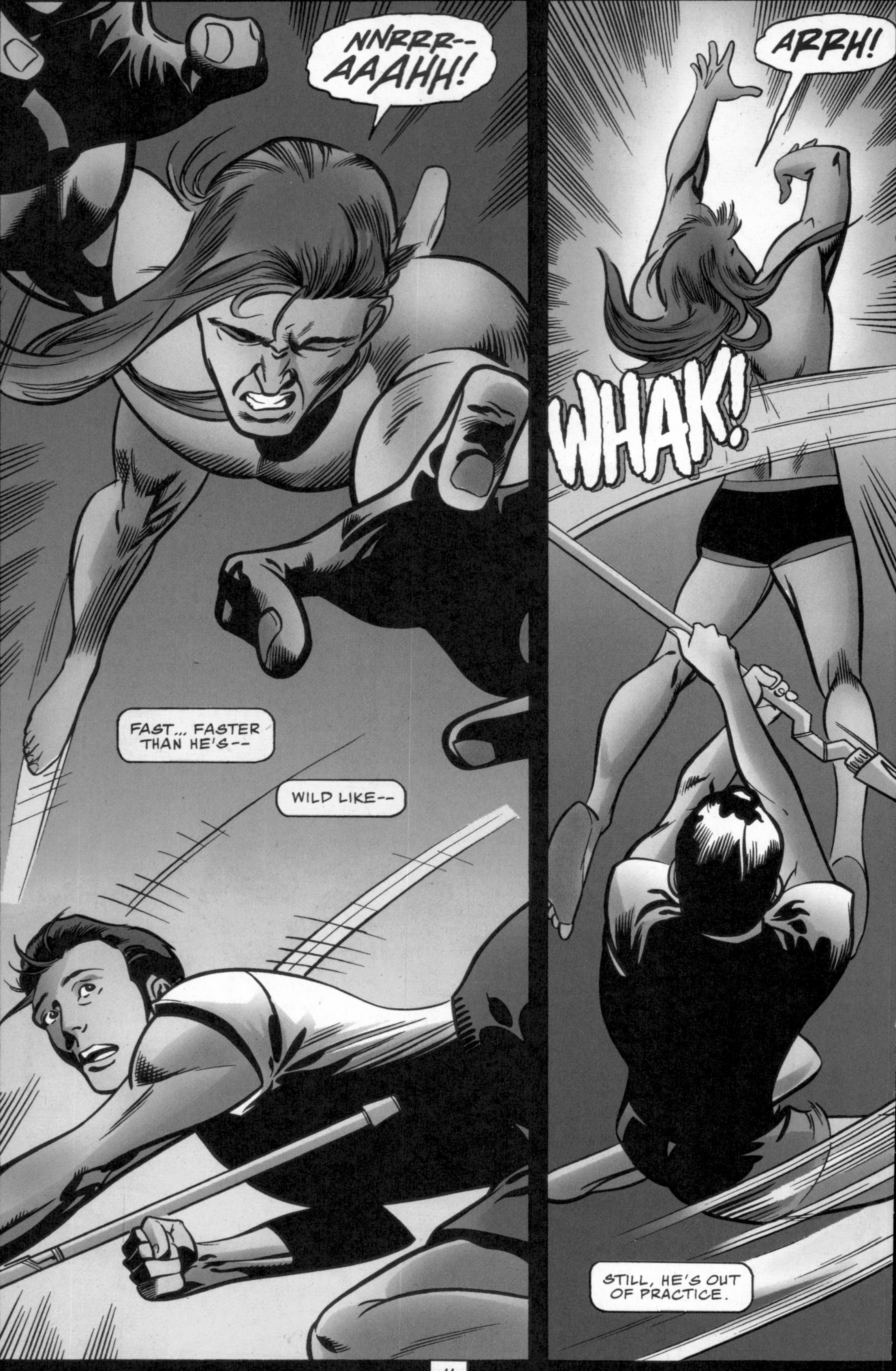
NNRRR--AAAHH!
FAST... FASTER THAN HE'S--
WILD LIKE--
ARRH!
WHAK!
STILL, HE'S OUT OF PRACTICE.

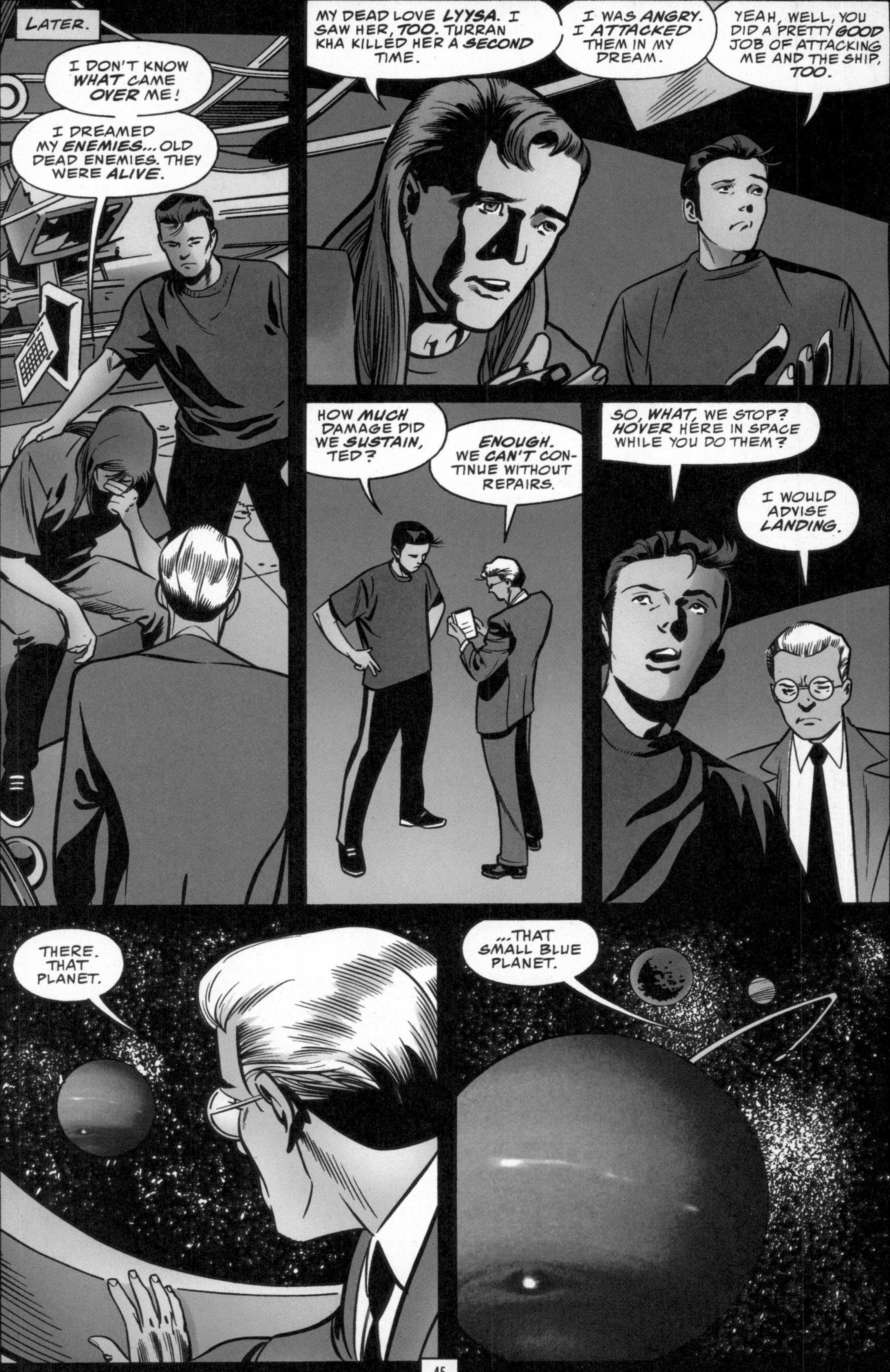
LATER.
I DON'T KNOW WHAT CAME OVER ME!
I DREAMED MY ENEMIES... OLD DEAD ENEMIES. THEY WERE ALIVE.
MY DEAD LOVE LYYSA. I SAW HER, TOO. TURRAN KHA KILLED HER A SECOND TIME.
I WAS ANGRY. I ATTACKED THEM IN MY DREAM.
YEAH, WELL, YOU DID A PRETTY GOOD JOB OF ATTACKING ME AND THE SHIP, TOO.
HOW MUCH DAMAGE DID WE SUSTAIN, TED?
ENOUGH. WE CAN'T CONTINUE WITHOUT REPAIRS.
SO, WHAT, WE STOP? HOVER HERE IN SPACE WHILE YOU DO THEM?
I WOULD ADVISE LANDING.
THERE. THAT PLANET.
...THAT SMALL BLUE PLANET.

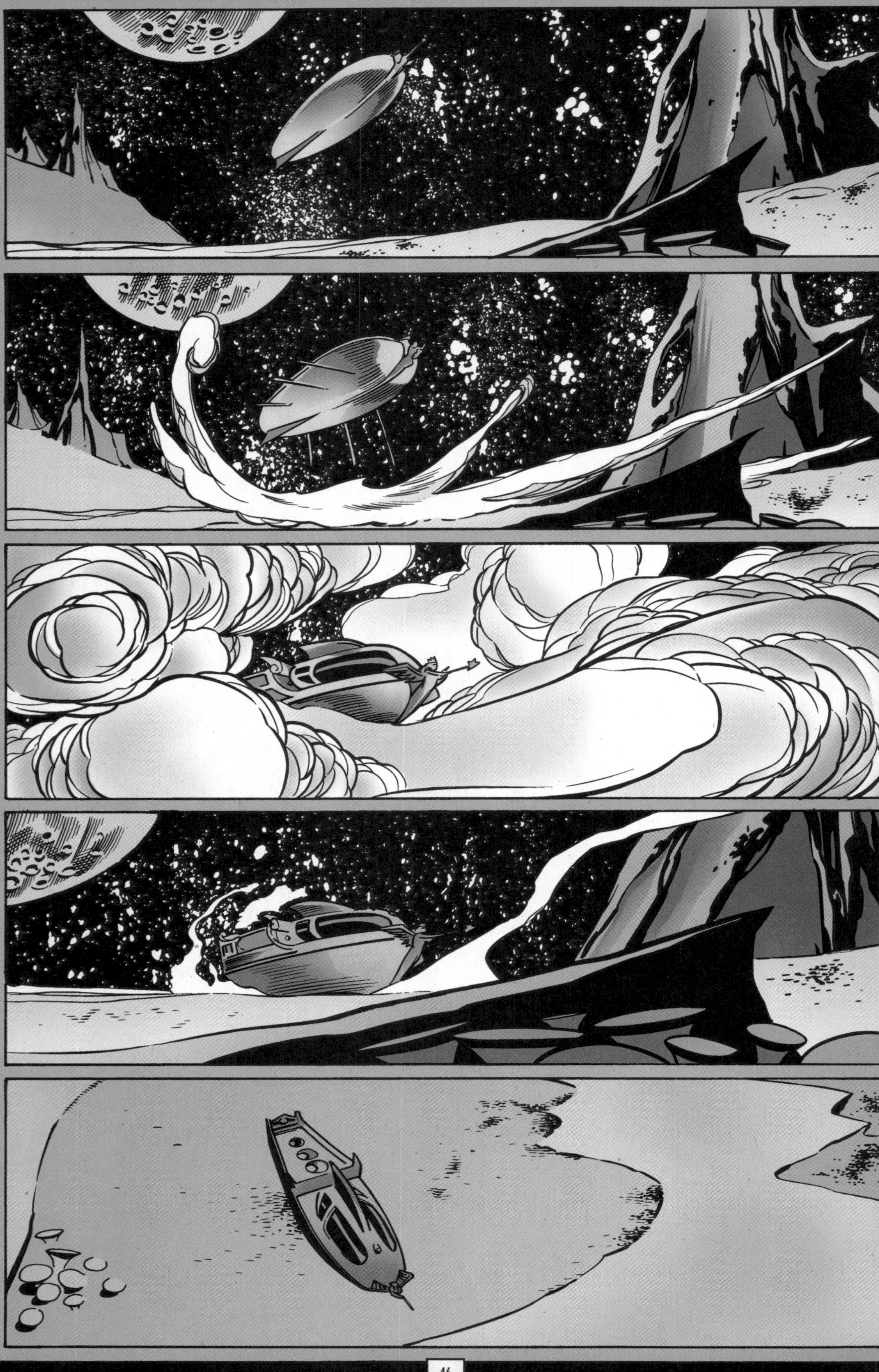

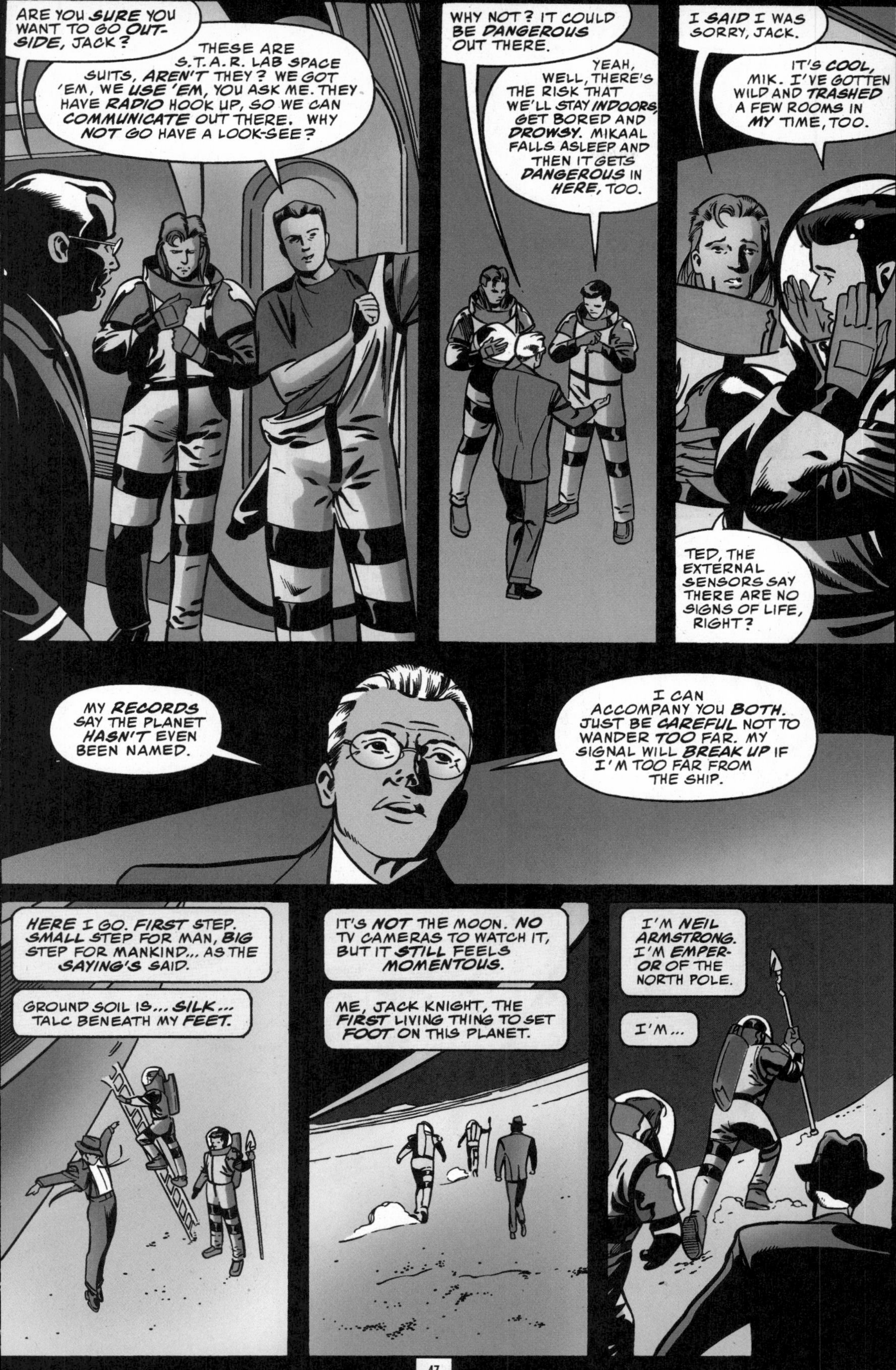

ARE YOU SURE YOU WANT TO GO OUT-SIDE, JACK?
THESE ARE S.T.A.R. LAB SPACE SUITS, AREN'T THEY? WE GOT 'EM, WE USE 'EM, YOU ASK ME. THEY HAVE RADIO HOOK UP, SO WE CAN COMMUNICATE OUT THERE. WHY NOT GO HAVE A LOOK-SEE?
WHY NOT? IT COULD BE DANGEROUS OUT THERE.
YEAH, WELL, THERE'S THE RISK THAT WE'LL STAY INDOORS, GET BORED AND DROWSY. MIKAAL FALLS ASLEEP AND THEN IT GETS DANGEROUS IN HERE, TOO.
I SAID I WAS SORRY, JACK.
IT'S COOL, MIK. I'VE GOTTEN WILD AND TRASHED A FEW ROOMS IN MY TIME, TOO.
TED, THE EXTERNAL SENSORS SAY THERE ARE NO SIGNS OF LIFE, RIGHT?
MY RECORDS SAY THE PLANET HASN'T EVEN BEEN NAMED.
I CAN ACCOMPANY YOU BOTH. JUST BE CAREFUL NOT TO WANDER TOO FAR. MY SIGNAL WILL BREAK UP IF I'M TOO FAR FROM THE SHIP.
HERE I GO. FIRST STEP. SMALL STEP FOR MAN, BIG STEP FOR MANKIND... AS THE SAYING'S SAID.
GROUND SOIL IS... SILK... TALC BENEATH MY FEET.
IT'S NOT THE MOON. NO TV CAMERAS TO WATCH IT, BUT IT STILL FEELS MOMENTOUS.
ME, JACK KNIGHT, THE FIRST LIVING THING TO SET FOOT ON THIS PLANET.
I'M NEIL ARMSTRONG. I'M EMPER-OR OF THE NORTH POLE.
I'M...

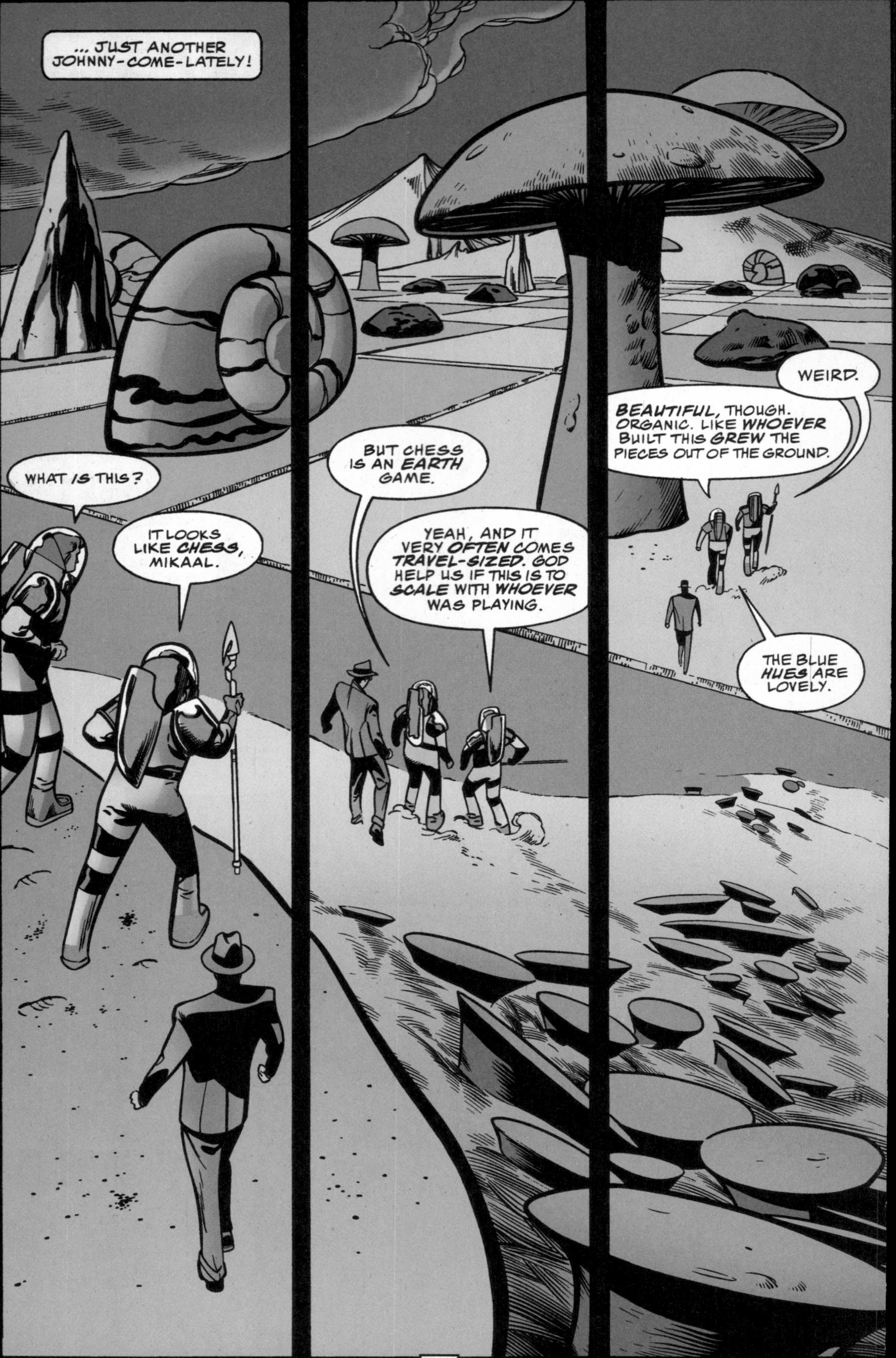
... JUST ANOTHER JOHNNY-COME-LATELY!
WHAT IS THIS?
IT LOOKS LIKE CHESS, MIKAAL.
BUT CHESS IS AN EARTH GAME.
YEAH, AND IT VERY OFTEN COMES TRAVEL-SIZED. GOD HELP US IF THIS IS TO SCALE WITH WHOEVER WAS PLAYING.
WEIRD.
BEAUTIFUL, THOUGH. ORGANIC. LIKE WHOEVER BUILT THIS GREW THE PIECES OUT OF THE GROUND.
THE BLUE HUES ARE LOVELY.

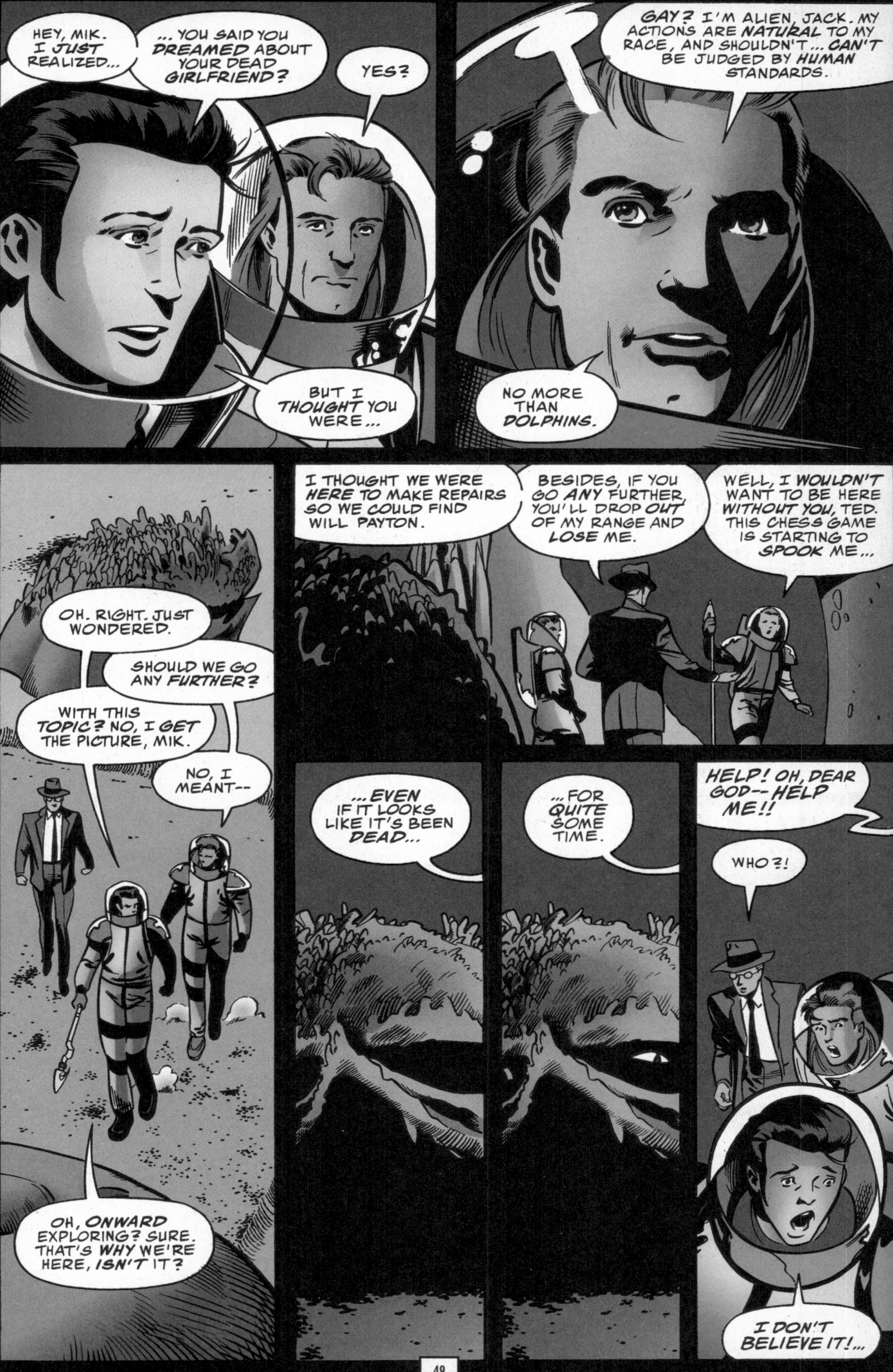
HEY, MIK. I JUST REALIZED...
...YOU SAID YOU DREAMED ABOUT YOUR DEAD GIRLFRIEND?
YES?
BUT I THOUGHT YOU WERE...
GAY? I'M ALIEN, JACK. MY ACTIONS ARE NATURAL TO MY RACE, AND SHOULDN'T... CAN'T BE JUDGED BY HUMAN STANDARDS.
NO MORE THAN DOLPHINS.
OH. RIGHT. JUST WONDERED.
SHOULD WE GO ANY FURTHER?
WITH THIS TOPIC? NO, I GET THE PICTURE, MIK.
NO, I MEANT--
OH, ONWARD EXPLORING? SURE. THAT'S WHY WE'RE HERE, ISN'T IT?
I THOUGHT WE WERE HERE TO MAKE REPAIRS SO WE COULD FIND WILL PAYTON.
BESIDES, IF YOU GO ANY FURTHER, YOU'LL DROP OUT OF MY RANGE AND LOSE ME.
WELL, I WOULDN'T WANT TO BE HERE WITHOUT YOU, TED. THIS CHESS GAME IS STARTING TO SPOOK ME...
...EVEN IF IT LOOKS LIKE IT'S BEEN DEAD...
...FOR QUITE SOME TIME.
HELP! OH, DEAR GOD-- HELP ME!!
WHO?!
I DON'T BELIEVE IT!...

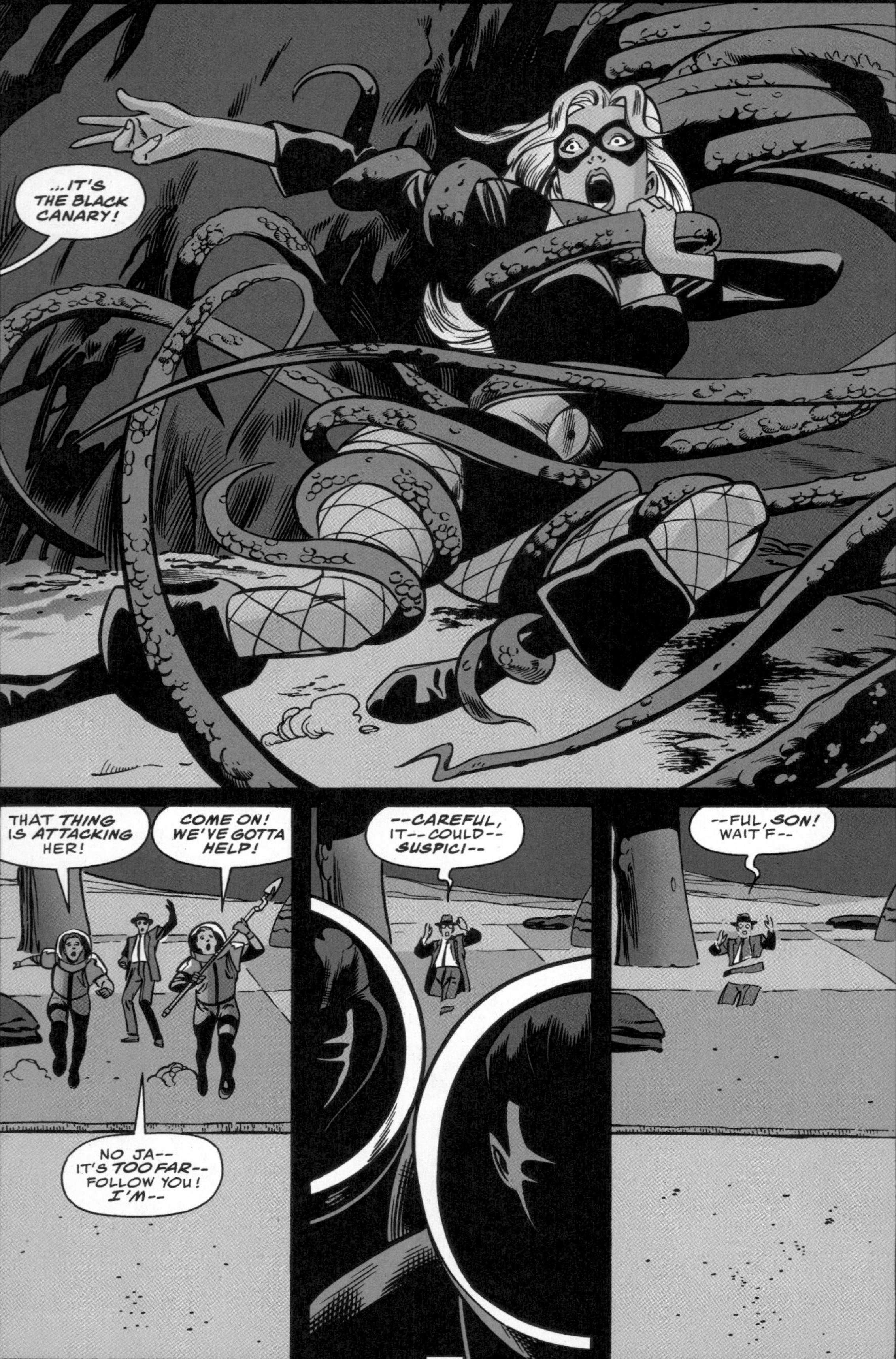

...IT'S THE BLACK CANARY!
THAT THING IS ATTACKING HER!
COME ON! WE'VE GOTTA HELP!
NO JA-- IT'S TOO FAR-- FOLLOW YOU! I'M--
--CAREFUL, IT--COULD-- SUSPICI--
--FUL, SON! WAIT F--

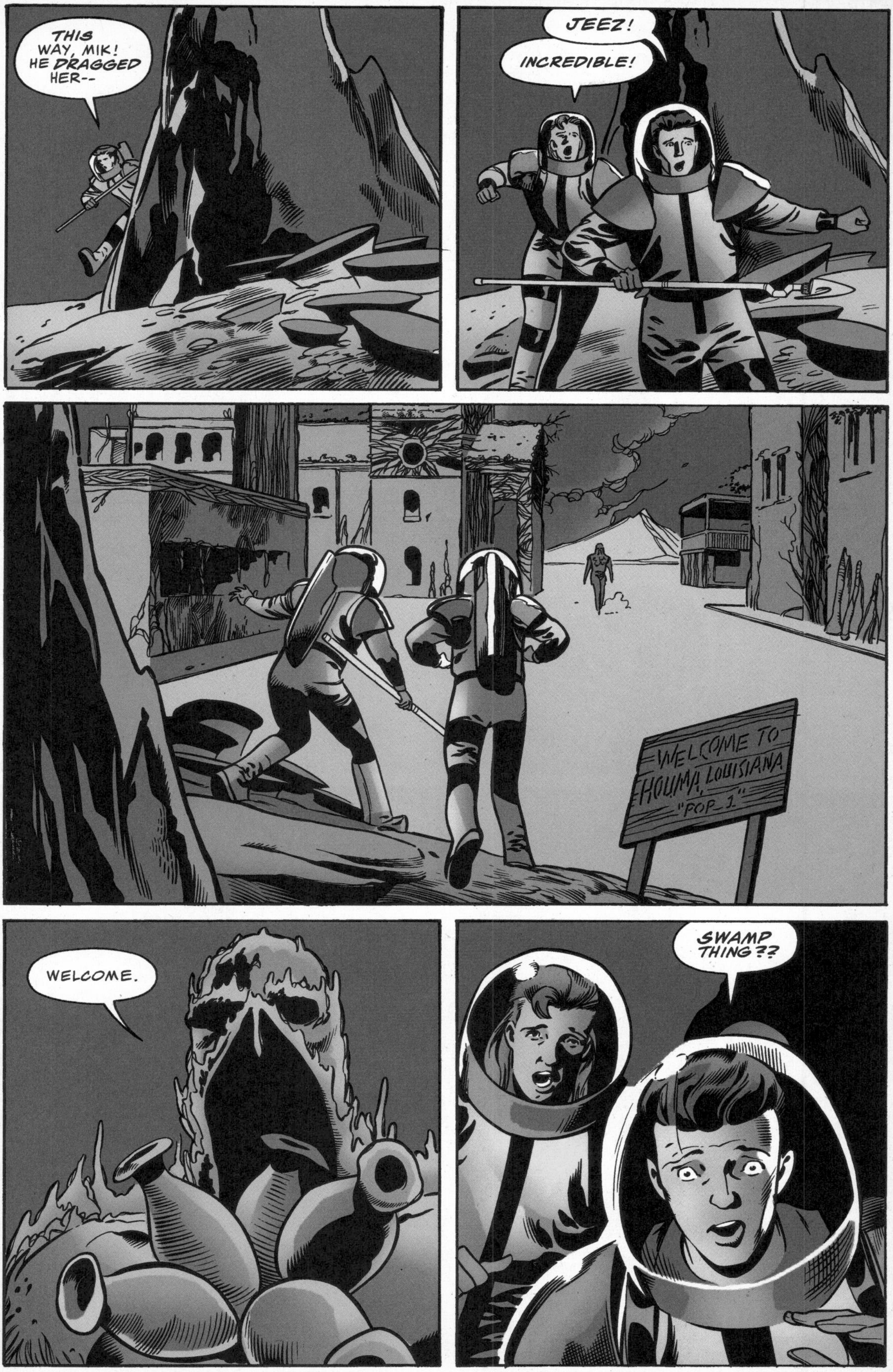
THIS WAY, MIK! HE DRAGGED HER--
JEEZ!
INCREDIBLE!
WELCOME TO HOUMA, LOUISIANA "POP_1"
WELCOME.
SWAMP THING??

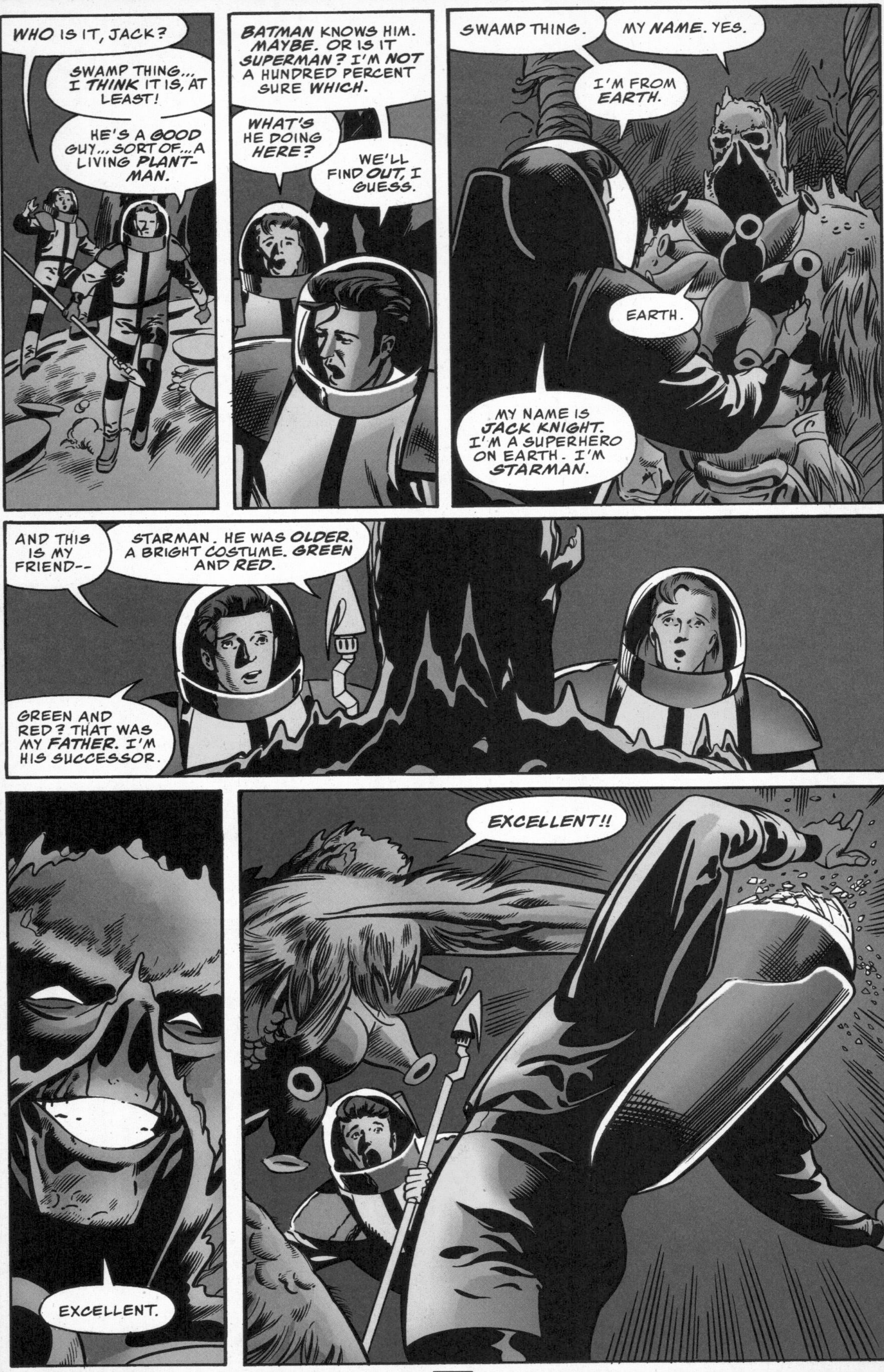
WHO IS IT, JACK?
SWAMP THING... I THINK IT IS, AT LEAST!
HE'S A GOOD GUY... SORT OF... A LIVING PLANT-MAN.
BATMAN KNOWS HIM. MAYBE. OR IS IT SUPERMAN? I'M NOT A HUNDRED PERCENT SURE WHICH.
WHAT'S HE DOING HERE?
WE'LL FIND OUT, I GUESS.
SWAMP THING.
MY NAME. YES.
I'M FROM EARTH.
EARTH.
MY NAME IS JACK KNIGHT. I'M A SUPERHERO ON EARTH. I'M STARMAN.
AND THIS IS MY FRIEND--
STARMAN. HE WAS OLDER. A BRIGHT COSTUME. GREEN AND RED.
GREEN AND RED? THAT WAS MY FATHER. I'M HIS SUCCESSOR.
EXCELLENT.
EXCELLENT!!

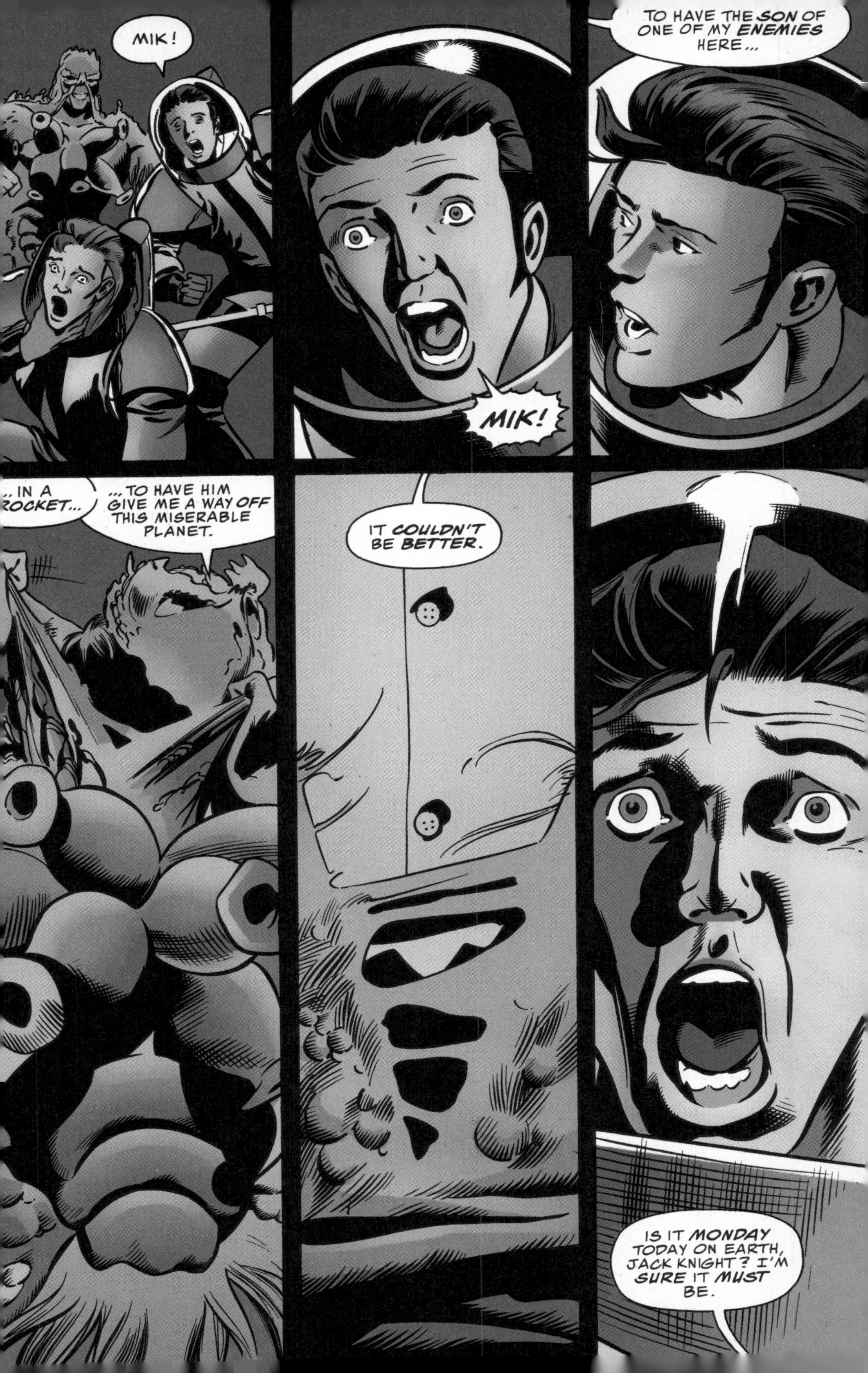
MIK!
MIK!
TO HAVE THE SON OF ONE OF MY ENEMIES HERE...
...IN A ROCKET...
...TO HAVE HIM GIVE ME A WAY OFF THIS MISERABLE PLANET.
IT COULDN'T BE BETTER.
IS IT MONDAY TODAY ON EARTH, JACK KNIGHT? I'M SURE IT MUST BE.

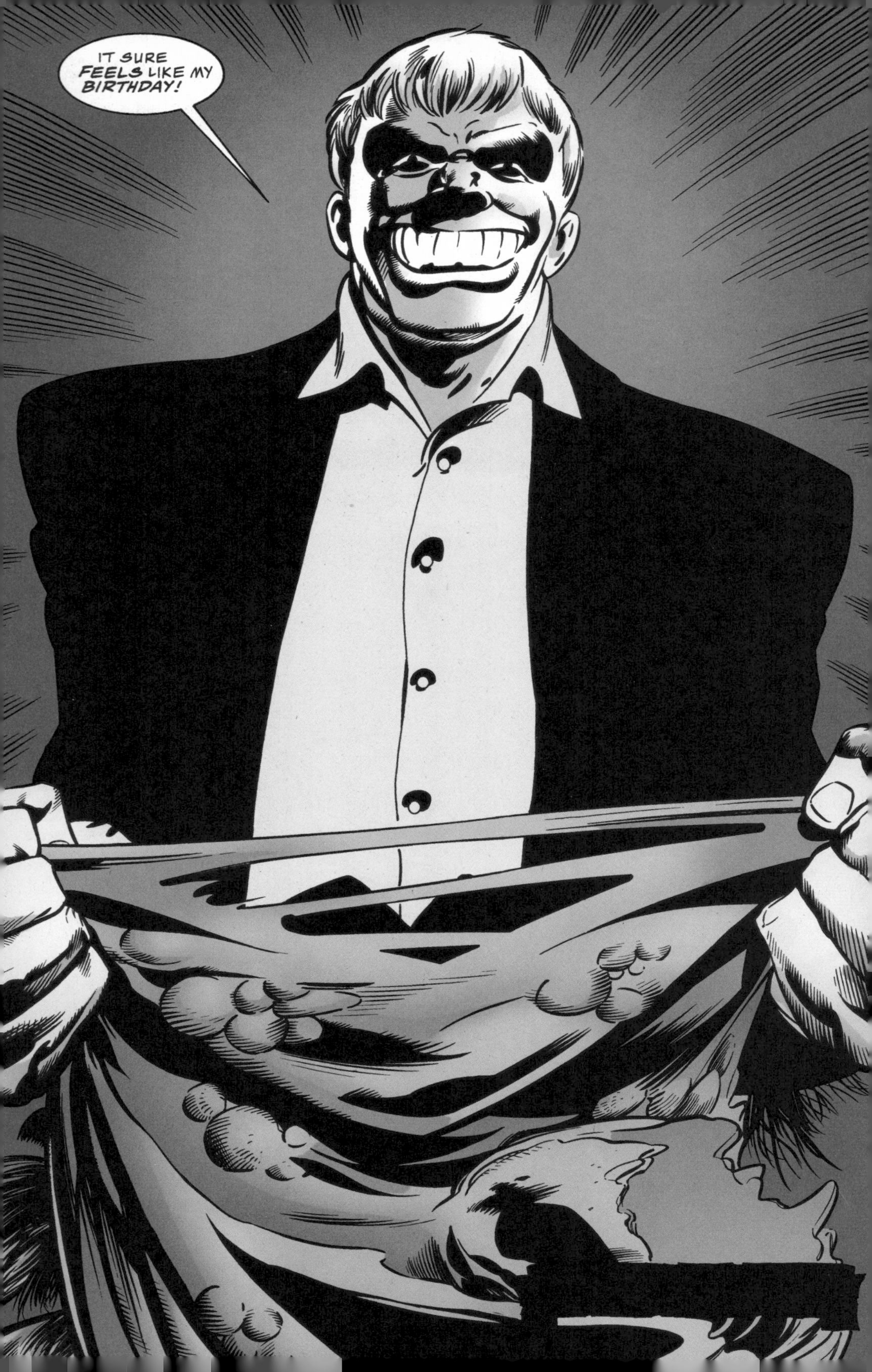
IT SURE FEELS LIKE MY BIRTHDAY!

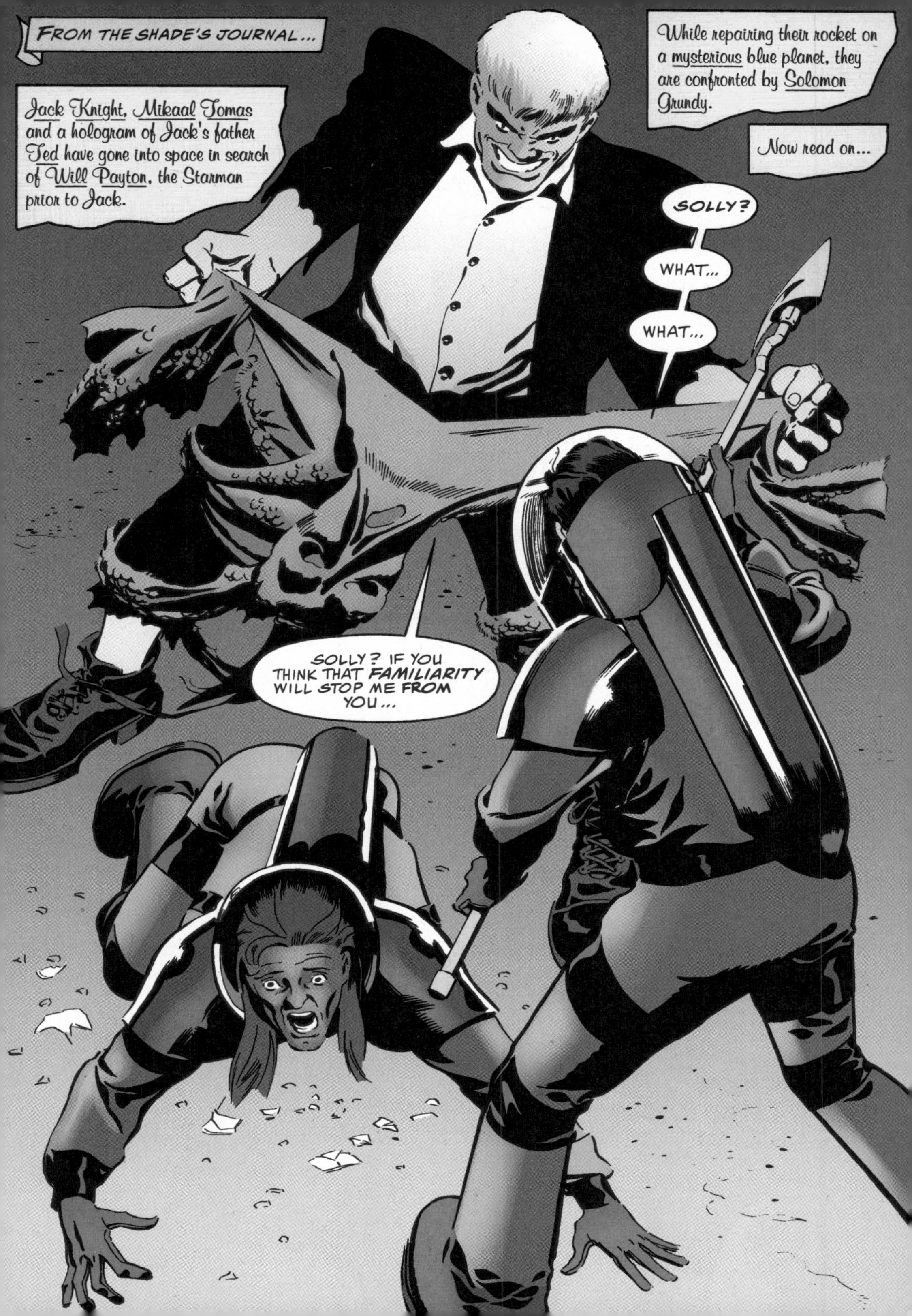
FROM THE SHADE'S JOURNAL...
Jack Knight, Mikaal Tomas and a hologram of Jack's father Ted have gone into space in search of Will Payton, the Starman prior to Jack.
While repairing their rocket on a mysterious blue planet, they are confronted by Solomon Grundy.
Now read on...
SOLLY?
WHAT...
WHAT...
SOLLY? IF YOU THINK THAT FAMILIARITY WILL STOP ME FROM YOU...

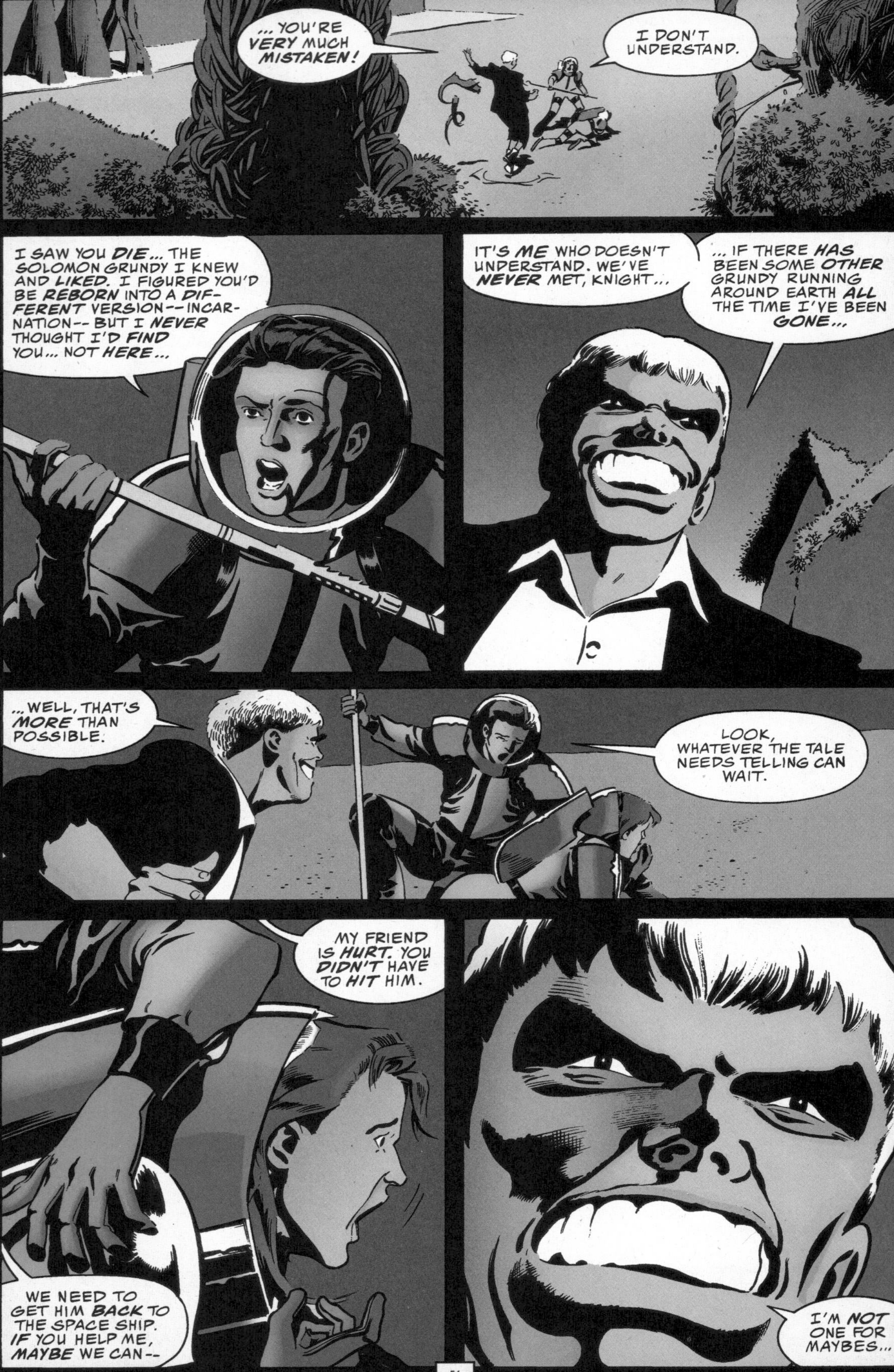
...YOU'RE VERY MUCH MISTAKEN!
I DON'T UNDERSTAND.
I SAW YOU DIE... THE SOLOMON GRUNDY I KNEW AND LIKED. I FIGURED YOU'D BE REBORN INTO A DIFFERENT VERSION--INCARNATION-- BUT I NEVER THOUGHT I'D FIND YOU... NOT HERE...
IT'S ME WHO DOESN'T UNDERSTAND. WE'VE NEVER MET, KNIGHT...
...IF THERE HAS BEEN SOME OTHER GRUNDY RUNNING AROUND EARTH ALL THE TIME I'VE BEEN GONE...
...WELL, THAT'S MORE THAN POSSIBLE.
LOOK, WHATEVER THE TALE NEEDS TELLING CAN WAIT.
MY FRIEND IS HURT. YOU DIDN'T HAVE TO HIT HIM.
WE NEED TO GET HIM BACK TO THE SPACE SHIP. IF YOU HELP ME, MAYBE WE CAN--
I'M NOT ONE FOR MAYBES...

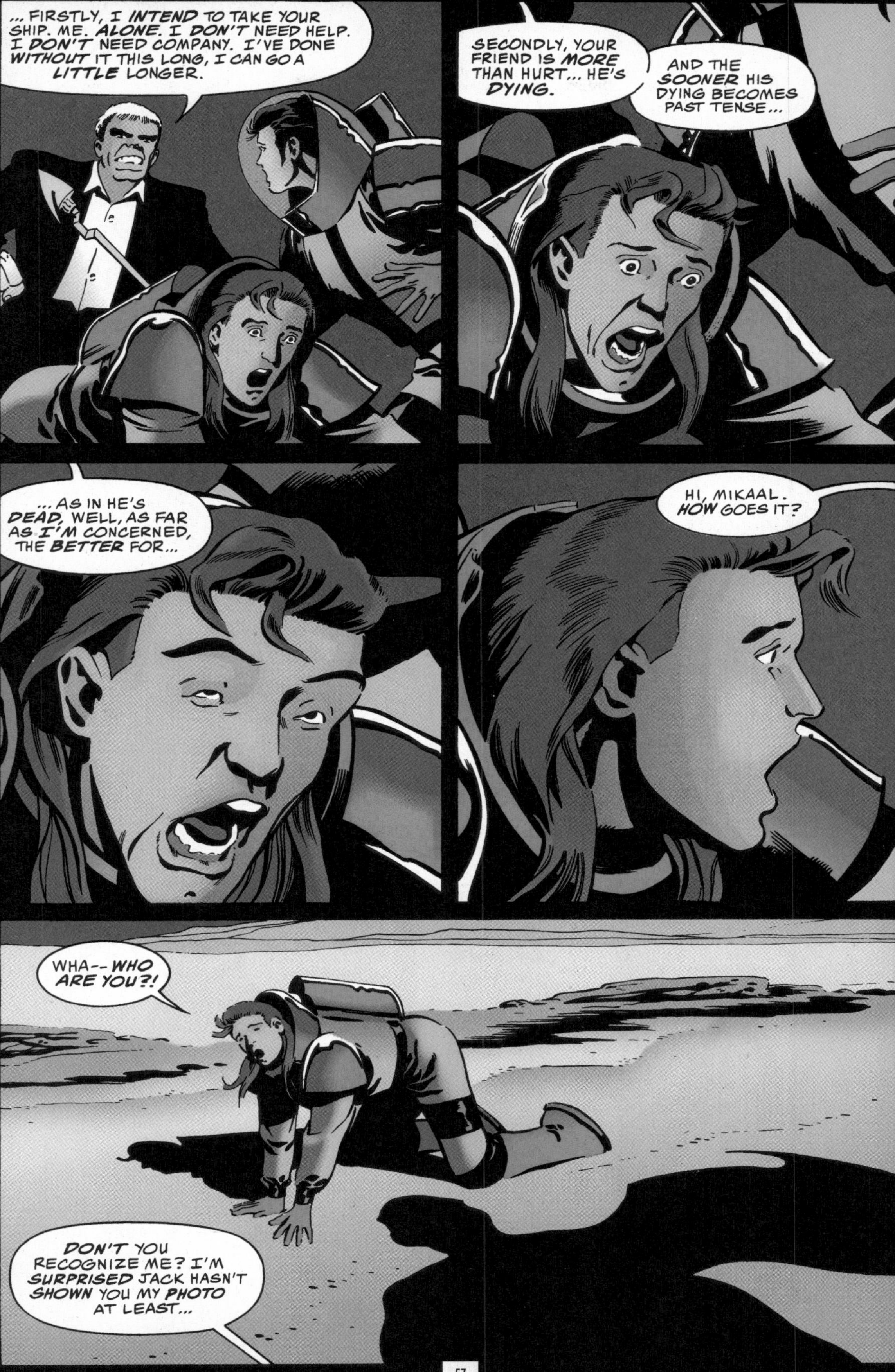
...FIRSTLY, I INTEND TO TAKE YOUR SHIP. ME. ALONE. I DON'T NEED HELP. I DON'T NEED COMPANY. I'VE DONE WITHOUT IT THIS LONG, I CAN GO A LITTLE LONGER.
SECONDLY, YOUR FRIEND IS MORE THAN HURT... HE'S DYING.
AND THE SOONER HIS DYING BECOMES PAST TENSE...
...AS IN HE'S DEAD, WELL, AS FAR AS I'M CONCERNED, THE BETTER FOR...
HI, MIKAAL. HOW GOES IT?
WHA--WHO ARE YOU?!
DON'T YOU RECOGNIZE ME? I'M SURPRISED JACK HASN'T SHOWN YOU MY PHOTO AT LEAST...

FIGHTING WITH GRUNDY;
Talking with David '99

ROBINSON & GOYER story	ROBINSON words	YEOWELL pencils & inks	OAKLEY letters	WRIGHT colors	GCW seps	TOMASI editor	GOODWIN guiding light

BUT YOU'RE--!

PLEASE, PLEASE, *PLEASE* DON'T SAY THE "D" WORD. IT *CREEPS* ME OUT.

I PREFER *MORTALLY CHALLENGED.*

DOES THAT MAKE *ME,* err... MORTALLY CHALLENGED, TOO?

YOU? HEAVENS, NO.

YOU'VE GOT A *FEW* MORE YEARS IN THAT OLD BLUE *CARCASS* OF YOURS. THIS? THIS IS JUST A *BAD SCENE.*

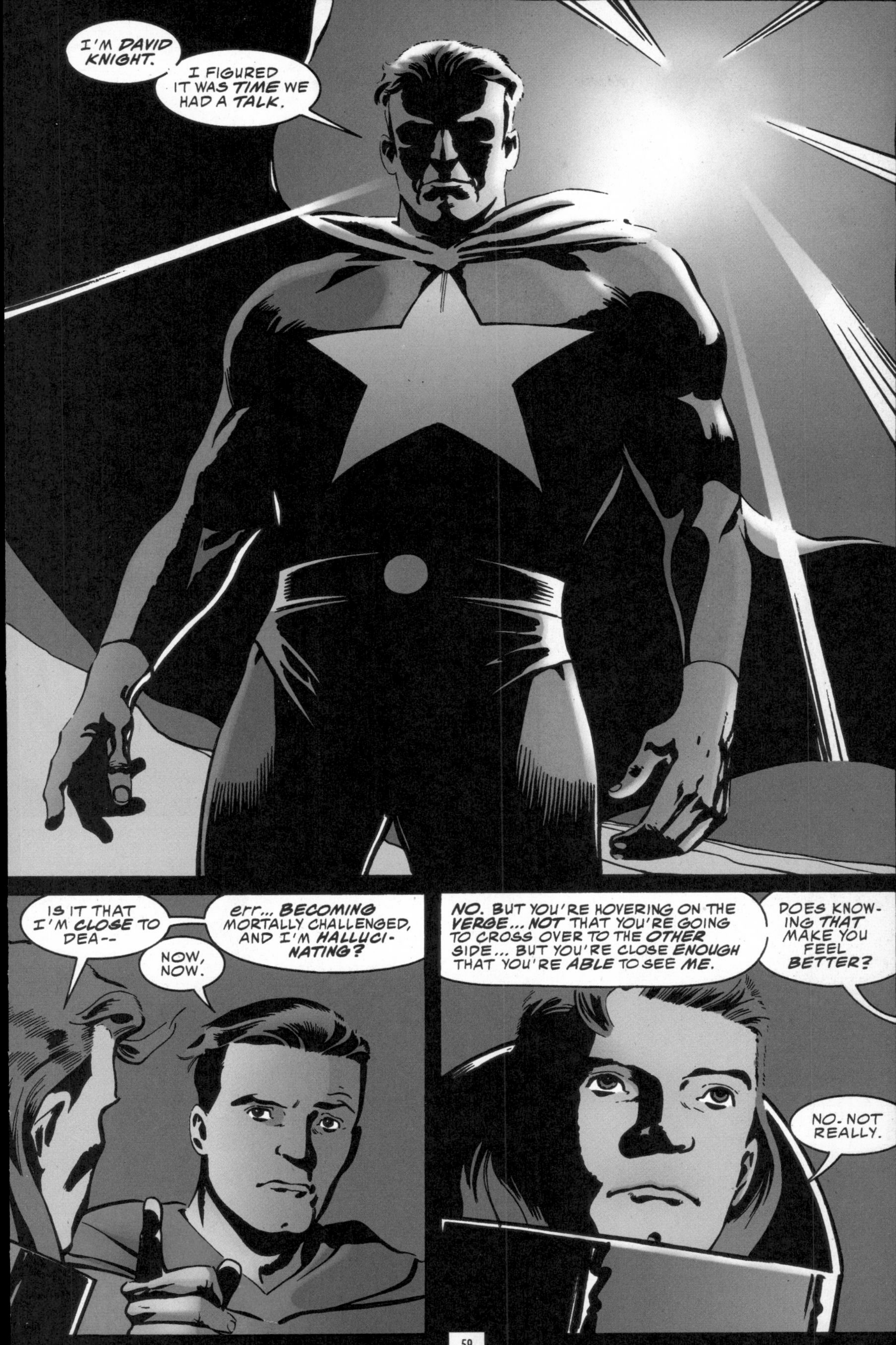
I'M DAVID KNIGHT.
I FIGURED IT WAS TIME WE HAD A TALK.
IS IT THAT I'M CLOSE TO DEA--
err... BECOMING MORTALLY CHALLENGED, AND I'M HALLUCINATING?
NOW, NOW.
NO. BUT YOU'RE HOVERING ON THE VERGE... NOT THAT YOU'RE GOING TO CROSS OVER TO THE OTHER SIDE... BUT YOU'RE CLOSE ENOUGH THAT YOU'RE ABLE TO SEE ME.
DOES KNOWING THAT MAKE YOU FEEL BETTER?
NO. NOT REALLY.

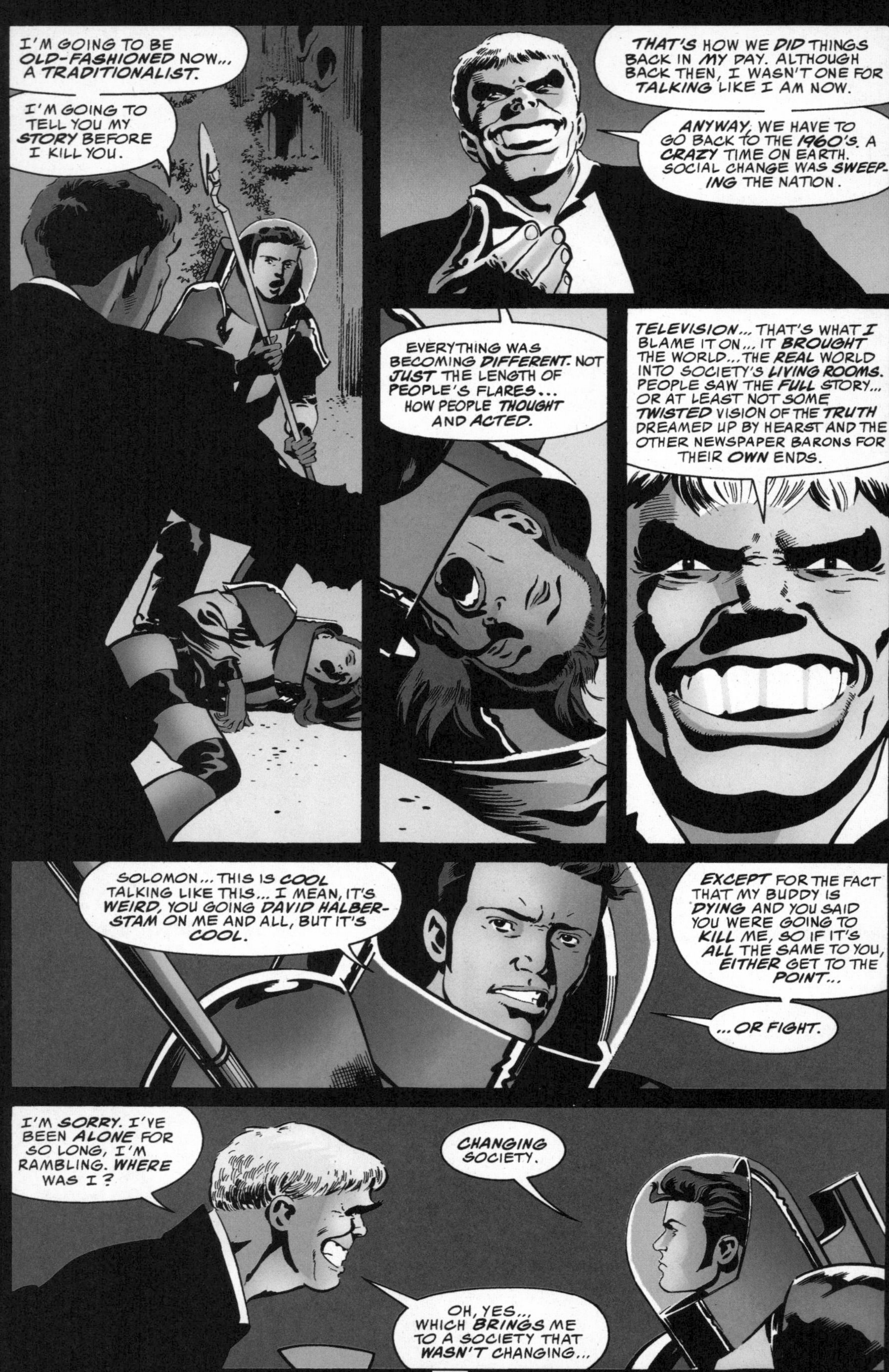
I'M GOING TO BE OLD-FASHIONED NOW... A TRADITIONALIST.
I'M GOING TO TELL YOU MY STORY BEFORE I KILL YOU.
THAT'S HOW WE DID THINGS BACK IN MY DAY. ALTHOUGH BACK THEN, I WASN'T ONE FOR TALKING LIKE I AM NOW.
ANYWAY, WE HAVE TO GO BACK TO THE 1960'S. A CRAZY TIME ON EARTH. SOCIAL CHANGE WAS SWEEPING THE NATION.
EVERYTHING WAS BECOMING DIFFERENT. NOT JUST THE LENGTH OF PEOPLE'S FLARES... HOW PEOPLE THOUGHT AND ACTED.
TELEVISION... THAT'S WHAT I BLAME IT ON... IT BROUGHT THE WORLD... THE REAL WORLD INTO SOCIETY'S LIVING ROOMS. PEOPLE SAW THE FULL STORY... OR AT LEAST NOT SOME TWISTED VISION OF THE TRUTH DREAMED UP BY HEARST AND THE OTHER NEWSPAPER BARONS FOR THEIR OWN ENDS.
SOLOMON... THIS IS COOL TALKING LIKE THIS... I MEAN, IT'S WEIRD, YOU GOING DAVID HALBERSTAM ON ME AND ALL, BUT IT'S COOL.
EXCEPT FOR THE FACT THAT MY BUDDY IS DYING AND YOU SAID YOU WERE GOING TO KILL ME, SO IF IT'S ALL THE SAME TO YOU, EITHER GET TO THE POINT...
...OR FIGHT.
I'M SORRY. I'VE BEEN ALONE FOR SO LONG, I'M RAMBLING. WHERE WAS I?
CHANGING SOCIETY.
OH, YES... WHICH BRINGS ME TO A SOCIETY THAT WASN'T CHANGING...

"...THE JUSTICE SOCIETY.

"THEY WERE THE *SAME* THEN AS THEY WERE IN THE 1940'S. 'BAD GUY DOES *WRONG. FIGHT* THE *BAD GUY. STOP* THE *BAD GUY.*'

"SO THERE I WAS IN THE '60S... I FORGET THE YEAR *EXACTLY,* IT WAS THAT LONG AGO...

"...AND I'M FIGHTING *DR. FATE* AND *HOURMAN* AND THE *GREEN LANTERN.*

"AND I *LOST.* THANKS IN NO *SMALL* PART TO GREEN LANTERN.

"AND THEY DECIDED TO *IMPRISON* ME BY SENDING ME INTO *SPACE.*

"WHICH I *RECALL* THINKING AT THE TIME WAS *OVERLY HARSH,* BUT WHATEVER.

"MAYBE I WAS SUPPOSED TO *STAY* IN EARTH'S ORBIT, BUT THINGS WENT *WRONG...*

"I DRIFTED AND DRIFTED AND DRIFTED...

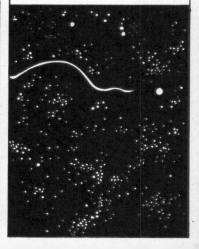

"SO I'M *UP* IN SPACE. AND THEN I *DIED.* I RAN *OUT OF AIR...* OR I GOT *TOO FAR* FROM THE SUN... OR *MAYBE* I WAS *BORED* TO DEATH."

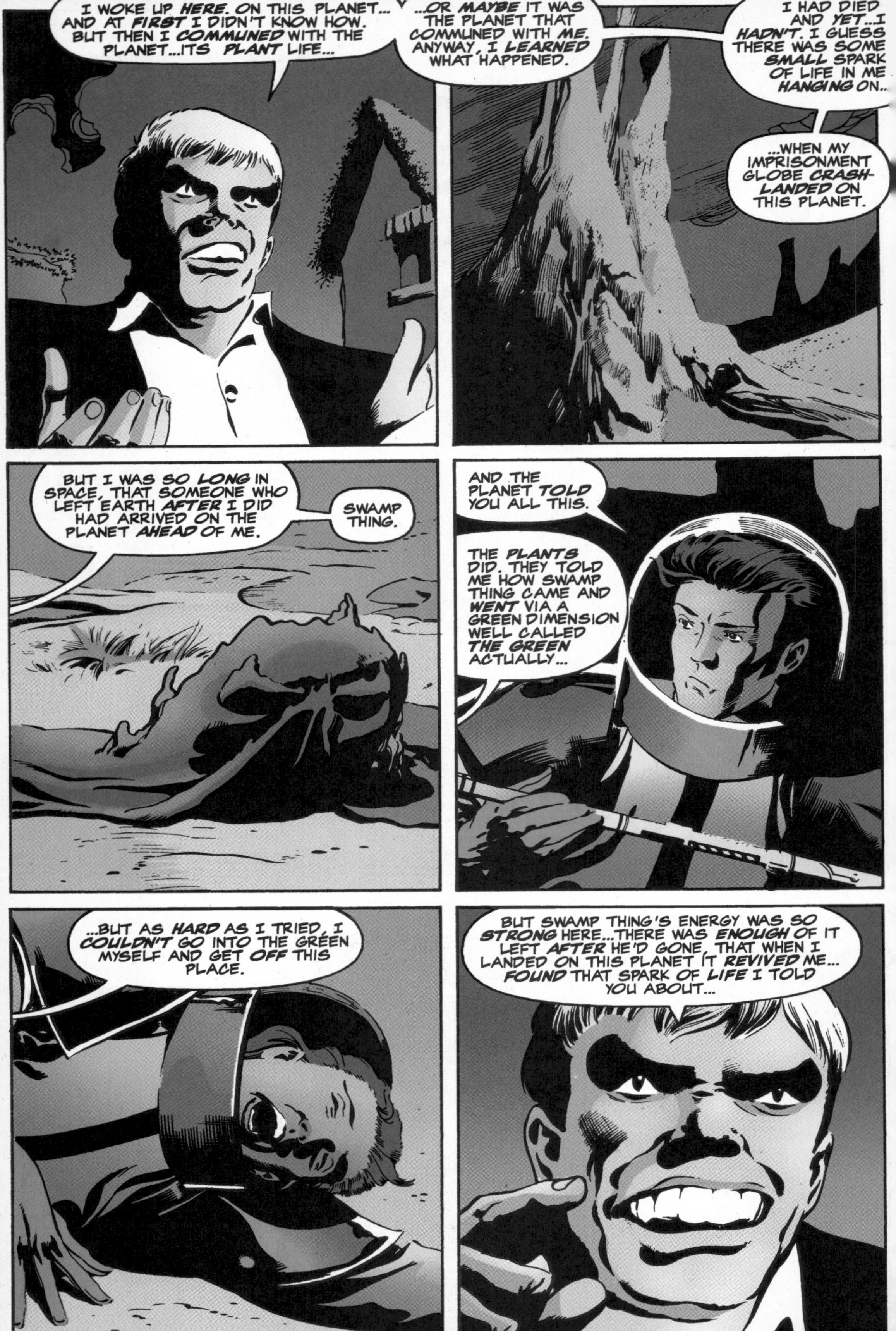
I WOKE UP HERE. ON THIS PLANET... AND AT FIRST I DIDN'T KNOW HOW. BUT THEN I COMMUNED WITH THE PLANET...ITS PLANT LIFE...
...OR MAYBE IT WAS THE PLANET THAT COMMUNED WITH ME. ANYWAY, I LEARNED WHAT HAPPENED.
I HAD DIED AND YET...I HADN'T. I GUESS THERE WAS SOME SMALL SPARK OF LIFE IN ME HANGING ON...
...WHEN MY IMPRISONMENT GLOBE CRASH-LANDED ON THIS PLANET.
BUT I WAS SO LONG IN SPACE, THAT SOMEONE WHO LEFT EARTH AFTER I DID HAD ARRIVED ON THE PLANET AHEAD OF ME.
SWAMP THING.
AND THE PLANET TOLD YOU ALL THIS.
THE PLANTS DID. THEY TOLD ME HOW SWAMP THING CAME AND WENT VIA A GREEN DIMENSION WELL CALLED THE GREEN ACTUALLY...
...BUT AS HARD AS I TRIED, I COULDN'T GO INTO THE GREEN MYSELF AND GET OFF THIS PLACE.
BUT SWAMP THING'S ENERGY WAS SO STRONG HERE...THERE WAS ENOUGH OF IT LEFT AFTER HE'D GONE, THAT WHEN I LANDED ON THIS PLANET IT REVIVED ME... FOUND THAT SPARK OF LIFE I TOLD YOU ABOUT...

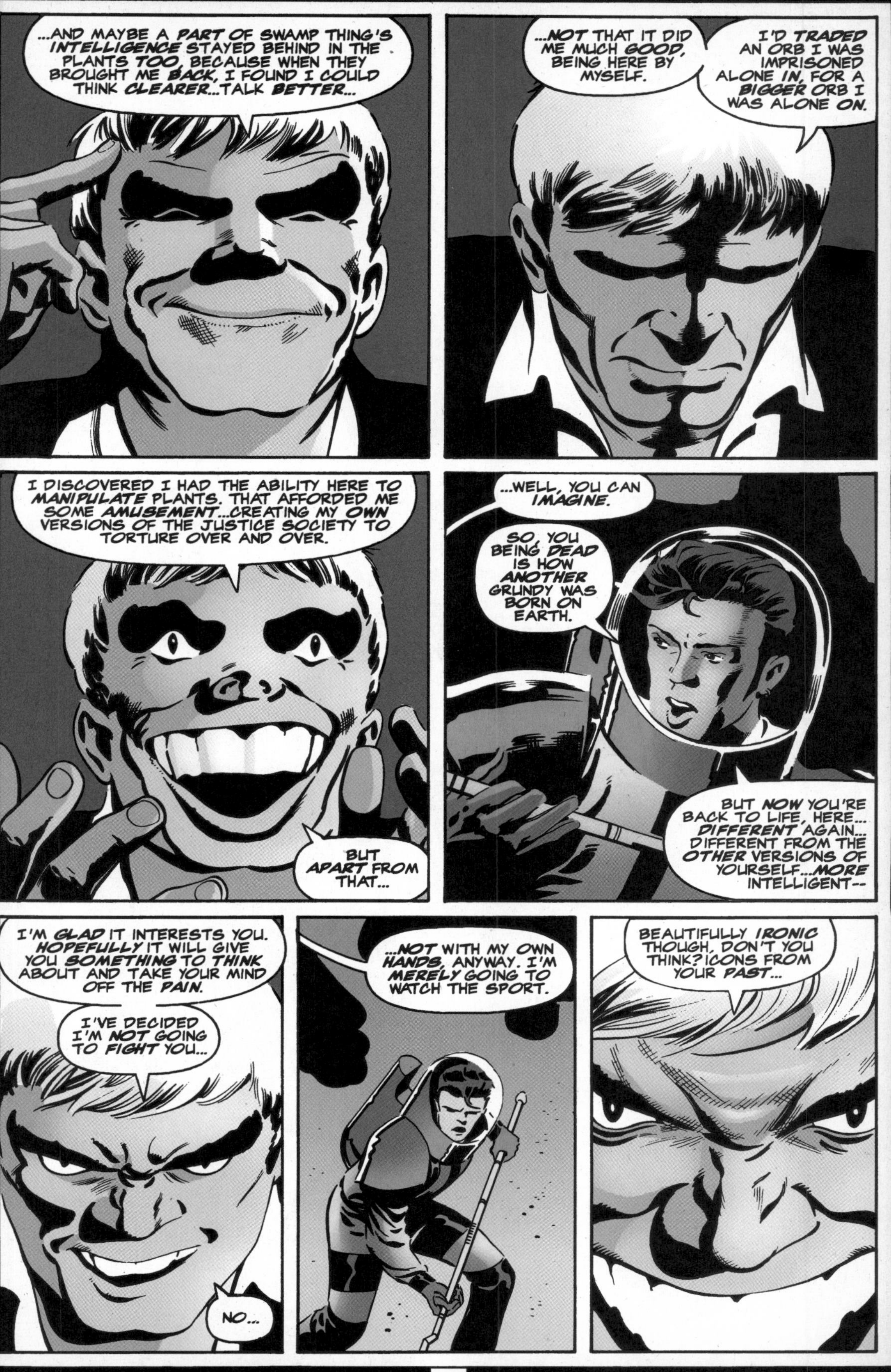
...AND MAYBE A PART OF SWAMP THING'S INTELLIGENCE STAYED BEHIND IN THE PLANTS TOO, BECAUSE WHEN THEY BROUGHT ME BACK, I FOUND I COULD THINK CLEARER...TALK BETTER...
I'D TRADED AN ORB I WAS IMPRISONED ALONE IN, FOR A BIGGER ORB I WAS ALONE ON.
...NOT THAT IT DID ME MUCH GOOD, BEING HERE BY MYSELF.
I DISCOVERED I HAD THE ABILITY HERE TO MANIPULATE PLANTS. THAT AFFORDED ME SOME AMUSEMENT...CREATING MY OWN VERSIONS OF THE JUSTICE SOCIETY TO TORTURE OVER AND OVER.
BUT APART FROM THAT...
...WELL, YOU CAN IMAGINE.
SO, YOU BEING DEAD IS HOW ANOTHER GRUNDY WAS BORN ON EARTH.
BUT NOW YOU'RE BACK TO LIFE, HERE... DIFFERENT AGAIN... DIFFERENT FROM THE OTHER VERSIONS OF YOURSELF...MORE INTELLIGENT--
I'M GLAD IT INTERESTS YOU. HOPEFULLY IT WILL GIVE YOU SOMETHING TO THINK ABOUT AND TAKE YOUR MIND OFF THE PAIN.
I'VE DECIDED I'M NOT GOING TO FIGHT YOU...
NO...
...NOT WITH MY OWN HANDS, ANYWAY. I'M MERELY GOING TO WATCH THE SPORT.
BEAUTIFULLY IRONIC THOUGH, DON'T YOU THINK? ICONS FROM YOUR PAST...

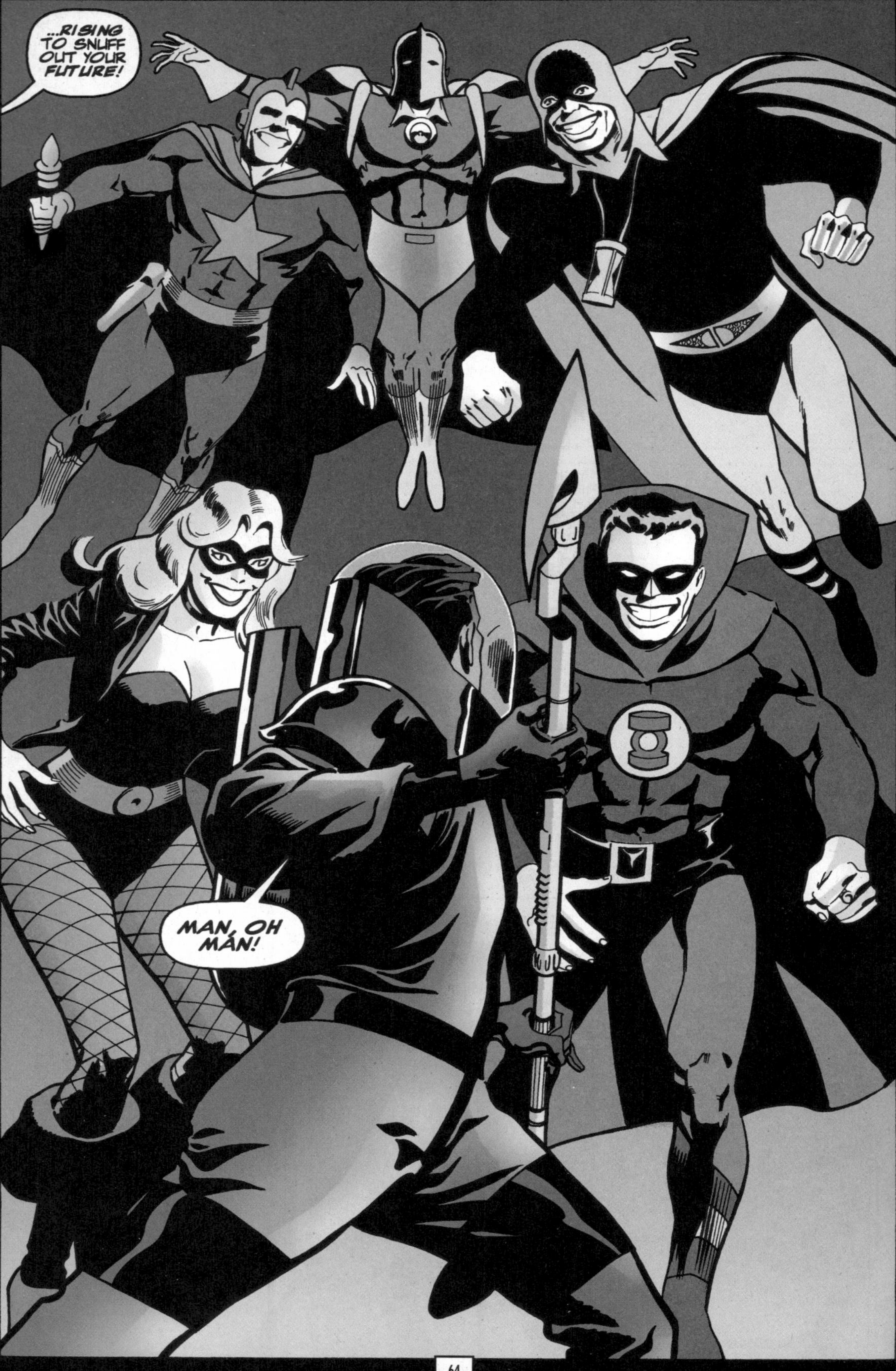
...RISING TO SNUFF OUT YOUR FUTURE!
MAN, OH MAN!

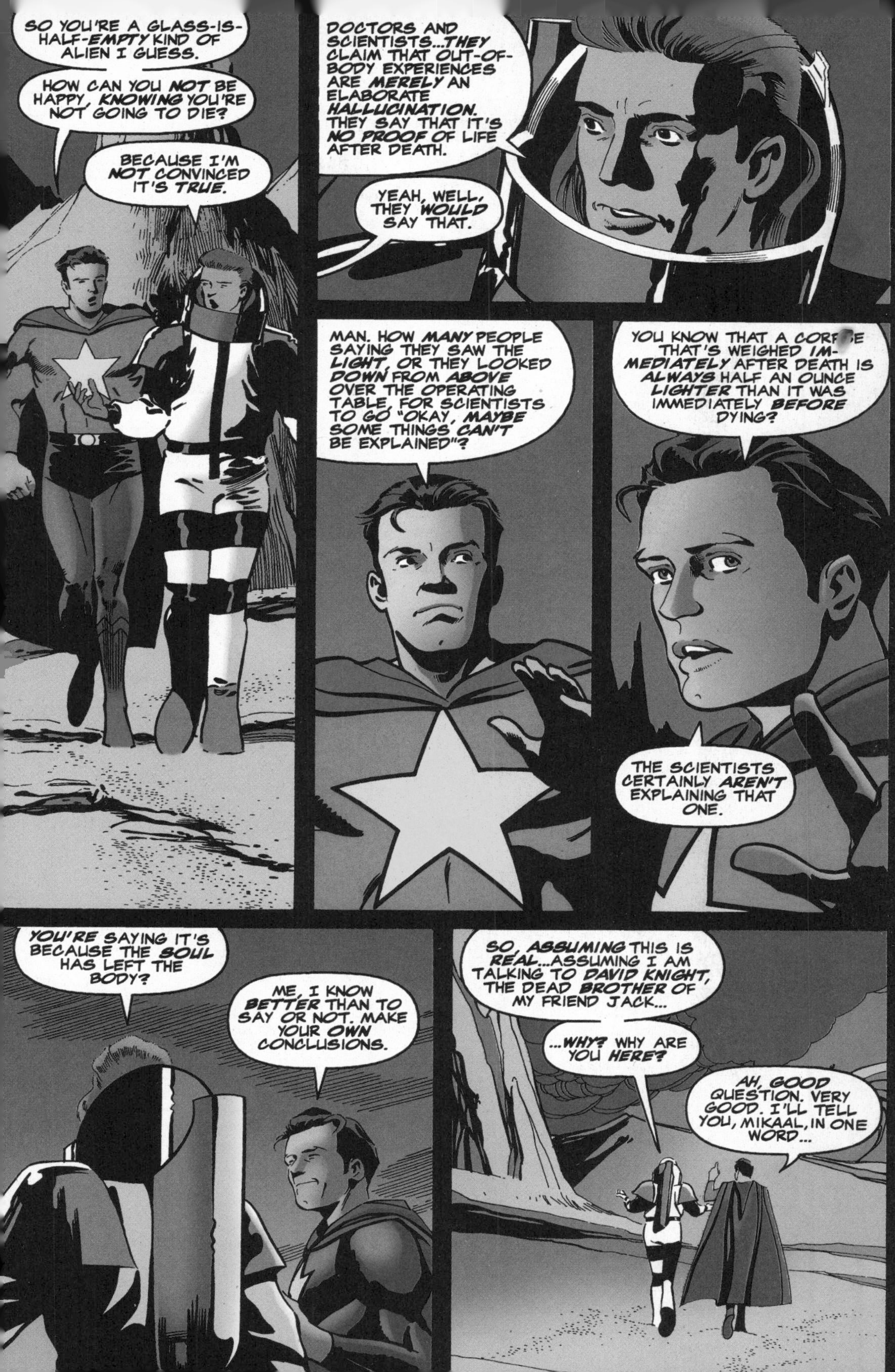
SO YOU'RE A GLASS-IS-HALF-EMPTY KIND OF ALIEN I GUESS.
HOW CAN YOU NOT BE HAPPY, KNOWING YOU'RE NOT GOING TO DIE?
BECAUSE I'M NOT CONVINCED IT'S TRUE.
DOCTORS AND SCIENTISTS...THEY CLAIM THAT OUT-OF-BODY EXPERIENCES ARE MERELY AN ELABORATE HALLUCINATION. THEY SAY THAT IT'S NO PROOF OF LIFE AFTER DEATH.
YEAH, WELL, THEY WOULD SAY THAT.
MAN. HOW MANY PEOPLE SAYING THEY SAW THE LIGHT, OR THEY LOOKED DOWN FROM ABOVE OVER THE OPERATING TABLE, FOR SCIENTISTS TO GO "OKAY, MAYBE SOME THINGS CAN'T BE EXPLAINED"?
YOU KNOW THAT A CORPSE THAT'S WEIGHED IM-MEDIATELY AFTER DEATH IS ALWAYS HALF AN OUNCE LIGHTER THAN IT WAS IMMEDIATELY BEFORE DYING?
THE SCIENTISTS CERTAINLY AREN'T EXPLAINING THAT ONE.
YOU'RE SAYING IT'S BECAUSE THE SOUL HAS LEFT THE BODY?
ME, I KNOW BETTER THAN TO SAY OR NOT. MAKE YOUR OWN CONCLUSIONS.
SO, ASSUMING THIS IS REAL...ASSUMING I AM TALKING TO DAVID KNIGHT, THE DEAD BROTHER OF MY FRIEND JACK...
...WHY? WHY ARE YOU HERE?
AH, GOOD QUESTION. VERY GOOD. I'LL TELL YOU, MIKAAL, IN ONE WORD...

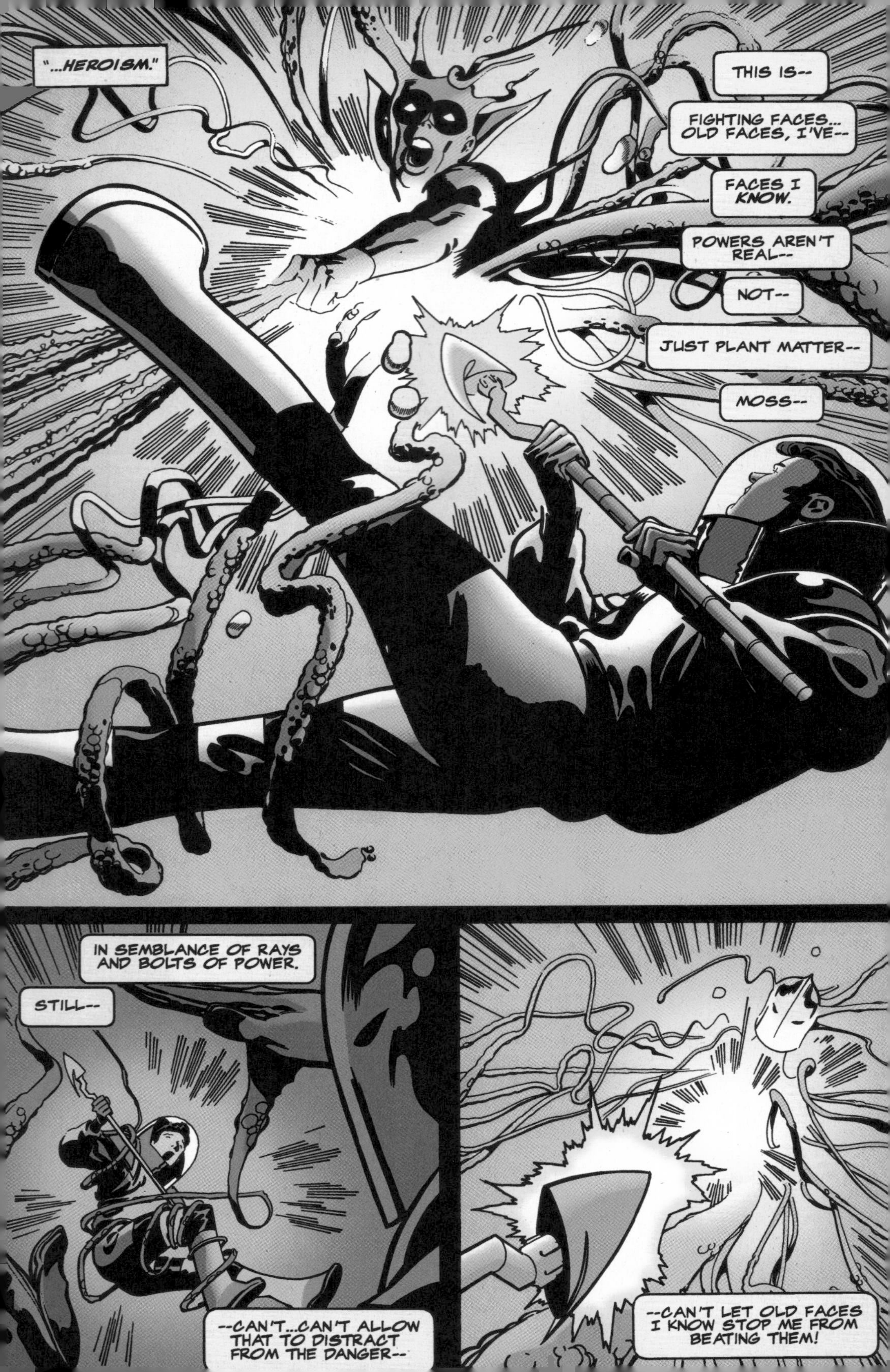
"...HEROISM."
THIS IS--
FIGHTING FACES... OLD FACES, I'VE--
FACES I KNOW.
POWERS AREN'T REAL--
NOT--
JUST PLANT MATTER--
MOSS--
IN SEMBLANCE OF RAYS AND BOLTS OF POWER.
STILL--
--CAN'T...CAN'T ALLOW THAT TO DISTRACT FROM THE DANGER--
--CAN'T LET OLD FACES I KNOW STOP ME FROM BEATING THEM!

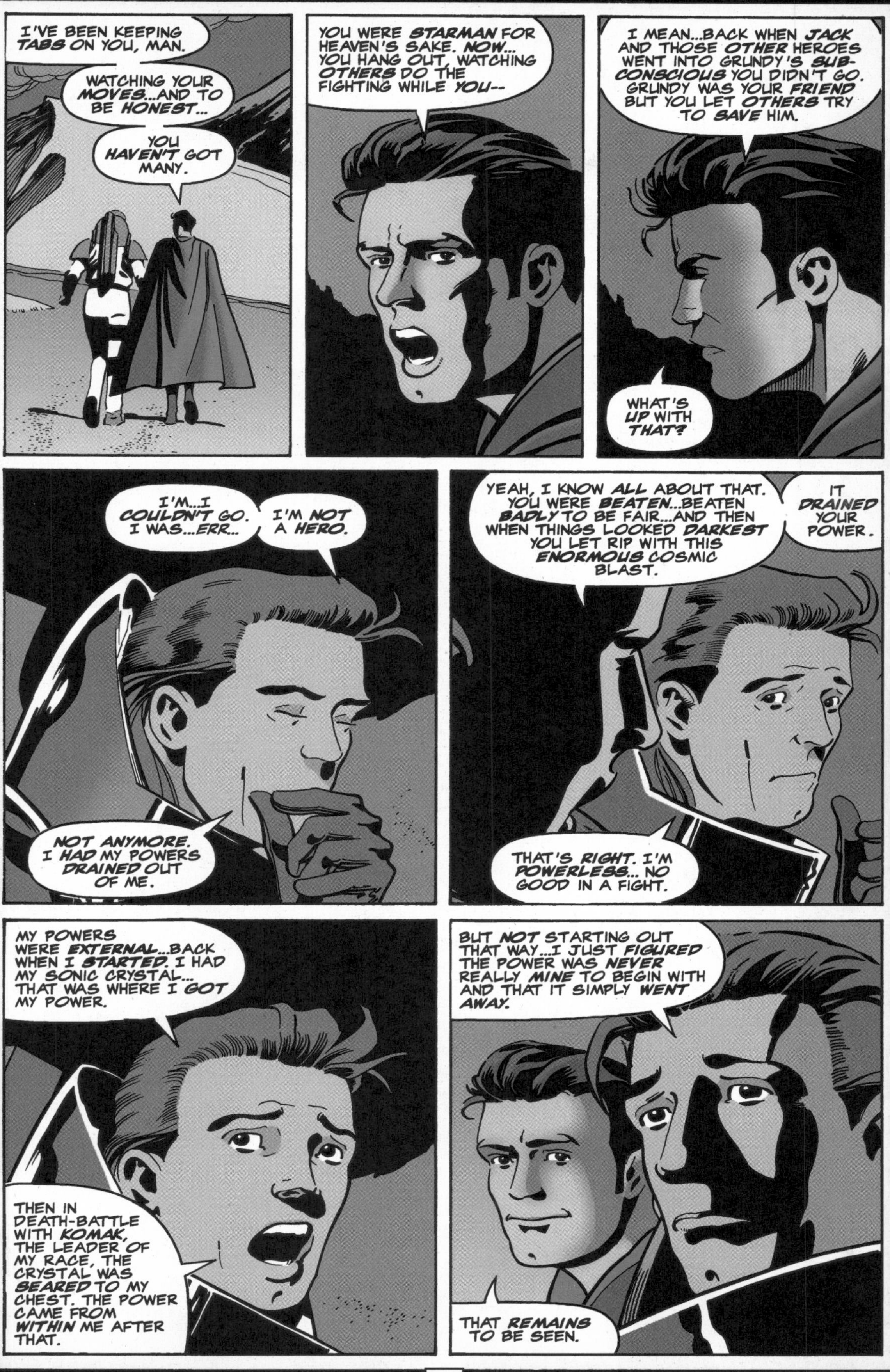
I'VE BEEN KEEPING TABS ON YOU, MAN.
WATCHING YOUR MOVES...AND TO BE HONEST...
YOU HAVEN'T GOT MANY.
YOU WERE STARMAN FOR HEAVEN'S SAKE. NOW... YOU HANG OUT, WATCHING OTHERS DO THE FIGHTING WHILE YOU--
I MEAN...BACK WHEN JACK AND THOSE OTHER HEROES WENT INTO GRUNDY'S SUB-CONSCIOUS YOU DIDN'T GO. GRUNDY WAS YOUR FRIEND BUT YOU LET OTHERS TRY TO SAVE HIM.
WHAT'S UP WITH THAT?
I'M...I COULDN'T GO. I WAS...ERR...
I'M NOT A HERO.
NOT ANYMORE. I HAD MY POWERS DRAINED OUT OF ME.
YEAH, I KNOW ALL ABOUT THAT. YOU WERE BEATEN...BEATEN BADLY TO BE FAIR...AND THEN WHEN THINGS LOOKED DARKEST YOU LET RIP WITH THIS ENORMOUS COSMIC BLAST.
IT DRAINED YOUR POWER.
THAT'S RIGHT. I'M POWERLESS... NO GOOD IN A FIGHT.
MY POWERS WERE EXTERNAL...BACK WHEN I STARTED. I HAD MY SONIC CRYSTAL... THAT WAS WHERE I GOT MY POWER.
THEN IN DEATH-BATTLE WITH KOMAK, THE LEADER OF MY RACE, THE CRYSTAL WAS SEARED TO MY CHEST. THE POWER CAME FROM WITHIN ME AFTER THAT.
BUT NOT STARTING OUT THAT WAY...I JUST FIGURED THE POWER WAS NEVER REALLY MINE TO BEGIN WITH AND THAT IT SIMPLY WENT AWAY.
THAT REMAINS TO BE SEEN.

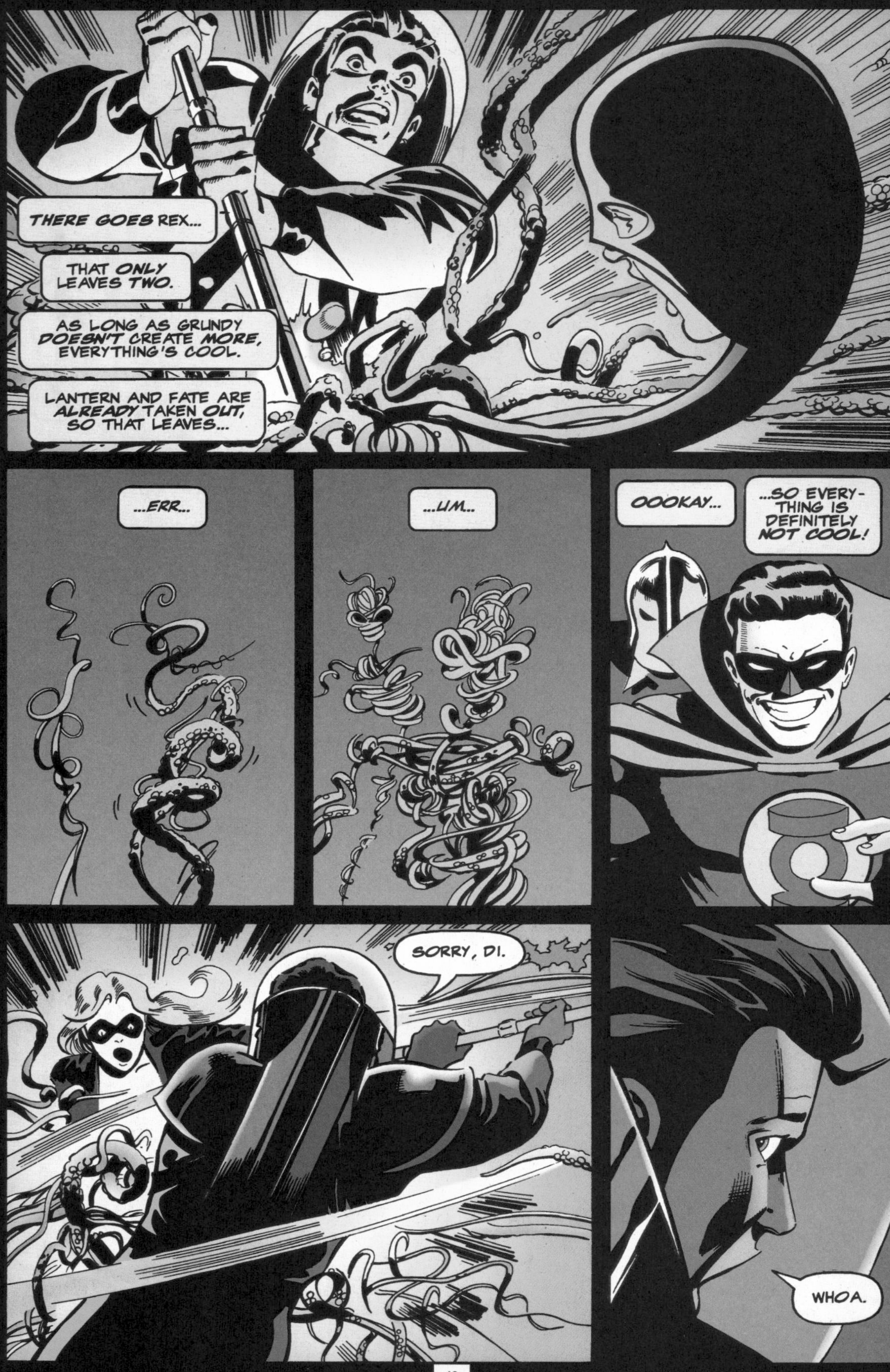

THERE GOES REX...
THAT ONLY LEAVES TWO.
AS LONG AS GRUNDY DOESN'T CREATE MORE, EVERYTHING'S COOL.
LANTERN AND FATE ARE ALREADY TAKEN OUT, SO THAT LEAVES...
...ERR...
...UM...
OOOKAY...
...SO EVERY-THING IS DEFINITELY NOT COOL!
SORRY, DI.
WHOA.

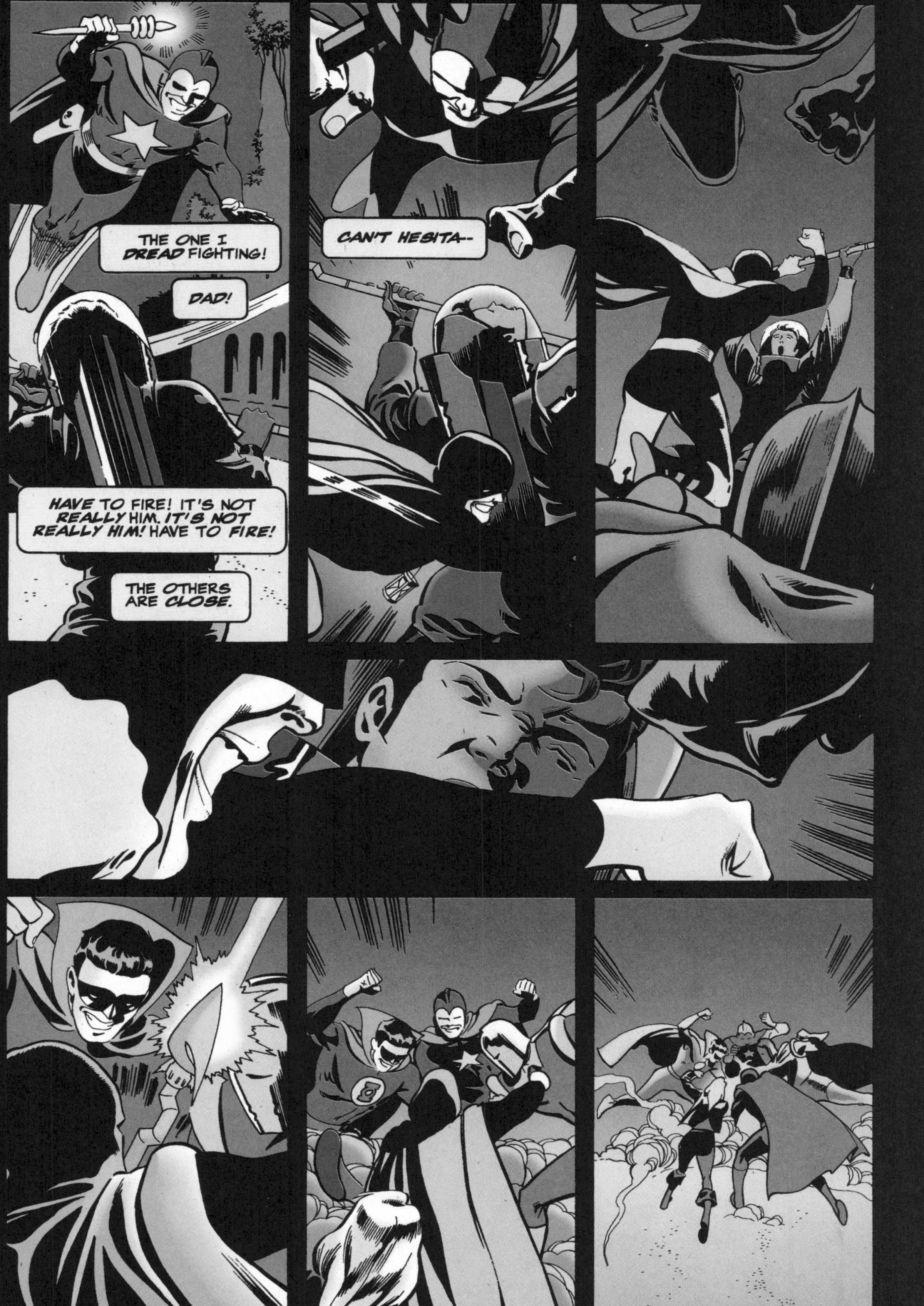

THE ONE I DREAD FIGHTING!
DAD!
HAVE TO FIRE! IT'S NOT REALLY HIM. IT'S NOT REALLY HIM! HAVE TO FIRE!
THE OTHERS ARE CLOSE.
CAN'T HESITA--

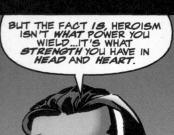

BUT THE FACT *IS*, HEROISM ISN'T *WHAT* POWER YOU WIELD...IT'S WHAT *STRENGTH* YOU HAVE IN *HEAD* AND *HEART*.

THAT'S WHAT MAKES A *GOOD* FIGHTER...A *GOOD* SOLDIER...AND *ESPECIALLY* A *GOOD* SUPERHERO.

MAYBE *THAT'S* WHY I WASN'T.

YOU'RE BEING *HARD* ON YOURSELF.

I'M BEING *HONEST*.

BUT ANYWAY, WE'RE *NOT* TALKING ABOUT *ME*. IT'S *YOU*, MIK.

LOOK, I'VE BEEN *MEETING* UP WITH JACK IN THIS WAY FOR A *WHILE*.

THIS WAY? *WHAT* WAY? *HOW* ARE WE DOING THIS?

I *CAN'T* SAY. NOT THE DE- TAILS. SUFFICE IT TO SAY JACK *DOESN'T* TALK ABOUT IT.

BUT I *TRY* TO FOREWARN HIM OF *THINGS*...WHEN I FEEL I *SHOULD*. AND IN *THIS* INSTANCE, I FELT IT WAS *MORE* IMPORTANT TO FOREWARN *YOU* INSTEAD.

OF WHAT?

THERE WILL *COME* A TIME WHEN YOU WILL *HAVE* TO BE THE HERO.

WHETHER YOU HAVE POWERS THEN OR *NOT*... IT'S WHAT IS *WITHIN* YOU... YOUR INNER STRENGTH THAT WILL BE *NEEDED*.

SO IF *I* WAS YOU, I'D START *THINKING* LIKE A HERO AGAIN. ACTING AND THINKING LIKE YOU *HAVE* GOT THE STUFF OF CHAMPIONS.

I'M *NOT* SURE I FOLLOW YOU.

WHEN WILL I HAVE TO *ACT* THIS WAY... WHILE I'M IN *SPACE* WITH JACK?

NOW? DO I HAVE TO DO SOMETHING TO *SAVE* HIM FROM GRUNDY?

NO...

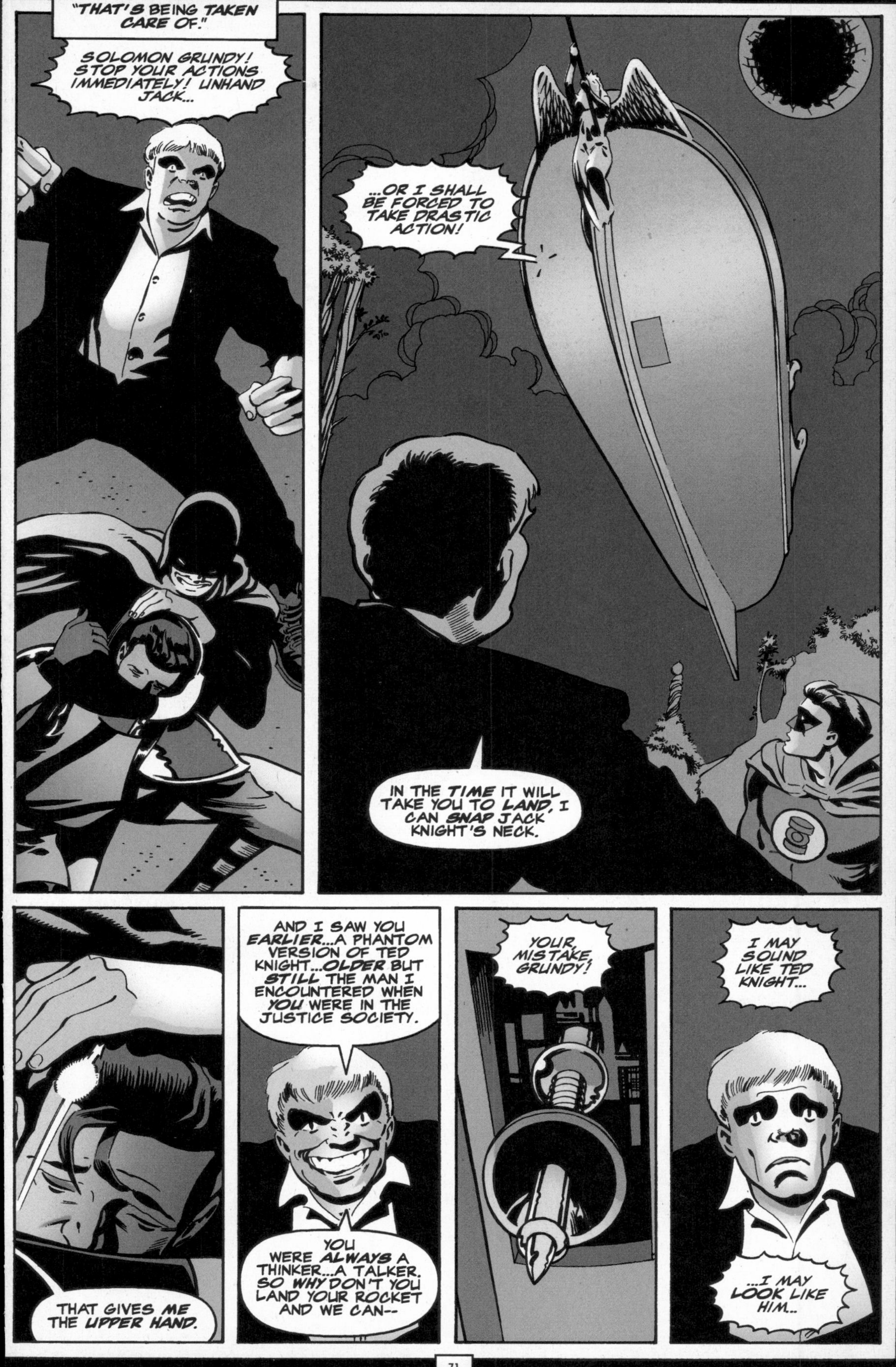
"THAT'S BEING TAKEN CARE OF."
SOLOMON GRUNDY! STOP YOUR ACTIONS IMMEDIATELY! UNHAND JACK...
...OR I SHALL BE FORCED TO TAKE DRASTIC ACTION!
IN THE TIME IT WILL TAKE YOU TO LAND, I CAN SNAP JACK KNIGHT'S NECK.
THAT GIVES ME THE UPPER HAND.
AND I SAW YOU EARLIER...A PHANTOM VERSION OF TED KNIGHT...OLDER BUT STILL THE MAN I ENCOUNTERED WHEN YOU WERE IN THE JUSTICE SOCIETY.
YOU WERE ALWAYS A THINKER...A TALKER. SO WHY DON'T YOU LAND YOUR ROCKET AND WE CAN--
YOUR MISTAKE, GRUNDY!
I MAY SOUND LIKE TED KNIGHT...
...I MAY LOOK LIKE HIM...

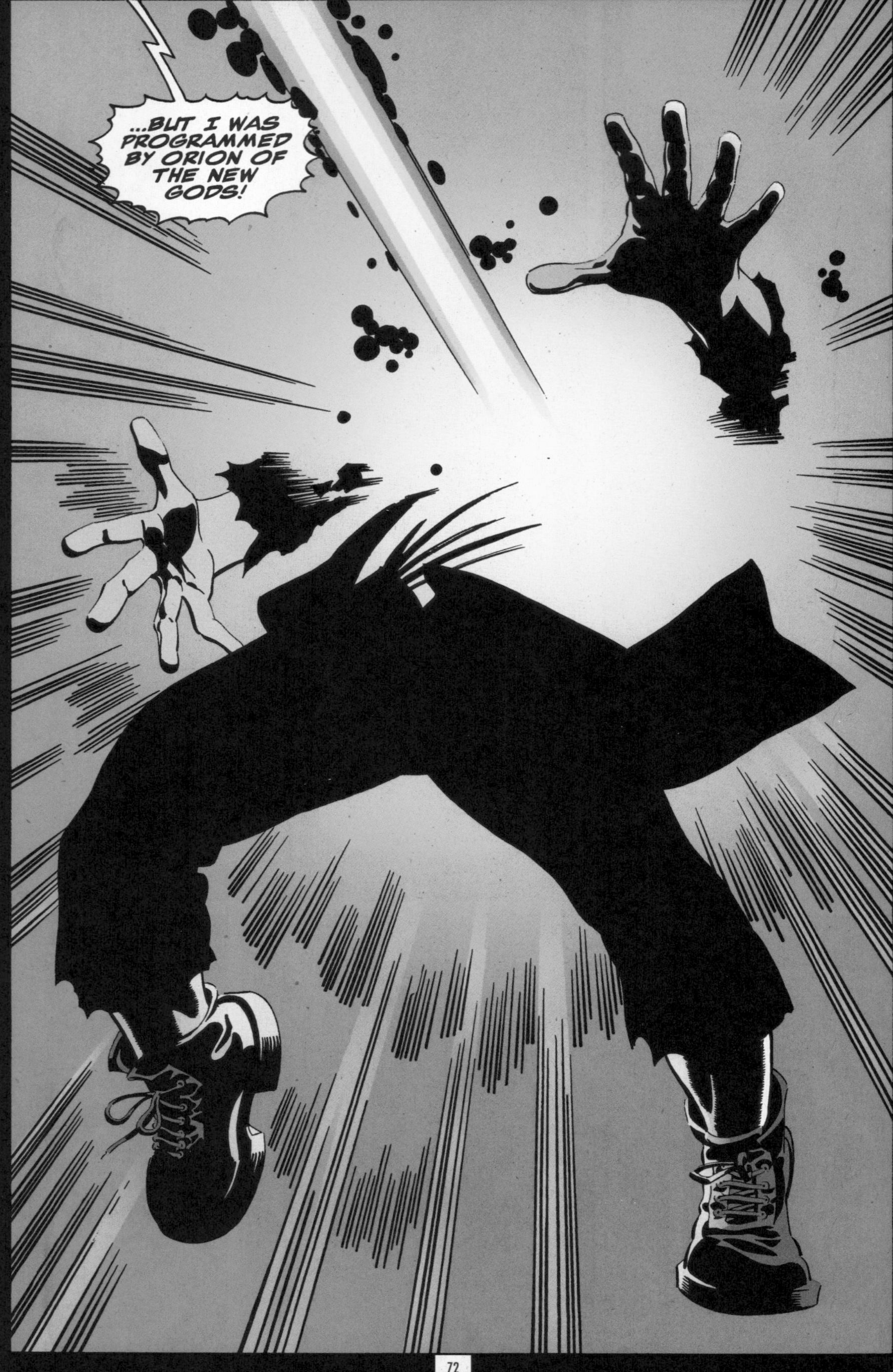
...BUT I WAS PROGRAMMED BY ORION OF THE NEW GODS!

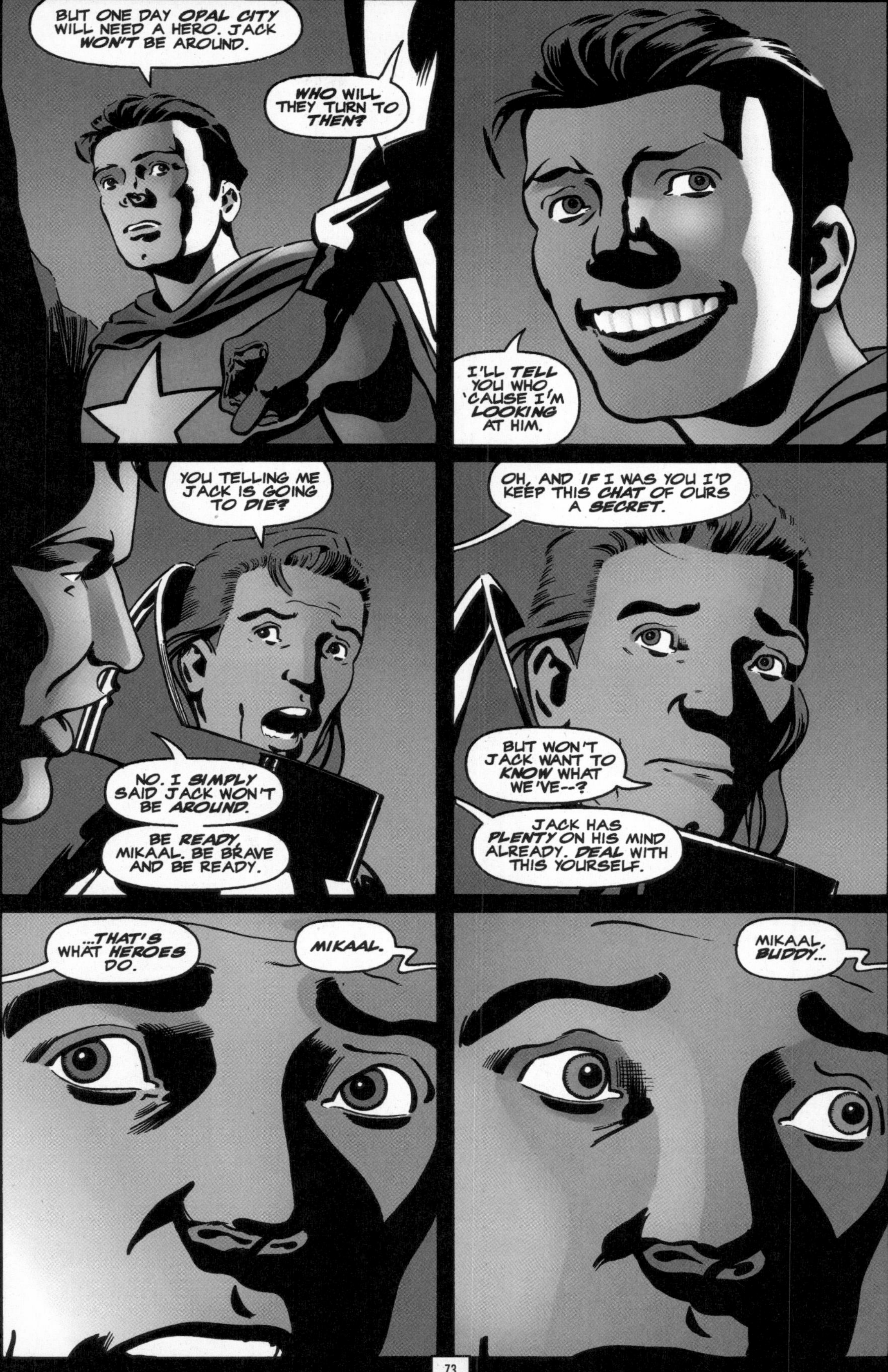
BUT ONE DAY OPAL CITY WILL NEED A HERO. JACK WON'T BE AROUND.
WHO WILL THEY TURN TO THEN?
I'LL TELL YOU WHO, 'CAUSE I'M LOOKING AT HIM.
YOU TELLING ME JACK IS GOING TO DIE?
NO. I SIMPLY SAID JACK WON'T BE AROUND.
BE READY, MIKAAL. BE BRAVE AND BE READY.
OH, AND IF I WAS YOU I'D KEEP THIS CHAT OF OURS A SECRET.
BUT WON'T JACK WANT TO KNOW WHAT WE'VE--?
JACK HAS PLENTY ON HIS MIND ALREADY. DEAL WITH THIS YOURSELF.
...THAT'S WHAT HEROES DO.
MIKAAL.
MIKAAL, BUDDY...

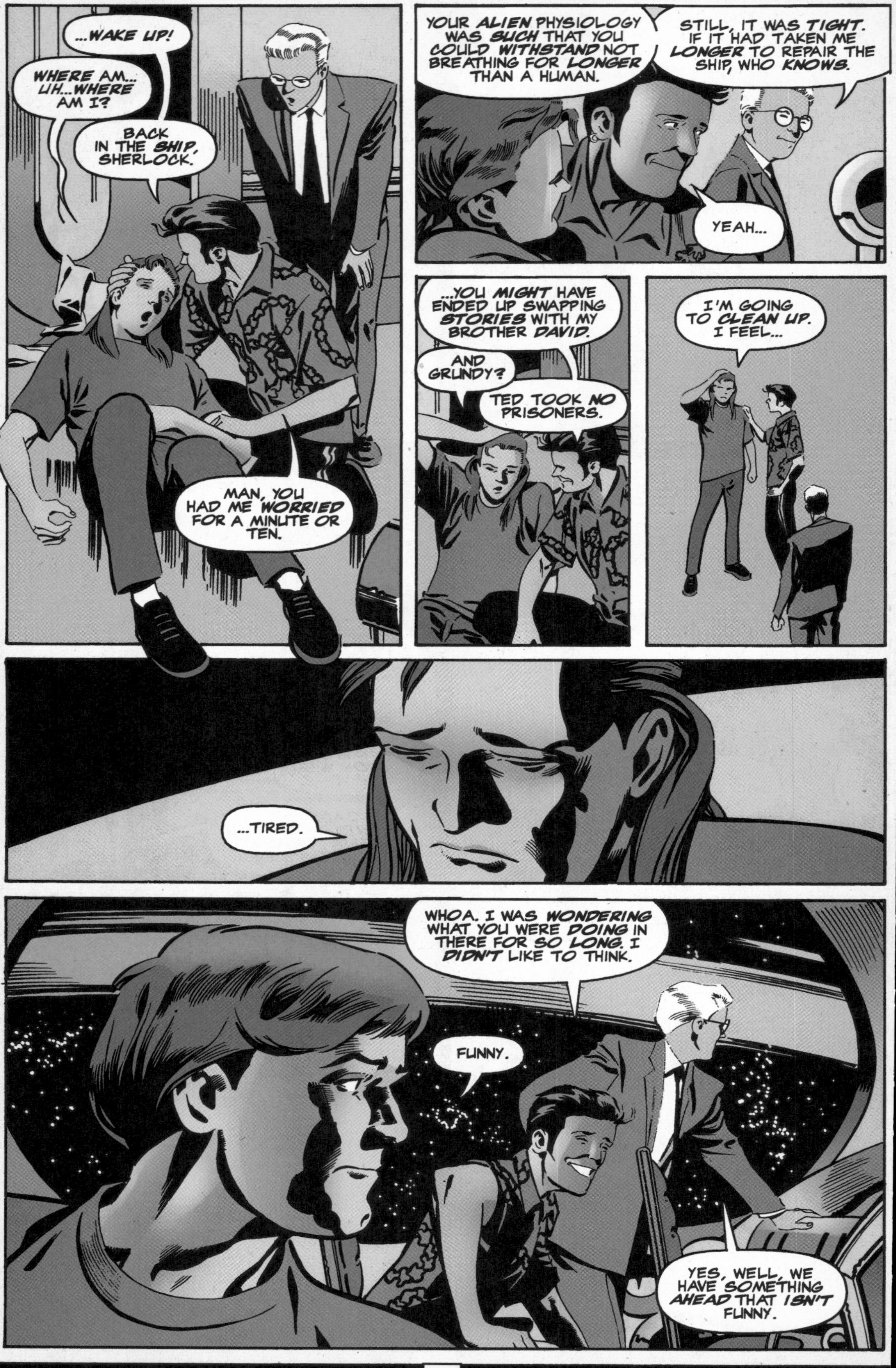

...WAKE UP!
WHERE AM... UH...WHERE AM I?
BACK IN THE SHIP, SHERLOCK.
MAN, YOU HAD ME WORRIED FOR A MINUTE OR TEN.
YOUR ALIEN PHYSIOLOGY WAS SUCH THAT YOU COULD WITHSTAND NOT BREATHING FOR LONGER THAN A HUMAN.
STILL, IT WAS TIGHT. IF IT HAD TAKEN ME LONGER TO REPAIR THE SHIP, WHO KNOWS.
YEAH...
...YOU MIGHT HAVE ENDED UP SWAPPING STORIES WITH MY BROTHER DAVID.
AND GRUNDY?
TED TOOK NO PRISONERS.
I'M GOING TO CLEAN UP. I FEEL...
...TIRED.
WHOA. I WAS WONDERING WHAT YOU WERE DOING IN THERE FOR SO LONG. I DIDN'T LIKE TO THINK.
FUNNY.
YES, WELL, WE HAVE SOMETHING AHEAD THAT ISN'T FUNNY.

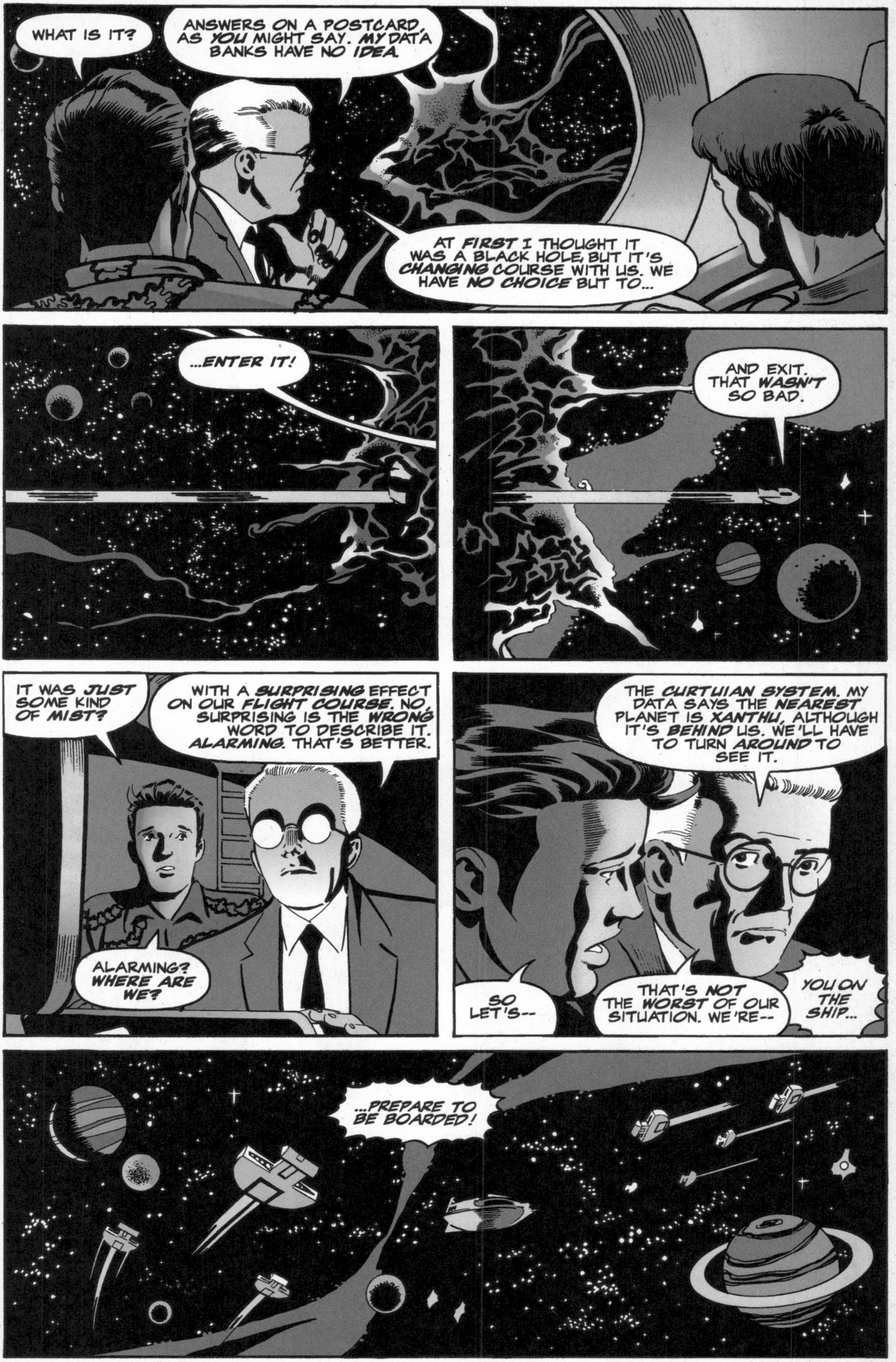

WHAT IS IT?
ANSWERS ON A POSTCARD, AS YOU MIGHT SAY. MY DATA BANKS HAVE NO IDEA.
AT FIRST I THOUGHT IT WAS A BLACK HOLE, BUT IT'S CHANGING COURSE WITH US. WE HAVE NO CHOICE BUT TO...
...ENTER IT!
AND EXIT. THAT WASN'T SO BAD.
IT WAS JUST SOME KIND OF MIST?
WITH A SURPRISING EFFECT ON OUR FLIGHT COURSE. NO, SURPRISING IS THE WRONG WORD TO DESCRIBE IT. ALARMING. THAT'S BETTER.
ALARMING? WHERE ARE WE?
THE CURTUIAN SYSTEM. MY DATA SAYS THE NEAREST PLANET IS XANTHU, ALTHOUGH IT'S BEHIND US. WE'LL HAVE TO TURN AROUND TO SEE IT.
SO LET'S--
THAT'S NOT THE WORST OF OUR SITUATION. WE'RE--
YOU ON THE SHIP...
...PREPARE TO BE BOARDED!

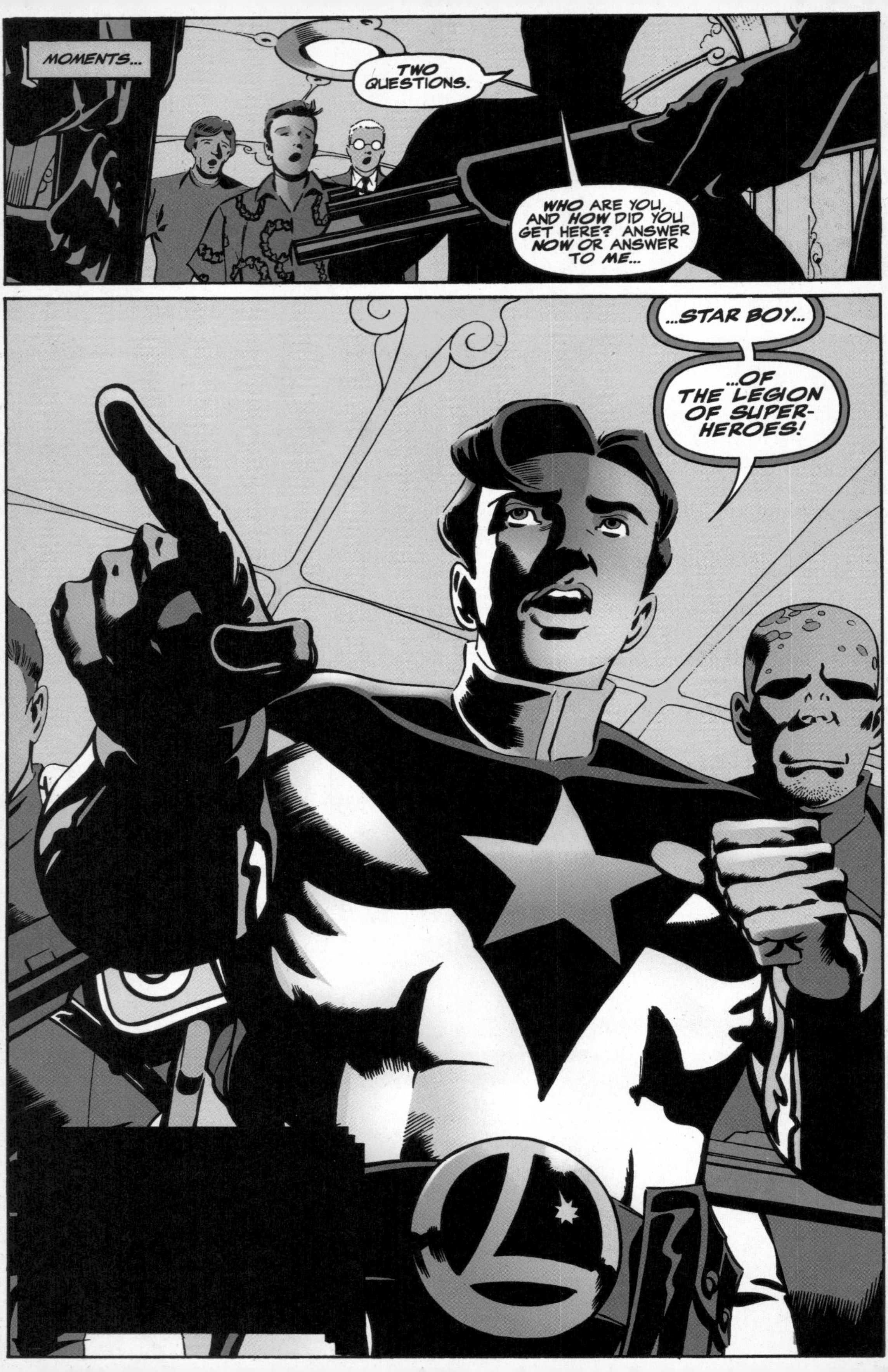
MOMENTS...
TWO QUESTIONS.
WHO ARE YOU, AND HOW DID YOU GET HERE? ANSWER NOW OR ANSWER TO ME...
...STAR BOY...
...OF THE LEGION OF SUPER-HEROES!

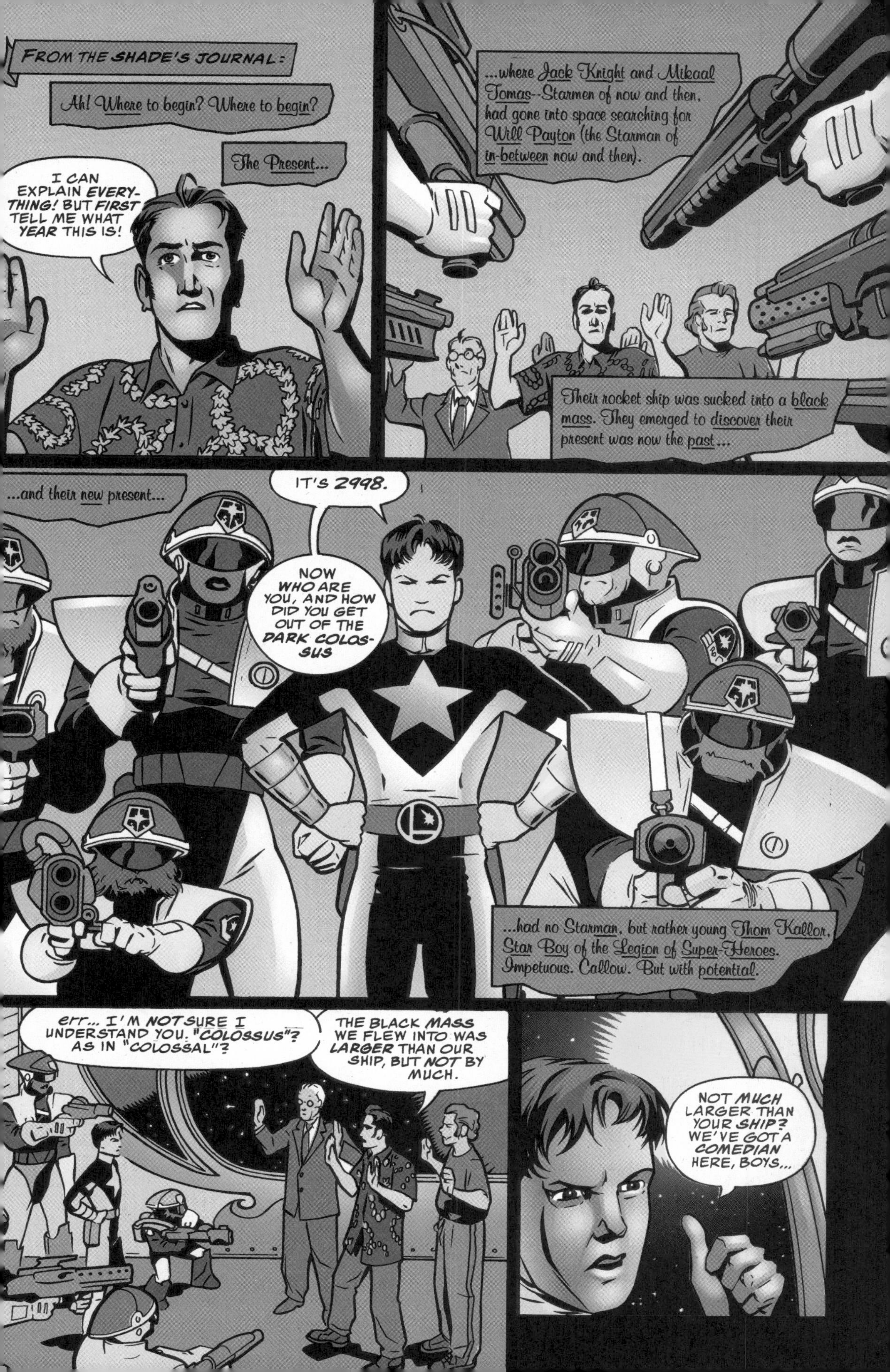
FROM THE SHADE'S JOURNAL:
Ah! Where to begin? Where to begin?
The Present...
I CAN EXPLAIN EVERYTHING! BUT FIRST TELL ME WHAT YEAR THIS IS!
...where Jack Knight and Mikaal Tomas--Starmen of now and then, had gone into space searching for Will Payton (the Starman of in-between now and then).
Their rocket ship was sucked into a black mass. They emerged to discover their present was now the past...
...and their new present...
IT'S 2998.
NOW WHO ARE YOU, AND HOW DID YOU GET OUT OF THE DARK COLOSSUS
...had no Starman, but rather young Thom Kallor, Star Boy of the Legion of Super-Heroes. Impetuous. Callow. But with potential.
err... I'M NOT SURE I UNDERSTAND YOU. "COLOSSUS"? AS IN "COLOSSAL"?
THE BLACK MASS WE FLEW INTO WAS LARGER THAN OUR SHIP, BUT NOT BY MUCH.
NOT MUCH LARGER THAN YOUR SHIP? WE'VE GOT A COMEDIAN HERE, BOYS...

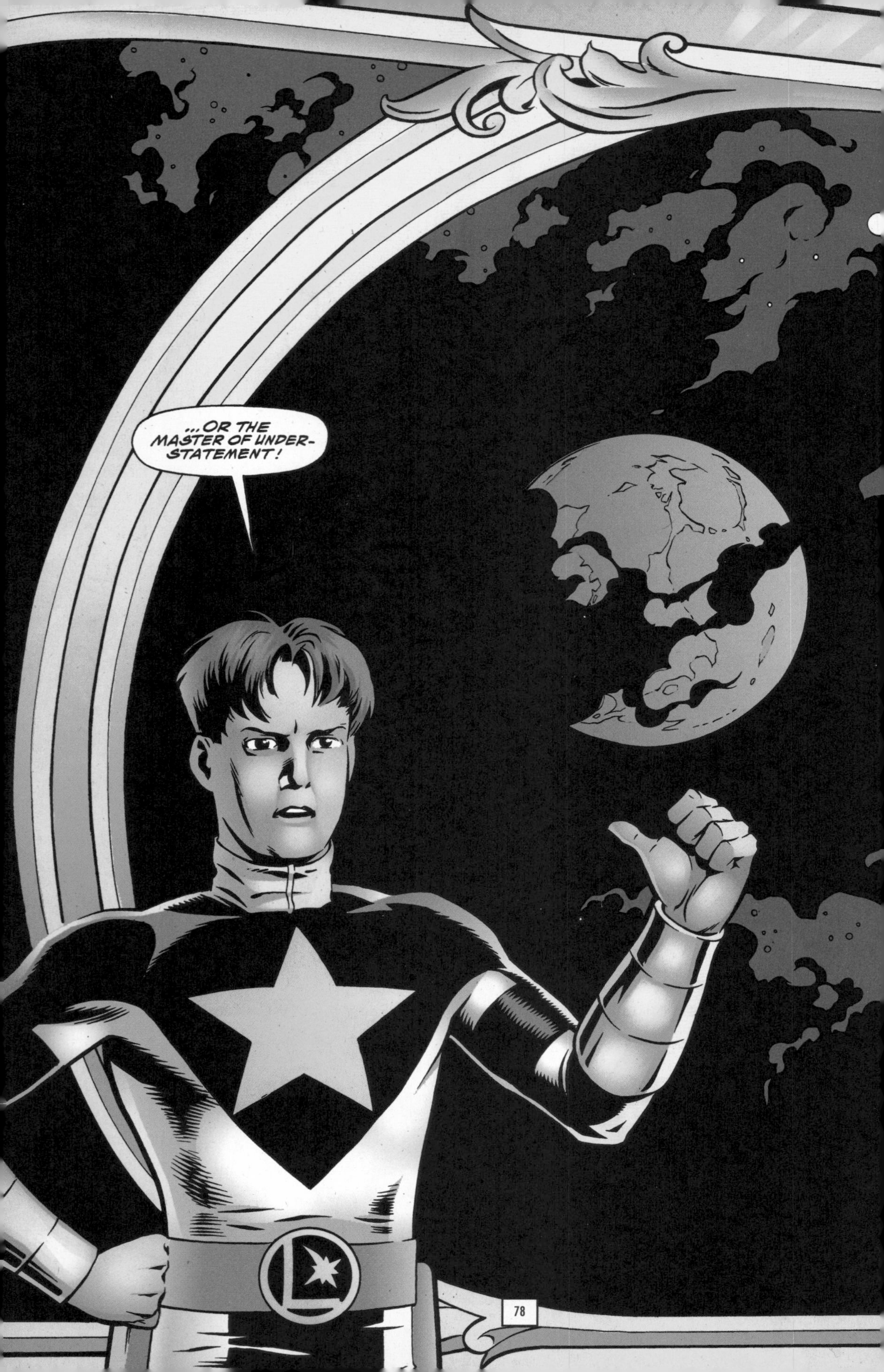
...OR THE MASTER OF UNDER-STATEMENT!

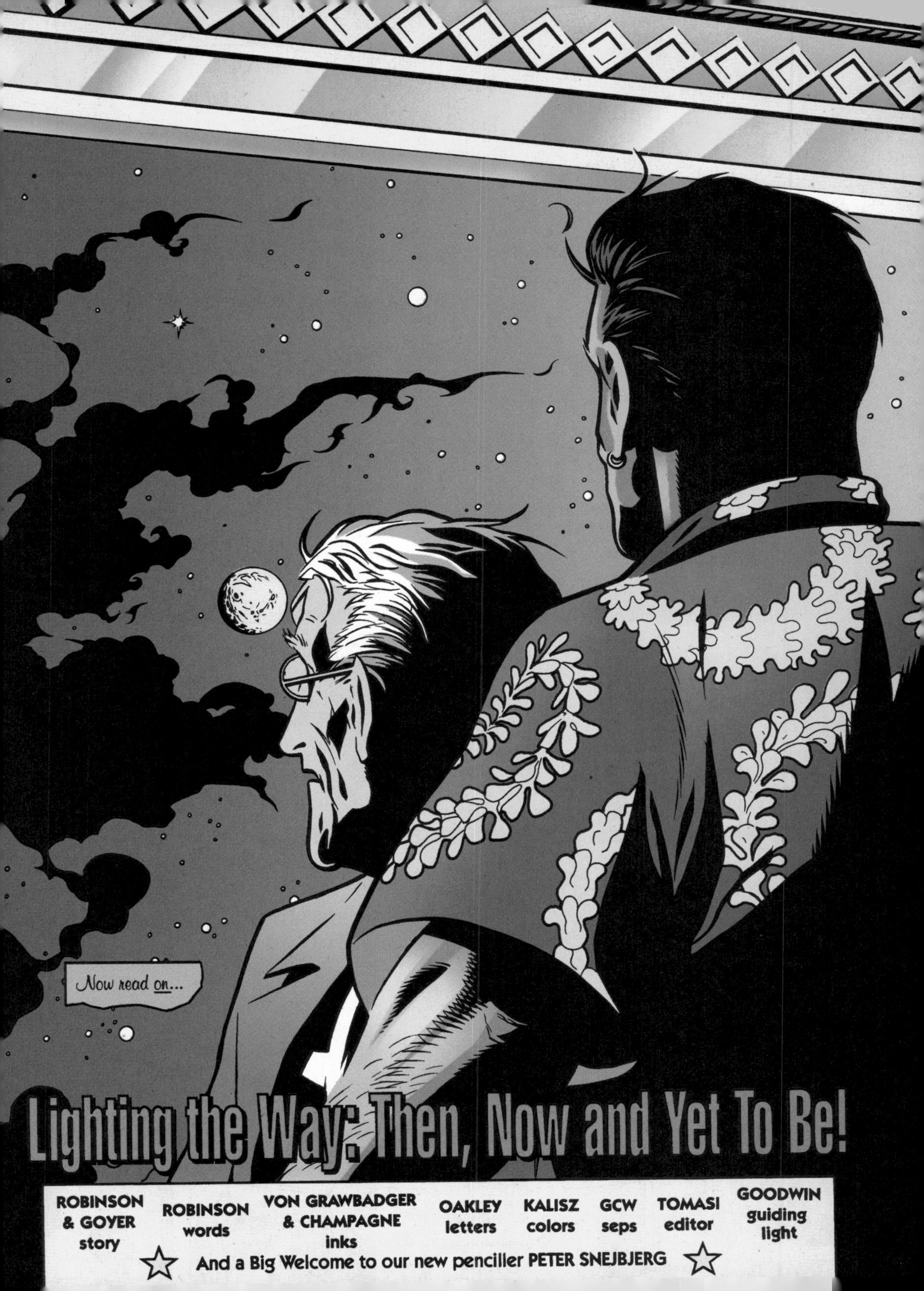

Now read on...
Lighting the Way: Then, Now and Yet To Be!
ROBINSON & GOYER story
ROBINSON words
VON GRAWBADGER & CHAMPAGNE inks
OAKLEY letters
KALISZ colors
GCW seps
TOMASI editor
GOODWIN guiding light
And a Big Welcome to our new penciller PETER SNEJBJERG

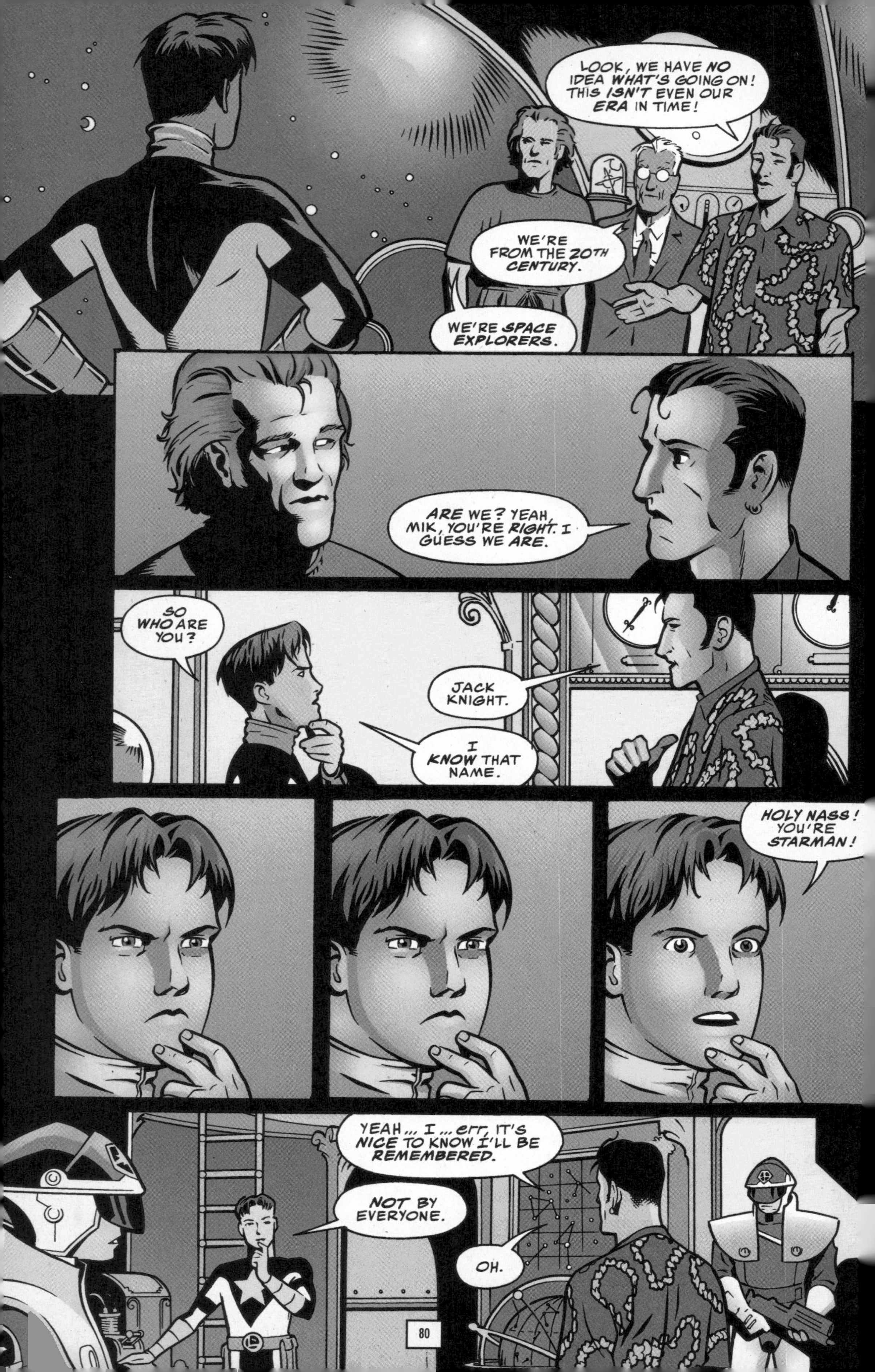

LOOK, WE HAVE NO IDEA WHAT'S GOING ON! THIS ISN'T EVEN OUR ERA IN TIME!
WE'RE FROM THE 20TH CENTURY.
WE'RE SPACE EXPLORERS.
ARE WE? YEAH, MIK, YOU'RE RIGHT. I GUESS WE ARE.
SO WHO ARE YOU?
JACK KNIGHT.
I KNOW THAT NAME.
HOLY NASS! YOU'RE STARMAN!
YEAH... I... err, IT'S NICE TO KNOW I'LL BE REMEMBERED.
NOT BY EVERYONE.
OH.

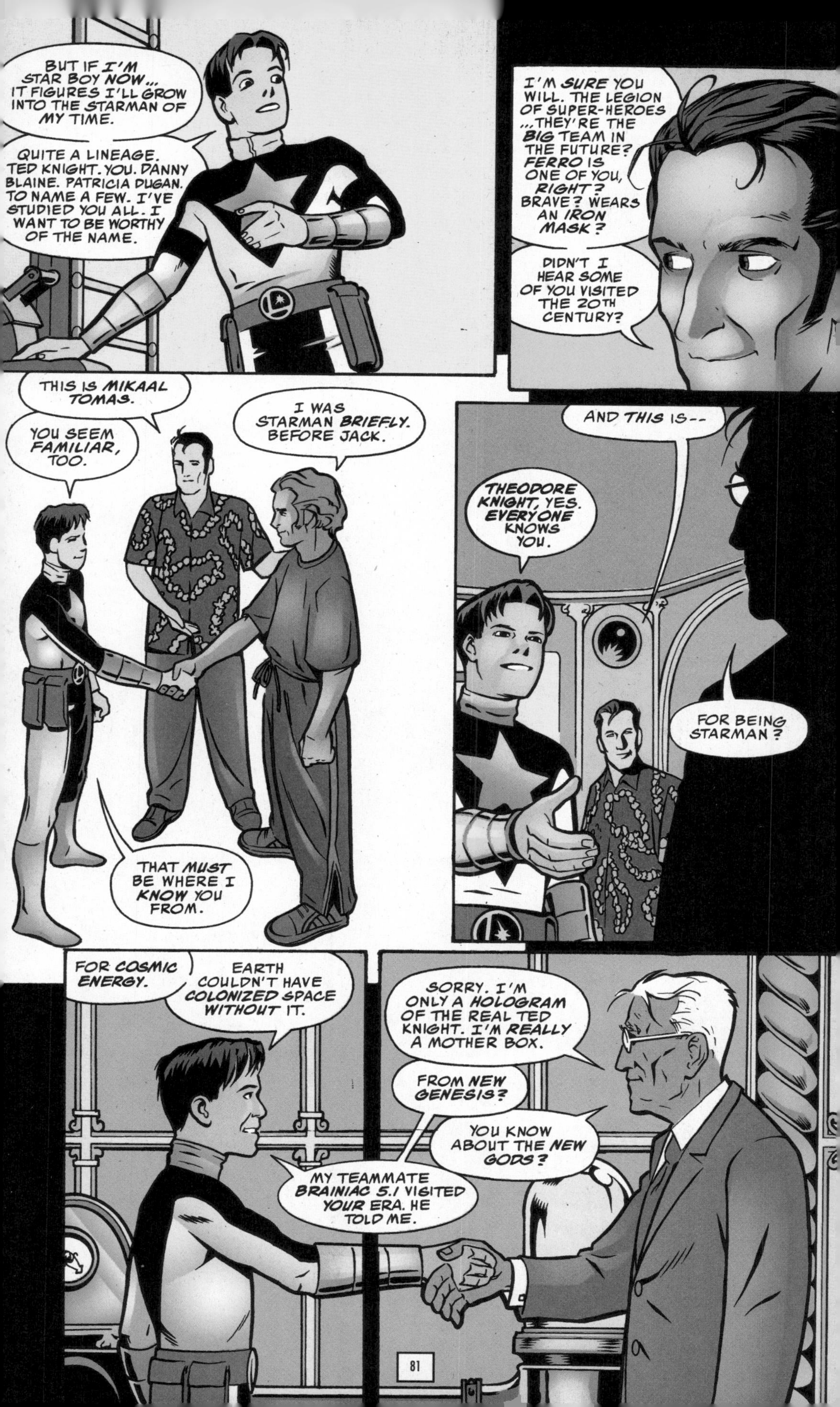
BUT IF I'M STAR BOY NOW... IT FIGURES I'LL GROW INTO THE STARMAN OF MY TIME.
QUITE A LINEAGE. TED KNIGHT. YOU. DANNY BLAINE. PATRICIA DUGAN. TO NAME A FEW. I'VE STUDIED YOU ALL. I WANT TO BE WORTHY OF THE NAME.
I'M SURE YOU WILL. THE LEGION OF SUPER-HEROES ...THEY'RE THE BIG TEAM IN THE FUTURE? FERRO IS ONE OF YOU, RIGHT? BRAVE? WEARS AN IRON MASK?
DIDN'T I HEAR SOME OF YOU VISITED THE 20TH CENTURY?
THIS IS MIKAAL TOMAS.
YOU SEEM FAMILIAR, TOO.
I WAS STARMAN BRIEFLY. BEFORE JACK.
THAT MUST BE WHERE I KNOW YOU FROM.
AND THIS IS--
THEODORE KNIGHT, YES. EVERYONE KNOWS YOU.
FOR BEING STARMAN?
FOR COSMIC ENERGY.
EARTH COULDN'T HAVE COLONIZED SPACE WITHOUT IT.
SORRY. I'M ONLY A HOLOGRAM OF THE REAL TED KNIGHT. I'M REALLY A MOTHER BOX.
FROM NEW GENESIS?
YOU KNOW ABOUT THE NEW GODS?
MY TEAMMATE BRAINIAC 5.1 VISITED YOUR ERA. HE TOLD ME.

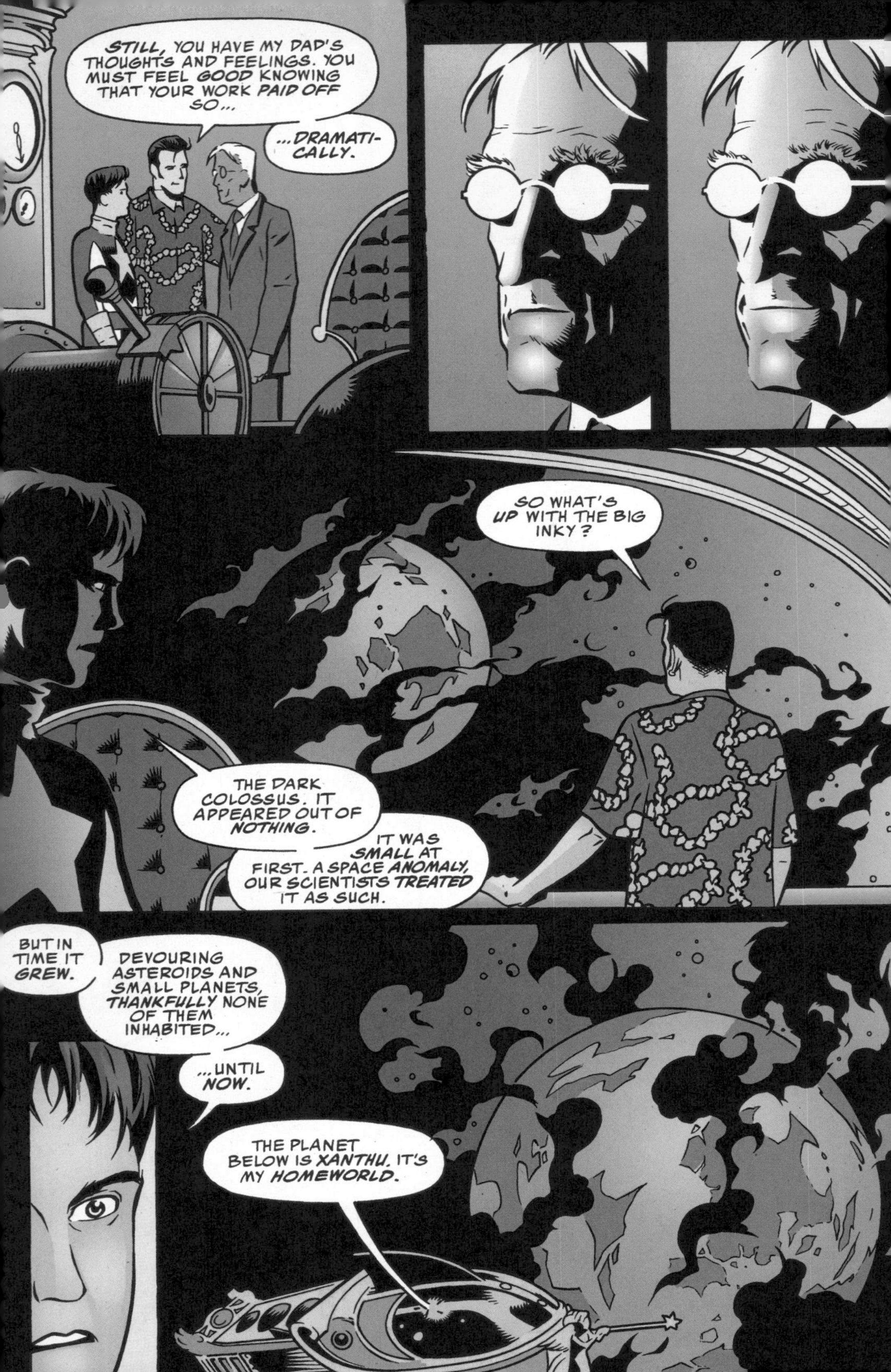
STILL, YOU HAVE MY DAD'S THOUGHTS AND FEELINGS. YOU MUST FEEL GOOD KNOWING THAT YOUR WORK PAID OFF SO...
...DRAMATICALLY.
SO WHAT'S UP WITH THE BIG INKY?
THE DARK COLOSSUS. IT APPEARED OUT OF NOTHING.
IT WAS SMALL AT FIRST. A SPACE ANOMALY, OUR SCIENTISTS TREATED IT AS SUCH.
BUT IN TIME IT GREW.
DEVOURING ASTEROIDS AND SMALL PLANETS, THANKFULLY NONE OF THEM INHABITED...
...UNTIL NOW.
THE PLANET BELOW IS XANTHU. IT'S MY HOMEWORLD.

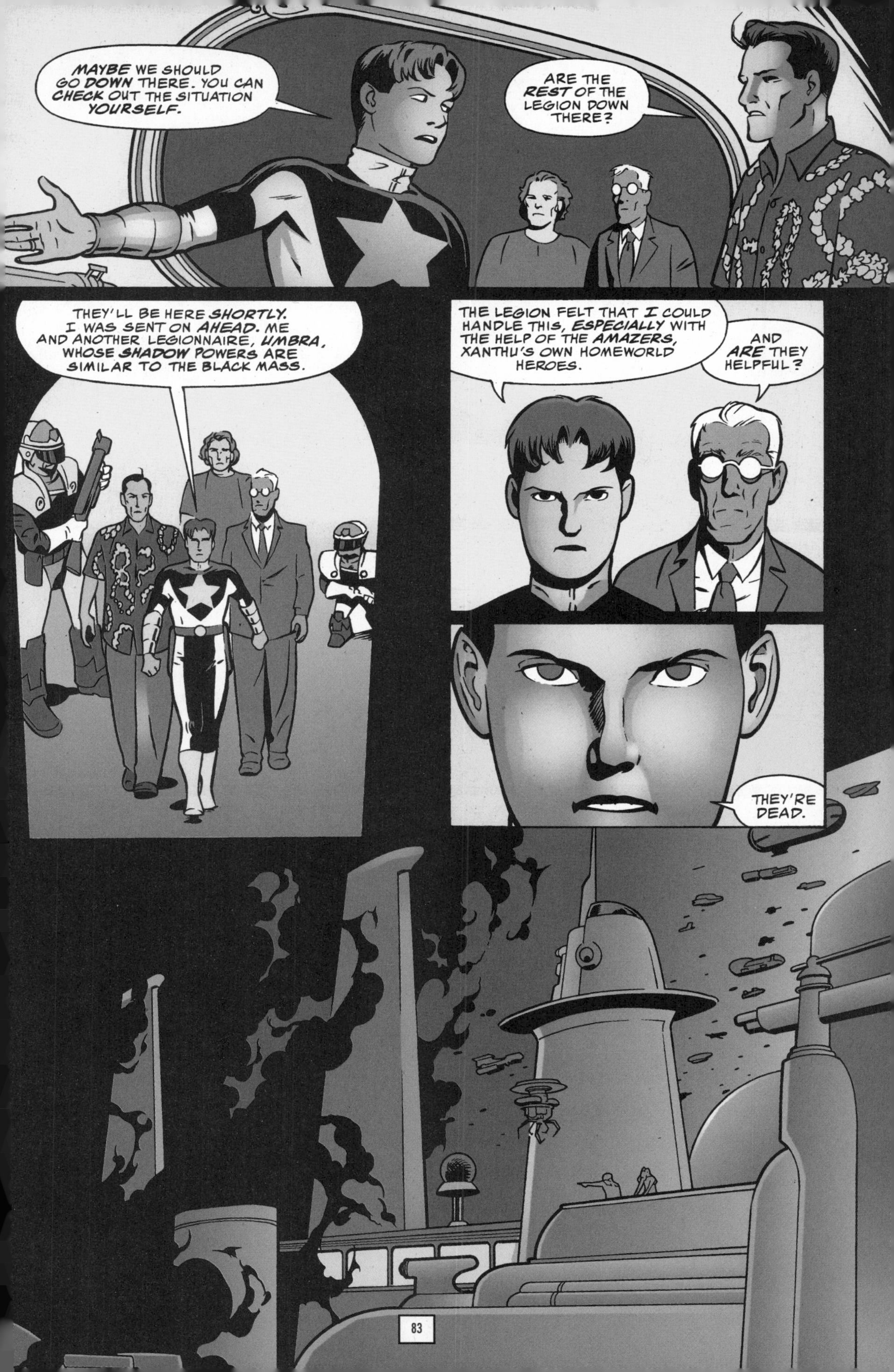
MAYBE WE SHOULD GO DOWN THERE. YOU CAN CHECK OUT THE SITUATION YOURSELF.
ARE THE REST OF THE LEGION DOWN THERE?
THEY'LL BE HERE SHORTLY. I WAS SENT ON AHEAD. ME AND ANOTHER LEGIONNAIRE, UMBRA, WHOSE SHADOW POWERS ARE SIMILAR TO THE BLACK MASS.
THE LEGION FELT THAT I COULD HANDLE THIS, ESPECIALLY WITH THE HELP OF THE AMAZERS, XANTHU'S OWN HOMEWORLD HEROES.
AND ARE THEY HELPFUL?
THEY'RE DEAD.

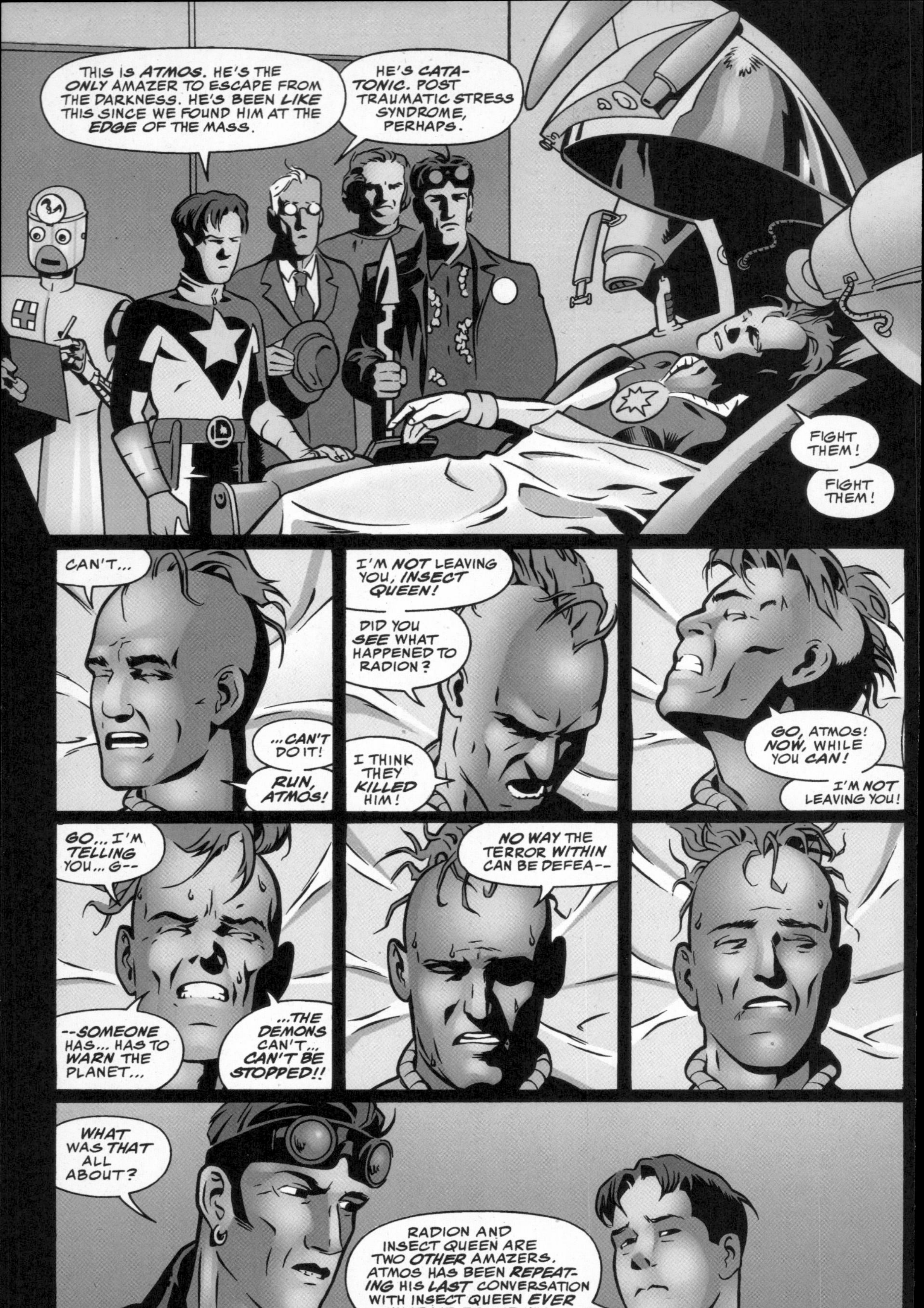

THIS IS ATMOS. HE'S THE ONLY AMAZER TO ESCAPE FROM THE DARKNESS. HE'S BEEN LIKE THIS SINCE WE FOUND HIM AT THE EDGE OF THE MASS.
HE'S CATATONIC. POST TRAUMATIC STRESS SYNDROME, PERHAPS.
FIGHT THEM!
FIGHT THEM!
CAN'T...
...CAN'T DO IT!
RUN, ATMOS!
I'M NOT LEAVING YOU, INSECT QUEEN!
DID YOU SEE WHAT HAPPENED TO RADION?
I THINK THEY KILLED HIM!
GO, ATMOS! NOW, WHILE YOU CAN!
I'M NOT LEAVING YOU!
GO... I'M TELLING YOU... G--
--SOMEONE HAS... HAS TO WARN THE PLANET...
...THE DEMONS CAN'T... CAN'T BE STOPPED!!
NO WAY THE TERROR WITHIN CAN BE DEFEA--
WHAT WAS THAT ALL ABOUT?
RADION AND INSECT QUEEN ARE TWO OTHER AMAZERS. ATMOS HAS BEEN REPEATING HIS LAST CONVERSATION WITH INSECT QUEEN EVER SINCE WE FOUND HIM.

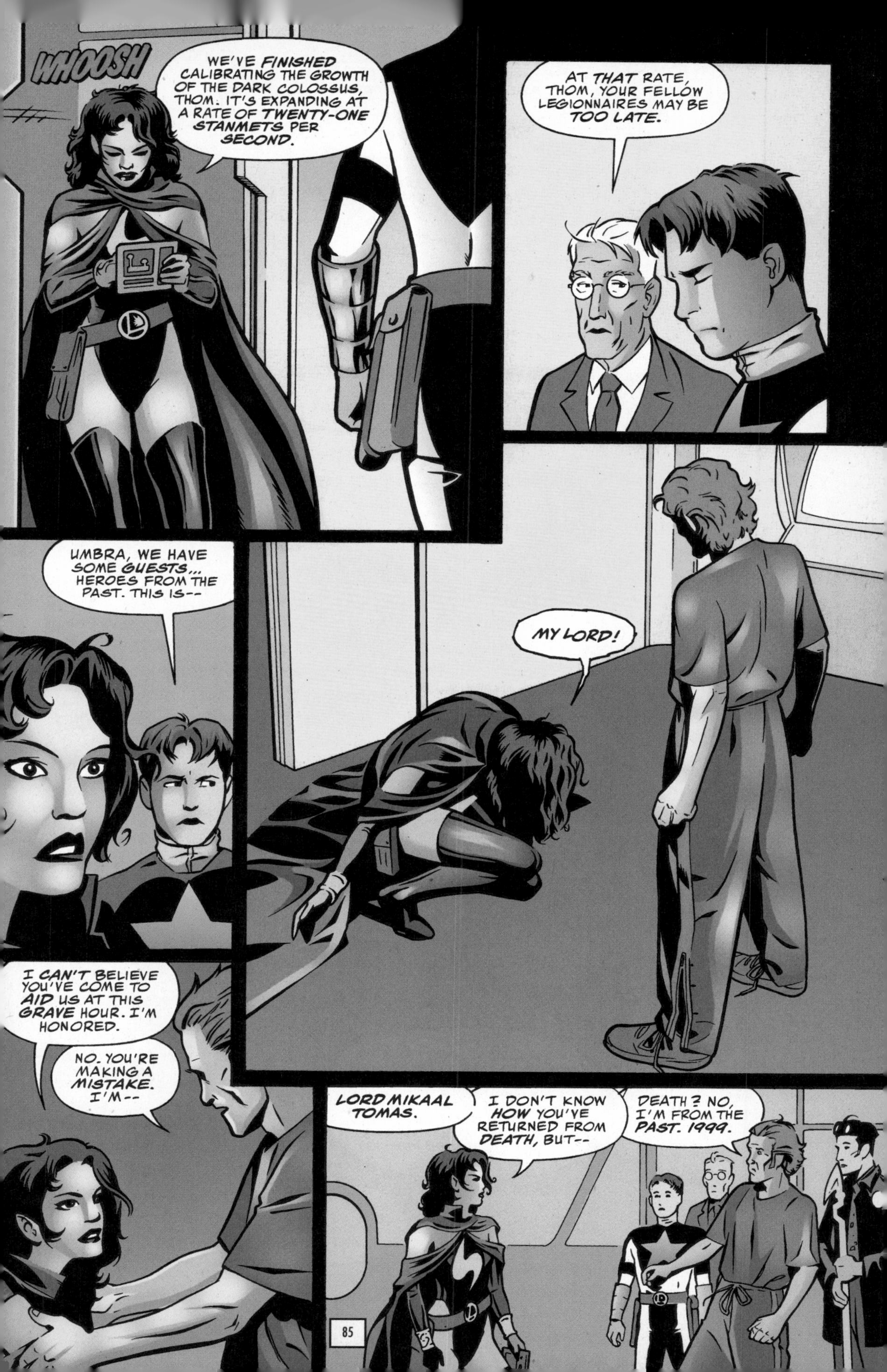

WHOOSH
WE'VE FINISHED CALIBRATING THE GROWTH OF THE DARK COLOSSUS, THOM. IT'S EXPANDING AT A RATE OF TWENTY-ONE STANMETS PER SECOND.
AT THAT RATE, THOM, YOUR FELLOW LEGIONNAIRES MAY BE TOO LATE.
UMBRA, WE HAVE SOME GUESTS... HEROES FROM THE PAST. THIS IS--
MY LORD!
I CAN'T BELIEVE YOU'VE COME TO AID US AT THIS GRAVE HOUR. I'M HONORED.
NO. YOU'RE MAKING A MISTAKE. I'M--
LORD MIKAAL TOMAS.
I DON'T KNOW HOW YOU'VE RETURNED FROM DEATH, BUT--
DEATH? NO, I'M FROM THE PAST. 1999.

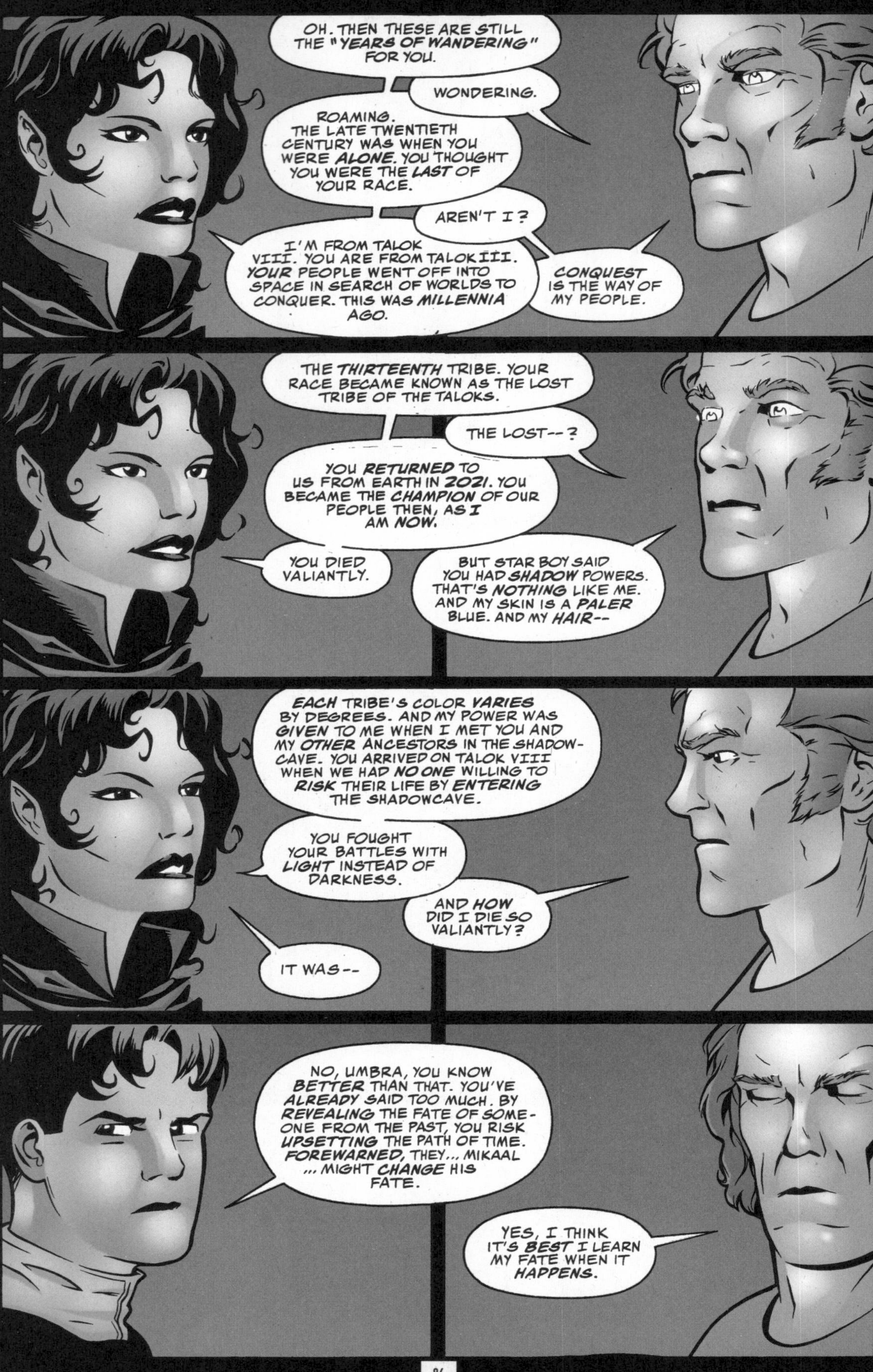

OH. THEN THESE ARE STILL THE "YEARS OF WANDERING" FOR YOU.
WONDERING.
ROAMING. THE LATE TWENTIETH CENTURY WAS WHEN YOU WERE ALONE. YOU THOUGHT YOU WERE THE LAST OF YOUR RACE.
AREN'T I?
I'M FROM TALOK VIII. YOU ARE FROM TALOK III. YOUR PEOPLE WENT OFF INTO SPACE IN SEARCH OF WORLDS TO CONQUER. THIS WAS MILLENNIA AGO.
CONQUEST IS THE WAY OF MY PEOPLE.
THE THIRTEENTH TRIBE. YOUR RACE BECAME KNOWN AS THE LOST TRIBE OF THE TALOKS.
THE LOST--?
YOU RETURNED TO US FROM EARTH IN 2021. YOU BECAME THE CHAMPION OF OUR PEOPLE THEN, AS I AM NOW.
YOU DIED VALIANTLY.
BUT STAR BOY SAID YOU HAD SHADOW POWERS. THAT'S NOTHING LIKE ME. AND MY SKIN IS A PALER BLUE. AND MY HAIR--
EACH TRIBE'S COLOR VARIES BY DEGREES. AND MY POWER WAS GIVEN TO ME WHEN I MET YOU AND MY OTHER ANCESTORS IN THE SHADOW-CAVE. YOU ARRIVED ON TALOK VIII WHEN WE HAD NO ONE WILLING TO RISK THEIR LIFE BY ENTERING THE SHADOWCAVE.
YOU FOUGHT YOUR BATTLES WITH LIGHT INSTEAD OF DARKNESS.
AND HOW DID I DIE SO VALIANTLY?
IT WAS--
NO, UMBRA, YOU KNOW BETTER THAN THAT. YOU'VE ALREADY SAID TOO MUCH. BY REVEALING THE FATE OF SOME-ONE FROM THE PAST, YOU RISK UPSETTING THE PATH OF TIME. FOREWARNED, THEY... MIKAAL ...MIGHT CHANGE HIS FATE.
YES, I THINK IT'S BEST I LEARN MY FATE WHEN IT HAPPENS.

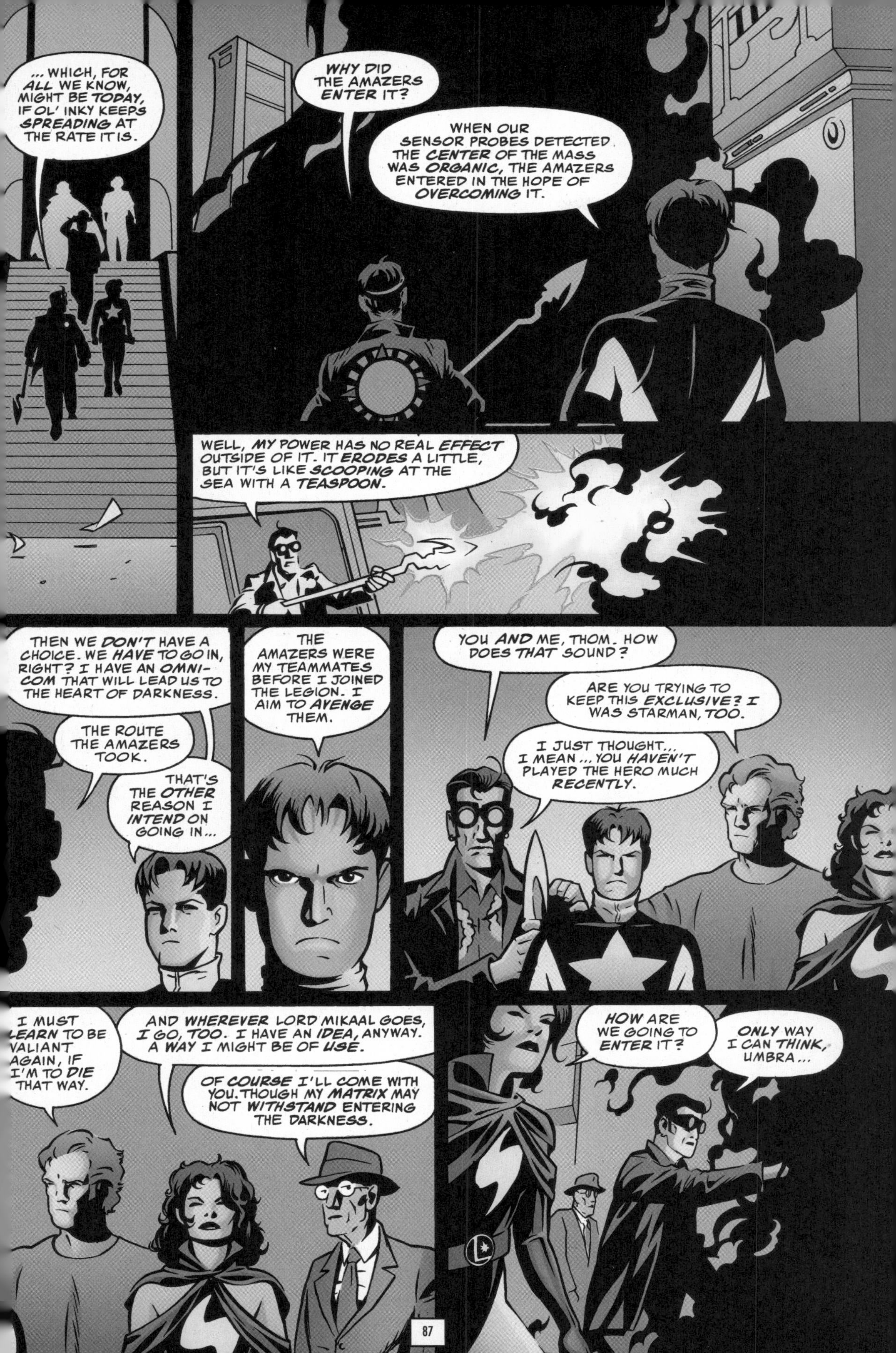

... WHICH, FOR ALL WE KNOW, MIGHT BE TODAY, IF OL' INKY KEEPS SPREADING AT THE RATE IT IS.
WHY DID THE AMAZERS ENTER IT?
WHEN OUR SENSOR PROBES DETECTED THE CENTER OF THE MASS WAS ORGANIC, THE AMAZERS ENTERED IN THE HOPE OF OVERCOMING IT.
WELL, MY POWER HAS NO REAL EFFECT OUTSIDE OF IT. IT ERODES A LITTLE, BUT IT'S LIKE SCOOPING AT THE SEA WITH A TEASPOON.
THEN WE DON'T HAVE A CHOICE. WE HAVE TO GO IN, RIGHT? I HAVE AN OMNI-COM THAT WILL LEAD US TO THE HEART OF DARKNESS.
THE ROUTE THE AMAZERS TOOK.
THAT'S THE OTHER REASON I INTEND ON GOING IN...
THE AMAZERS WERE MY TEAMMATES BEFORE I JOINED THE LEGION. I AIM TO AVENGE THEM.
YOU AND ME, THOM. HOW DOES THAT SOUND?
ARE YOU TRYING TO KEEP THIS EXCLUSIVE? I WAS STARMAN, TOO.
I JUST THOUGHT... I MEAN ... YOU HAVEN'T PLAYED THE HERO MUCH RECENTLY.
I MUST LEARN TO BE VALIANT AGAIN, IF I'M TO DIE THAT WAY.
AND WHEREVER LORD MIKAAL GOES, I GO, TOO. I HAVE AN IDEA, ANYWAY. A WAY I MIGHT BE OF USE.
OF COURSE I'LL COME WITH YOU. THOUGH MY MATRIX MAY NOT WITHSTAND ENTERING THE DARKNESS.
HOW ARE WE GOING TO ENTER IT?
ONLY WAY I CAN THINK, UMBRA...

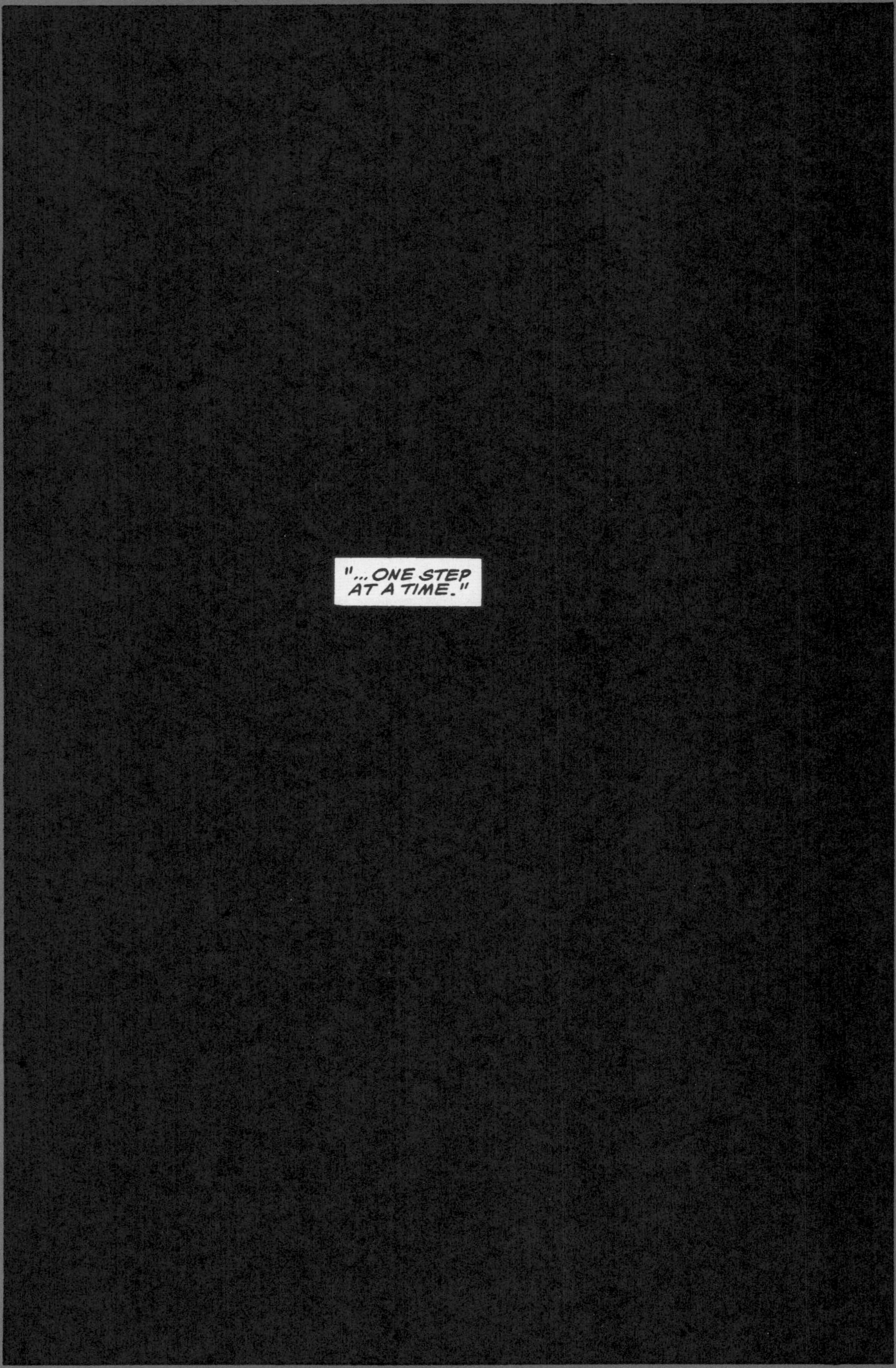
"...ONE STEP AT A TIME."

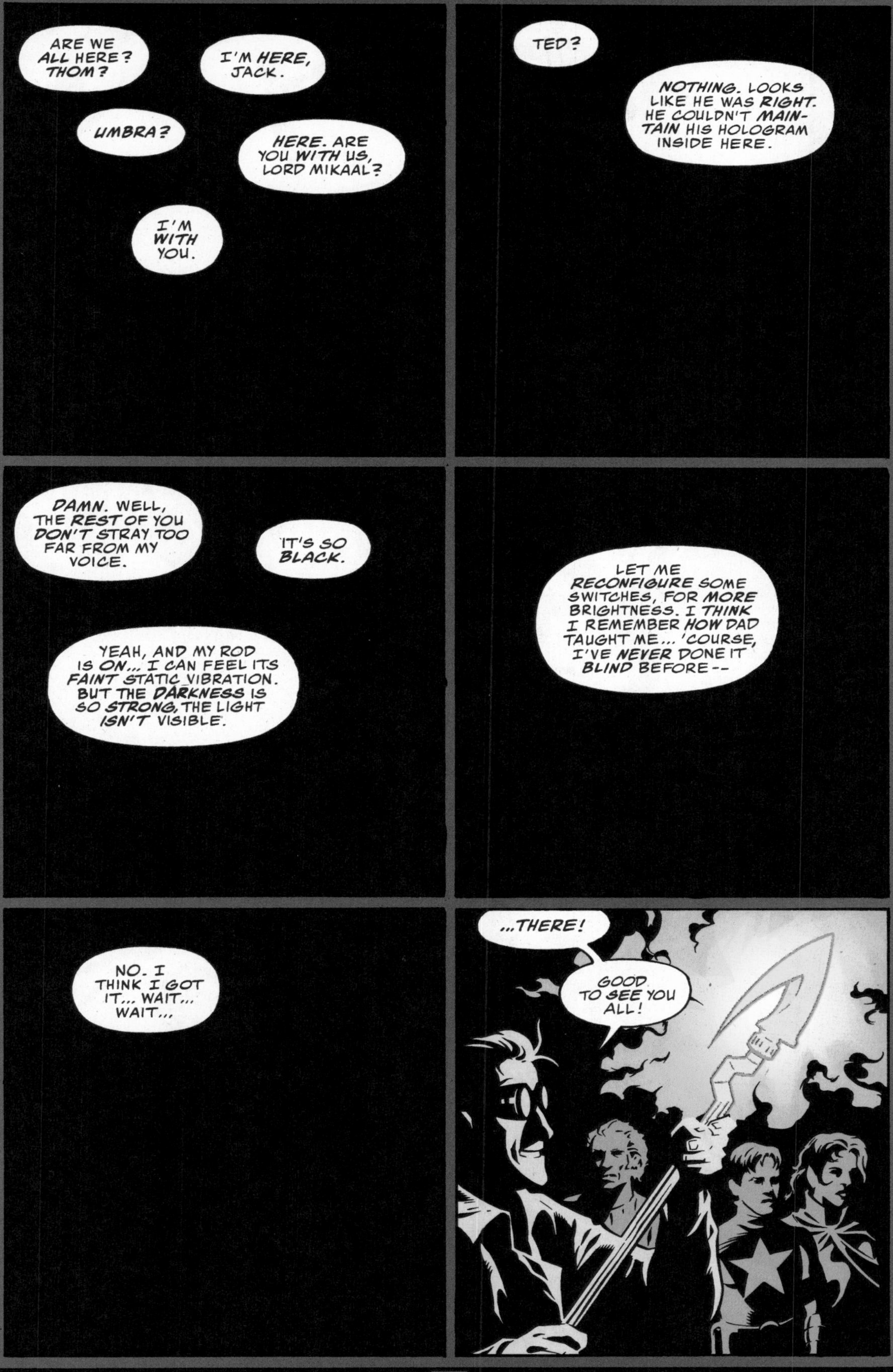
ARE WE ALL HERE? THOM?
I'M HERE, JACK.
UMBRA?
HERE. ARE YOU WITH US, LORD MIKAAL?
I'M WITH YOU.
TED?
NOTHING. LOOKS LIKE HE WAS RIGHT. HE COULDN'T MAIN-TAIN HIS HOLOGRAM INSIDE HERE.
DAMN. WELL, THE REST OF YOU DON'T STRAY TOO FAR FROM MY VOICE.
IT'S SO BLACK.
YEAH, AND MY ROD IS ON... I CAN FEEL ITS FAINT STATIC VIBRATION. BUT THE DARKNESS IS SO STRONG, THE LIGHT ISN'T VISIBLE.
LET ME RECONFIGURE SOME SWITCHES, FOR MORE BRIGHTNESS. I THINK I REMEMBER HOW DAD TAUGHT ME... 'COURSE, I'VE NEVER DONE IT BLIND BEFORE--
NO. I THINK I GOT IT... WAIT... WAIT...
...THERE!
GOOD TO SEE YOU ALL!

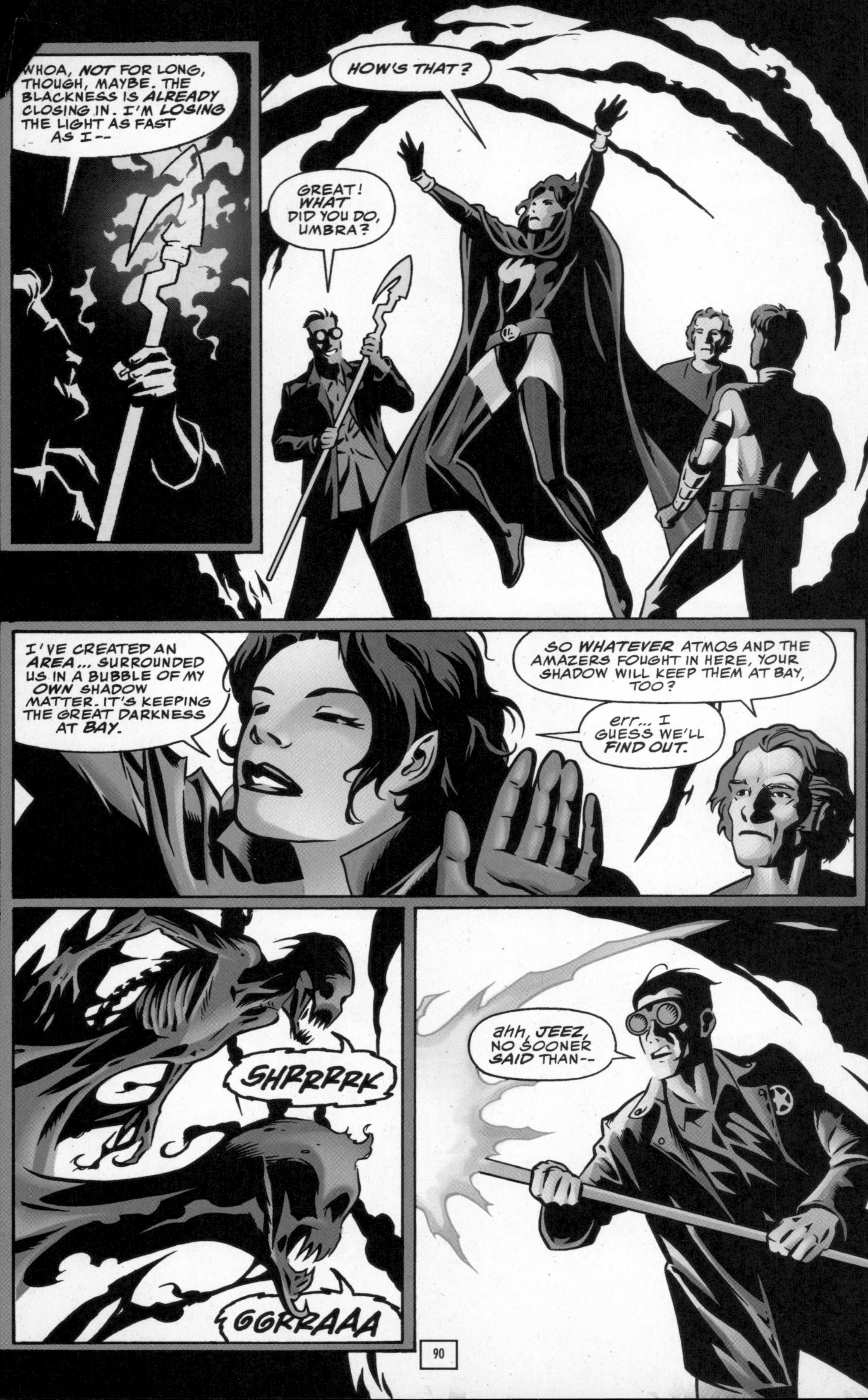
WHOA, NOT FOR LONG, THOUGH, MAYBE. THE BLACKNESS IS ALREADY CLOSING IN. I'M LOSING THE LIGHT AS FAST AS I--
HOW'S THAT?
GREAT! WHAT DID YOU DO, UMBRA?
I'VE CREATED AN AREA... SURROUNDED US IN A BUBBLE OF MY OWN SHADOW MATTER. IT'S KEEPING THE GREAT DARKNESS AT BAY.
SO WHATEVER ATMOS AND THE AMAZERS FOUGHT IN HERE, YOUR SHADOW WILL KEEP THEM AT BAY, TOO?
err... I GUESS WE'LL FIND OUT.
SHRRRRK
GGRRAAA
ahh, JEEZ, NO SOONER SAID THAN--

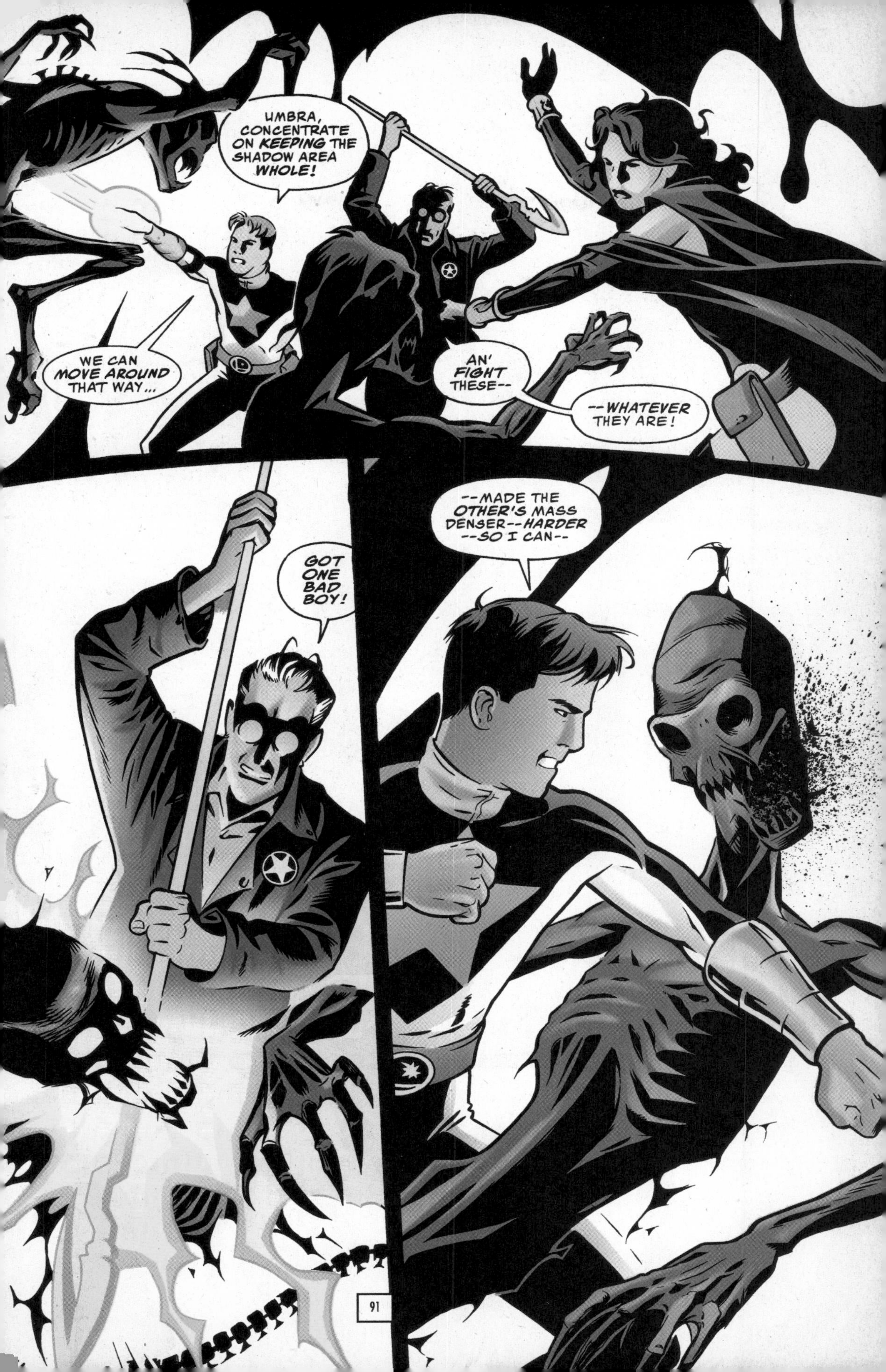
UMBRA, CONCENTRATE ON KEEPING THE SHADOW AREA WHOLE!
WE CAN MOVE AROUND THAT WAY...
AN' FIGHT THESE--
--WHATEVER THEY ARE!
GOT ONE BAD BOY!
--MADE THE OTHER'S MASS DENSER--HARDER --SO I CAN--

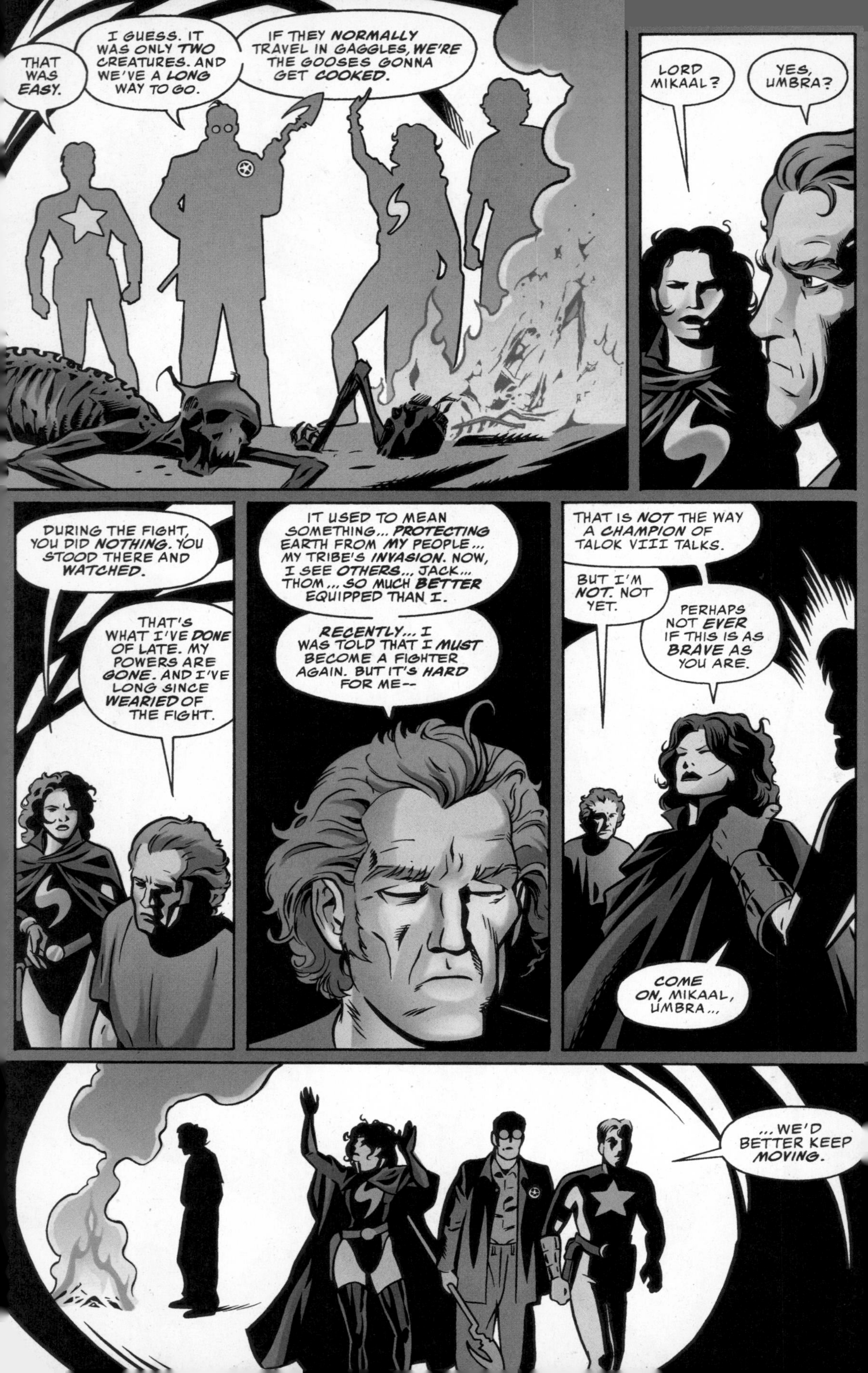
THAT WAS EASY.
I GUESS. IT WAS ONLY TWO CREATURES. AND WE'VE A LONG WAY TO GO.
IF THEY NORMALLY TRAVEL IN GAGGLES, WE'RE THE GOOSES GONNA GET COOKED.
LORD MIKAAL?
YES, UMBRA?
DURING THE FIGHT, YOU DID NOTHING. YOU STOOD THERE AND WATCHED.
THAT'S WHAT I'VE DONE OF LATE. MY POWERS ARE GONE. AND I'VE LONG SINCE WEARIED OF THE FIGHT.
IT USED TO MEAN SOMETHING... PROTECTING EARTH FROM MY PEOPLE... MY TRIBE'S INVASION. NOW, I SEE OTHERS... JACK... THOM... SO MUCH BETTER EQUIPPED THAN I.
RECENTLY... I WAS TOLD THAT I MUST BECOME A FIGHTER AGAIN. BUT IT'S HARD FOR ME--
THAT IS NOT THE WAY A CHAMPION OF TALOK VIII TALKS.
BUT I'M NOT. NOT YET.
PERHAPS NOT EVER IF THIS IS AS BRAVE AS YOU ARE.
COME ON, MIKAAL, UMBRA...
...WE'D BETTER KEEP MOVING.

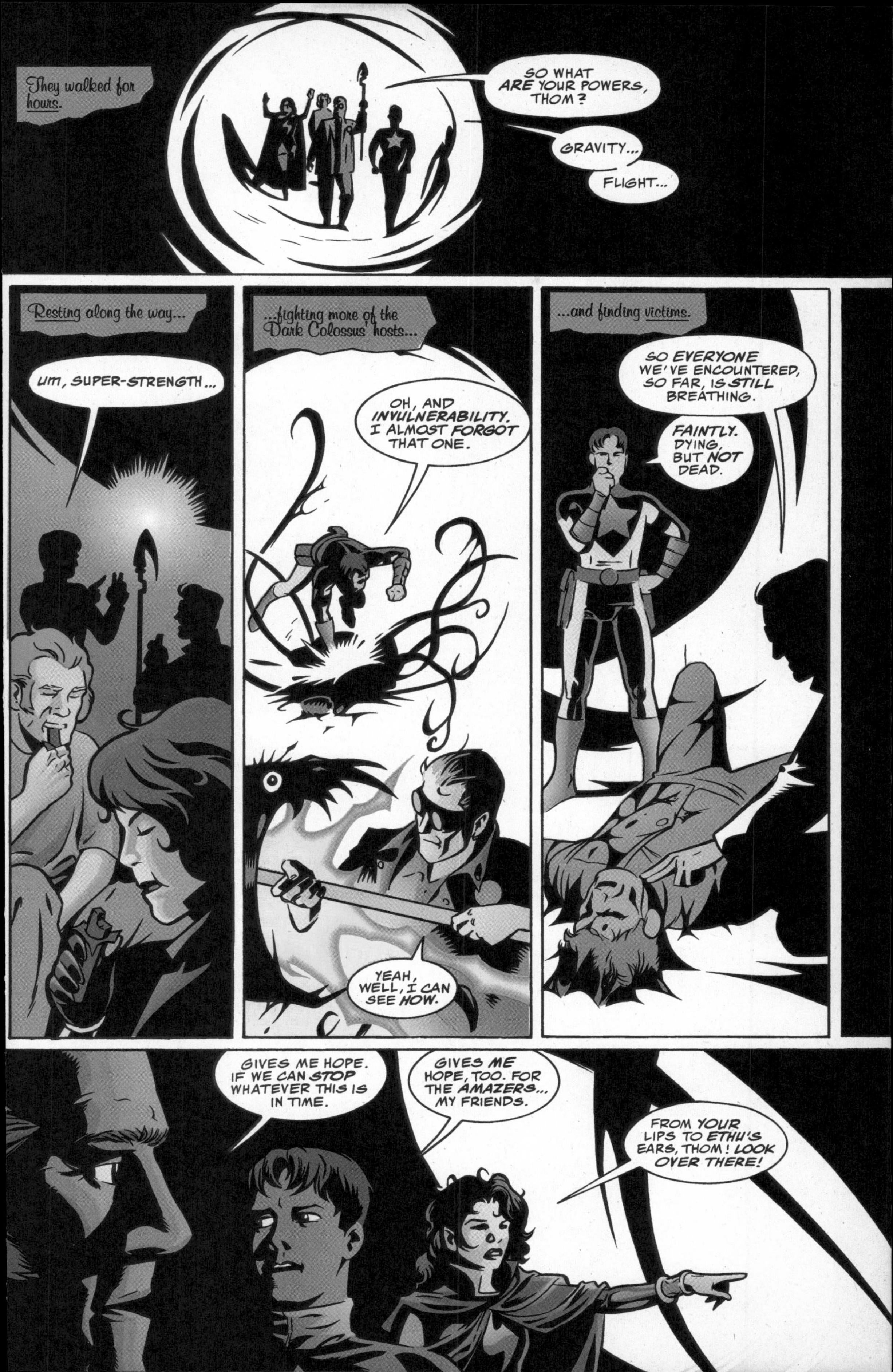
They walked for hours.
SO WHAT ARE YOUR POWERS, THOM?
GRAVITY...
FLIGHT...
Resting along the way...
UM, SUPER-STRENGTH...
...fighting more of the Dark Colossus' hosts...
OH, AND INVULNERABILITY. I ALMOST FORGOT THAT ONE.
YEAH, WELL, I CAN SEE HOW.
...and finding victims.
SO EVERYONE WE'VE ENCOUNTERED, SO FAR, IS STILL BREATHING.
FAINTLY. DYING, BUT NOT DEAD.
GIVES ME HOPE. IF WE CAN STOP WHATEVER THIS IS IN TIME.
GIVES ME HOPE, TOO. FOR THE AMAZERS... MY FRIENDS.
FROM YOUR LIPS TO ETHU'S EARS, THOM! LOOK OVER THERE!

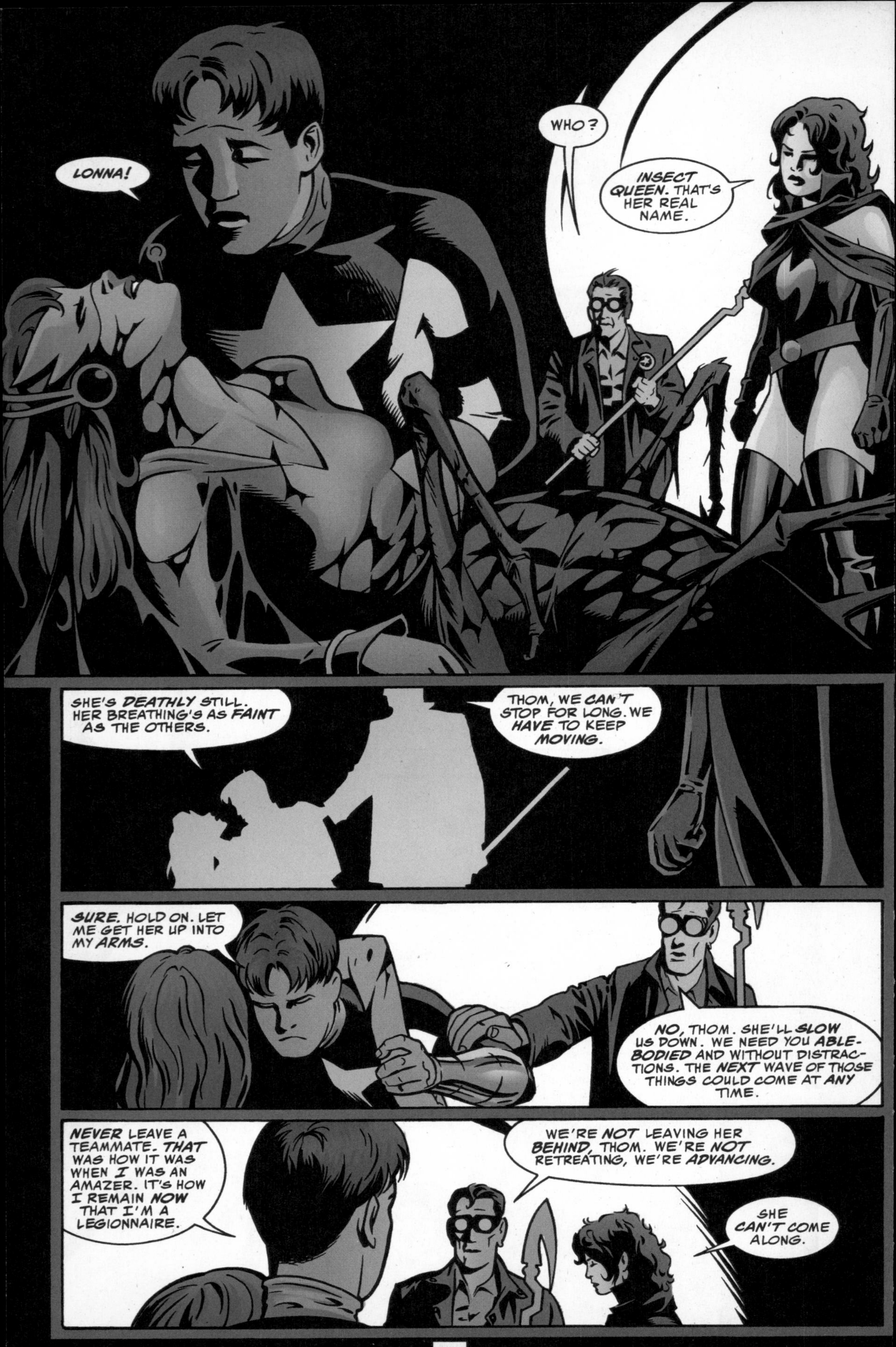
LONNA!
WHO?
INSECT QUEEN. THAT'S HER REAL NAME.
SHE'S DEATHLY STILL. HER BREATHING'S AS FAINT AS THE OTHERS.
THOM, WE CAN'T STOP FOR LONG. WE HAVE TO KEEP MOVING.
SURE. HOLD ON. LET ME GET HER UP INTO MY ARMS.
NO, THOM. SHE'LL SLOW US DOWN. WE NEED YOU ABLE-BODIED AND WITHOUT DISTRACTIONS. THE NEXT WAVE OF THOSE THINGS COULD COME AT ANY TIME.
NEVER LEAVE A TEAMMATE. THAT WAS HOW IT WAS WHEN I WAS AN AMAZER. IT'S HOW I REMAIN NOW THAT I'M A LEGIONNAIRE.
WE'RE NOT LEAVING HER BEHIND, THOM. WE'RE NOT RETREATING, WE'RE ADVANCING.
SHE CAN'T COME ALONG.

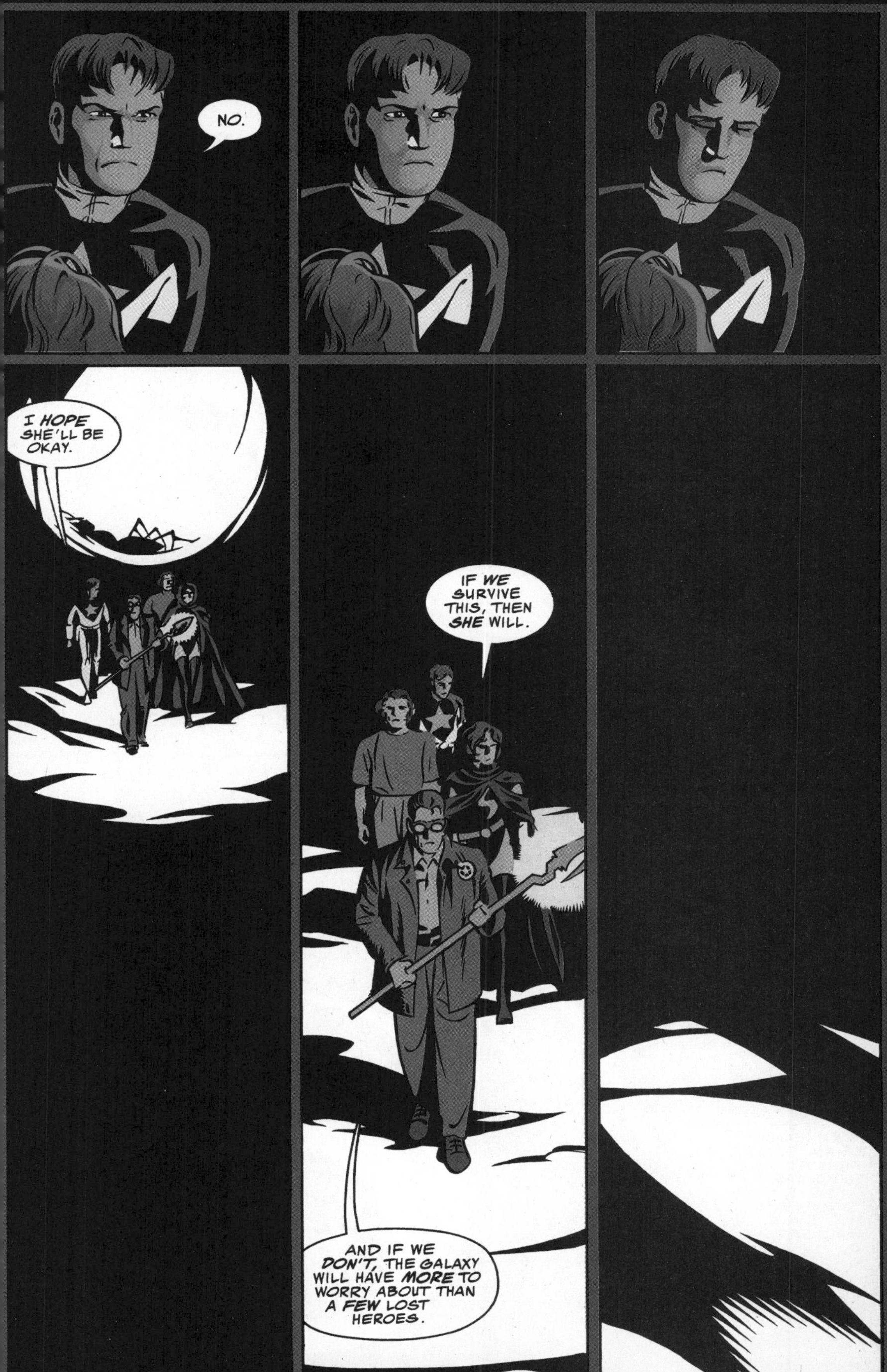
NO.
I HOPE SHE'LL BE OKAY.
IF WE SURVIVE THIS, THEN SHE WILL.
AND IF WE DON'T, THE GALAXY WILL HAVE MORE TO WORRY ABOUT THAN A FEW LOST HEROES.

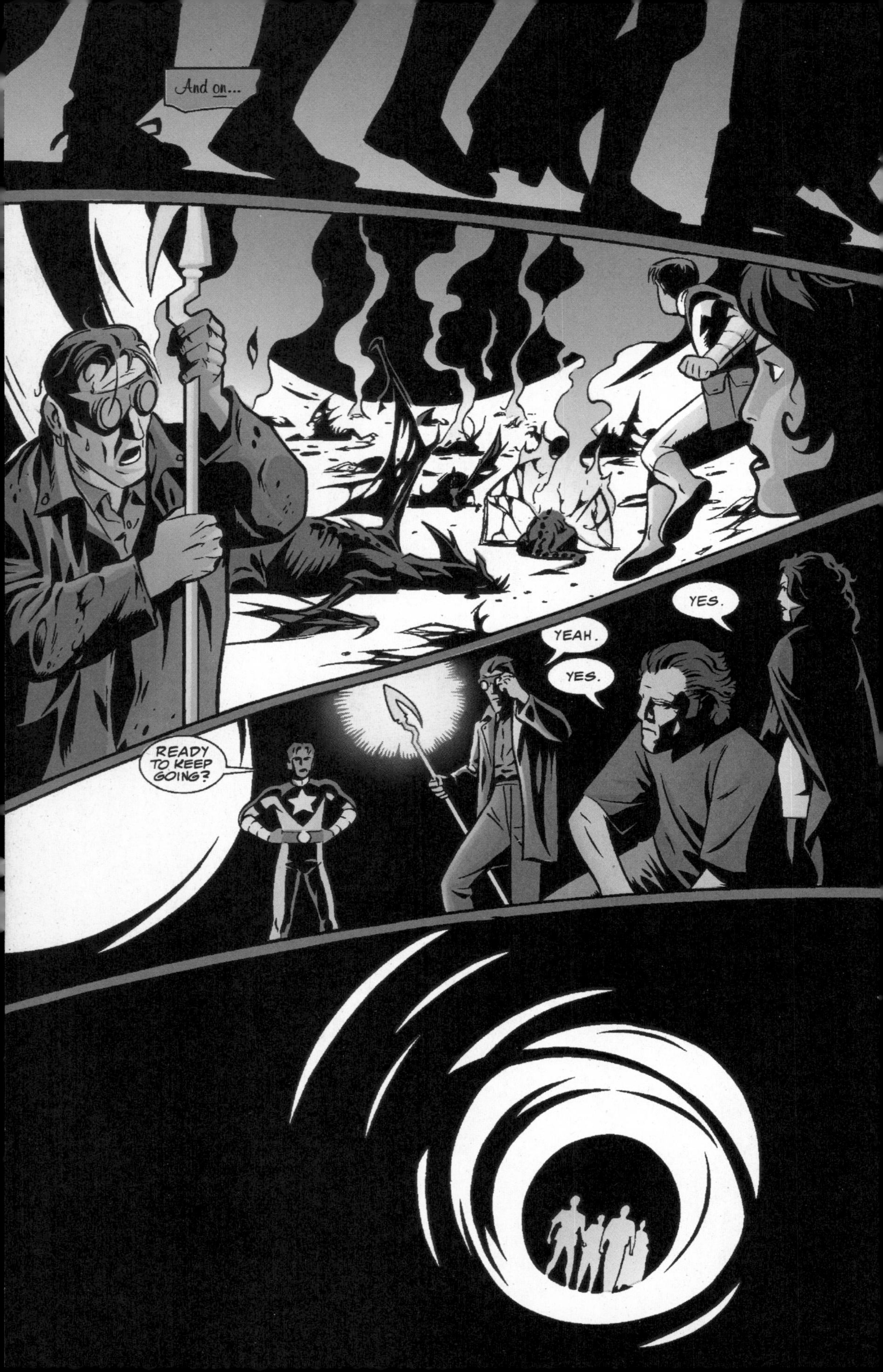
And on...
YES.
YEAH.
YES.
READY TO KEEP GOING?

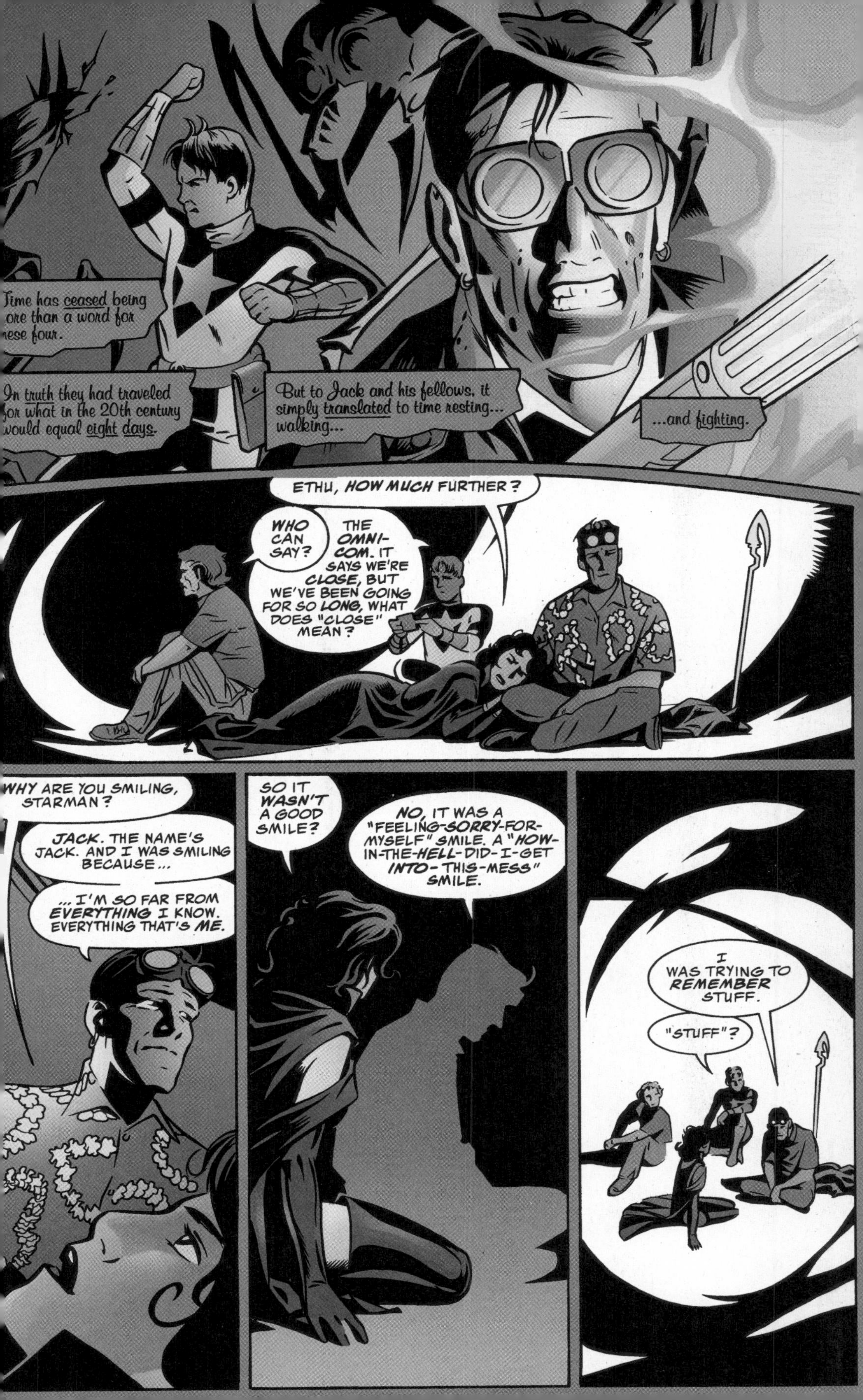

Time has ceased being more than a word for these four.
In truth they had traveled for what in the 20th century would equal eight days.
But to Jack and his fellows, it simply translated to time resting... walking...
...and fighting.
ETHU, HOW MUCH FURTHER?
WHO CAN SAY?
THE OMNI-COM. IT SAYS WE'RE CLOSE, BUT WE'VE BEEN GOING FOR SO LONG, WHAT DOES "CLOSE" MEAN?
WHY ARE YOU SMILING, STARMAN?
JACK. THE NAME'S JACK. AND I WAS SMILING BECAUSE...
... I'M SO FAR FROM EVERYTHING I KNOW. EVERYTHING THAT'S ME.
SO IT WASN'T A GOOD SMILE?
NO, IT WAS A "FEELING-SORRY-FOR-MYSELF" SMILE. A "HOW-IN-THE-HELL-DID-I-GET INTO-THIS-MESS" SMILE.
I WAS TRYING TO REMEMBER STUFF.
"STUFF"?

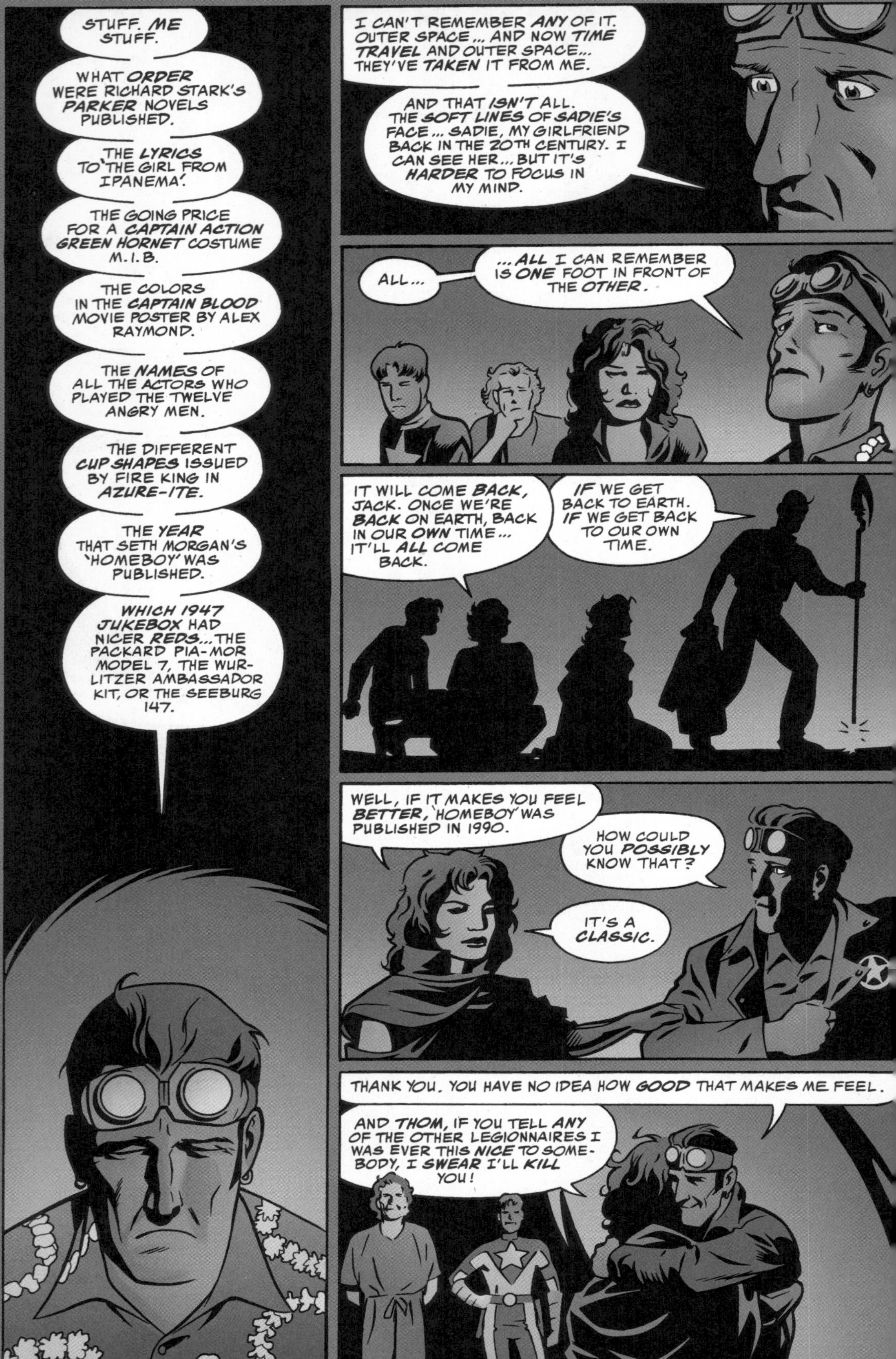
STUFF. ME STUFF.
WHAT ORDER WERE RICHARD STARK'S PARKER NOVELS PUBLISHED.
THE LYRICS TO 'THE GIRL FROM IPANEMA'.
THE GOING PRICE FOR A CAPTAIN ACTION GREEN HORNET COSTUME M.I.B.
THE COLORS IN THE CAPTAIN BLOOD MOVIE POSTER BY ALEX RAYMOND.
THE NAMES OF ALL THE ACTORS WHO PLAYED THE TWELVE ANGRY MEN.
THE DIFFERENT CUP SHAPES ISSUED BY FIRE KING IN AZURE-ITE.
THE YEAR THAT SETH MORGAN'S 'HOMEBOY' WAS PUBLISHED.
WHICH 1947 JUKEBOX HAD NICER REDS... THE PACKARD PIA-MOR MODEL 7, THE WURLITZER AMBASSADOR KIT, OR THE SEEBURG 147.
I CAN'T REMEMBER ANY OF IT. OUTER SPACE... AND NOW TIME TRAVEL AND OUTER SPACE... THEY'VE TAKEN IT FROM ME.
AND THAT ISN'T ALL. THE SOFT LINES OF SADIE'S FACE... SADIE, MY GIRLFRIEND BACK IN THE 20TH CENTURY. I CAN SEE HER... BUT IT'S HARDER TO FOCUS IN MY MIND.
ALL...
...ALL I CAN REMEMBER IS ONE FOOT IN FRONT OF THE OTHER.
IT WILL COME BACK, JACK. ONCE WE'RE BACK ON EARTH, BACK IN OUR OWN TIME... IT'LL ALL COME BACK.
IF WE GET BACK TO EARTH. IF WE GET BACK TO OUR OWN TIME.
WELL, IF IT MAKES YOU FEEL BETTER, 'HOMEBOY' WAS PUBLISHED IN 1990.
HOW COULD YOU POSSIBLY KNOW THAT?
IT'S A CLASSIC.
THANK YOU. YOU HAVE NO IDEA HOW GOOD THAT MAKES ME FEEL.
AND THOM, IF YOU TELL ANY OF THE OTHER LEGIONNAIRES I WAS EVER THIS NICE TO SOMEBODY, I SWEAR I'LL KILL YOU!

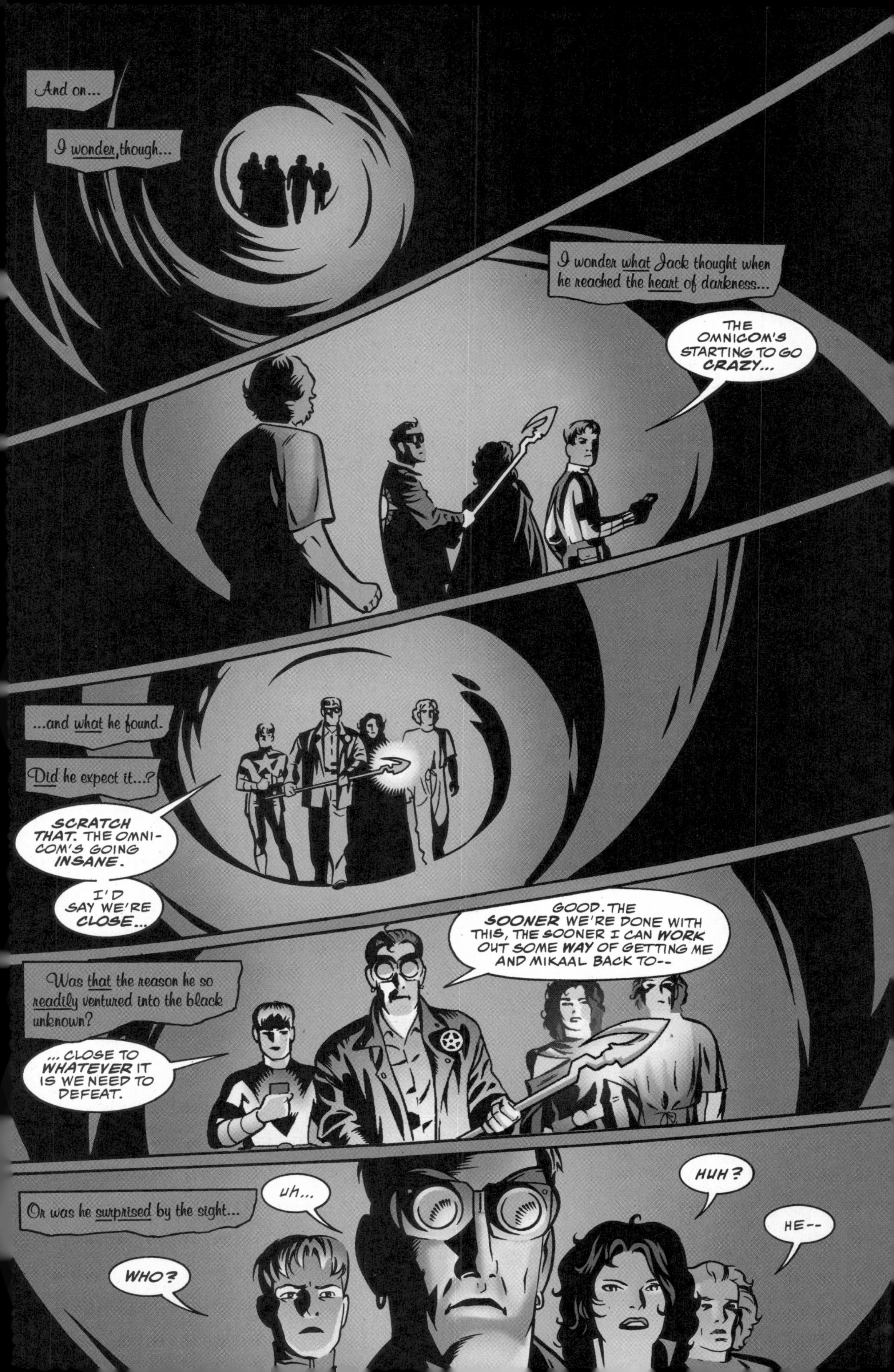
And on...
I wonder, though...
I wonder what Jack thought when he reached the heart of darkness...
THE OMNICOM'S STARTING TO GO CRAZY...
...and what he found.
Did he expect it...?
SCRATCH THAT. THE OMNI-COM'S GOING INSANE.
I'D SAY WE'RE CLOSE...
GOOD. THE SOONER WE'RE DONE WITH THIS, THE SOONER I CAN WORK OUT SOME WAY OF GETTING ME AND MIKAAL BACK TO--
Was that the reason he so readily ventured into the black unknown?
... CLOSE TO WHATEVER IT IS WE NEED TO DEFEAT.
Or was he surprised by the sight...
uh...
HUH?
HE--
WHO?

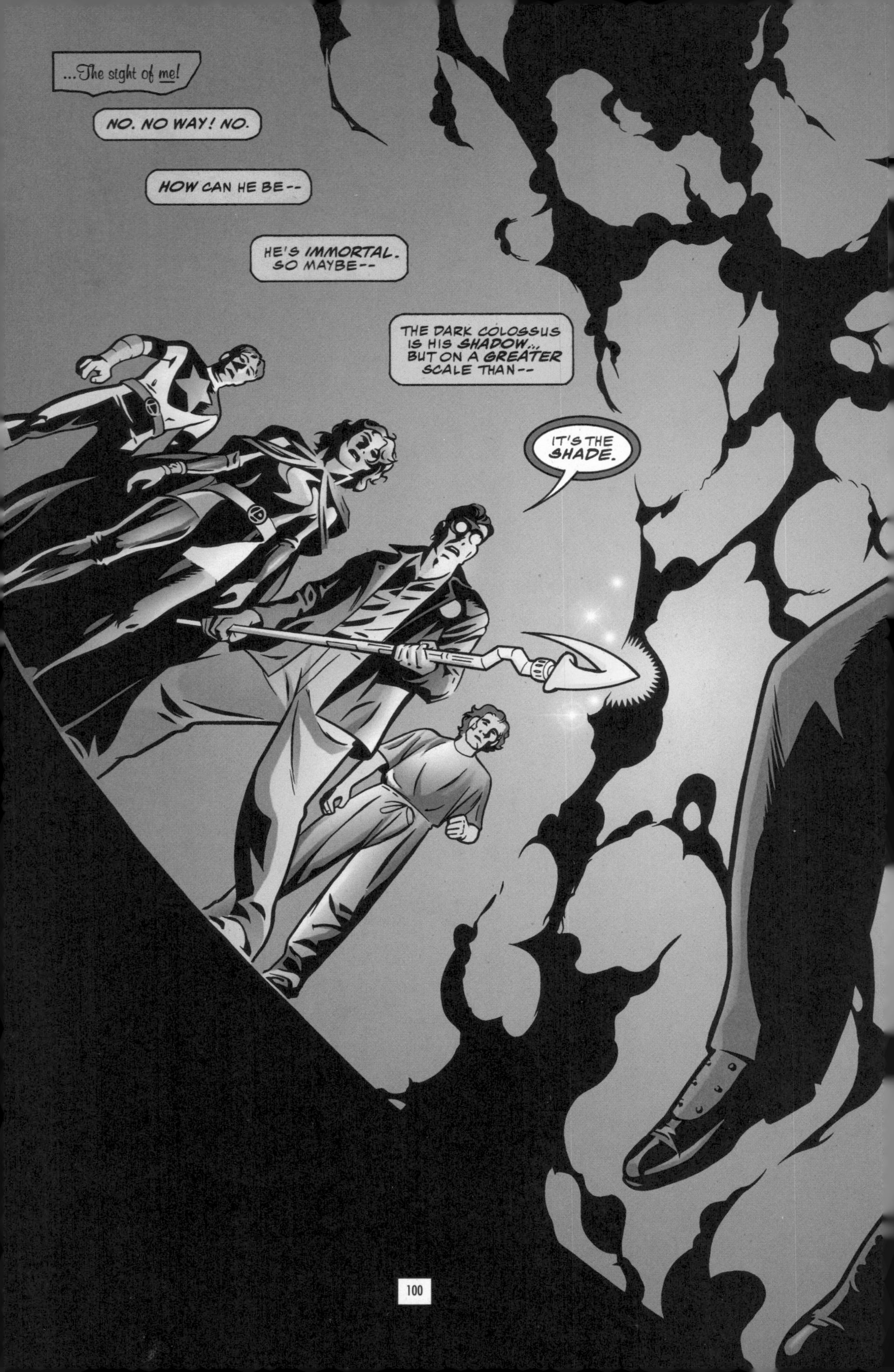
...The sight of me!
NO. NO WAY! NO.
HOW CAN HE BE--
HE'S IMMORTAL. SO MAYBE--
THE DARK COLOSSUS IS HIS SHADOW... BUT ON A GREATER SCALE THAN--
IT'S THE SHADE.

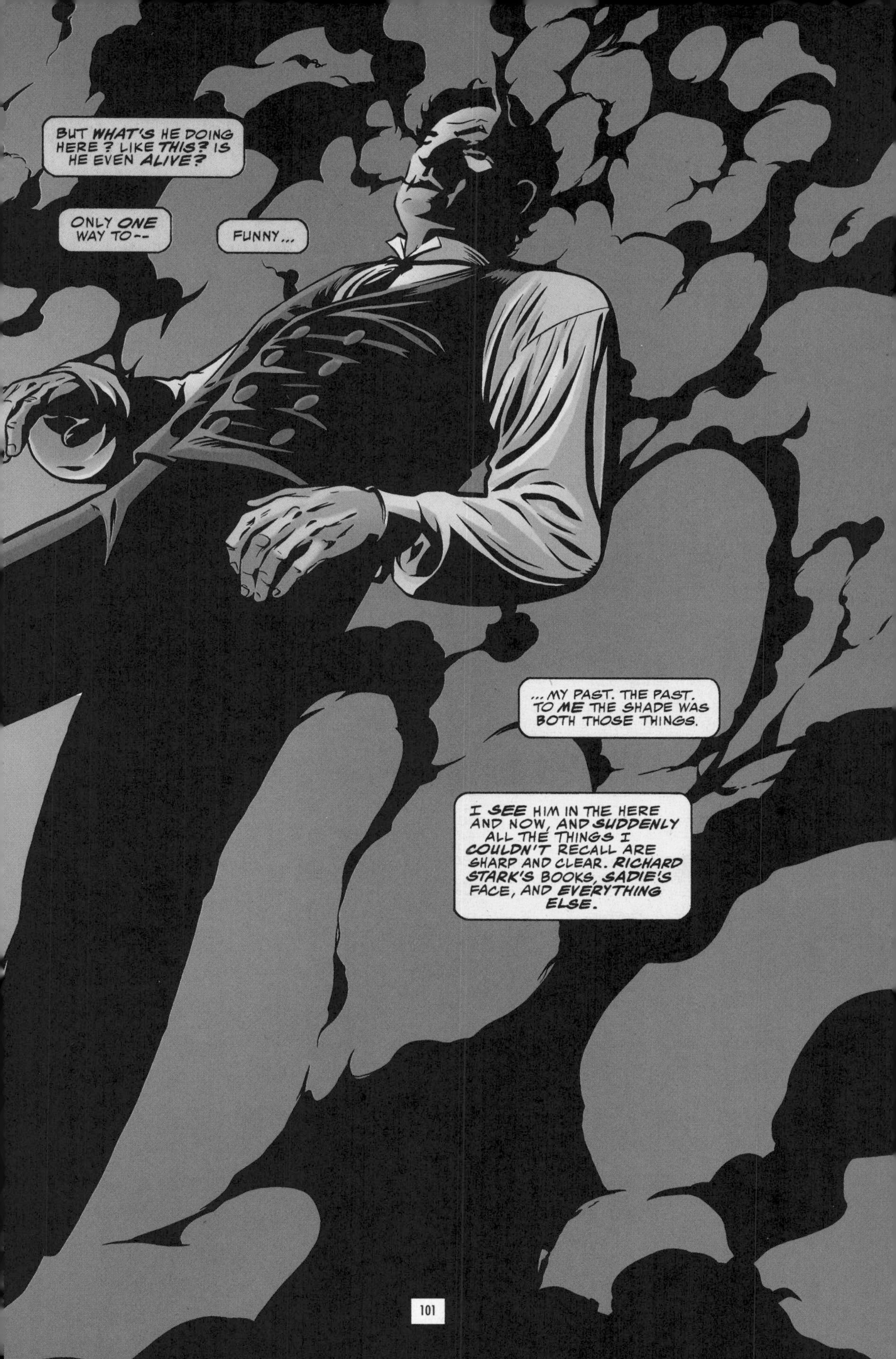
BUT WHAT'S HE DOING HERE? LIKE THIS? IS HE EVEN ALIVE?
ONLY ONE WAY TO--
FUNNY...
...MY PAST. THE PAST. TO ME THE SHADE WAS BOTH THOSE THINGS.
I SEE HIM IN THE HERE AND NOW, AND SUDDENLY ALL THE THINGS I COULDN'T RECALL ARE SHARP AND CLEAR. RICHARD STARK'S BOOKS, SADIE'S FACE, AND EVERYTHING ELSE.

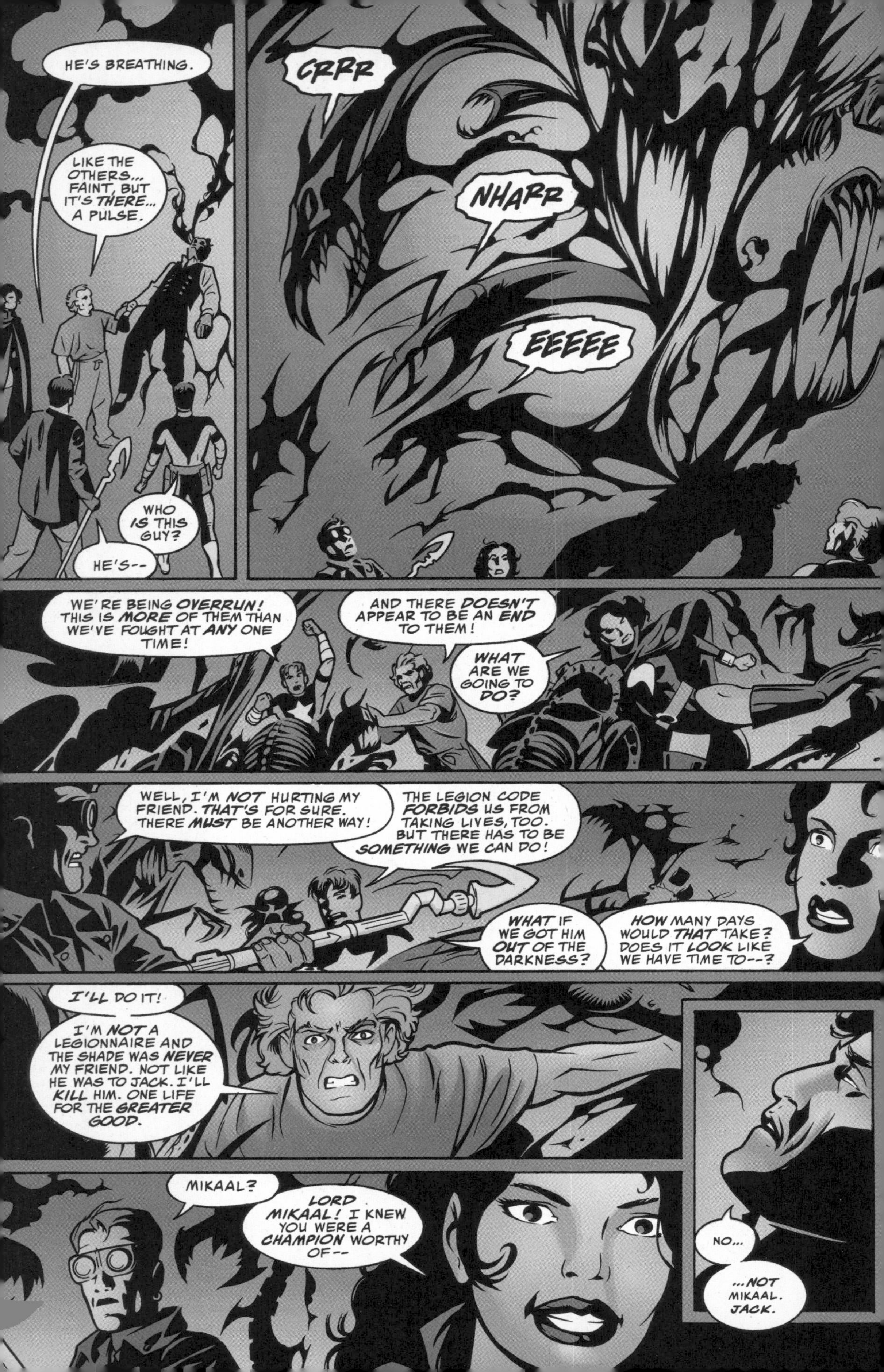

HE'S BREATHING.
LIKE THE OTHERS... FAINT, BUT IT'S THERE... A PULSE.
WHO IS THIS GUY?
HE'S--
CRRR
NHARR
EEEEE
WE'RE BEING OVERRUN! THIS IS MORE OF THEM THAN WE'VE FOUGHT AT ANY ONE TIME!
AND THERE DOESN'T APPEAR TO BE AN END TO THEM!
WHAT ARE WE GOING TO DO?
WELL, I'M NOT HURTING MY FRIEND. THAT'S FOR SURE. THERE MUST BE ANOTHER WAY!
THE LEGION CODE FORBIDS US FROM TAKING LIVES, TOO. BUT THERE HAS TO BE SOMETHING WE CAN DO!
WHAT IF WE GOT HIM OUT OF THE DARKNESS?
HOW MANY DAYS WOULD THAT TAKE? DOES IT LOOK LIKE WE HAVE TIME TO--?
I'LL DO IT!
I'M NOT A LEGIONNAIRE AND THE SHADE WAS NEVER MY FRIEND. NOT LIKE HE WAS TO JACK. I'LL KILL HIM. ONE LIFE FOR THE GREATER GOOD.
MIKAAL?
LORD MIKAAL! I KNEW YOU WERE A CHAMPION WORTHY OF--
NO...
...NOT MIKAAL. JACK.

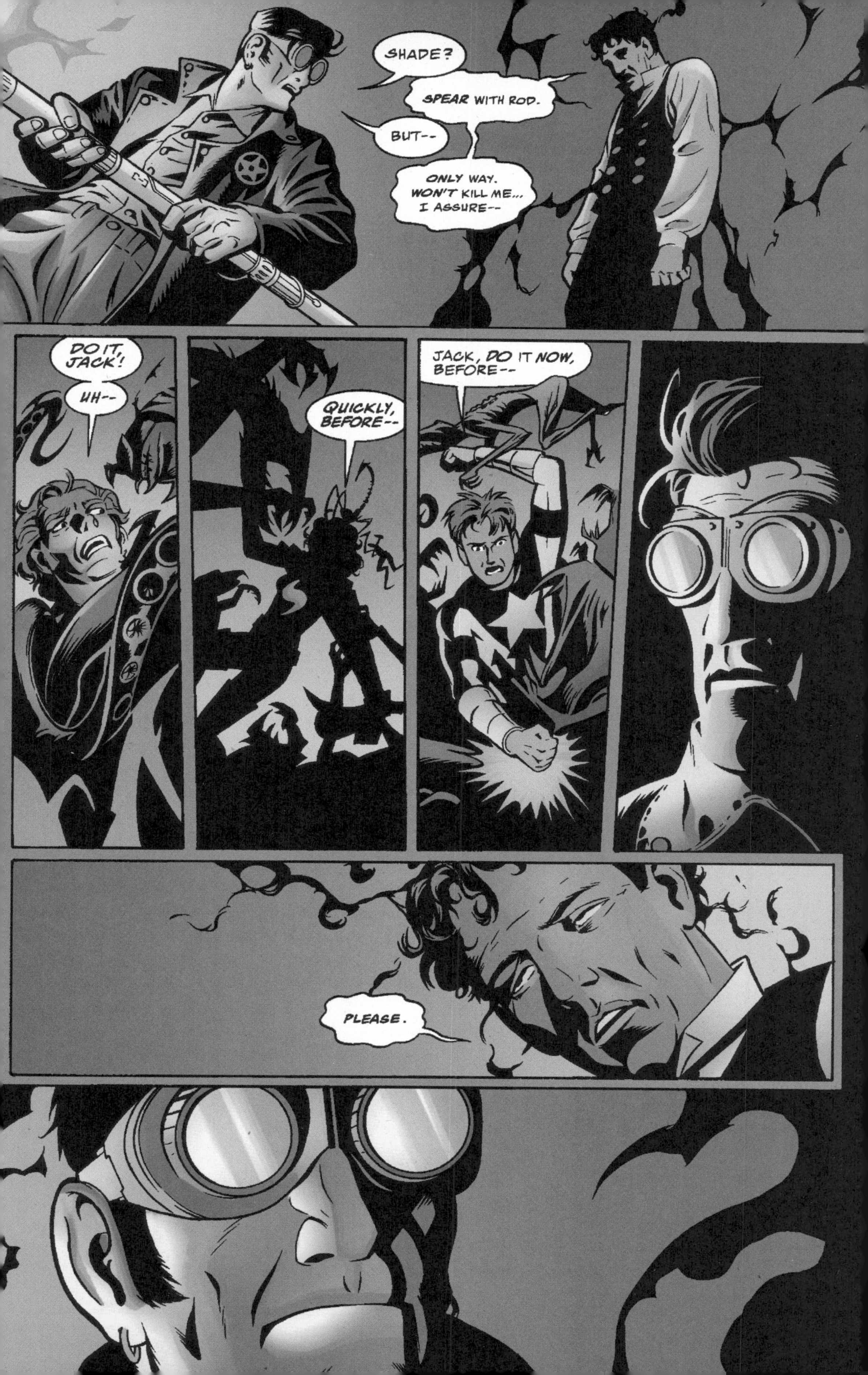
SHADE?
SPEAR WITH ROD.
BUT--
ONLY WAY. WON'T KILL ME... I ASSURE--
DO IT, JACK!
UH--
QUICKLY, BEFORE--
JACK, DO IT NOW, BEFORE--
PLEASE.

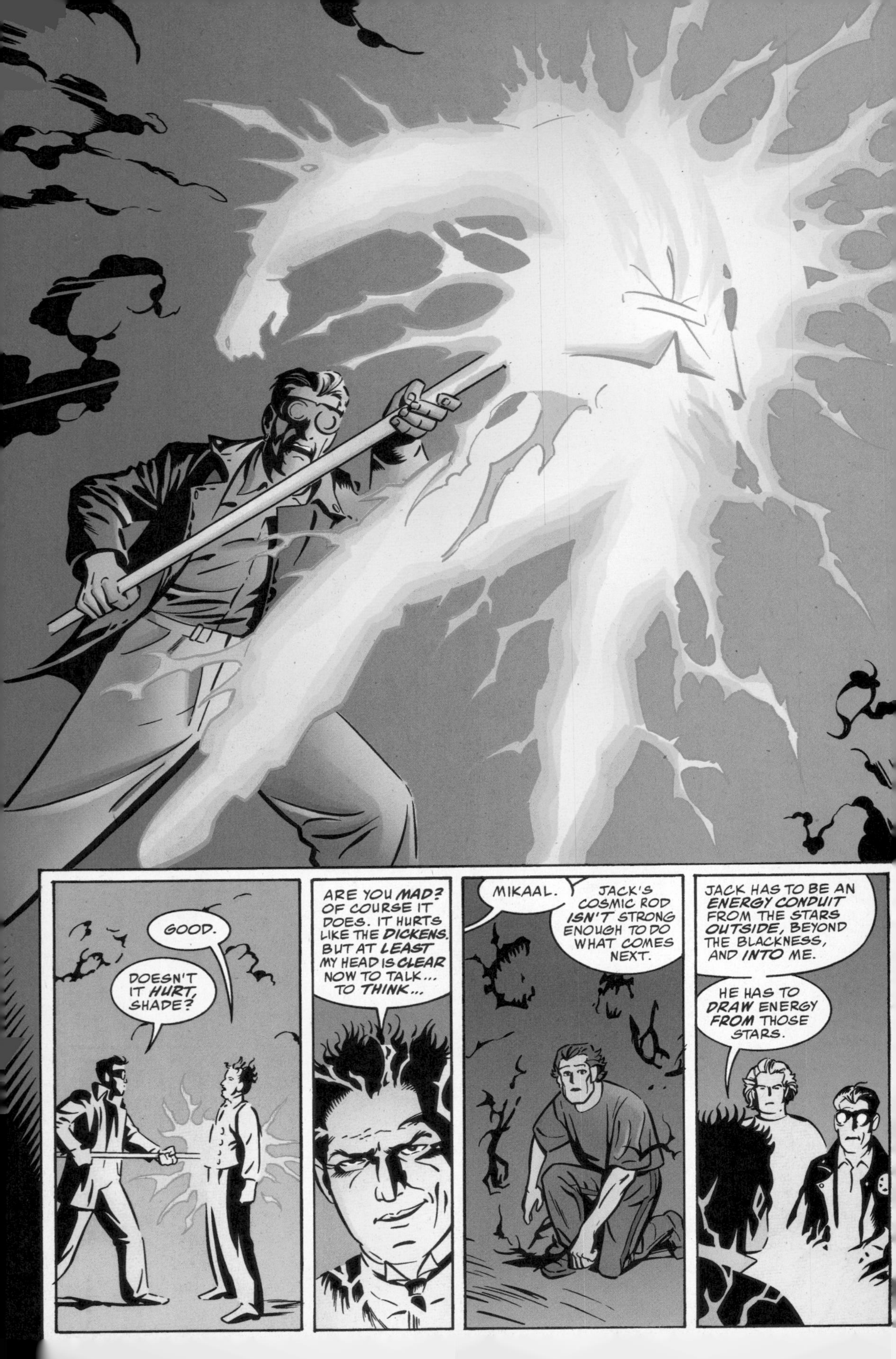
GOOD.
DOESN'T IT HURT, SHADE?
ARE YOU MAD? OF COURSE IT DOES. IT HURTS LIKE THE DICKENS. BUT AT LEAST MY HEAD IS CLEAR NOW TO TALK... TO THINK...
MIKAAL.
JACK'S COSMIC ROD ISN'T STRONG ENOUGH TO DO WHAT COMES NEXT.
JACK HAS TO BE AN ENERGY CONDUIT FROM THE STARS OUTSIDE, BEYOND THE BLACKNESS, AND INTO ME.
HE HAS TO DRAW ENERGY FROM THOSE STARS.

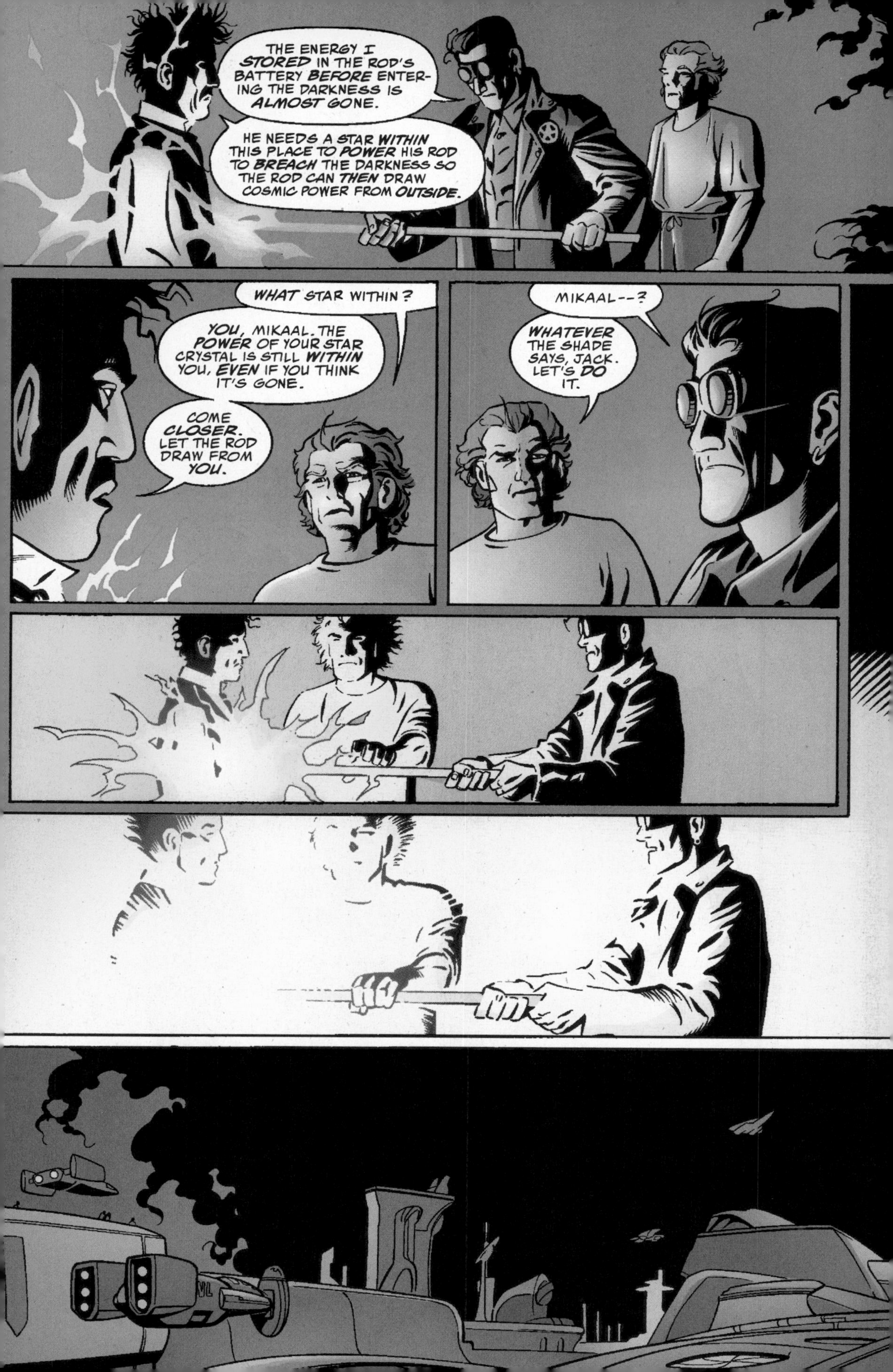

THE ENERGY I STORED IN THE ROD'S BATTERY BEFORE ENTERING THE DARKNESS IS ALMOST GONE.
HE NEEDS A STAR WITHIN THIS PLACE TO POWER HIS ROD TO BREACH THE DARKNESS SO THE ROD CAN THEN DRAW COSMIC POWER FROM OUTSIDE.
WHAT STAR WITHIN?
YOU, MIKAAL. THE POWER OF YOUR STAR CRYSTAL IS STILL WITHIN YOU, EVEN IF YOU THINK IT'S GONE.
COME CLOSER. LET THE ROD DRAW FROM YOU.
MIKAAL--?
WHATEVER THE SHADE SAYS, JACK. LET'S DO IT.

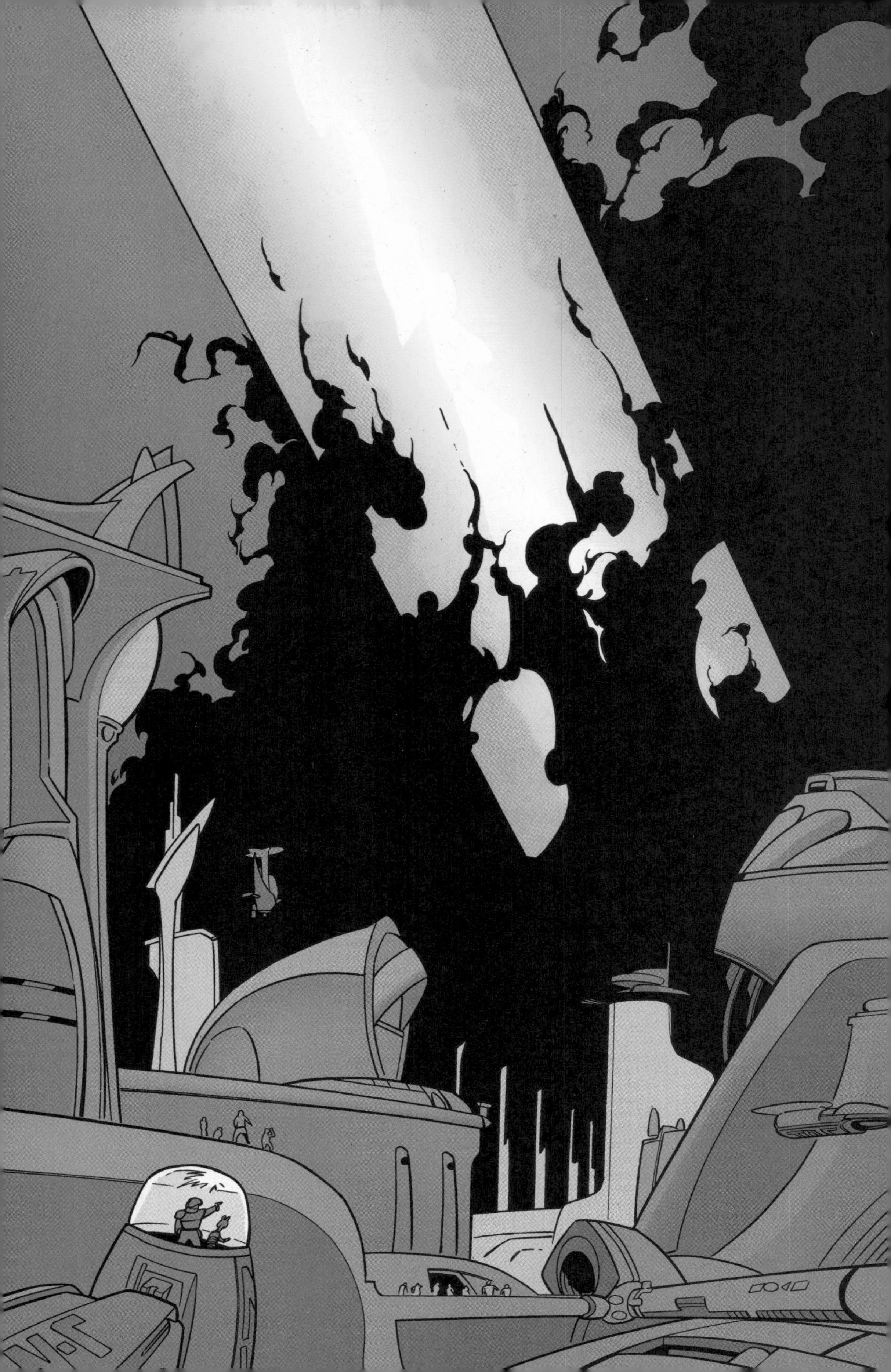

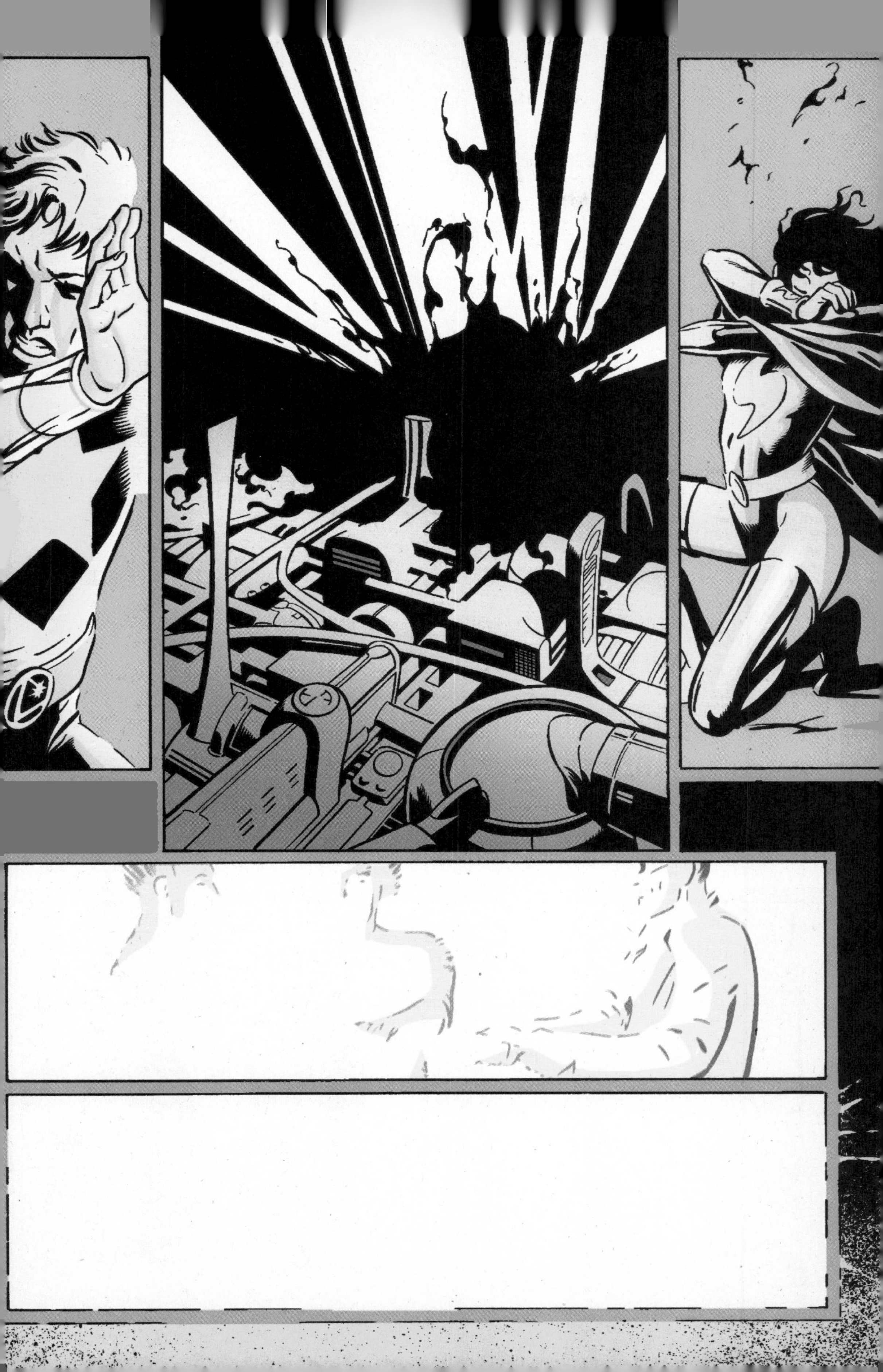

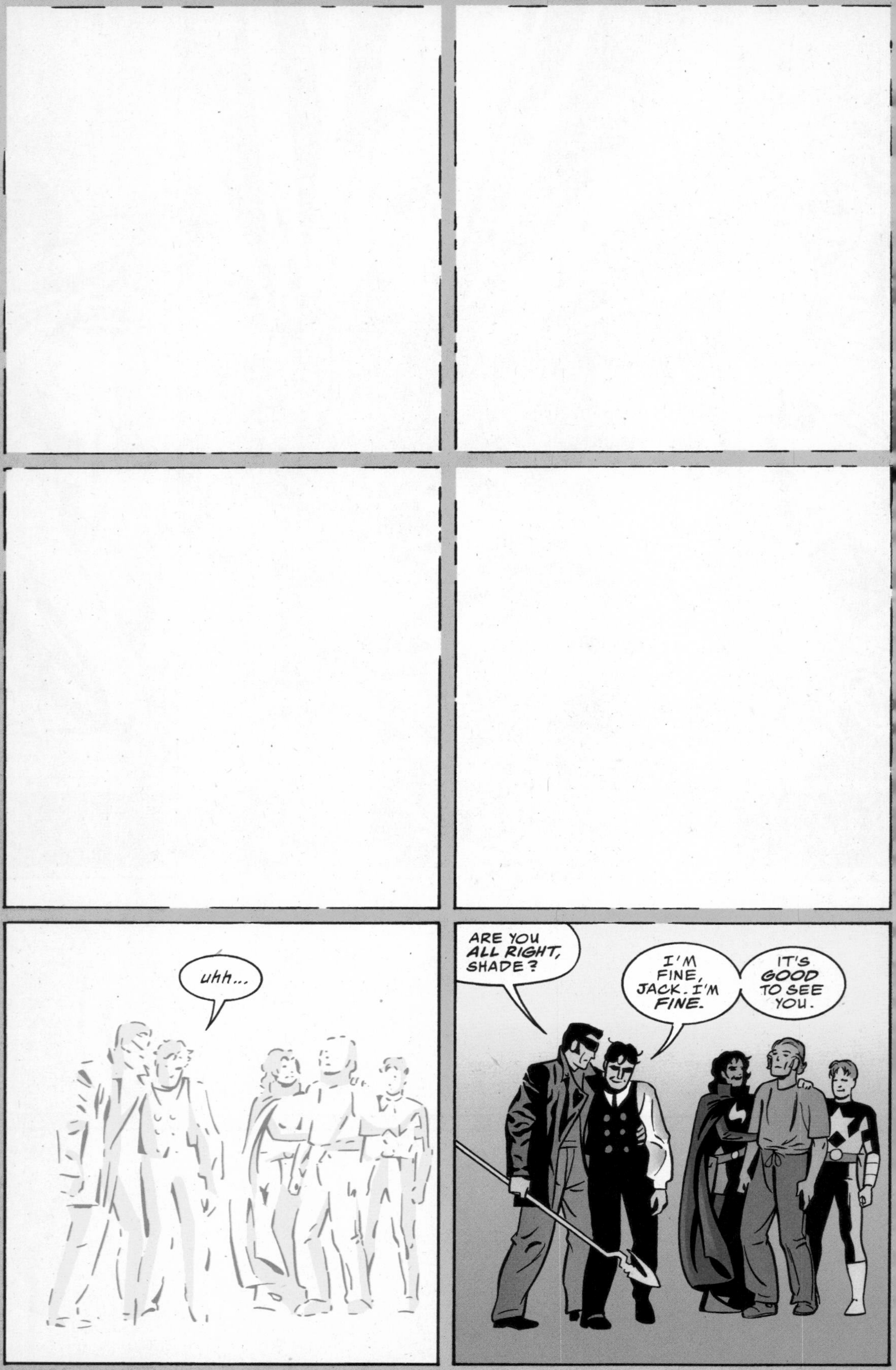
uhh...
ARE YOU ALL RIGHT, SHADE?
I'M FINE, JACK. I'M FINE.
IT'S GOOD TO SEE YOU.

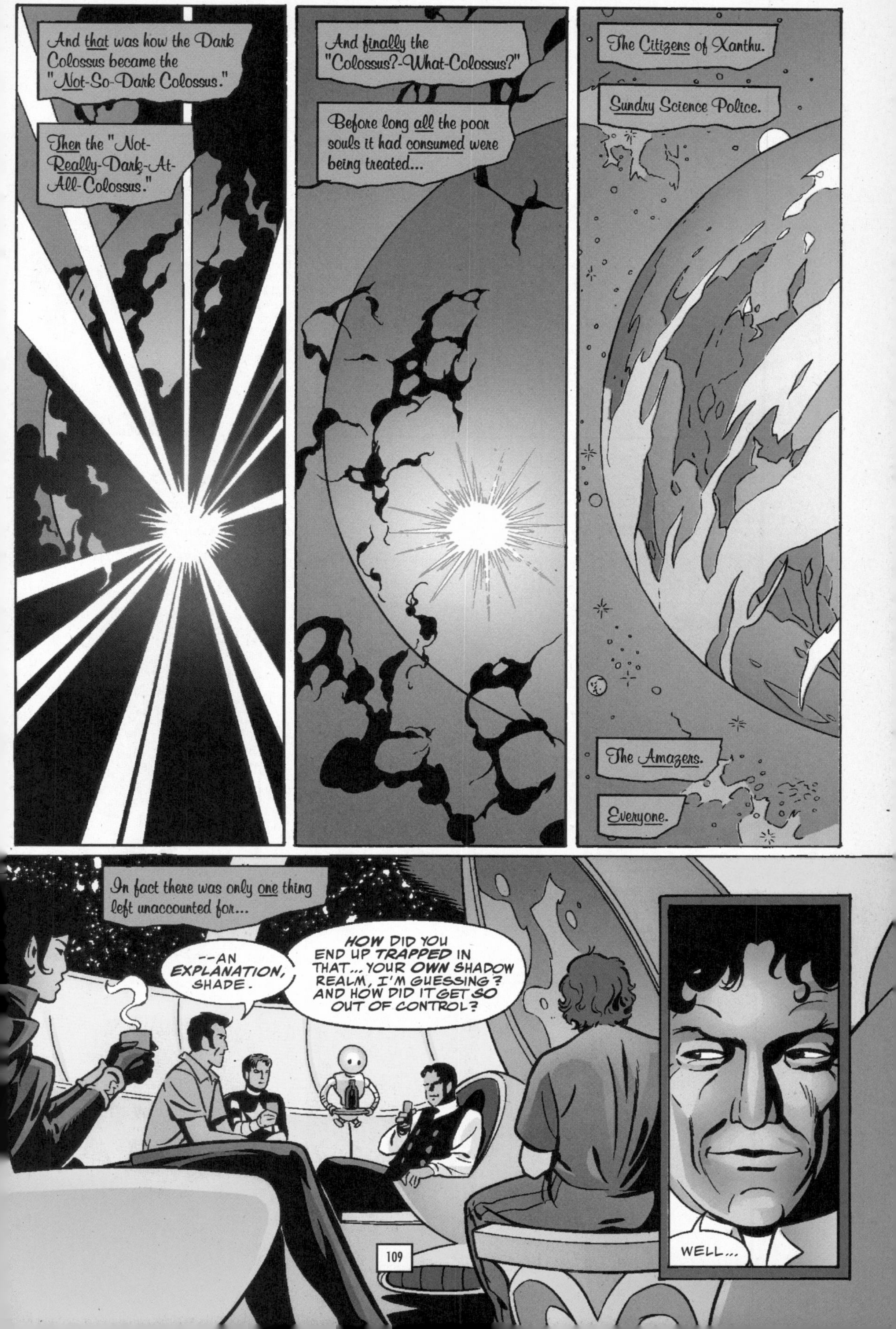

And that was how the Dark Colossus became the "Not-So-Dark Colossus."
Then the "Not-Really-Dark-At-All-Colossus."
And finally the "Colossus?-What-Colossus?"
Before long all the poor souls it had consumed were being treated...
The Citizens of Xanthu.
Sundry Science Police.
The Amazers.
Everyone.
In fact there was only one thing left unaccounted for...
--AN EXPLANATION, SHADE.
HOW DID YOU END UP TRAPPED IN THAT... YOUR OWN SHADOW REALM, I'M GUESSING? AND HOW DID IT GET SO OUT OF CONTROL?
WELL...

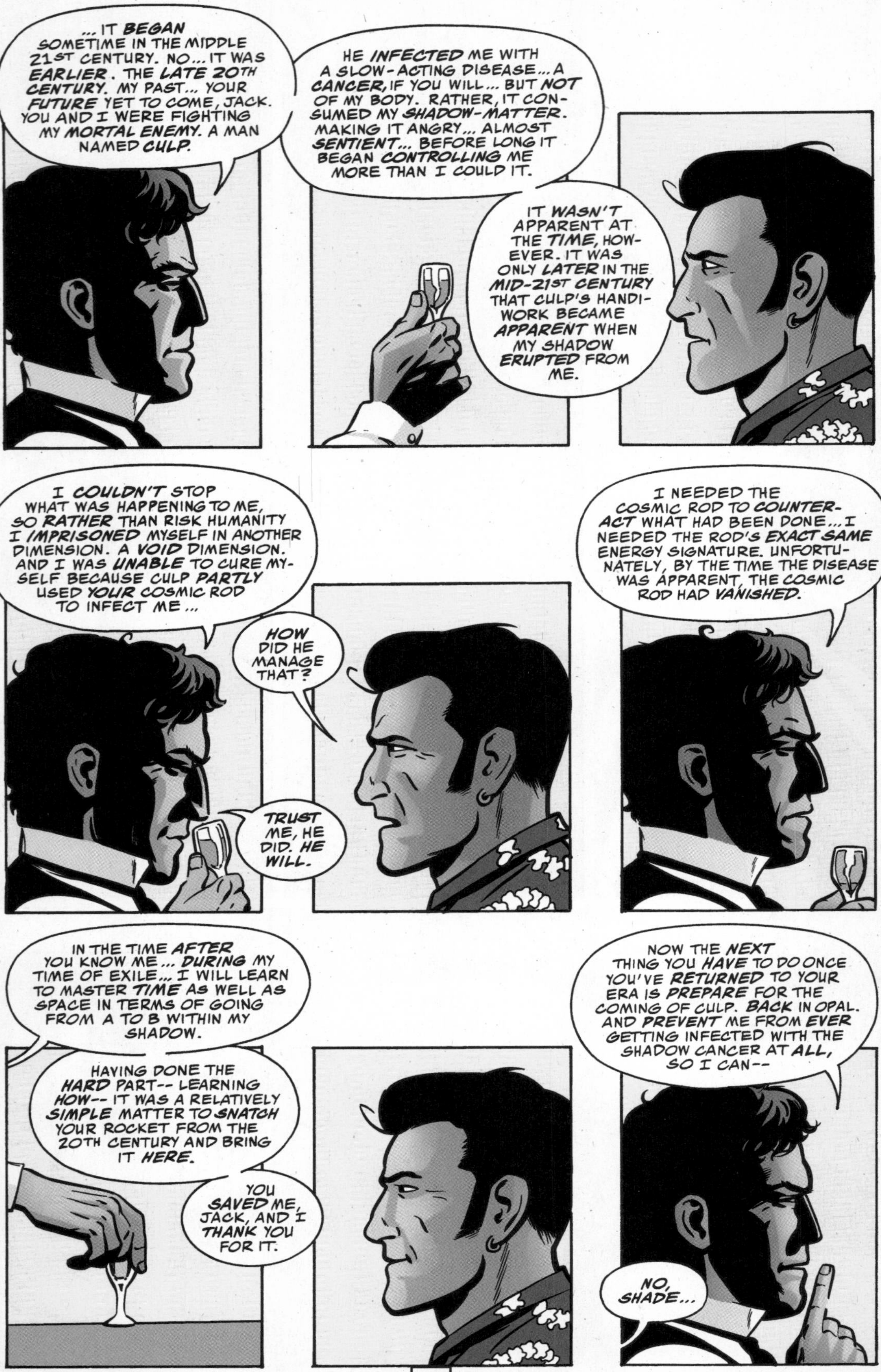

...IT BEGAN SOMETIME IN THE MIDDLE 21ST CENTURY. NO... IT WAS EARLIER. THE LATE 20TH CENTURY. MY PAST... YOUR FUTURE YET TO COME, JACK. YOU AND I WERE FIGHTING MY MORTAL ENEMY. A MAN NAMED CULP.
HE INFECTED ME WITH A SLOW-ACTING DISEASE... A CANCER, IF YOU WILL... BUT NOT OF MY BODY. RATHER, IT CONSUMED MY SHADOW-MATTER. MAKING IT ANGRY... ALMOST SENTIENT... BEFORE LONG IT BEGAN CONTROLLING ME MORE THAN I COULD IT.
IT WASN'T APPARENT AT THE TIME, HOWEVER. IT WAS ONLY LATER IN THE MID-21ST CENTURY THAT CULP'S HANDIWORK BECAME APPARENT WHEN MY SHADOW ERUPTED FROM ME.
I COULDN'T STOP WHAT WAS HAPPENING TO ME, SO RATHER THAN RISK HUMANITY I IMPRISONED MYSELF IN ANOTHER DIMENSION. A VOID DIMENSION. AND I WAS UNABLE TO CURE MYSELF BECAUSE CULP PARTLY USED YOUR COSMIC ROD TO INFECT ME...
HOW DID HE MANAGE THAT?
TRUST ME, HE DID. HE WILL.
I NEEDED THE COSMIC ROD TO COUNTERACT WHAT HAD BEEN DONE... I NEEDED THE ROD'S EXACT SAME ENERGY SIGNATURE. UNFORTUNATELY, BY THE TIME THE DISEASE WAS APPARENT, THE COSMIC ROD HAD VANISHED.
IN THE TIME AFTER YOU KNOW ME... DURING MY TIME OF EXILE... I WILL LEARN TO MASTER TIME AS WELL AS SPACE IN TERMS OF GOING FROM A TO B WITHIN MY SHADOW.
HAVING DONE THE HARD PART-- LEARNING HOW-- IT WAS A RELATIVELY SIMPLE MATTER TO SNATCH YOUR ROCKET FROM THE 20TH CENTURY AND BRING IT HERE.
YOU SAVED ME, JACK, AND I THANK YOU FOR IT.
NOW THE NEXT THING YOU HAVE TO DO ONCE YOU'VE RETURNED TO YOUR ERA IS PREPARE FOR THE COMING OF CULP. BACK IN OPAL. AND PREVENT ME FROM EVER GETTING INFECTED WITH THE SHADOW CANCER AT ALL, SO I CAN--
NO, SHADE...

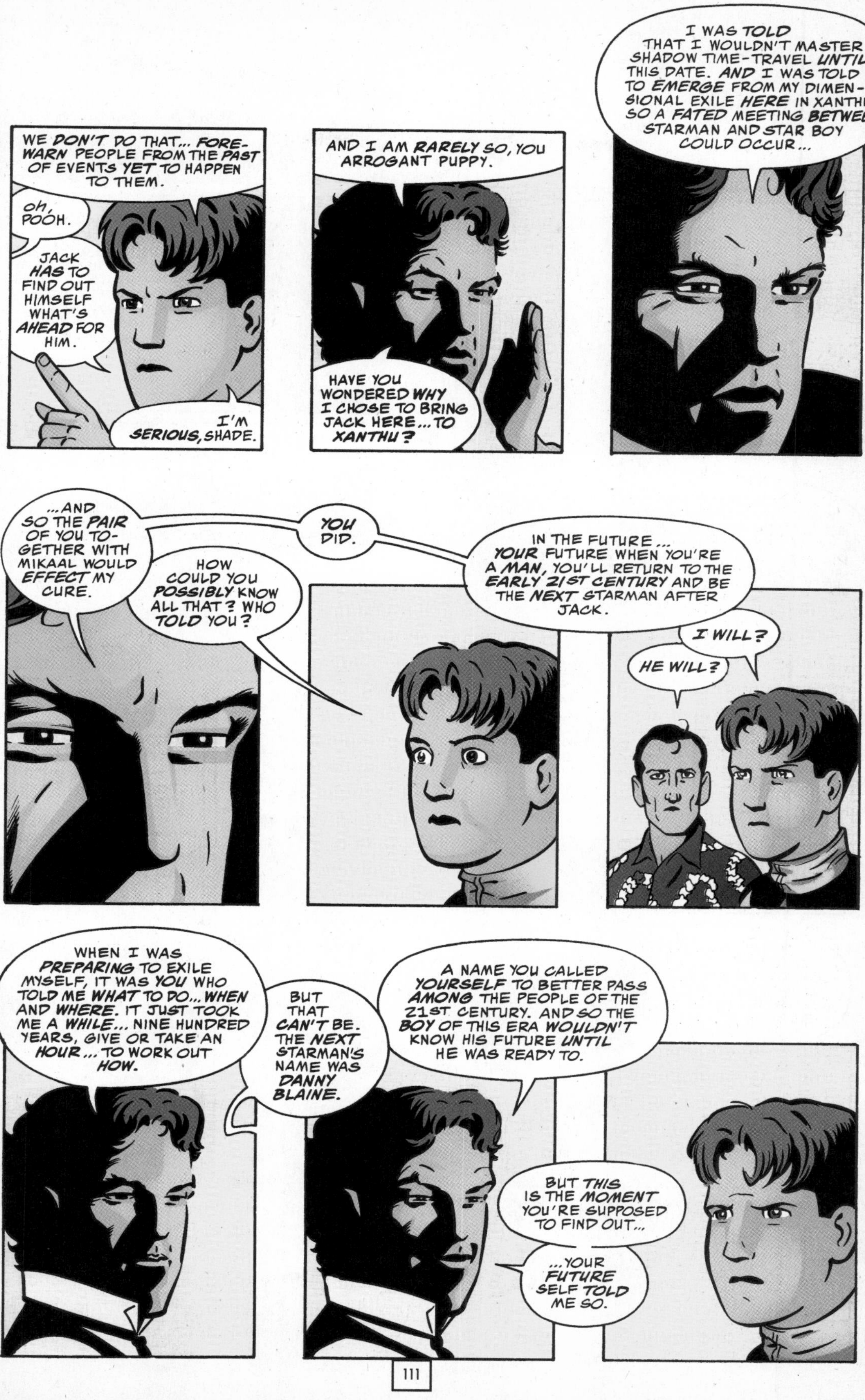
WE DON'T DO THAT... FOREWARN PEOPLE FROM THE PAST OF EVENTS YET TO HAPPEN TO THEM.
oh, POOH.
JACK HAS TO FIND OUT HIMSELF WHAT'S AHEAD FOR HIM.
I'M SERIOUS, SHADE.
AND I AM RARELY SO, YOU ARROGANT PUPPY.
HAVE YOU WONDERED WHY I CHOSE TO BRING JACK HERE... TO XANTHU?
I WAS TOLD THAT I WOULDN'T MASTER SHADOW TIME-TRAVEL UNTIL THIS DATE. AND I WAS TOLD TO EMERGE FROM MY DIMENSIONAL EXILE HERE IN XANTHU SO A FATED MEETING BETWEEN STARMAN AND STAR BOY COULD OCCUR...
...AND SO THE PAIR OF YOU TOGETHER WITH MIKAAL WOULD EFFECT MY CURE.
HOW COULD YOU POSSIBLY KNOW ALL THAT? WHO TOLD YOU?
YOU DID.
IN THE FUTURE... YOUR FUTURE WHEN YOU'RE A MAN, YOU'LL RETURN TO THE EARLY 21ST CENTURY AND BE THE NEXT STARMAN AFTER JACK.
I WILL?
HE WILL?
WHEN I WAS PREPARING TO EXILE MYSELF, IT WAS YOU WHO TOLD ME WHAT TO DO... WHEN AND WHERE. IT JUST TOOK ME A WHILE... NINE HUNDRED YEARS, GIVE OR TAKE AN HOUR... TO WORK OUT HOW.
BUT THAT CAN'T BE. THE NEXT STARMAN'S NAME WAS DANNY BLAINE.
A NAME YOU CALLED YOURSELF TO BETTER PASS AMONG THE PEOPLE OF THE 21ST CENTURY. AND SO THE BOY OF THIS ERA WOULDN'T KNOW HIS FUTURE UNTIL HE WAS READY TO.
BUT THIS IS THE MOMENT YOU'RE SUPPOSED TO FIND OUT...
...YOUR FUTURE SELF TOLD ME SO.

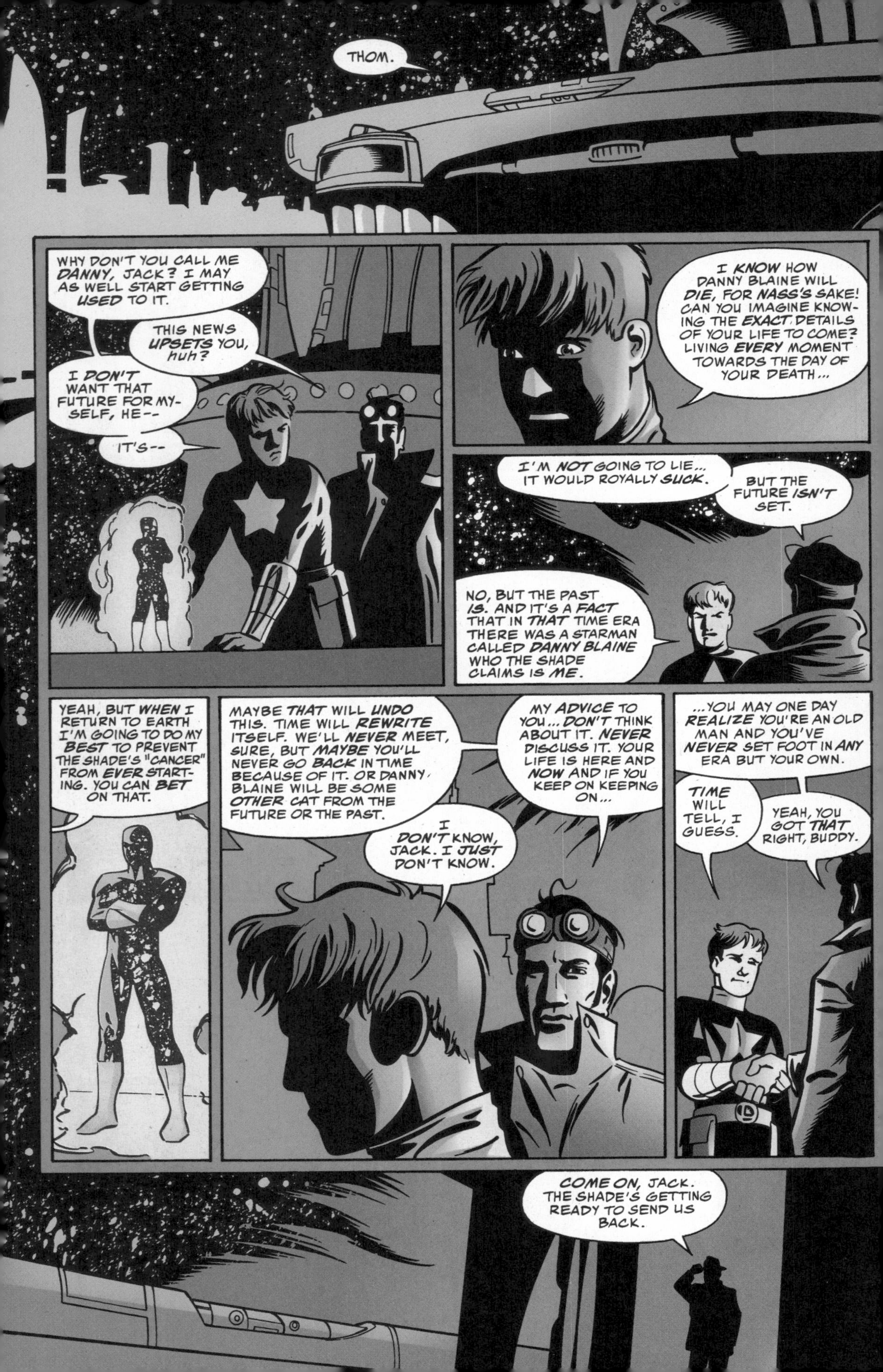
THOM.
WHY DON'T YOU CALL ME DANNY, JACK? I MAY AS WELL START GETTING USED TO IT.
THIS NEWS UPSETS YOU, HUH?
I DON'T WANT THAT FUTURE FOR MYSELF, HE--
IT'S--
I KNOW HOW DANNY BLAINE WILL DIE, FOR NASS'S SAKE! CAN YOU IMAGINE KNOWING THE EXACT DETAILS OF YOUR LIFE TO COME? LIVING EVERY MOMENT TOWARDS THE DAY OF YOUR DEATH...
I'M NOT GOING TO LIE... IT WOULD ROYALLY SUCK.
BUT THE FUTURE ISN'T SET.
NO, BUT THE PAST IS. AND IT'S A FACT THAT IN THAT TIME ERA THERE WAS A STARMAN CALLED DANNY BLAINE WHO THE SHADE CLAIMS IS ME.
YEAH, BUT WHEN I RETURN TO EARTH I'M GOING TO DO MY BEST TO PREVENT THE SHADE'S "CANCER" FROM EVER STARTING. YOU CAN BET ON THAT.
MAYBE THAT WILL UNDO THIS. TIME WILL REWRITE ITSELF. WE'LL NEVER MEET, SURE, BUT MAYBE YOU'LL NEVER GO BACK IN TIME BECAUSE OF IT. OR DANNY BLAINE WILL BE SOME OTHER CAT FROM THE FUTURE OR THE PAST.
MY ADVICE TO YOU... DON'T THINK ABOUT IT. NEVER DISCUSS IT. YOUR LIFE IS HERE AND NOW AND IF YOU KEEP ON KEEPING ON...
I DON'T KNOW, JACK. I JUST DON'T KNOW.
...YOU MAY ONE DAY REALIZE YOU'RE AN OLD MAN AND YOU'VE NEVER SET FOOT IN ANY ERA BUT YOUR OWN.
TIME WILL TELL, I GUESS.
YEAH, YOU GOT THAT RIGHT, BUDDY.
COME ON, JACK. THE SHADE'S GETTING READY TO SEND US BACK.

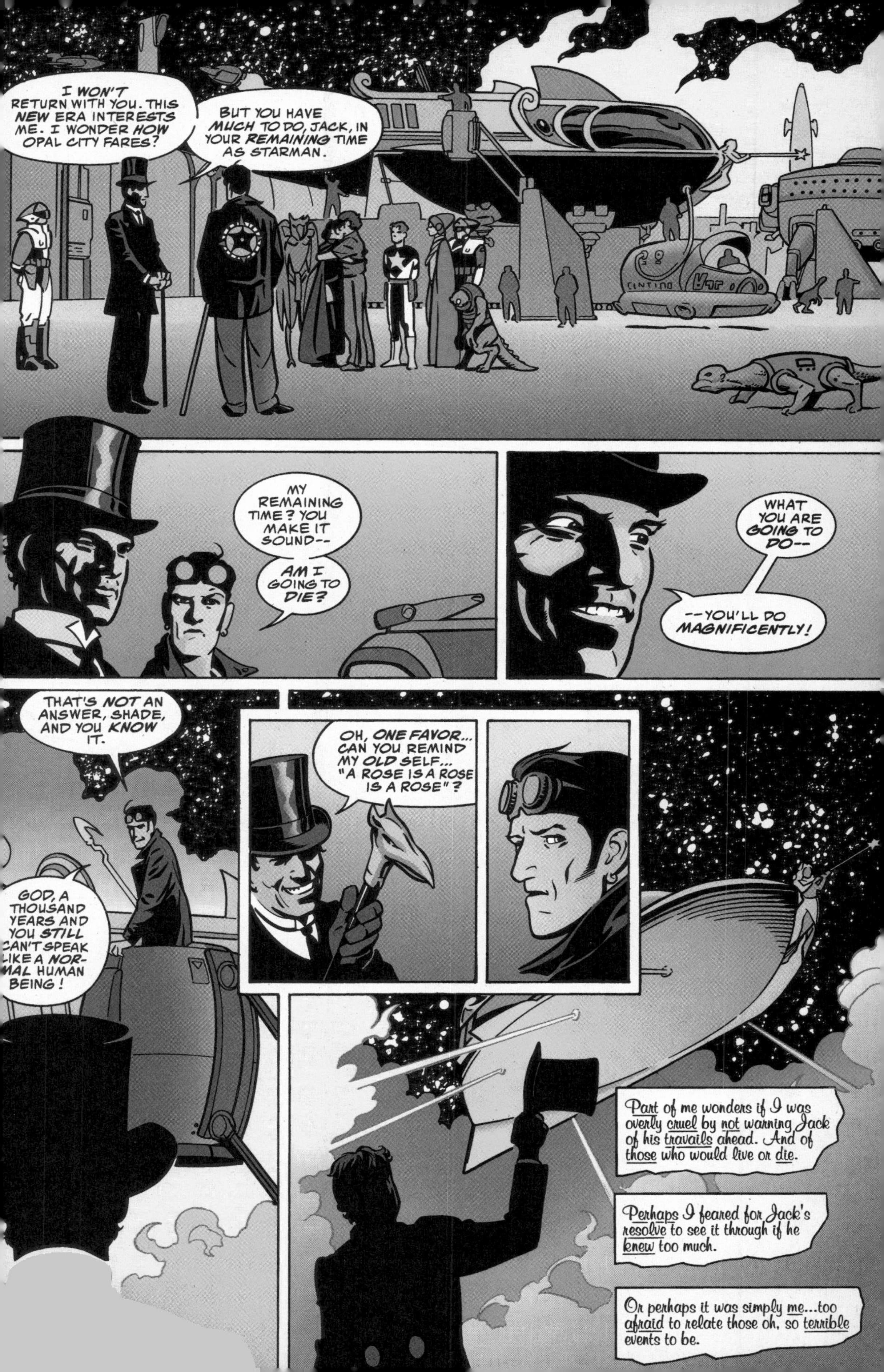
I WON'T RETURN WITH YOU. THIS NEW ERA INTERESTS ME. I WONDER HOW OPAL CITY FARES?
BUT YOU HAVE MUCH TO DO, JACK, IN YOUR REMAINING TIME AS STARMAN.
MY REMAINING TIME? YOU MAKE IT SOUND--
AM I GOING TO DIE?
WHAT YOU ARE GOING TO DO--
--YOU'LL DO MAGNIFICENTLY!
THAT'S NOT AN ANSWER, SHADE, AND YOU KNOW IT.
OH, ONE FAVOR... CAN YOU REMIND MY OLD SELF... "A ROSE IS A ROSE IS A ROSE"?
GOD, A THOUSAND YEARS AND YOU STILL CAN'T SPEAK LIKE A NORMAL HUMAN BEING!
Part of me wonders if I was overly cruel by not warning Jack of his travails ahead. And of those who would live or die.
Perhaps I feared for Jack's resolve to see it through if he knew too much.
Or perhaps it was simply me...too afraid to relate those oh, so terrible events to be.

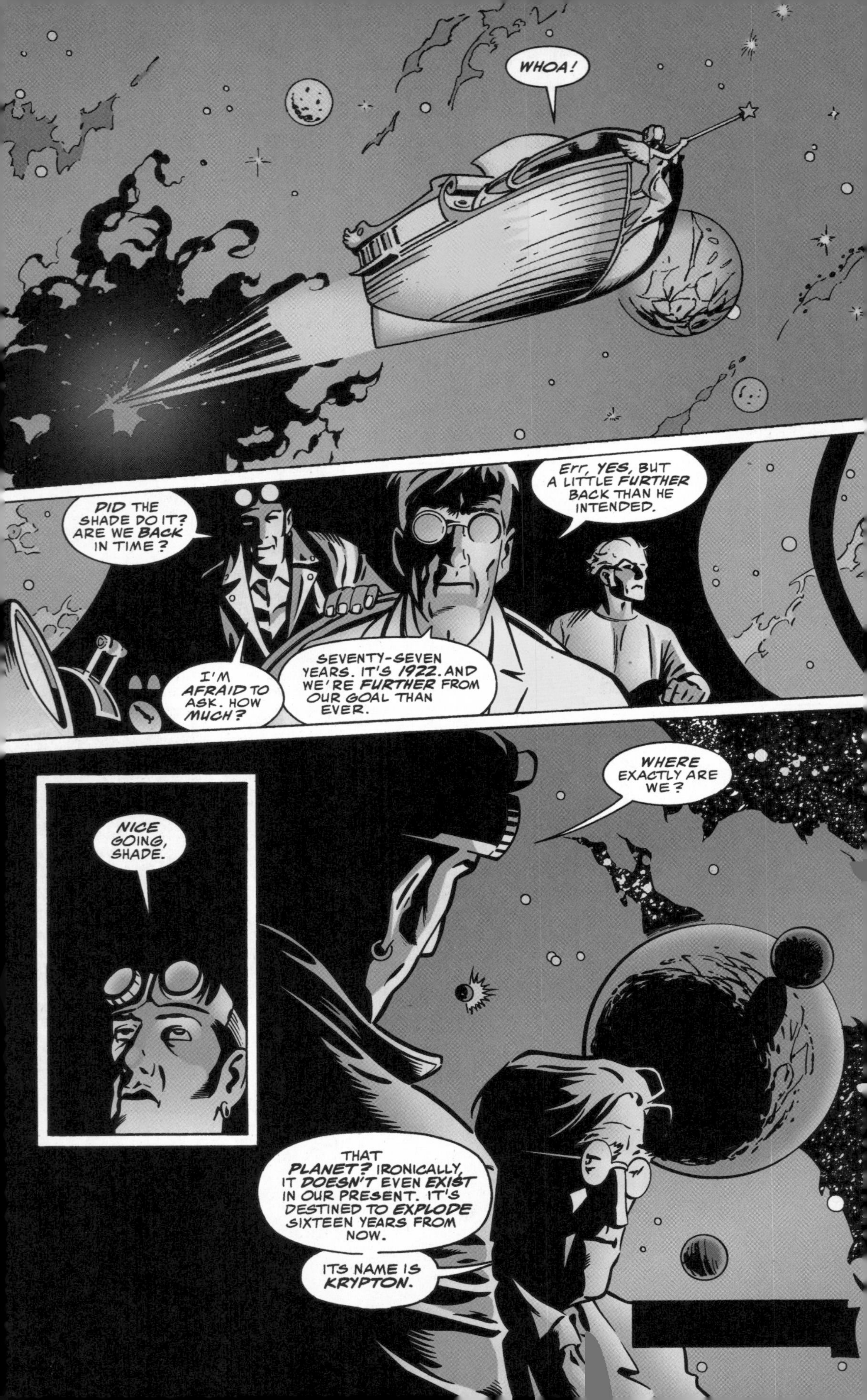
WHOA!
DID THE SHADE DO IT? ARE WE BACK IN TIME?
Err, YES, BUT A LITTLE FURTHER BACK THAN HE INTENDED.
I'M AFRAID TO ASK. HOW MUCH?
SEVENTY-SEVEN YEARS. IT'S 1922. AND WE'RE FURTHER FROM OUR GOAL THAN EVER.
NICE GOING, SHADE.
WHERE EXACTLY ARE WE?
THAT PLANET? IRONICALLY, IT DOESN'T EVEN EXIST IN OUR PRESENT. IT'S DESTINED TO EXPLODE SIXTEEN YEARS FROM NOW.
ITS NAME IS KRYPTON.

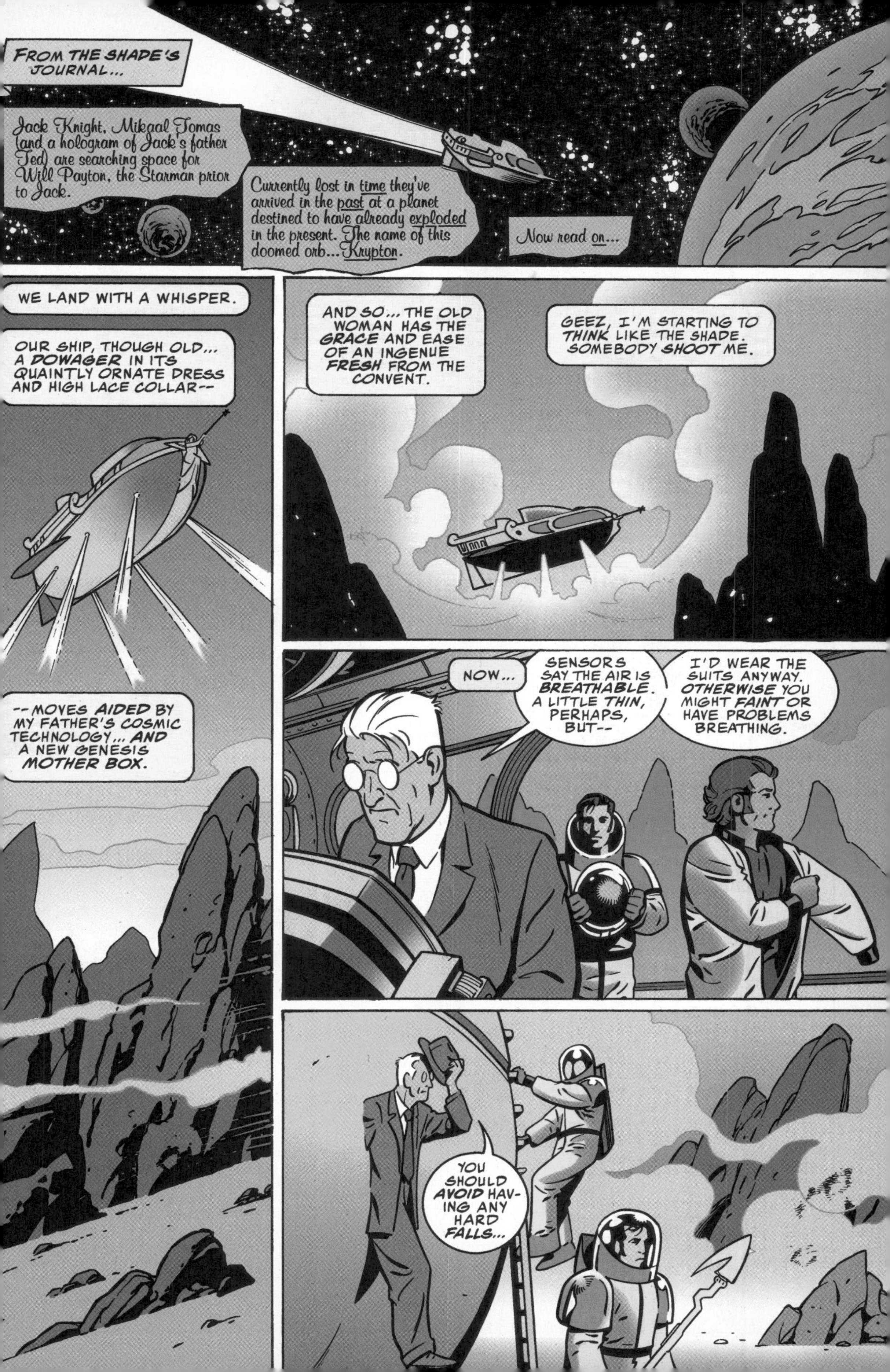

FROM THE SHADE'S JOURNAL...
Jack Knight, Mikaal Tomas (and a hologram of Jack's father Ted) are searching space for Will Payton, the Starman prior to Jack.
Currently lost in time they've arrived in the past at a planet destined to have already exploded in the present. The name of this doomed orb...Krypton.
Now read on...
WE LAND WITH A WHISPER.
OUR SHIP, THOUGH OLD... A DOWAGER IN ITS QUAINTLY ORNATE DRESS AND HIGH LACE COLLAR--
--MOVES AIDED BY MY FATHER'S COSMIC TECHNOLOGY... AND A NEW GENESIS MOTHER BOX.
AND SO... THE OLD WOMAN HAS THE GRACE AND EASE OF AN INGENUE FRESH FROM THE CONVENT.
GEEZ, I'M STARTING TO THINK LIKE THE SHADE. SOMEBODY SHOOT ME.
NOW...
SENSORS SAY THE AIR IS BREATHABLE. A LITTLE THIN, PERHAPS, BUT--
I'D WEAR THE SUITS ANYWAY. OTHERWISE YOU MIGHT FAINT OR HAVE PROBLEMS BREATHING.
YOU SHOULD AVOID HAVING ANY HARD FALLS...

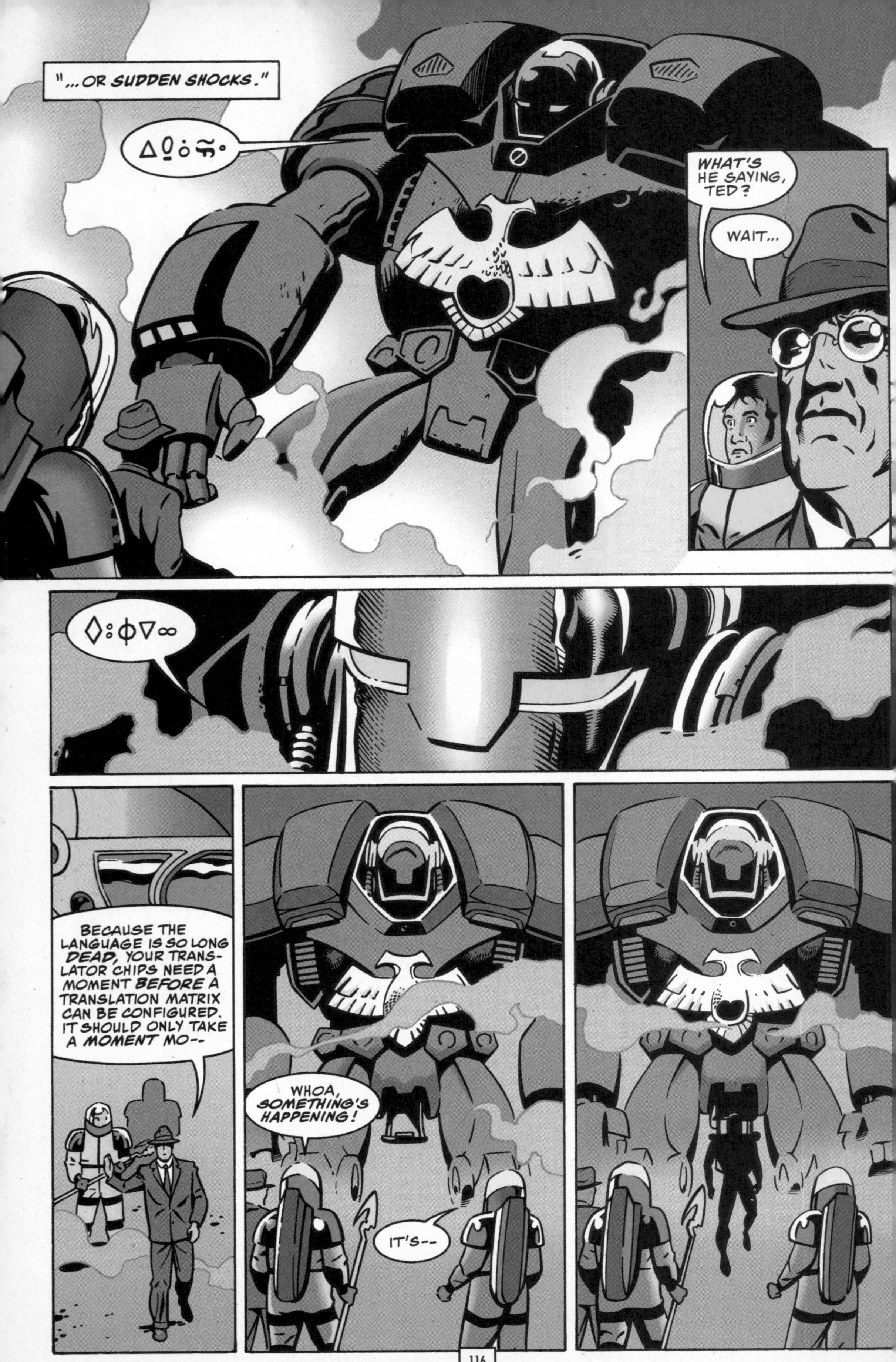
"...OR SUDDEN SHOCKS."
WHAT'S HE SAYING, TED?
WAIT...
BECAUSE THE LANGUAGE IS SO LONG DEAD, YOUR TRANSLATOR CHIPS NEED A MOMENT BEFORE A TRANSLATION MATRIX CAN BE CONFIGURED. IT SHOULD ONLY TAKE A MOMENT MO--
WHOA, SOMETHING'S HAPPENING!
IT'S--

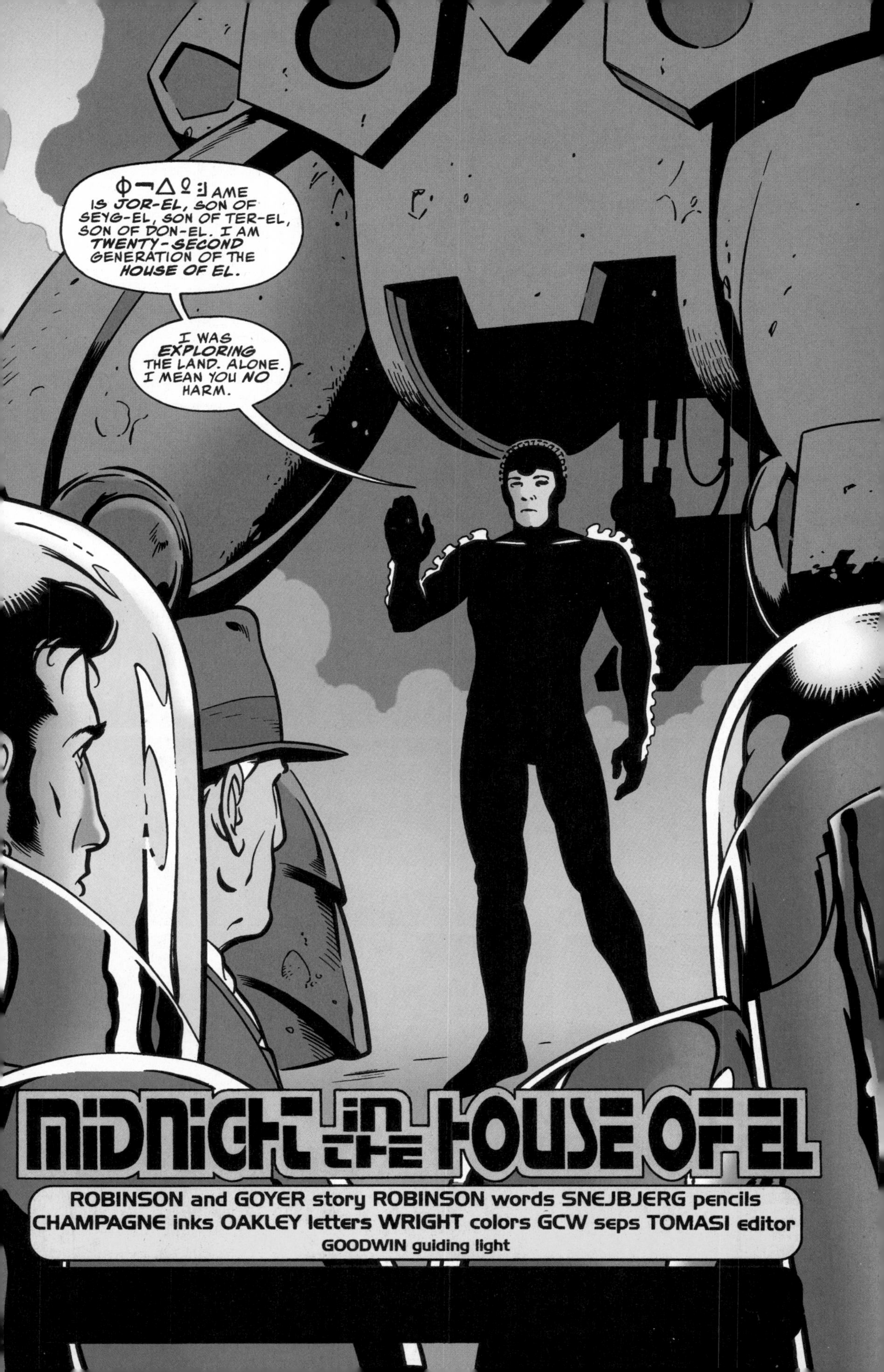
AME IS JOR-EL, SON OF SEYG-EL, SON OF TER-EL, SON OF DON-EL. I AM TWENTY-SECOND GENERATION OF THE HOUSE OF EL.
I WAS EXPLORING THE LAND. ALONE. I MEAN YOU NO HARM.
MIDNIGHT IN THE HOUSE OF EL
ROBINSON and GOYER story ROBINSON words SNEJBJERG pencils CHAMPAGNE inks OAKLEY letters WRIGHT colors GCW seps TOMASI editor
GOODWIN guiding light

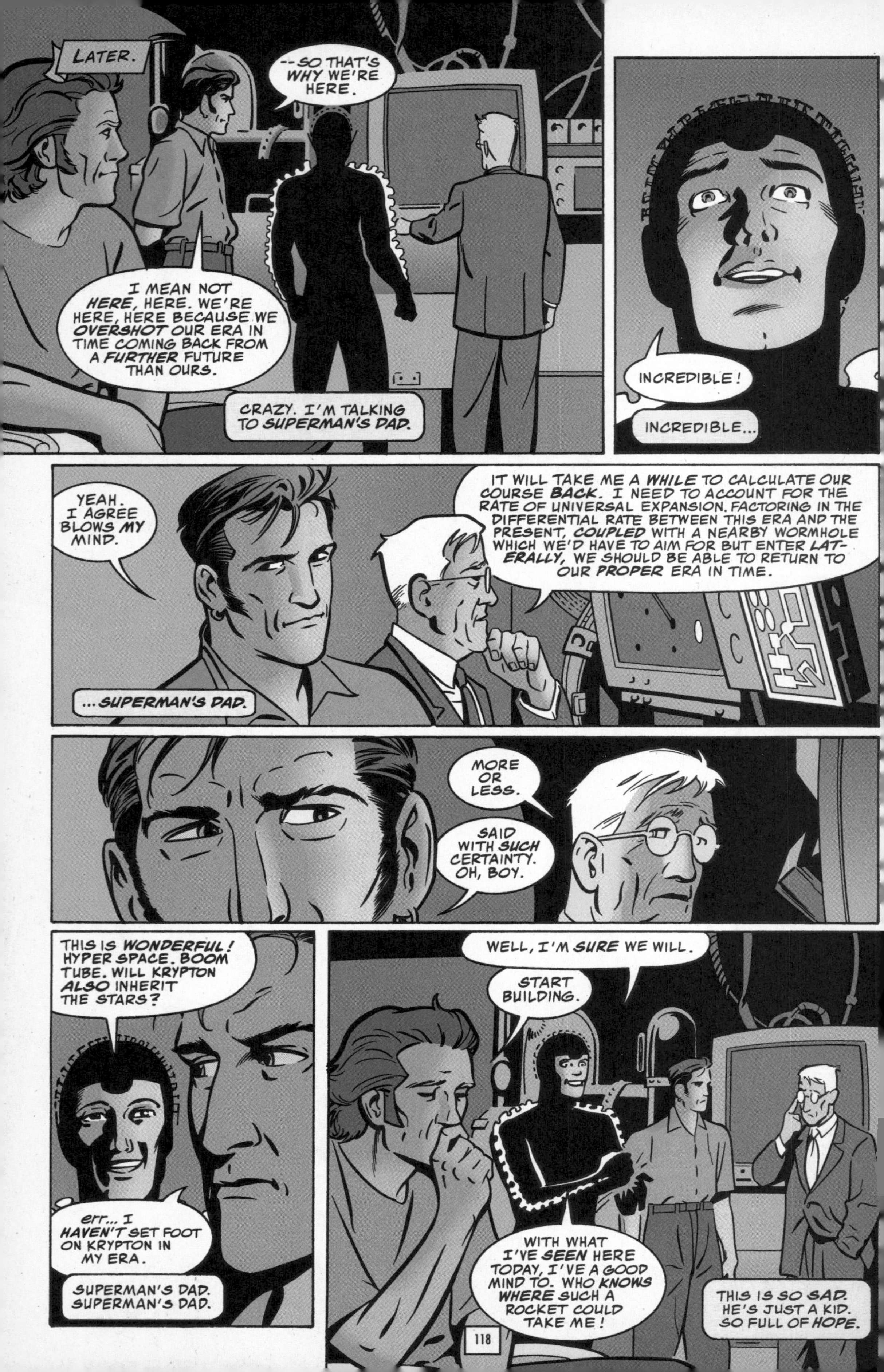
LATER.
--SO THAT'S WHY WE'RE HERE.
I MEAN NOT HERE, HERE. WE'RE HERE, HERE BECAUSE WE OVERSHOT OUR ERA IN TIME COMING BACK FROM A FURTHER FUTURE THAN OURS.
CRAZY. I'M TALKING TO SUPERMAN'S DAD.
INCREDIBLE!
INCREDIBLE...
YEAH. I AGREE BLOWS MY MIND.
IT WILL TAKE ME A WHILE TO CALCULATE OUR COURSE BACK. I NEED TO ACCOUNT FOR THE RATE OF UNIVERSAL EXPANSION. FACTORING IN THE DIFFERENTIAL RATE BETWEEN THIS ERA AND THE PRESENT, COUPLED WITH A NEARBY WORMHOLE WHICH WE'D HAVE TO AIM FOR BUT ENTER LATERALLY, WE SHOULD BE ABLE TO RETURN TO OUR PROPER ERA IN TIME.
...SUPERMAN'S DAD.
MORE OR LESS.
SAID WITH SUCH CERTAINTY. OH, BOY.
THIS IS WONDERFUL! HYPER SPACE. BOOM TUBE. WILL KRYPTON ALSO INHERIT THE STARS?
err... I HAVEN'T SET FOOT ON KRYPTON IN MY ERA.
SUPERMAN'S DAD. SUPERMAN'S DAD.
WELL, I'M SURE WE WILL.
START BUILDING.
WITH WHAT I'VE SEEN HERE TODAY, I'VE A GOOD MIND TO. WHO KNOWS WHERE SUCH A ROCKET COULD TAKE ME!
THIS IS SO SAD. HE'S JUST A KID. SO FULL OF HOPE.

WHY, I *MIGHT* EVEN VISIT YOUR WORLD.

URTH.

EARTH. HERE, I CAN EVEN SHOW YOU *WHERE.*

IT'S IN THE VIRGO CLUSTER.

VERGO? I DON'T UNDERSTAND.

HEY, COULDN'T YOU GIVE HIM THE CO-ORDINATES AS A *BINARY* FORMULA? THAT'S A *UNIVERSAL* LANGUAGE, ISN'T IT?

I DON'T BELIEVE YOU KNOW THAT!

YOU KNOW, I DON'T BELIEVE I KNOW THAT, *EITHER.*

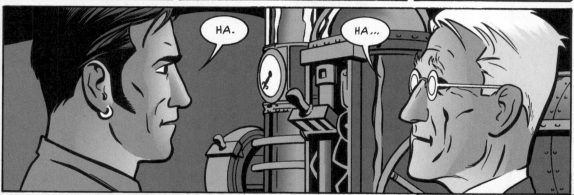

HA.

HA...

HA HA HA HA HA!

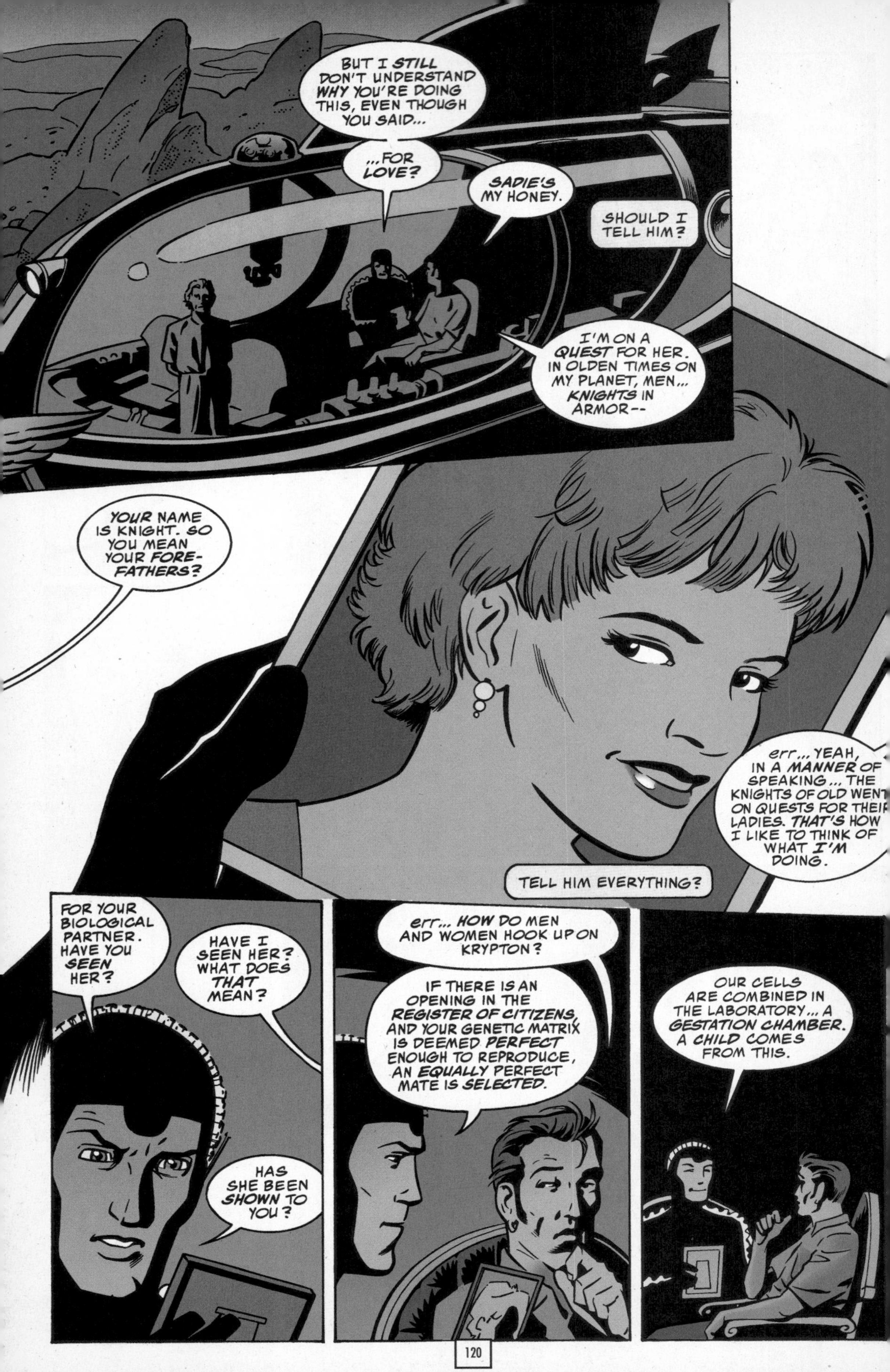
BUT I STILL DON'T UNDERSTAND WHY YOU'RE DOING THIS, EVEN THOUGH YOU SAID...
...FOR LOVE?
SADIE'S MY HONEY.
SHOULD I TELL HIM?
I'M ON A QUEST FOR HER. IN OLDEN TIMES ON MY PLANET, MEN... KNIGHTS IN ARMOR--
YOUR NAME IS KNIGHT. SO YOU MEAN YOUR FORE-FATHERS?
err... YEAH, IN A MANNER OF SPEAKING... THE KNIGHTS OF OLD WENT ON QUESTS FOR THEIR LADIES. THAT'S HOW I LIKE TO THINK OF WHAT I'M DOING.
TELL HIM EVERYTHING?
FOR YOUR BIOLOGICAL PARTNER. HAVE YOU SEEN HER?
HAVE I SEEN HER? WHAT DOES THAT MEAN?
HAS SHE BEEN SHOWN TO YOU?
err... HOW DO MEN AND WOMEN HOOK UP ON KRYPTON?
IF THERE IS AN OPENING IN THE REGISTER OF CITIZENS, AND YOUR GENETIC MATRIX IS DEEMED PERFECT ENOUGH TO REPRODUCE, AN EQUALLY PERFECT MATE IS SELECTED.
OUR CELLS ARE COMBINED IN THE LABORATORY... A GESTATION CHAMBER. A CHILD COMES FROM THIS.

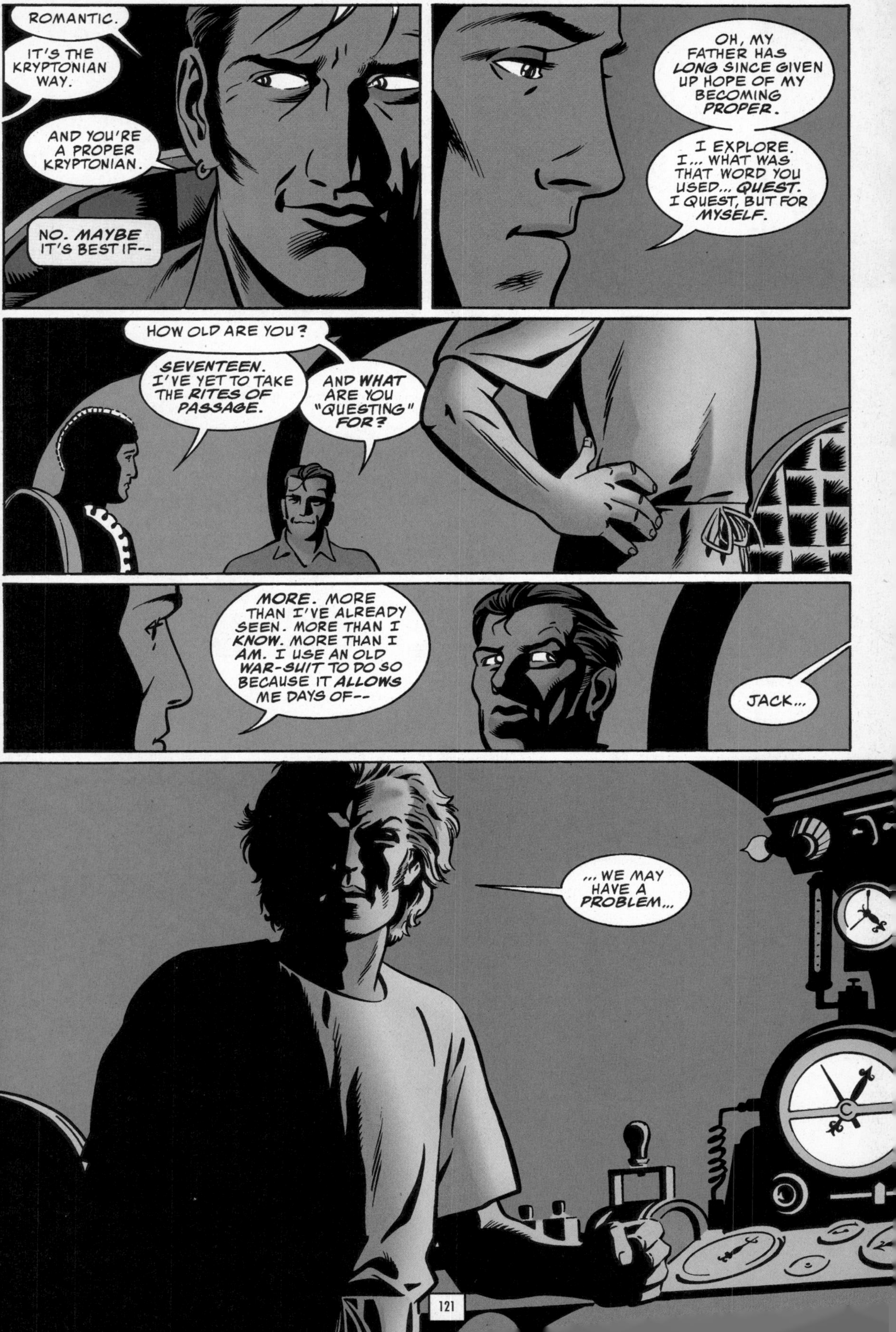
ROMANTIC.
IT'S THE KRYPTONIAN WAY.
AND YOU'RE A PROPER KRYPTONIAN.
NO. MAYBE IT'S BEST IF--
OH, MY FATHER HAS LONG SINCE GIVEN UP HOPE OF MY BECOMING PROPER.
I EXPLORE. I... WHAT WAS THAT WORD YOU USED... QUEST. I QUEST, BUT FOR MYSELF.
HOW OLD ARE YOU?
SEVENTEEN. I'VE YET TO TAKE THE RITES OF PASSAGE.
AND WHAT ARE YOU "QUESTING" FOR?
MORE. MORE THAN I'VE ALREADY SEEN. MORE THAN I KNOW. MORE THAN I AM. I USE AN OLD WAR-SUIT TO DO SO BECAUSE IT ALLOWS ME DAYS OF--
JACK...
...WE MAY HAVE A PROBLEM...

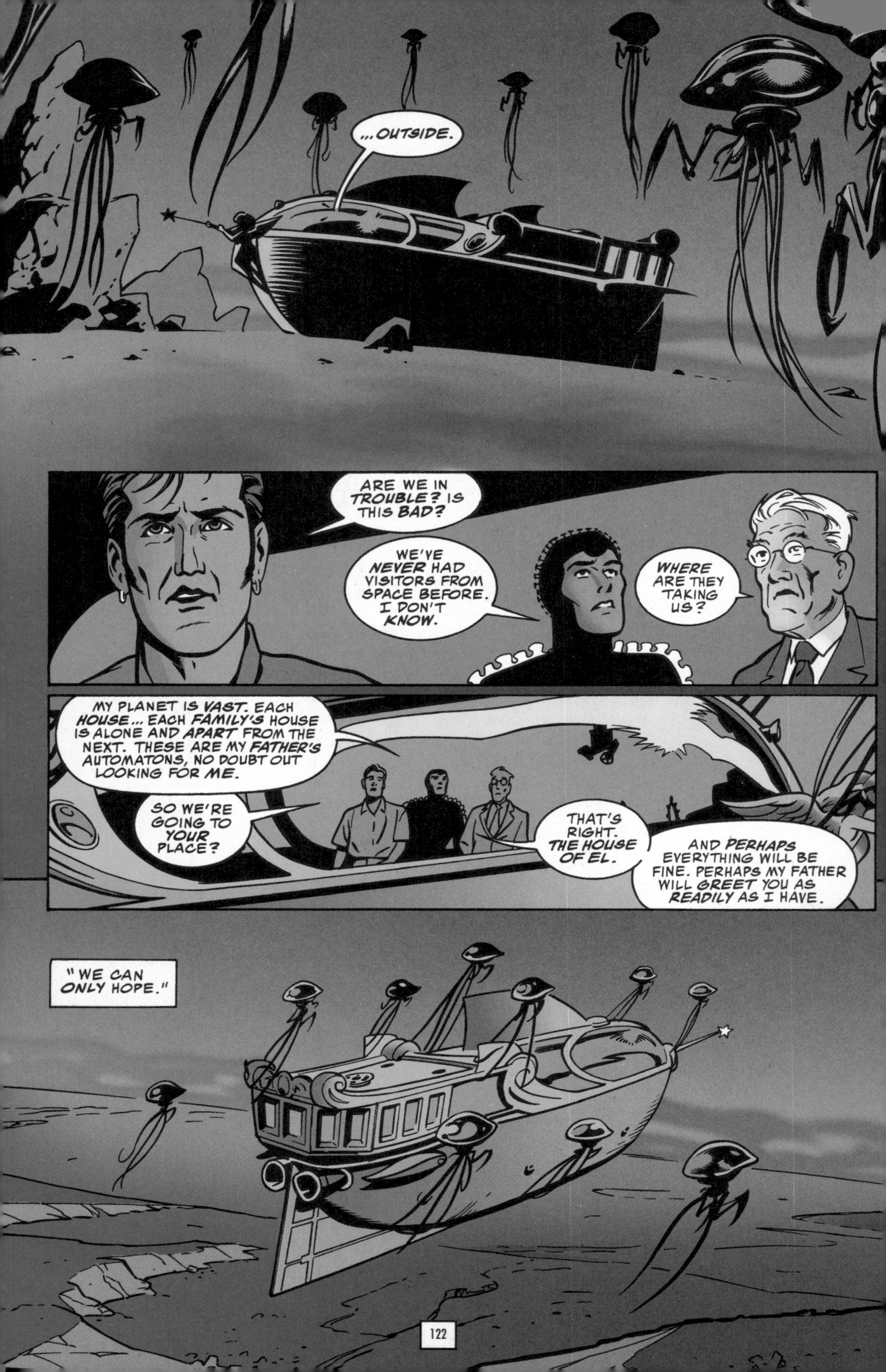
...OUTSIDE.
ARE WE IN TROUBLE? IS THIS BAD?
WE'VE NEVER HAD VISITORS FROM SPACE BEFORE. I DON'T KNOW.
WHERE ARE THEY TAKING US?
MY PLANET IS VAST. EACH HOUSE... EACH FAMILY'S HOUSE IS ALONE AND APART FROM THE NEXT. THESE ARE MY FATHER'S AUTOMATONS, NO DOUBT OUT LOOKING FOR ME.
SO WE'RE GOING TO YOUR PLACE?
THAT'S RIGHT. THE HOUSE OF EL.
AND PERHAPS EVERYTHING WILL BE FINE. PERHAPS MY FATHER WILL GREET YOU AS READILY AS I HAVE.
"WE CAN ONLY HOPE."

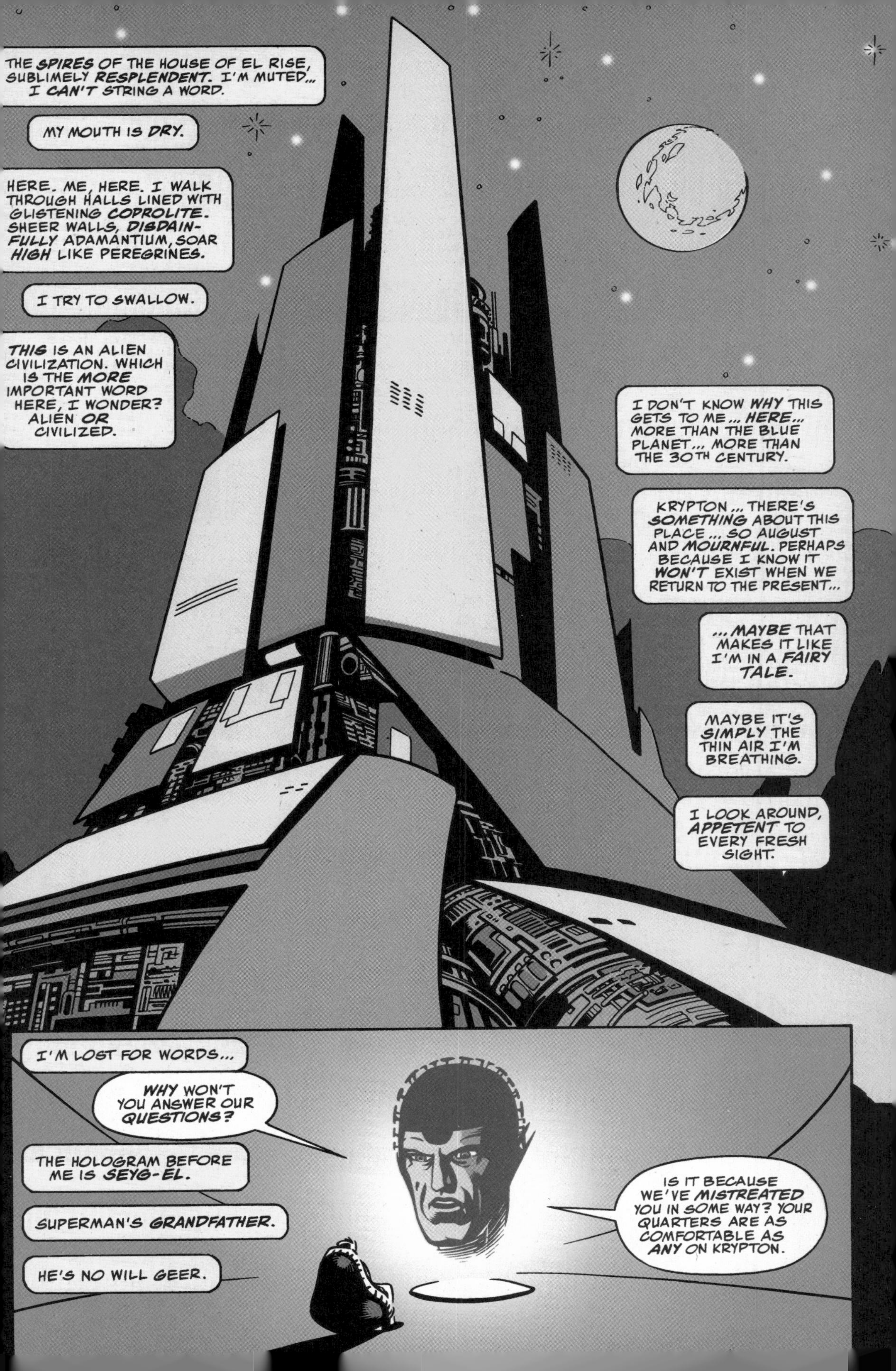
THE SPIRES OF THE HOUSE OF EL RISE, SUBLIMELY RESPLENDENT. I'M MUTED... I CAN'T STRING A WORD.
MY MOUTH IS DRY.
HERE. ME, HERE. I WALK THROUGH HALLS LINED WITH GLISTENING COPROLITE. SHEER WALLS, DISDAINFULLY ADAMANTIUM, SOAR HIGH LIKE PEREGRINES.
I TRY TO SWALLOW.
THIS IS AN ALIEN CIVILIZATION. WHICH IS THE MORE IMPORTANT WORD HERE, I WONDER? ALIEN OR CIVILIZED.
I DON'T KNOW WHY THIS GETS TO ME... HERE... MORE THAN THE BLUE PLANET... MORE THAN THE 30TH CENTURY.
KRYPTON... THERE'S SOMETHING ABOUT THIS PLACE... SO AUGUST AND MOURNFUL. PERHAPS BECAUSE I KNOW IT WON'T EXIST WHEN WE RETURN TO THE PRESENT...
...MAYBE THAT MAKES IT LIKE I'M IN A FAIRY TALE.
MAYBE IT'S SIMPLY THE THIN AIR I'M BREATHING.
I LOOK AROUND, APPETENT TO EVERY FRESH SIGHT.
I'M LOST FOR WORDS...
WHY WON'T YOU ANSWER OUR QUESTIONS?
THE HOLOGRAM BEFORE ME IS SEYG-EL.
SUPERMAN'S GRANDFATHER.
HE'S NO WILL GEER.
IS IT BECAUSE WE'VE MISTREATED YOU IN SOME WAY? YOUR QUARTERS ARE AS COMFORTABLE AS ANY ON KRYPTON.

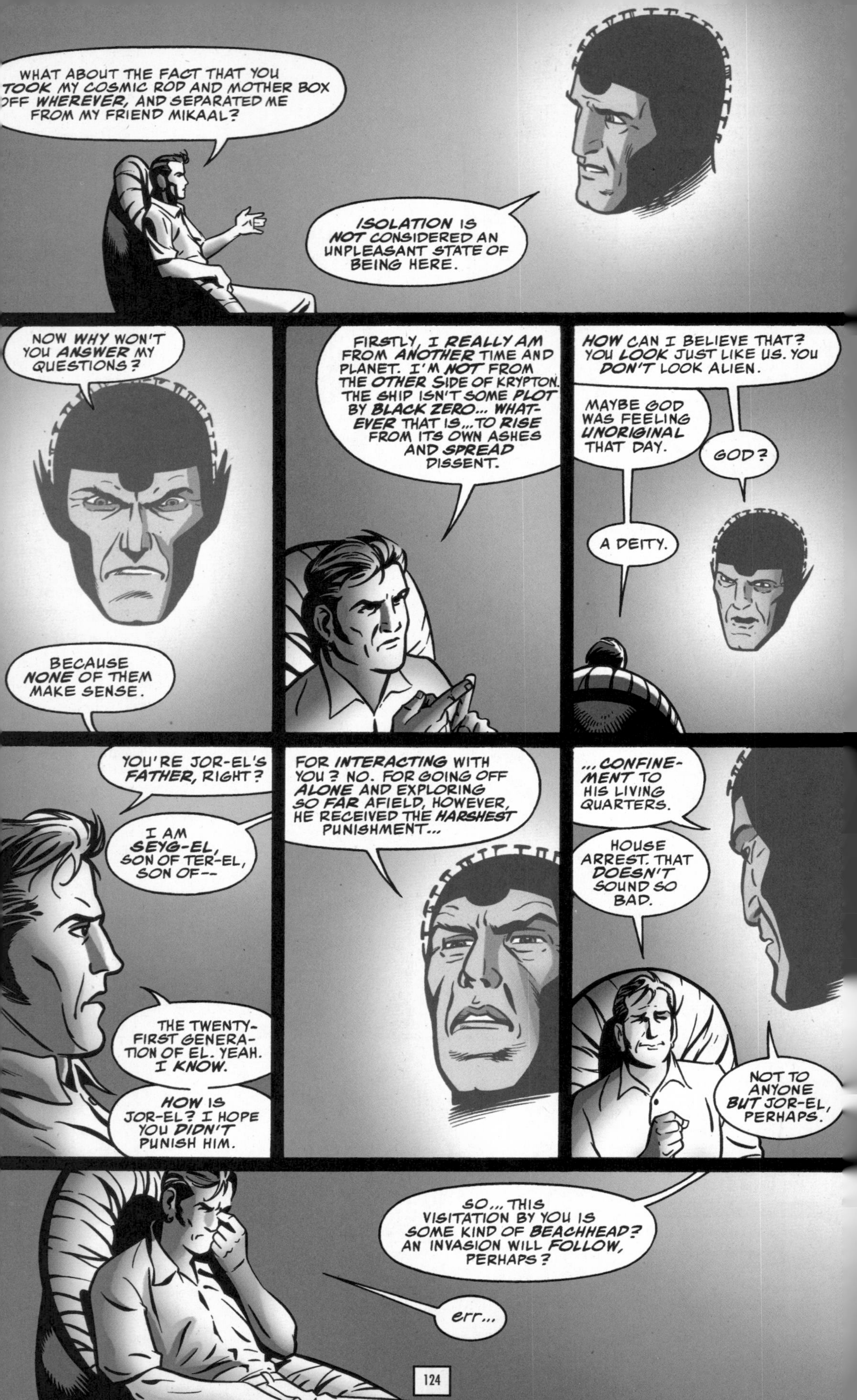

WHAT ABOUT THE FACT THAT YOU TOOK MY COSMIC ROD AND MOTHER BOX OFF WHEREVER, AND SEPARATED ME FROM MY FRIEND MIKAAL?
ISOLATION IS NOT CONSIDERED AN UNPLEASANT STATE OF BEING HERE.
NOW WHY WON'T YOU ANSWER MY QUESTIONS?
BECAUSE NONE OF THEM MAKE SENSE.
FIRSTLY, I REALLY AM FROM ANOTHER TIME AND PLANET. I'M NOT FROM THE OTHER SIDE OF KRYPTON. THE SHIP ISN'T SOME PLOT BY BLACK ZERO... WHATEVER THAT IS... TO RISE FROM ITS OWN ASHES AND SPREAD DISSENT.
HOW CAN I BELIEVE THAT? YOU LOOK JUST LIKE US. YOU DON'T LOOK ALIEN.
MAYBE GOD WAS FEELING UNORIGINAL THAT DAY.
GOD?
A DEITY.
YOU'RE JOR-EL'S FATHER, RIGHT?
I AM SEYG-EL, SON OF TER-EL, SON OF--
THE TWENTY-FIRST GENERATION OF EL. YEAH. I KNOW.
HOW IS JOR-EL? I HOPE YOU DIDN'T PUNISH HIM.
FOR INTERACTING WITH YOU? NO. FOR GOING OFF ALONE AND EXPLORING SO FAR AFIELD, HOWEVER, HE RECEIVED THE HARSHEST PUNISHMENT...
...CONFINEMENT TO HIS LIVING QUARTERS.
HOUSE ARREST. THAT DOESN'T SOUND SO BAD.
NOT TO ANYONE BUT JOR-EL, PERHAPS.
SO... THIS VISITATION BY YOU IS SOME KIND OF BEACHHEAD? AN INVASION WILL FOLLOW, PERHAPS?
err...

YOUR *FRIEND* REVEALED YOU *INTEND* TO INVADE US.

E DOUBT ACK SAID NYTHING F THE IND.

HE TOLD US *EVERY-THING.* HE IS WILLING TO *BETRAY* YOU FOR HIS OWN LIBERTY.

HE TALKED OF *DETESTING* YOU... YOUR BLUE SKIN.

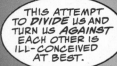

THIS ATTEMPT TO *DIVIDE* US AND TURN US *AGAINST* EACH OTHER IS ILL-CONCEIVED AT BEST.

I'M *WISE* TO YOU.

YOU *GOTTA* UNDERSTAND, ON MY PLANET THERE'S A MEANS OF MASS ENTERTAINMENT CALLED *TELEVISION.* ON TELEVISION ARE DRAMAS ABOUT LAW ENFORCERS. *COPS,* WE CALL THEM.

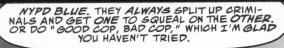

NYPD BLUE. THEY *ALWAYS* SPLIT UP CRIMI-NALS AND GET *ONE* TO SQUEAL ON THE *OTHER.* OR DO *"GOOD COP, BAD COP,"* WHICH I'M *GLAD* YOU HAVEN'T TRIED.

THE IDEA OF *"GOOD HEAD, BAD HEAD"* WOULD HAVE HAD ME IN *STITCHES.*

YOUR WORLD SOUNDS SO VERY *DIFFERENT* FROM OURS.

WE *INTERACT* TOGETHER *MORE,* FOR ONE. WE LAUGH. WE MAKE WAR. WE CONCEIVE OUR CHILDREN THE *GOOD* WAY...

...SWEATY AND *SQUIRTY.*

YOUR WORLD IS *SO STERILE,* I BET YOU *DON'T* EVEN KNOW *WHAT* I'M TALKING ABOUT.

BARBARIAN.

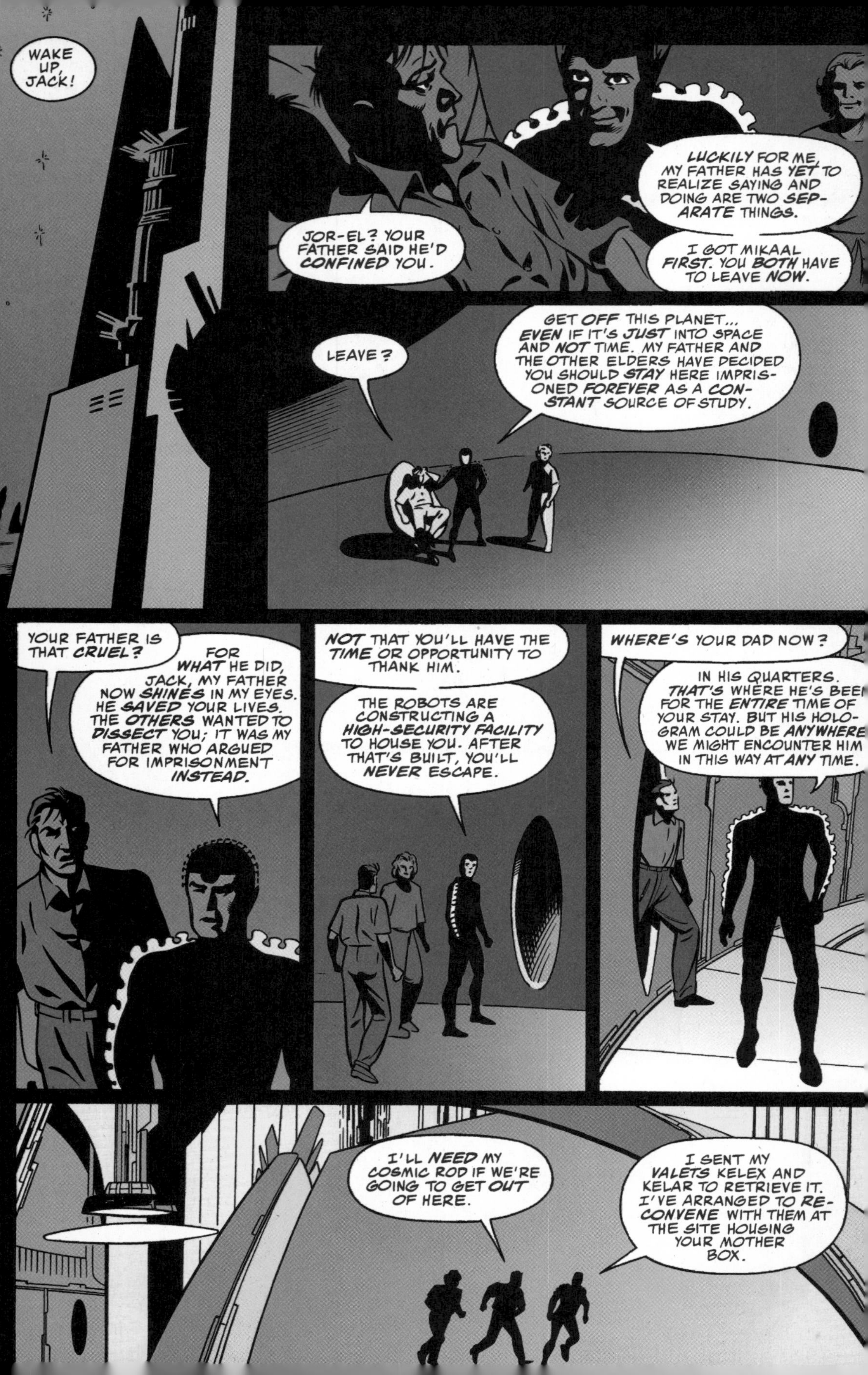
WAKE UP, JACK!
LUCKILY FOR ME, MY FATHER HAS YET TO REALIZE SAYING AND DOING ARE TWO SEP-ARATE THINGS.
JOR-EL? YOUR FATHER SAID HE'D CONFINED YOU.
I GOT MIKAAL FIRST. YOU BOTH HAVE TO LEAVE NOW.
LEAVE?
GET OFF THIS PLANET... EVEN IF IT'S JUST INTO SPACE AND NOT TIME. MY FATHER AND THE OTHER ELDERS HAVE DECIDED YOU SHOULD STAY HERE IMPRIS-ONED FOREVER AS A CON-STANT SOURCE OF STUDY.
YOUR FATHER IS THAT CRUEL?
FOR WHAT HE DID, JACK, MY FATHER NOW SHINES IN MY EYES. HE SAVED YOUR LIVES. THE OTHERS WANTED TO DISSECT YOU; IT WAS MY FATHER WHO ARGUED FOR IMPRISONMENT INSTEAD.
NOT THAT YOU'LL HAVE THE TIME OR OPPORTUNITY TO THANK HIM.
THE ROBOTS ARE CONSTRUCTING A HIGH-SECURITY FACILITY TO HOUSE YOU. AFTER THAT'S BUILT, YOU'LL NEVER ESCAPE.
WHERE'S YOUR DAD NOW?
IN HIS QUARTERS. THAT'S WHERE HE'S BEEN FOR THE ENTIRE TIME OF YOUR STAY. BUT HIS HOLO-GRAM COULD BE ANYWHERE. WE MIGHT ENCOUNTER HIM IN THIS WAY AT ANY TIME.
I'LL NEED MY COSMIC ROD IF WE'RE GOING TO GET OUT OF HERE.
I SENT MY VALETS KELEX AND KELAR TO RETRIEVE IT. I'VE ARRANGED TO RE-CONVENE WITH THEM AT THE SITE HOUSING YOUR MOTHER BOX.

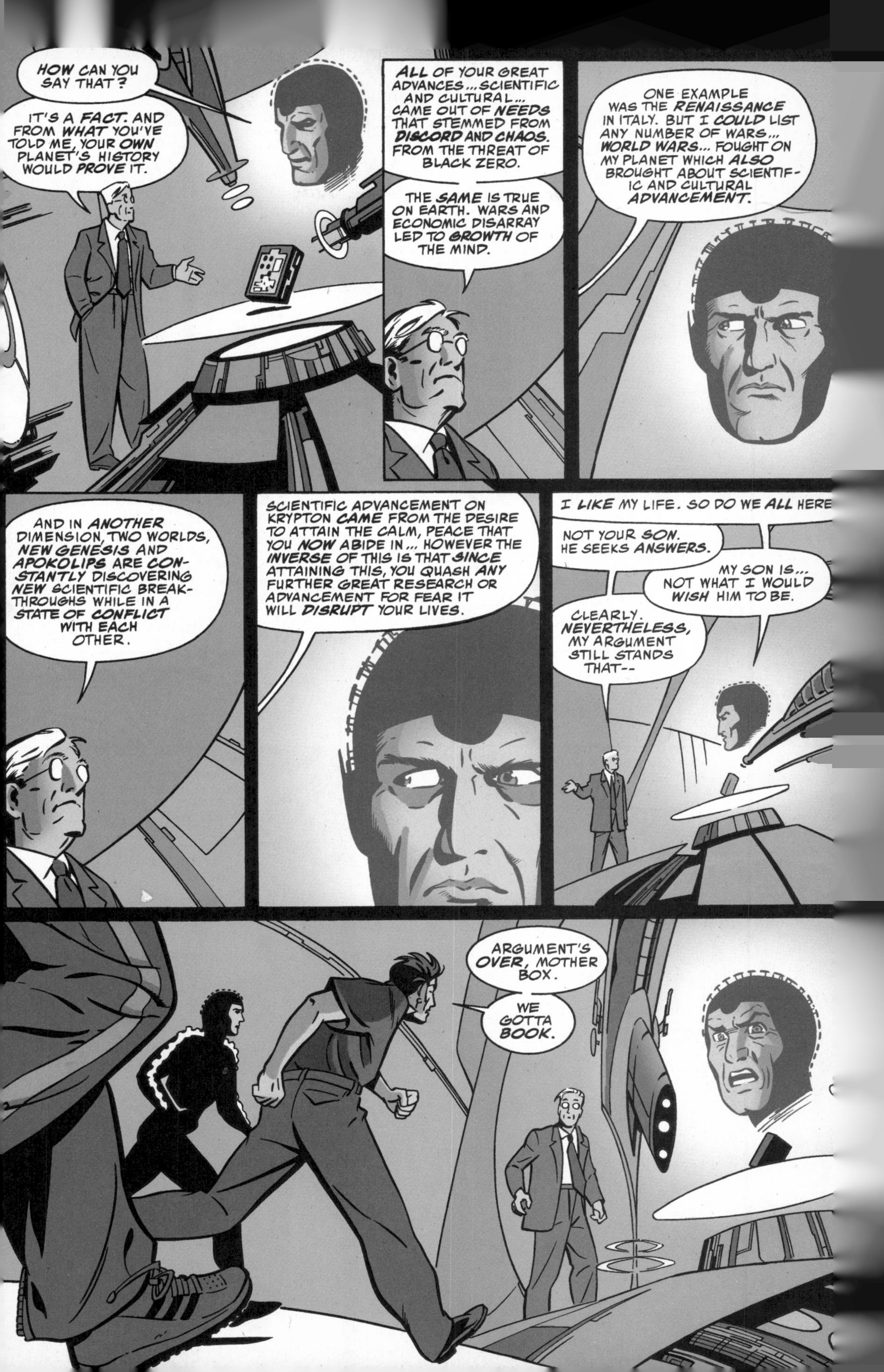
HOW CAN YOU SAY THAT?
IT'S A FACT. AND FROM WHAT YOU'VE TOLD ME, YOUR OWN PLANET'S HISTORY WOULD PROVE IT.
ALL OF YOUR GREAT ADVANCES... SCIENTIFIC AND CULTURAL... CAME OUT OF NEEDS THAT STEMMED FROM DISCORD AND CHAOS. FROM THE THREAT OF BLACK ZERO.
THE SAME IS TRUE ON EARTH. WARS AND ECONOMIC DISARRAY LED TO GROWTH OF THE MIND.
ONE EXAMPLE WAS THE RENAISSANCE IN ITALY. BUT I COULD LIST ANY NUMBER OF WARS... WORLD WARS... FOUGHT ON MY PLANET WHICH ALSO BROUGHT ABOUT SCIENTIFIC AND CULTURAL ADVANCEMENT.
AND IN ANOTHER DIMENSION, TWO WORLDS, NEW GENESIS AND APOKOLIPS ARE CONSTANTLY DISCOVERING NEW SCIENTIFIC BREAKTHROUGHS WHILE IN A STATE OF CONFLICT WITH EACH OTHER.
SCIENTIFIC ADVANCEMENT ON KRYPTON CAME FROM THE DESIRE TO ATTAIN THE CALM, PEACE THAT YOU NOW ABIDE IN... HOWEVER THE INVERSE OF THIS IS THAT SINCE ATTAINING THIS, YOU QUASH ANY FURTHER GREAT RESEARCH OR ADVANCEMENT FOR FEAR IT WILL DISRUPT YOUR LIVES.
I LIKE MY LIFE. SO DO WE ALL HERE
NOT YOUR SON. HE SEEKS ANSWERS.
MY SON IS... NOT WHAT I WOULD WISH HIM TO BE.
CLEARLY. NEVERTHELESS, MY ARGUMENT STILL STANDS THAT--
ARGUMENT'S OVER, MOTHER BOX.
WE GOTTA BOOK.

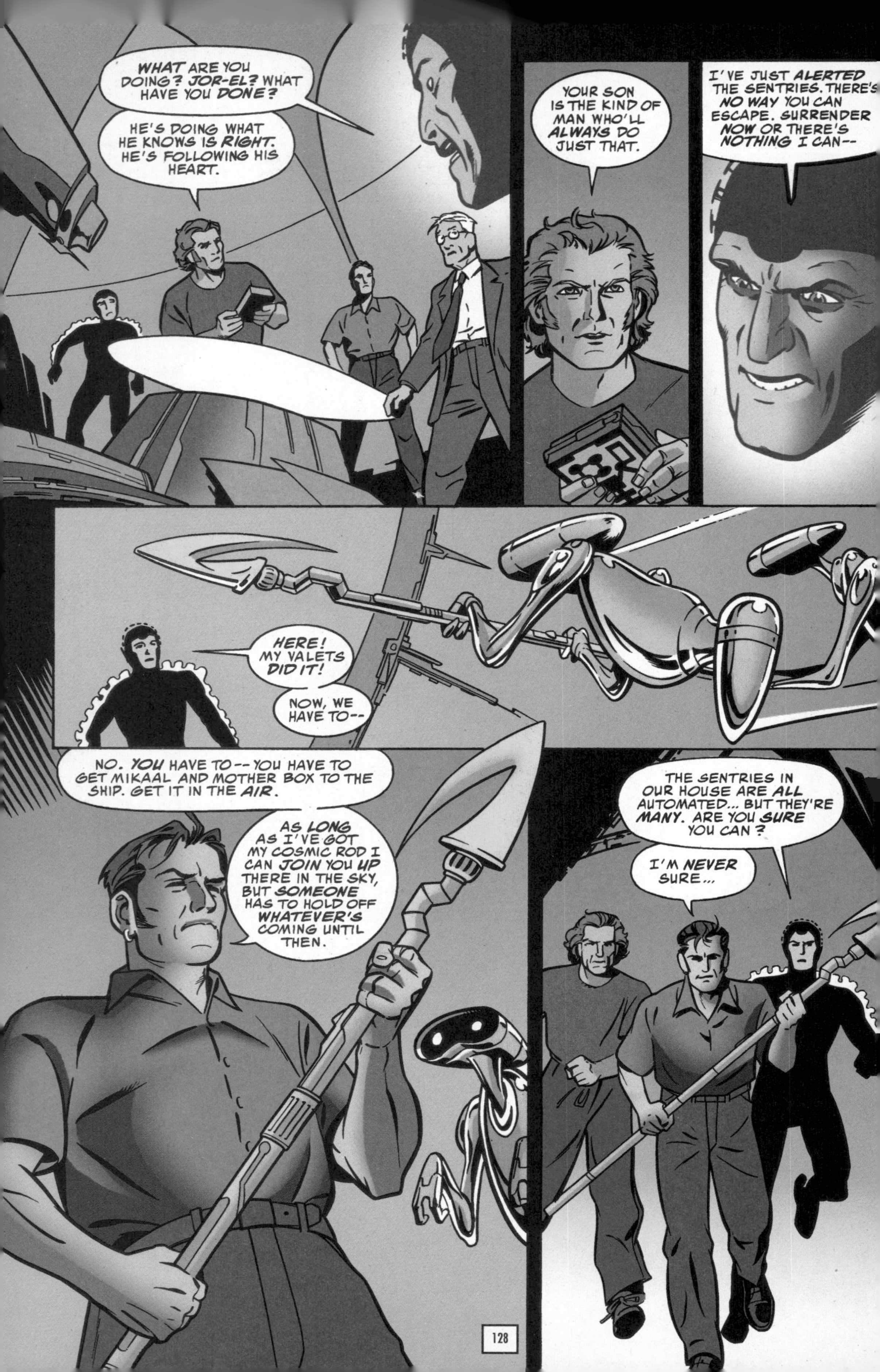

WHAT ARE YOU DOING? JOR-EL? WHAT HAVE YOU DONE?
HE'S DOING WHAT HE KNOWS IS RIGHT. HE'S FOLLOWING HIS HEART.
YOUR SON IS THE KIND OF MAN WHO'LL ALWAYS DO JUST THAT.
I'VE JUST ALERTED THE SENTRIES. THERE'S NO WAY YOU CAN ESCAPE. SURRENDER NOW OR THERE'S NOTHING I CAN--
HERE! MY VALETS DID IT!
NOW, WE HAVE TO--
NO. YOU HAVE TO-- YOU HAVE TO GET MIKAAL AND MOTHER BOX TO THE SHIP. GET IT IN THE AIR.
AS LONG AS I'VE GOT MY COSMIC ROD I CAN JOIN YOU UP THERE IN THE SKY, BUT SOMEONE HAS TO HOLD OFF WHATEVER'S COMING UNTIL THEN.
THE SENTRIES IN OUR HOUSE ARE ALL AUTOMATED... BUT THEY'RE MANY. ARE YOU SURE YOU CAN?
I'M NEVER SURE...

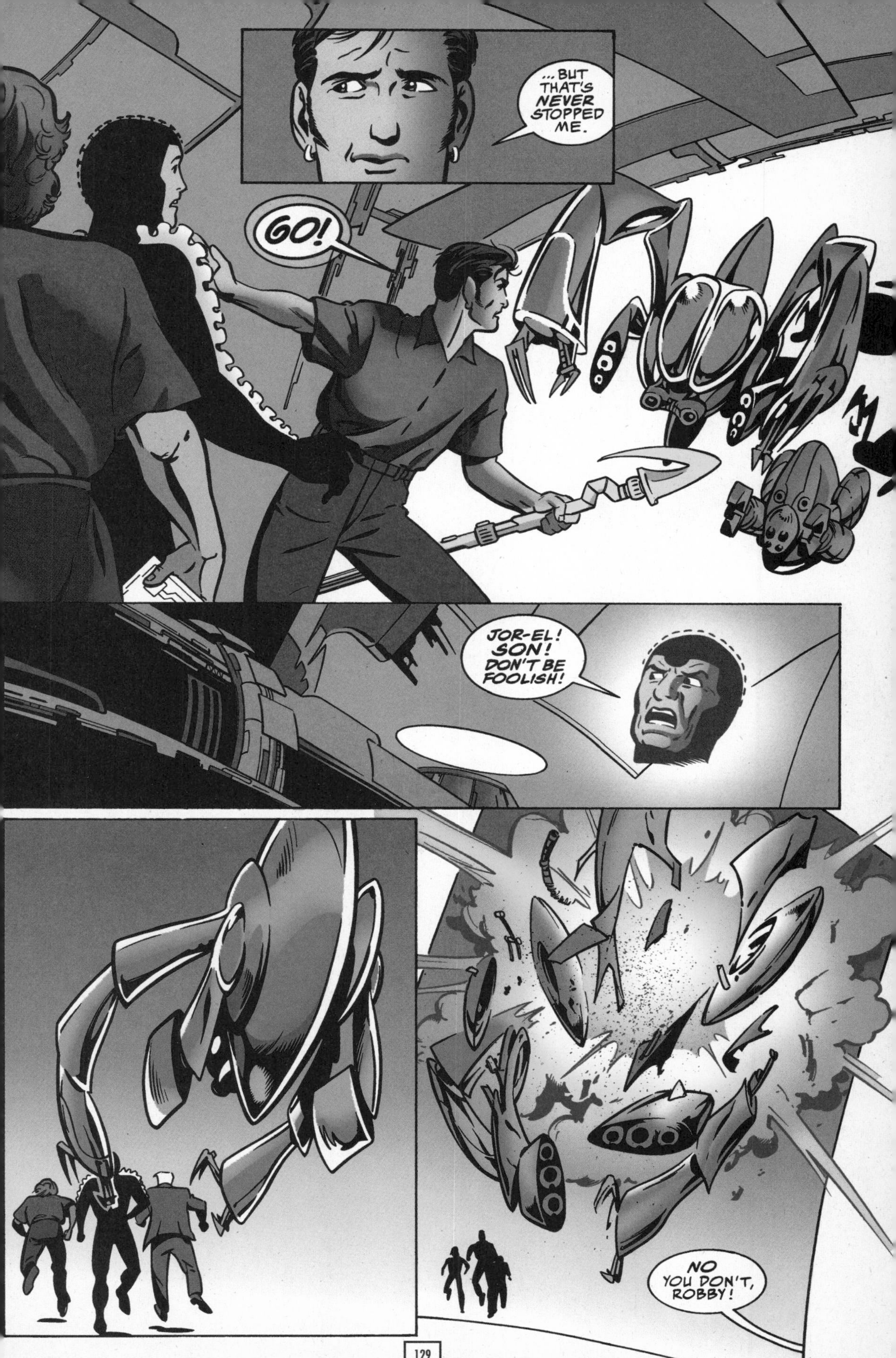
...BUT THAT'S NEVER STOPPED ME.
GO!
JOR-EL! SON! DON'T BE FOOLISH!
NO YOU DON'T, ROBBY!

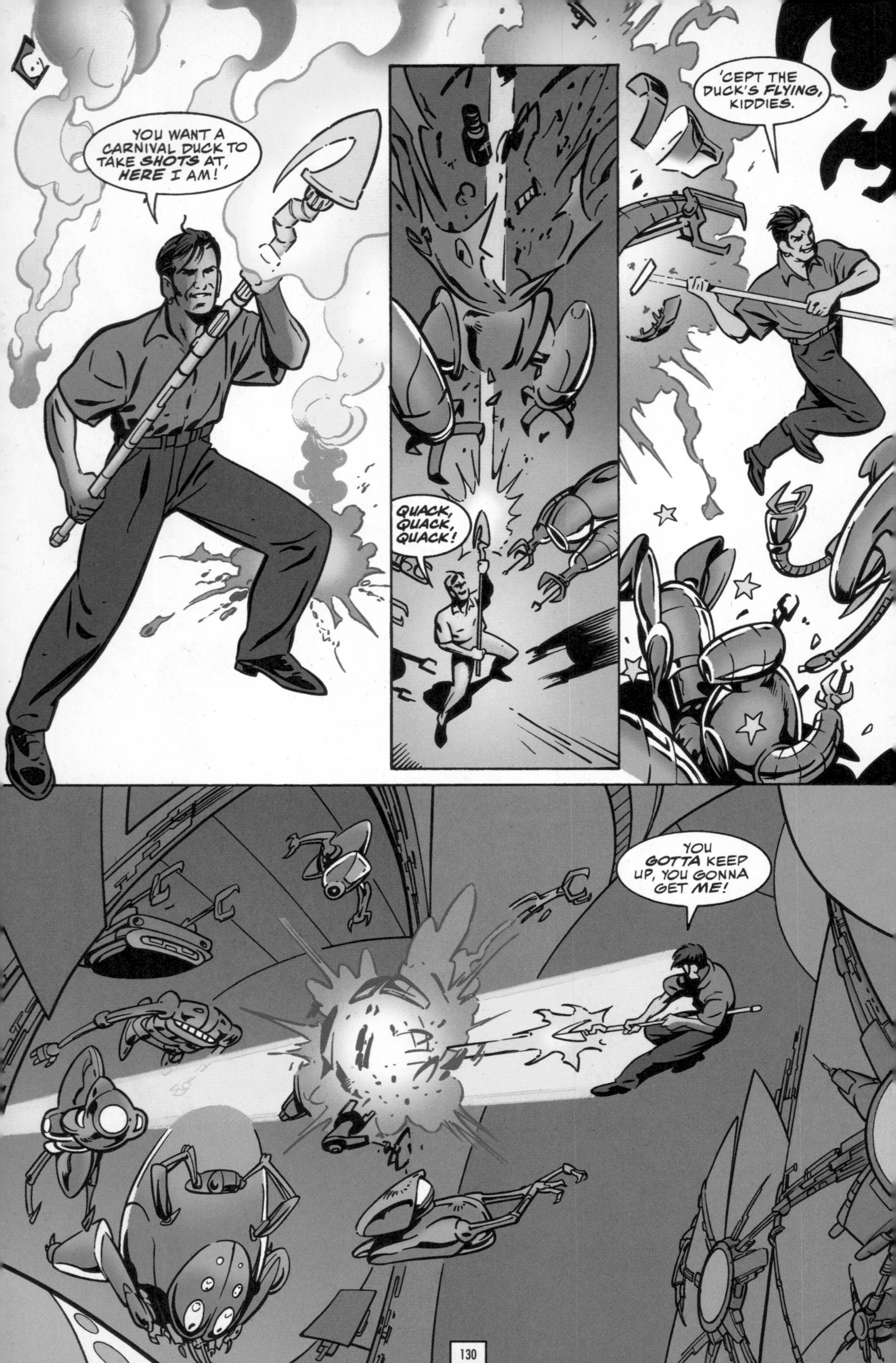
YOU WANT A CARNIVAL DUCK TO TAKE SHOTS AT, HERE I AM!
QUACK, QUACK, QUACK!
'CEPT THE DUCK'S FLYING, KIDDIES.
YOU GOTTA KEEP UP, YOU GONNA GET ME!

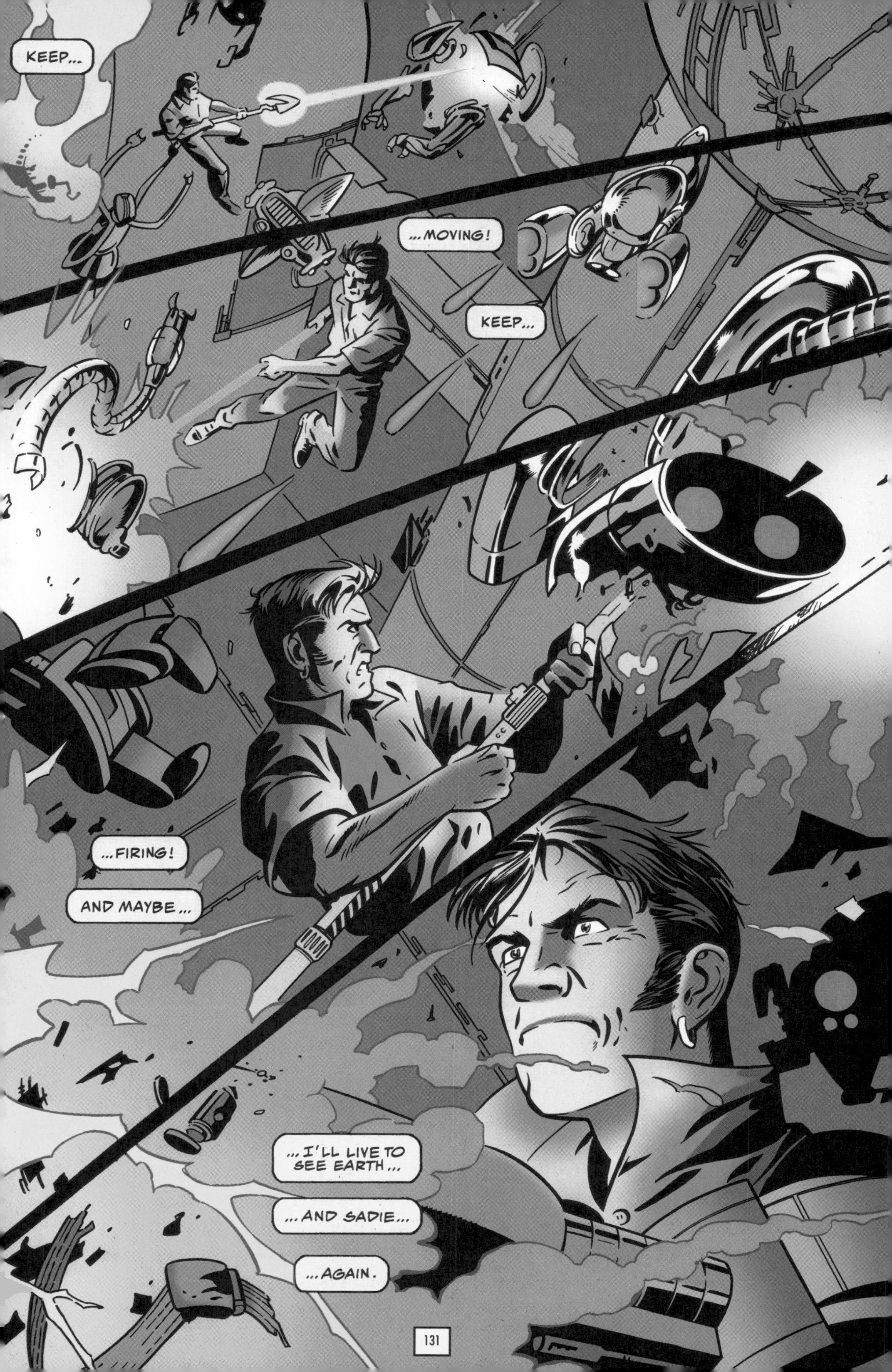
KEEP...
...MOVING!
KEEP...
...FIRING!
AND MAYBE...
...I'LL LIVE TO SEE EARTH...
...AND SADIE...
...AGAIN.

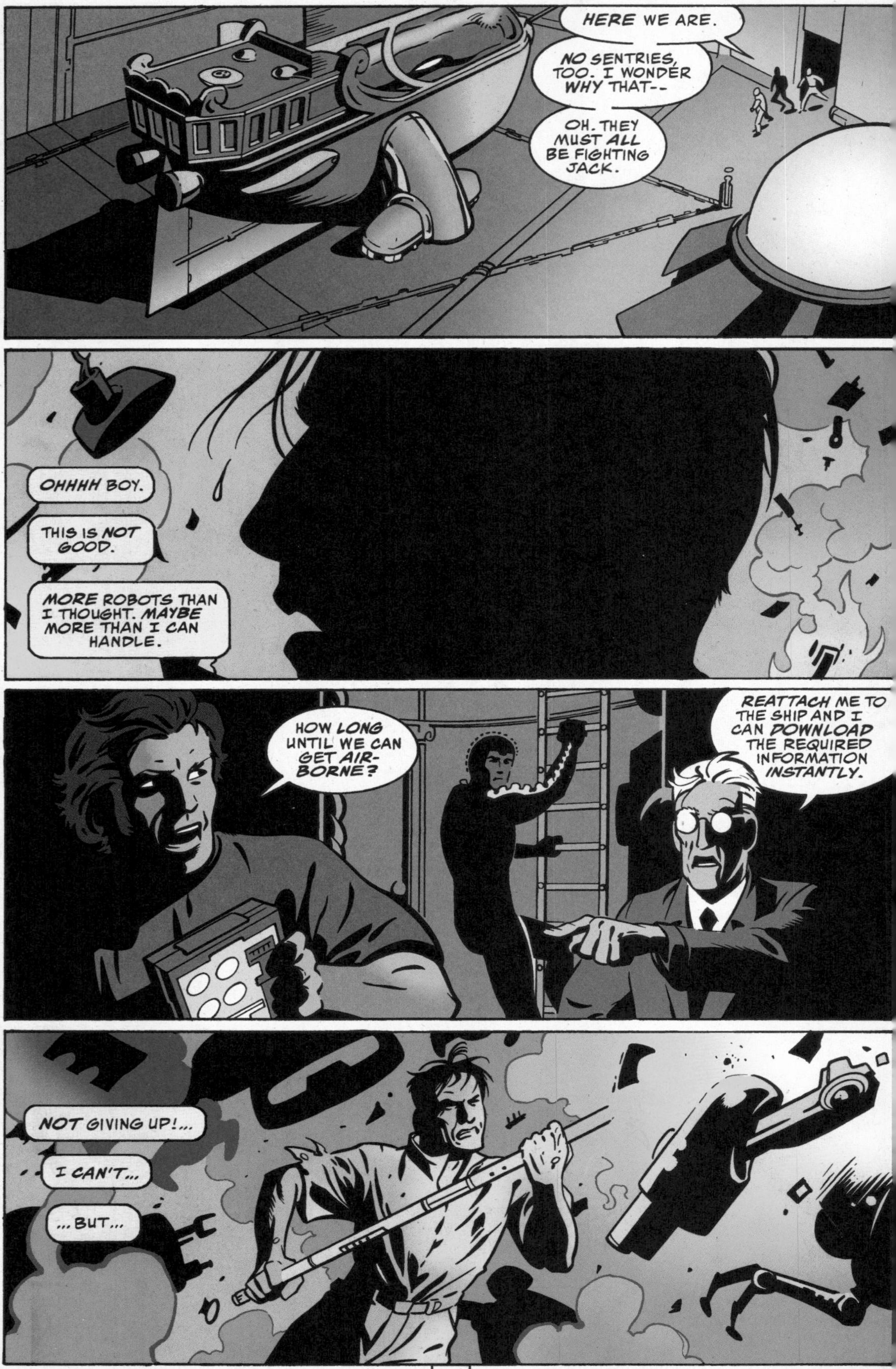
HERE WE ARE.
NO SENTRIES, TOO. I WONDER WHY THAT--
OH. THEY MUST ALL BE FIGHTING JACK.
OHHHH BOY.
THIS IS NOT GOOD.
MORE ROBOTS THAN I THOUGHT. MAYBE MORE THAN I CAN HANDLE.
HOW LONG UNTIL WE CAN GET AIR-BORNE?
REATTACH ME TO THE SHIP AND I CAN DOWNLOAD THE REQUIRED INFORMATION INSTANTLY.
NOT GIVING UP!...
I CAN'T...
...BUT...

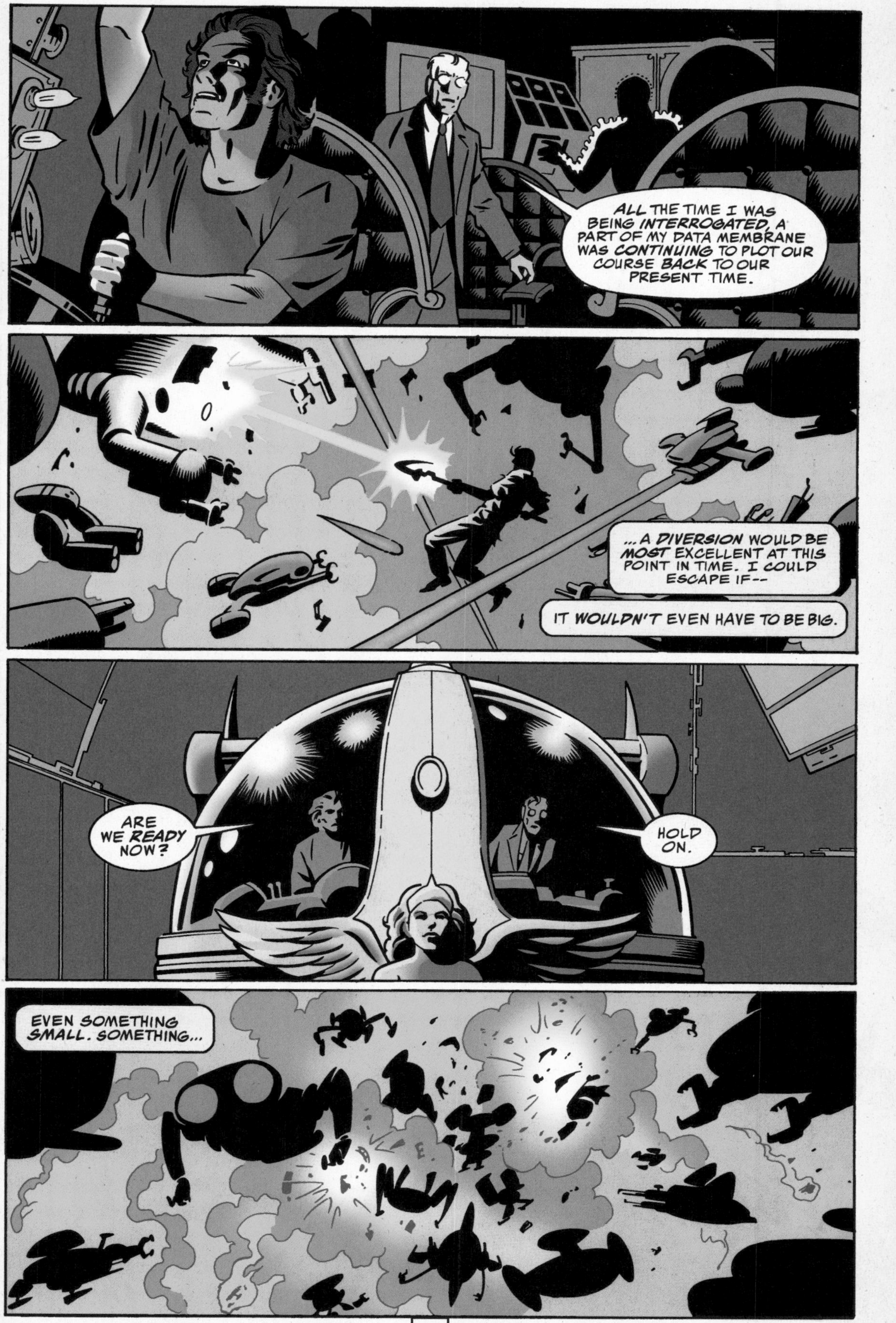
ALL THE TIME I WAS BEING INTERROGATED, A PART OF MY DATA MEMBRANE WAS CONTINUING TO PLOT OUR COURSE BACK TO OUR PRESENT TIME.
...A DIVERSION WOULD BE MOST EXCELLENT AT THIS POINT IN TIME. I COULD ESCAPE IF--
IT WOULDN'T EVEN HAVE TO BE BIG.
ARE WE READY NOW?
HOLD ON.
EVEN SOMETHING SMALL. SOMETHING...

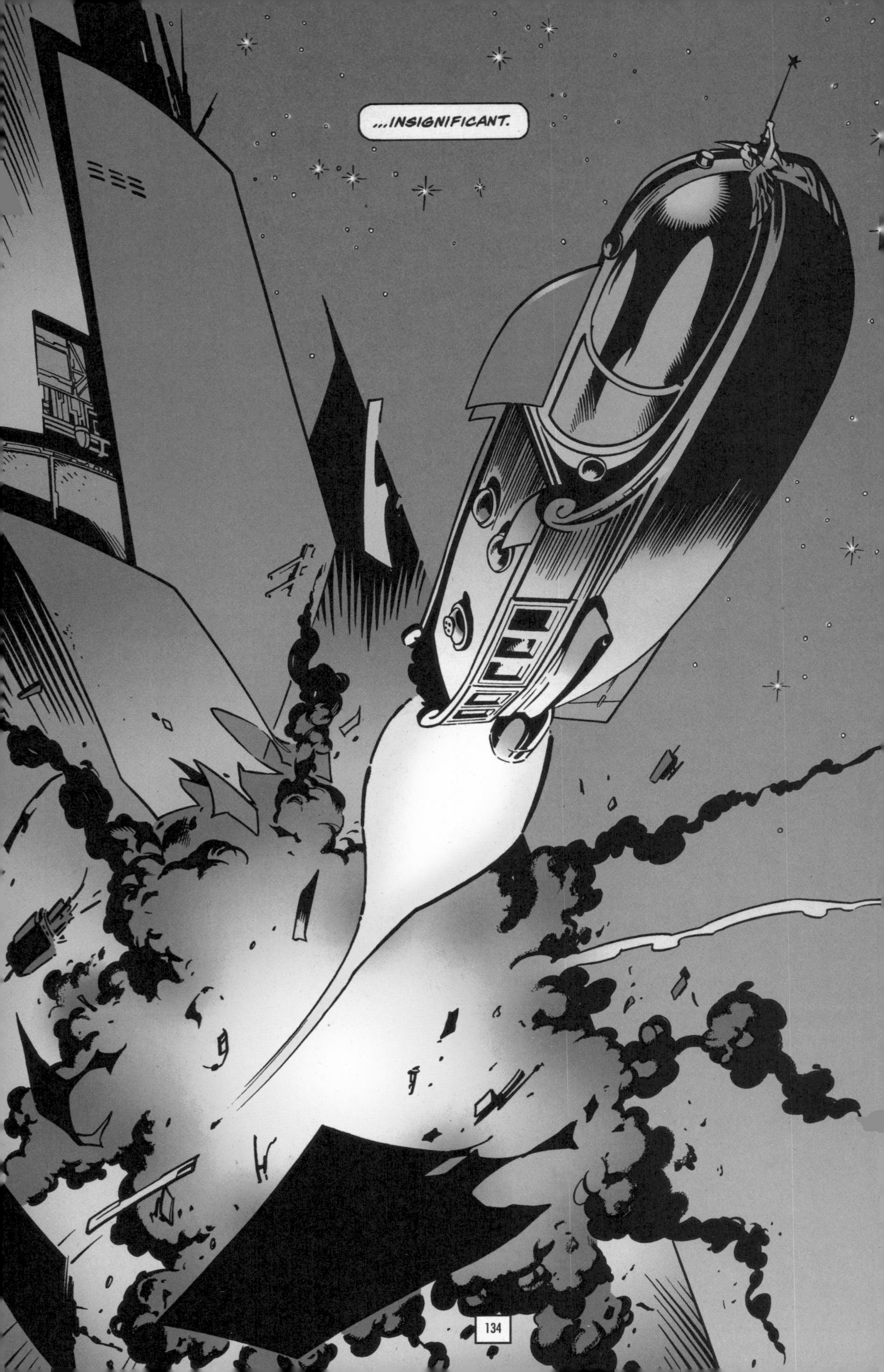
...INSIGNIFICANT.

IT *ALLOWS* ME MY *ESCAPE.* I MEET MY *FRIENDS.*

BUT *FURTHER* OFF WE *LAND.*

AFTER ALL...

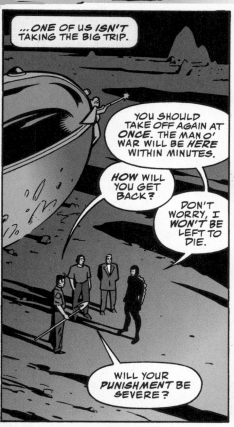

...ONE OF US *ISN'T* TAKING THE BIG TRIP.

YOU SHOULD TAKE OFF AGAIN AT *ONCE.* THE MAN O' *WAR* WILL BE *HERE* WITHIN MINUTES.

HOW WILL YOU GET *BACK?*

DON'T WORRY, I *WON'T* BE LEFT TO *DIE.*

WILL YOUR *PUNISHMENT* BE *SEVERE?*

ONE *GOOD* THING ABOUT MY WORLD IS THAT PUNISHMENT *LACKS* BOTH *SEVERITY* AND *IMAGINATION.* I'LL BE *CONFINED.* MY SECURITY WILL BE *INCREASED.*

SO IT MIGHT TAKE ME *TWO* DAYS TO THINK OF A WAY OUT *INSTEAD* OF ONE AS IT *USUALLY* DOES.

LOOK, THEY *APPROACH!* YOU *MUST* GO!

HERE, A *PARTING GIFT.*

THIS DEVICE CONTAINS THE *BINARY CODE* COORDINATES OF *EARTH.* VISUAL DATA, TOO... *PICTURES,* SO YOU WON'T *FORGET* WHAT EARTH AND ITS *PEOPLE* LOOK LIKE. FOR IF YOU *EVER* DO GET THAT ROCKET BUILT.

I'LL DO MY *BEST.* PERHAPS ONE DAY. AND IF *NOT* ME...

...PERHAPS I'LL HAVE A *SON.*

MAY GREAT *RAO* GUIDE YOU *ONWARD.*

AND MAY THE *MANY GODS* OF MY WORLD WATCH OVER *YOU...*

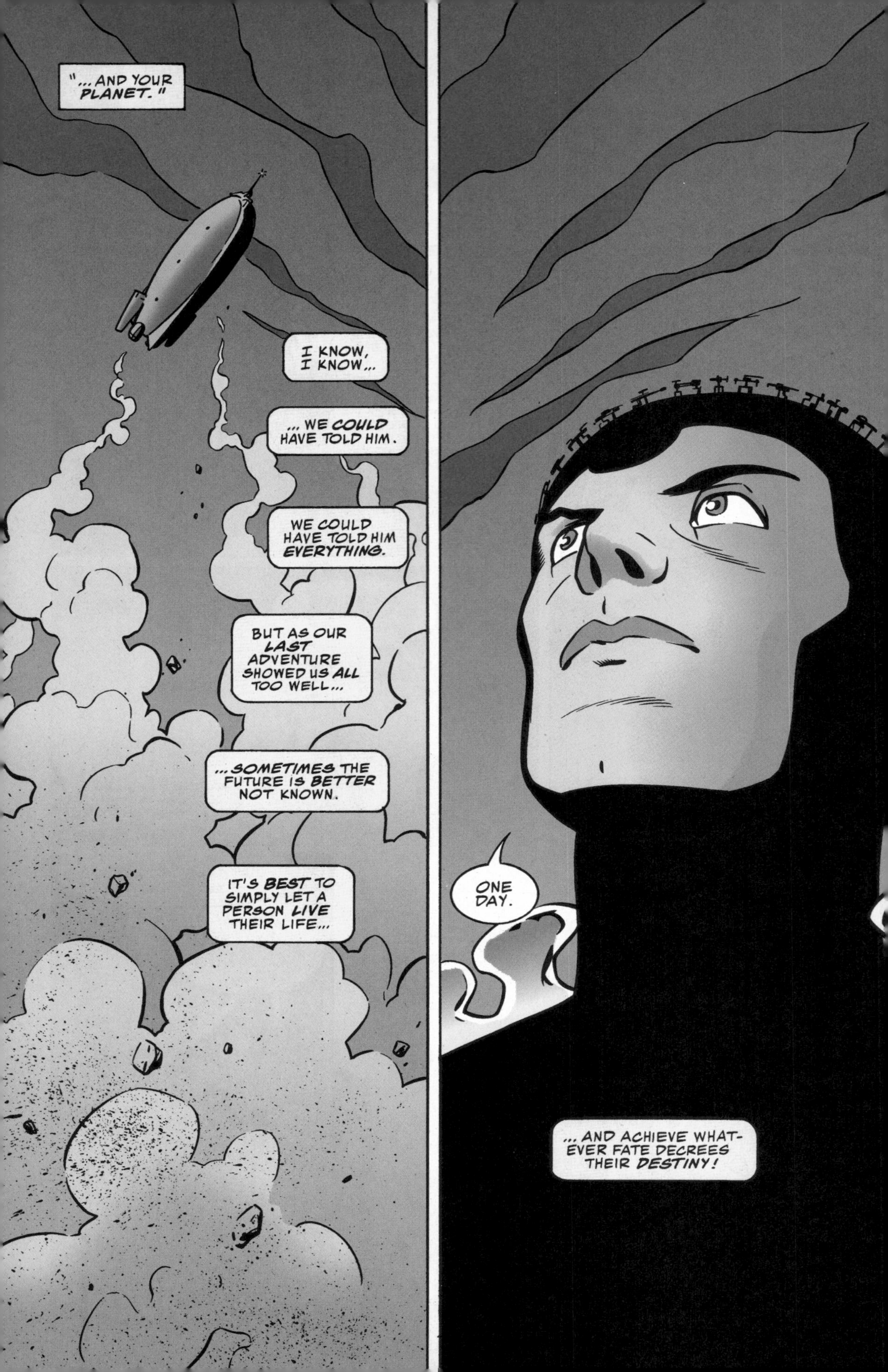
"...AND YOUR PLANET."
I KNOW, I KNOW...
...WE COULD HAVE TOLD HIM.
WE COULD HAVE TOLD HIM EVERYTHING.
BUT AS OUR LAST ADVENTURE SHOWED US ALL TOO WELL...
...SOMETIMES THE FUTURE IS BETTER NOT KNOWN.
IT'S BEST TO SIMPLY LET A PERSON LIVE THEIR LIFE...
ONE DAY.
...AND ACHIEVE WHAT-EVER FATE DECREES THEIR DESTINY!

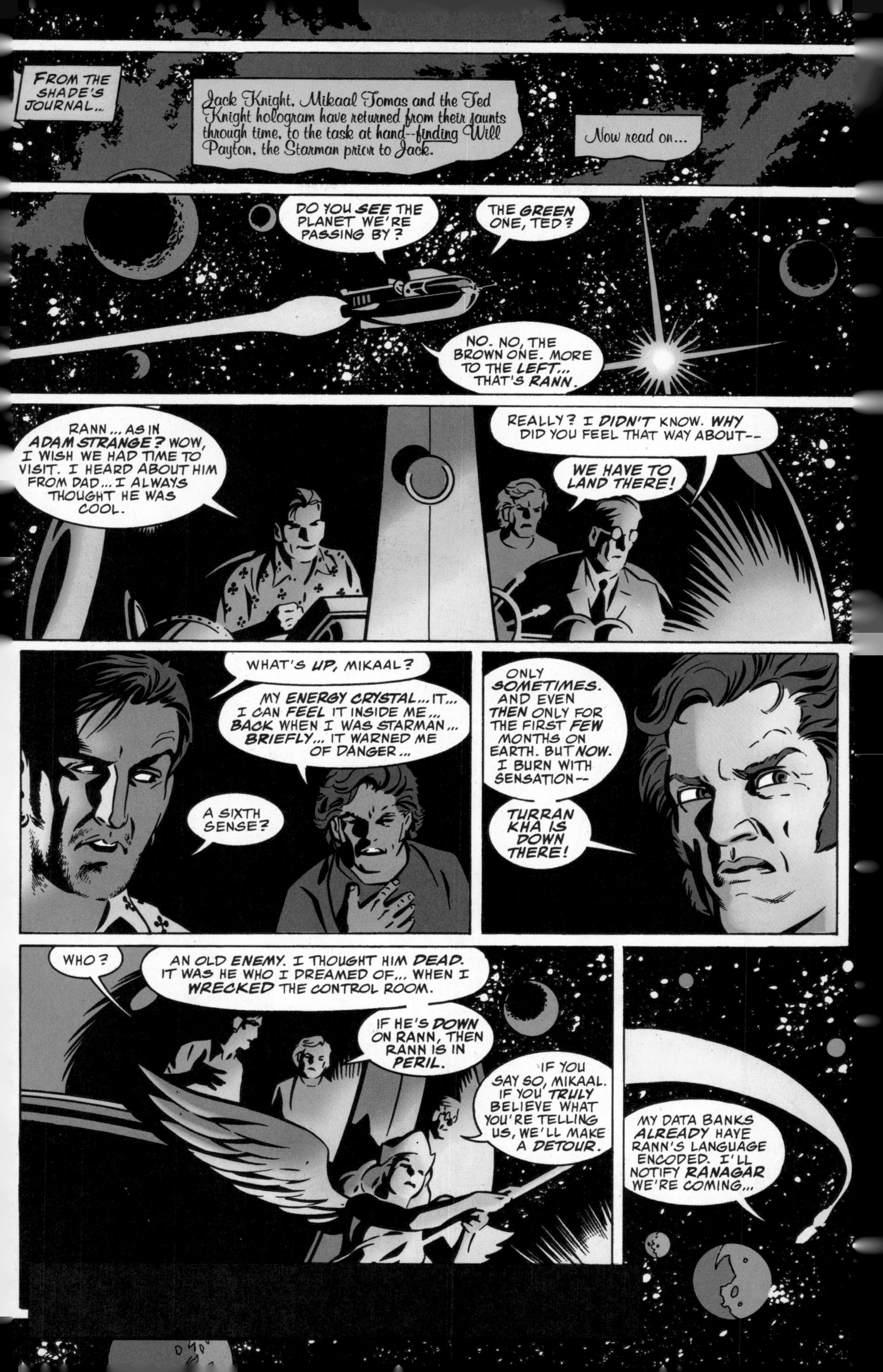
FROM THE SHADE'S JOURNAL...
Jack Knight, Mikaal Tomas and the Ted Knight hologram have returned from their jaunts through time, to the task at hand--finding Will Payton, the Starman prior to Jack.
Now read on...
DO YOU SEE THE PLANET WE'RE PASSING BY?
THE GREEN ONE, TED?
NO. NO, THE BROWN ONE. MORE TO THE LEFT... THAT'S RANN.
RANN... AS IN ADAM STRANGE? WOW, I WISH WE HAD TIME TO VISIT. I HEARD ABOUT HIM FROM DAD... I ALWAYS THOUGHT HE WAS COOL.
REALLY? I DIDN'T KNOW. WHY DID YOU FEEL THAT WAY ABOUT--
WE HAVE TO LAND THERE!
WHAT'S UP, MIKAAL?
MY ENERGY CRYSTAL... IT... I CAN FEEL IT INSIDE ME... BACK WHEN I WAS STARMAN... BRIEFLY... IT WARNED ME OF DANGER...
A SIXTH SENSE?
ONLY SOMETIMES. AND EVEN THEN ONLY FOR THE FIRST FEW MONTHS ON EARTH. BUT NOW. I BURN WITH SENSATION--
TURRAN KHA IS DOWN THERE!
WHO?
AN OLD ENEMY. I THOUGHT HIM DEAD. IT WAS HE WHO I DREAMED OF... WHEN I WRECKED THE CONTROL ROOM.
IF HE'S DOWN ON RANN, THEN RANN IS IN PERIL.
IF YOU SAY SO, MIKAAL. IF YOU TRULY BELIEVE WHAT YOU'RE TELLING US, WE'LL MAKE A DETOUR.
MY DATA BANKS ALREADY HAVE RANN'S LANGUAGE ENCODED. I'LL NOTIFY RANAGAR WE'RE COMING...

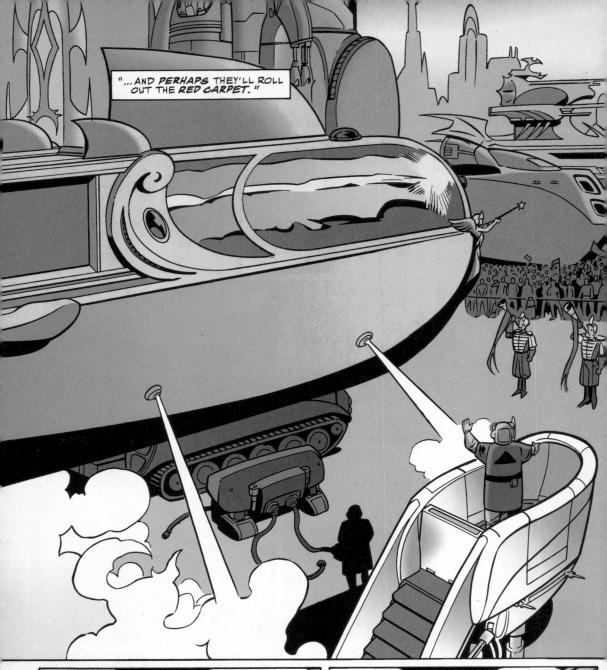

"...AND *PERHAPS* THEY'LL ROLL OUT THE *RED CARPET*."

WOW, WHEN YOU SAID THAT, I THOUGHT YOU WERE JOKING.

I WAS.

I'M *NOT* SURE THE RANNIANS THINK SO. IT'S A REAL *DEMILLE* PRODUCTION OUT THERE.

MAYBE THEY GREET *ALL* THEIR VISITORS THIS WAY.

MAYBE.

BUT I GOTTA SAY I'M *DOUBTFUL.*

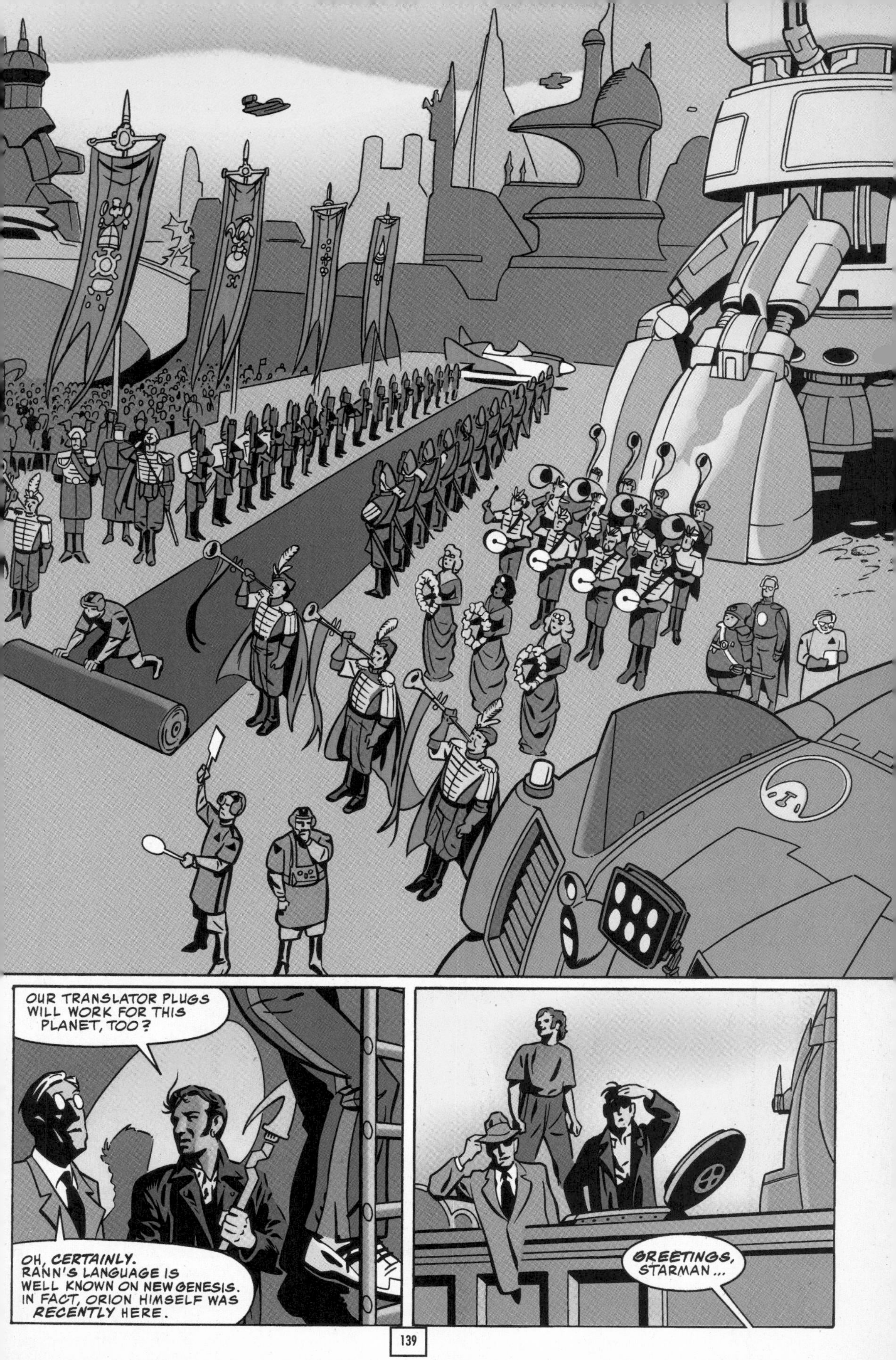
OUR TRANSLATOR PLUGS WILL WORK FOR THIS PLANET, TOO?
OH, CERTAINLY. RANN'S LANGUAGE IS WELL KNOWN ON NEW GENESIS. IN FACT, ORION HIMSELF WAS RECENTLY HERE.
GREETINGS, STARMAN...

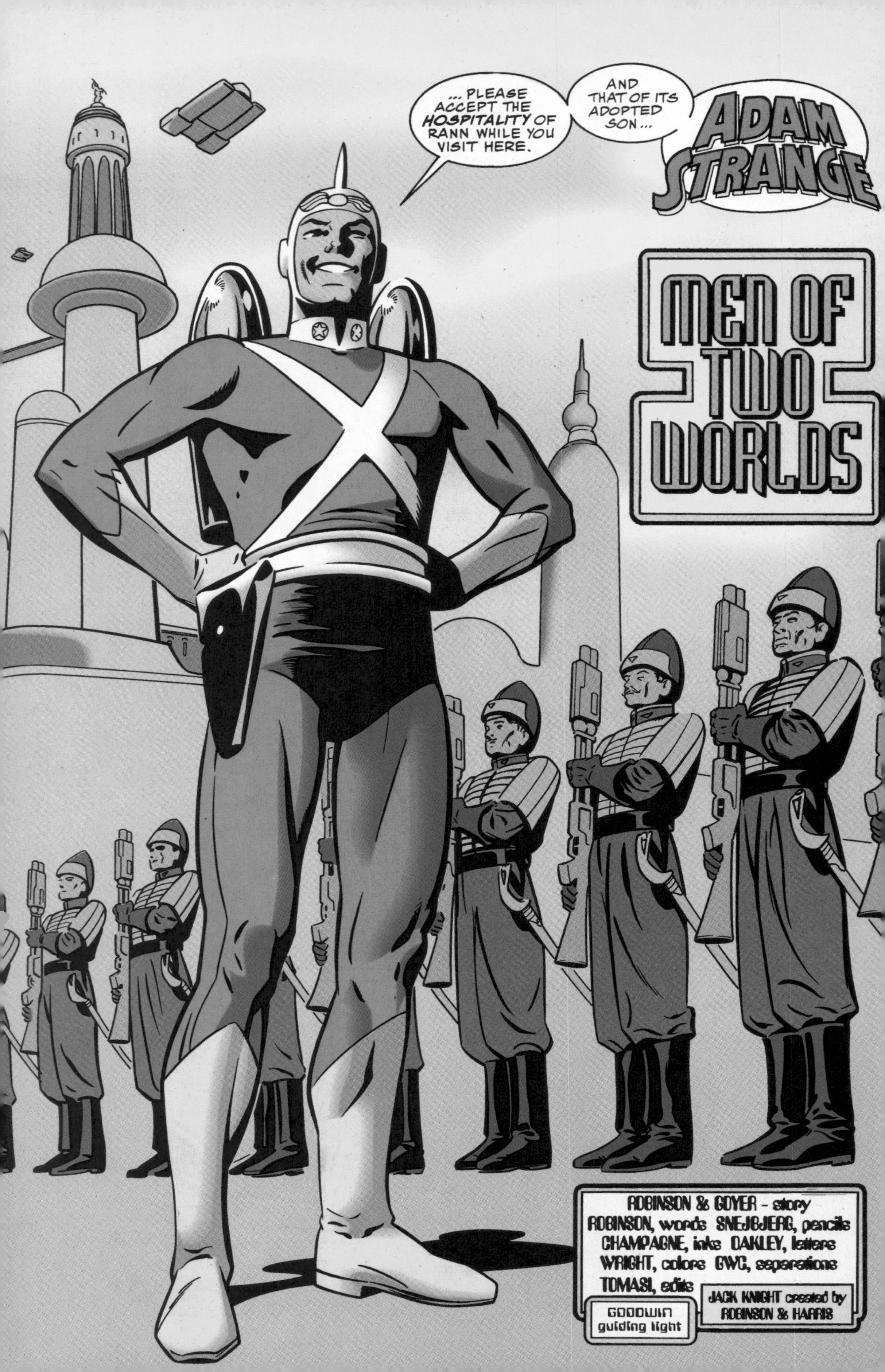

... PLEASE ACCEPT THE HOSPITALITY OF RANN WHILE YOU VISIT HERE.
AND THAT OF ITS ADOPTED SON...
ADAM STRANGE
MEN OF TWO WORLDS
ROBINSON & GOYER - story
ROBINSON, words SNEJBJERG, pencils
CHAMPAGNE, inks OAKLEY, letters
WRIGHT, colors GWC, separations
TOMASI, edits
GOODWIN guiding light
JACK KNIGHT created by ROBINSON & HARRIS

LATER, AFTER THE TRUMPETS SOUND, THE CYMBALS CRASH. LATER. QUIET AND CALM.

I HAVE A CONFESSION. THE WELCOME YOU RECEIVED IS SOMEWHAT *MORE* THAN YOU WOULD HAVE GOTTEN ON ANY *OTHER* DAY.

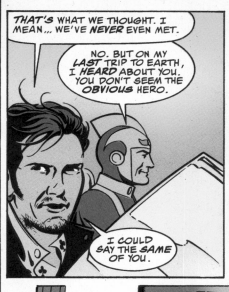

THAT'S WHAT WE THOUGHT. I MEAN... WE'VE *NEVER* EVEN MET.

NO. BUT ON MY *LAST* TRIP TO EARTH, I *HEARD* ABOUT YOU. YOU DON'T SEEM THE *OBVIOUS* HERO.

I COULD SAY THE *SAME* OF YOU.

JACK TOLD ME JUST NOW, HOW *MUCH* HE ADMIRED YOU.

I JUST THINK THE IDEA OF *CROSSING* SPACE OUT OF *LOVE* FROM YOUR SWEETHEART, IT'S LIKE THE *STUFF* OF FAIRY TALES OR ANCIENT MYTHS.

I COULD SAY THE *SAME* OF YOU.

ANYWAY, *WHY* THE POMP AND CIRCUMSTANCE?

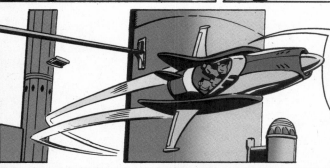

RANN... THE NEW, *IMPROVED* RANN I'M HELPING TO BRING ABOUT... IT'S *DONE* WITH PETTY WARS. WE *FOUGHT* ONE WITH THANAGAR SOME YEARS AGO, THAT WE COULD *SCARCE* AFFORD.

OTHER TERRITORIAL *SQUABBLES* OVER SPACE QUADRANTS CAUSE SABER RATTLING AND THE THREAT OF COMBAT.

WE SEEK AN *END* TO IT.

HOW SO?

A TREATY.

RANN AND MANY OF ITS ADJOINING PLANETS. LIKE THE *LEAGUE OF NATIONS* ON EARTH... A *LEAGUE OF PLANETS.* MY HOPE IS THIS TREATY WILL *GROW* FROM BEING A LEAGUE OF PLANETS AND INTO THE *UNITED PLANETS.*

WE'VE BEEN *WELCOMING* REPRESENTATIVES FROM THESE *WORLDS* ALL DAY. YOUR ARRIVAL WAS THE *LAST* SUCH LANDING. THE BAND WAS *STILL* IN PLACE, SO I THOUGHT... *HEY,* WHY NOT GIVE A REPRESENTATIVE FROM EARTH THE *SAME* HONOR?

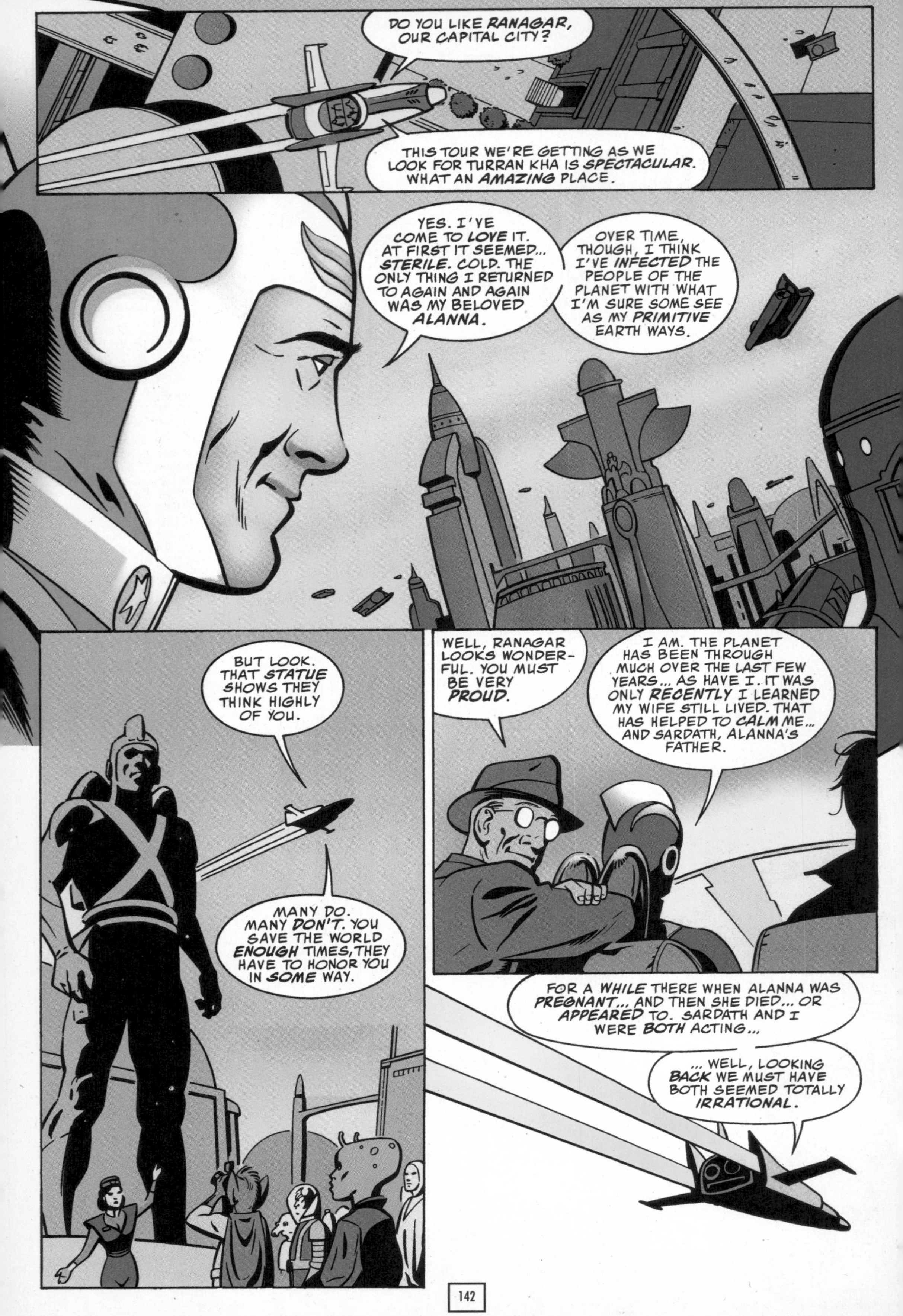
DO YOU LIKE RANAGAR, OUR CAPITAL CITY?
THIS TOUR WE'RE GETTING AS WE LOOK FOR TURRAN KHA IS SPECTACULAR. WHAT AN AMAZING PLACE.
YES. I'VE COME TO LOVE IT. AT FIRST IT SEEMED... STERILE. COLD. THE ONLY THING I RETURNED TO AGAIN AND AGAIN WAS MY BELOVED ALANNA.
OVER TIME, THOUGH, I THINK I'VE INFECTED THE PEOPLE OF THE PLANET WITH WHAT I'M SURE SOME SEE AS MY PRIMITIVE EARTH WAYS.
BUT LOOK. THAT STATUE SHOWS THEY THINK HIGHLY OF YOU.
MANY DO. MANY DON'T. YOU SAVE THE WORLD ENOUGH TIMES, THEY HAVE TO HONOR YOU IN SOME WAY.
WELL, RANAGAR LOOKS WONDERFUL. YOU MUST BE VERY PROUD.
I AM. THE PLANET HAS BEEN THROUGH MUCH OVER THE LAST FEW YEARS... AS HAVE I. IT WAS ONLY RECENTLY I LEARNED MY WIFE STILL LIVED. THAT HAS HELPED TO CALM ME... AND SARDATH, ALANNA'S FATHER.
FOR A WHILE THERE WHEN ALANNA WAS PREGNANT... AND THEN SHE DIED... OR APPEARED TO. SARDATH AND I WERE BOTH ACTING...
... WELL, LOOKING BACK WE MUST HAVE BOTH SEEMED TOTALLY IRRATIONAL.

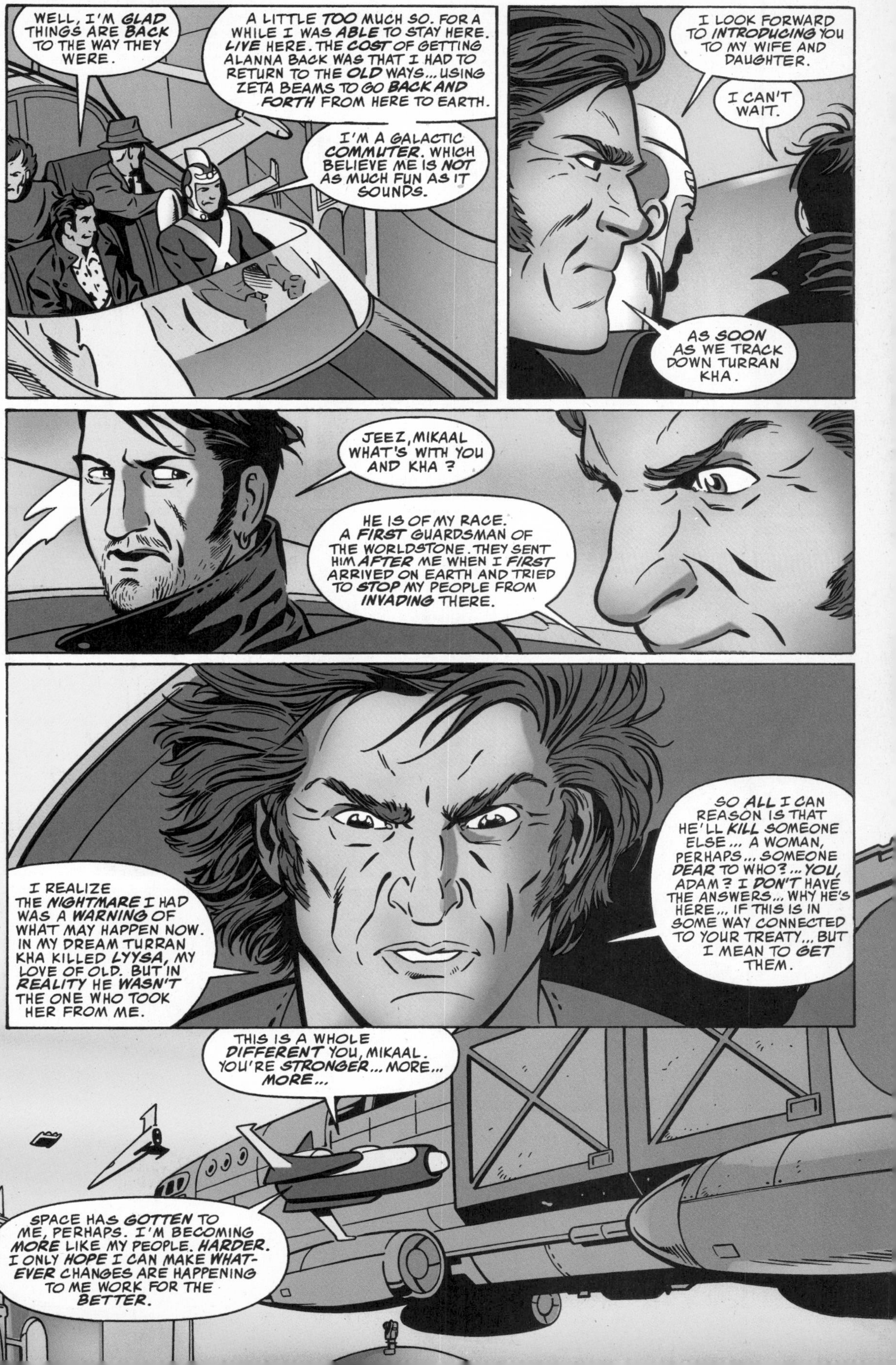
WELL, I'M GLAD THINGS ARE BACK TO THE WAY THEY WERE.
A LITTLE TOO MUCH SO. FOR A WHILE I WAS ABLE TO STAY HERE. LIVE HERE. THE COST OF GETTING ALANNA BACK WAS THAT I HAD TO RETURN TO THE OLD WAYS... USING ZETA BEAMS TO GO BACK AND FORTH FROM HERE TO EARTH.
I'M A GALACTIC COMMUTER. WHICH BELIEVE ME IS NOT AS MUCH FUN AS IT SOUNDS.
I LOOK FORWARD TO INTRODUCING YOU TO MY WIFE AND DAUGHTER.
I CAN'T WAIT.
AS SOON AS WE TRACK DOWN TURRAN KHA.
JEEZ, MIKAAL WHAT'S WITH YOU AND KHA ?
HE IS OF MY RACE. A FIRST GUARDSMAN OF THE WORLDSTONE. THEY SENT HIM AFTER ME WHEN I FIRST ARRIVED ON EARTH AND TRIED TO STOP MY PEOPLE FROM INVADING THERE.
I REALIZE THE NIGHTMARE I HAD WAS A WARNING OF WHAT MAY HAPPEN NOW. IN MY DREAM TURRAN KHA KILLED LYYSA, MY LOVE OF OLD. BUT IN REALITY HE WASN'T THE ONE WHO TOOK HER FROM ME.
SO ALL I CAN REASON IS THAT HE'LL KILL SOMEONE ELSE... A WOMAN, PERHAPS... SOMEONE DEAR TO WHO?... YOU, ADAM? I DON'T HAVE THE ANSWERS... WHY HE'S HERE... IF THIS IS IN SOME WAY CONNECTED TO YOUR TREATY... BUT I MEAN TO GET THEM.
THIS IS A WHOLE DIFFERENT YOU, MIKAAL. YOU'RE STRONGER... MORE... MORE...
SPACE HAS GOTTEN TO ME, PERHAPS. I'M BECOMING MORE LIKE MY PEOPLE. HARDER. I ONLY HOPE I CAN MAKE WHATEVER CHANGES ARE HAPPENING TO ME WORK FOR THE BETTER.

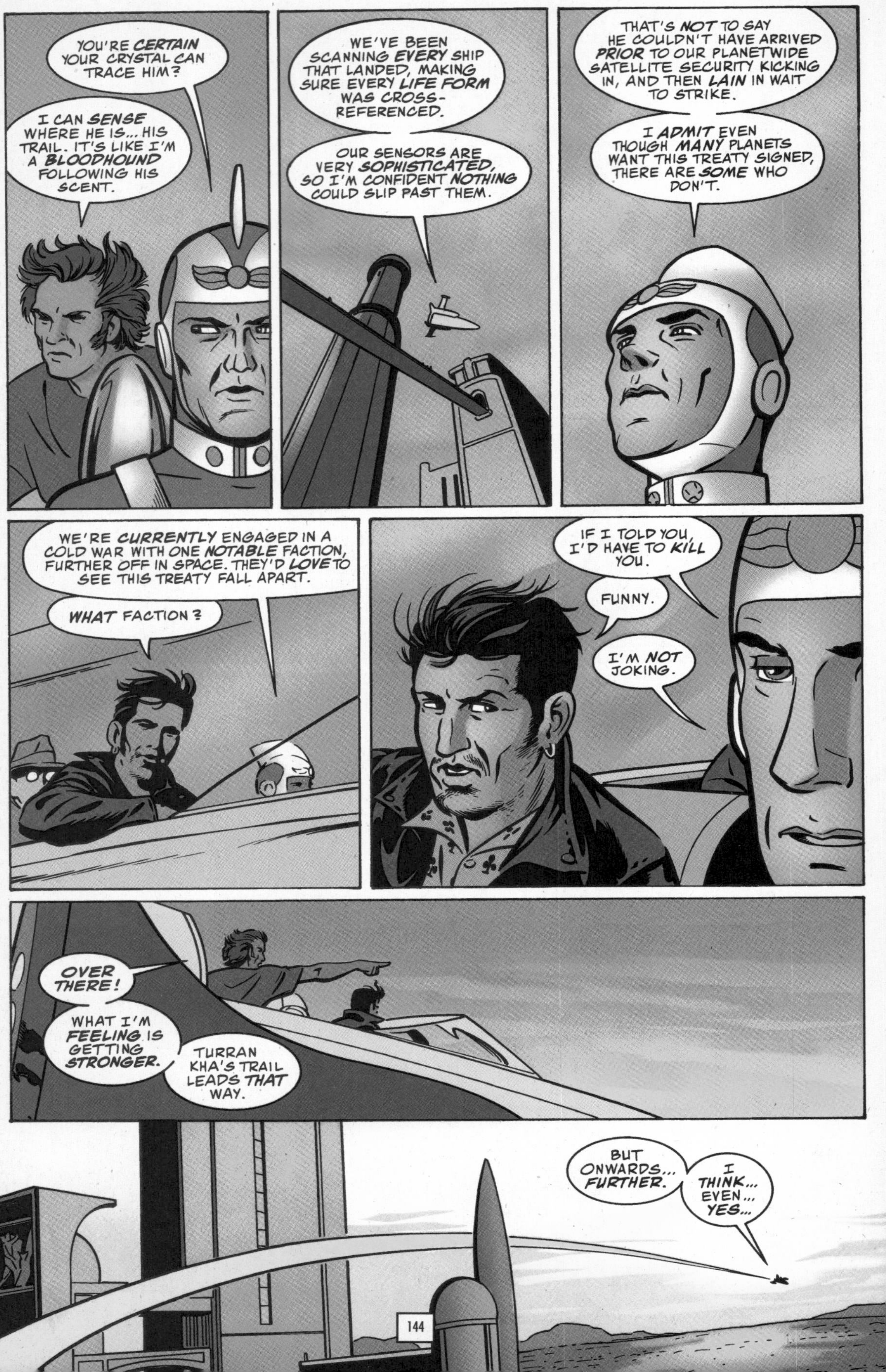
YOU'RE CERTAIN YOUR CRYSTAL CAN TRACE HIM?
I CAN SENSE WHERE HE IS... HIS TRAIL. IT'S LIKE I'M A BLOODHOUND FOLLOWING HIS SCENT.
WE'VE BEEN SCANNING EVERY SHIP THAT LANDED, MAKING SURE EVERY LIFE FORM WAS CROSS-REFERENCED.
OUR SENSORS ARE VERY SOPHISTICATED, SO I'M CONFIDENT NOTHING COULD SLIP PAST THEM.
THAT'S NOT TO SAY HE COULDN'T HAVE ARRIVED PRIOR TO OUR PLANETWIDE SATELLITE SECURITY KICKING IN, AND THEN LAIN IN WAIT TO STRIKE.
I ADMIT EVEN THOUGH MANY PLANETS WANT THIS TREATY SIGNED, THERE ARE SOME WHO DON'T.
WE'RE CURRENTLY ENGAGED IN A COLD WAR WITH ONE NOTABLE FACTION, FURTHER OFF IN SPACE. THEY'D LOVE TO SEE THIS TREATY FALL APART.
WHAT FACTION?
IF I TOLD YOU, I'D HAVE TO KILL YOU.
FUNNY.
I'M NOT JOKING.
OVER THERE!
WHAT I'M FEELING IS GETTING STRONGER.
TURRAN KHA'S TRAIL LEADS THAT WAY.
BUT ONWARDS... FURTHER.
I THINK... EVEN... YES...

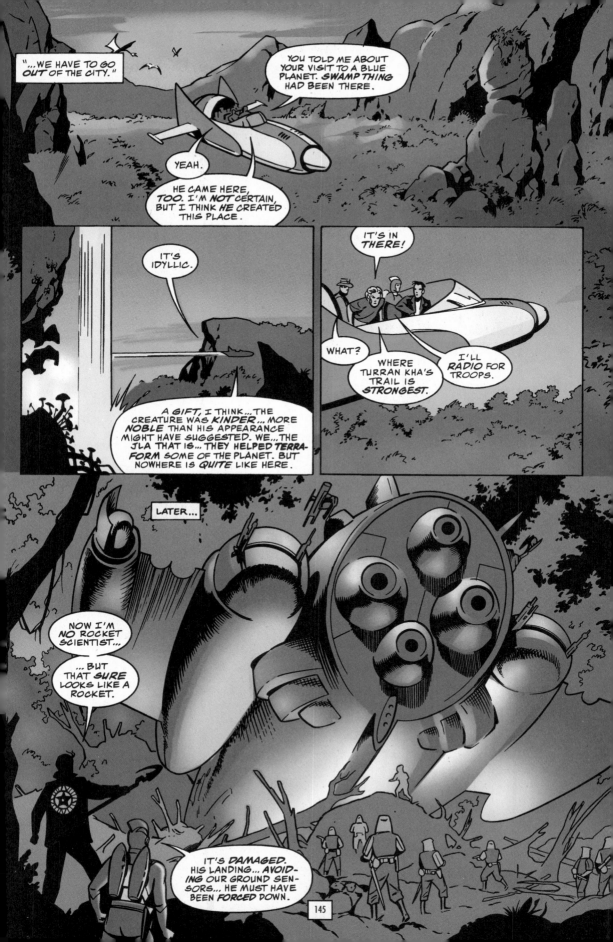

"...WE HAVE TO GO *OUT* OF THE CITY."

YOU TOLD ME ABOUT YOUR VISIT TO A BLUE PLANET. *SWAMP THING* HAD BEEN THERE.

YEAH.

HE CAME HERE, *TOO.* I'M *NOT* CERTAIN, BUT I THINK *HE CREATED* THIS PLACE.

IT'S *IDYLLIC.*

A *GIFT,* I THINK... THE CREATURE WAS *KINDER*... MORE *NOBLE* THAN HIS APPEARANCE MIGHT HAVE SUGGESTED. WE... THE JLA THAT IS... THEY HELPED *TERRA-FORM* SOME OF THE PLANET. BUT NOWHERE IS *QUITE* LIKE HERE.

IT'S IN *THERE!*

WHAT?

WHERE TURRAN KHA'S TRAIL IS *STRONGEST.*

I'LL *RADIO* FOR TROOPS.

LATER...

NOW I'M *NO ROCKET SCIENTIST*...

... BUT THAT *SURE* LOOKS LIKE A *ROCKET.*

IT'S *DAMAGED.* HIS LANDING... AVOID-ING OUR GROUND SEN-SORS... HE MUST HAVE BEEN *FORCED* DOWN.

145

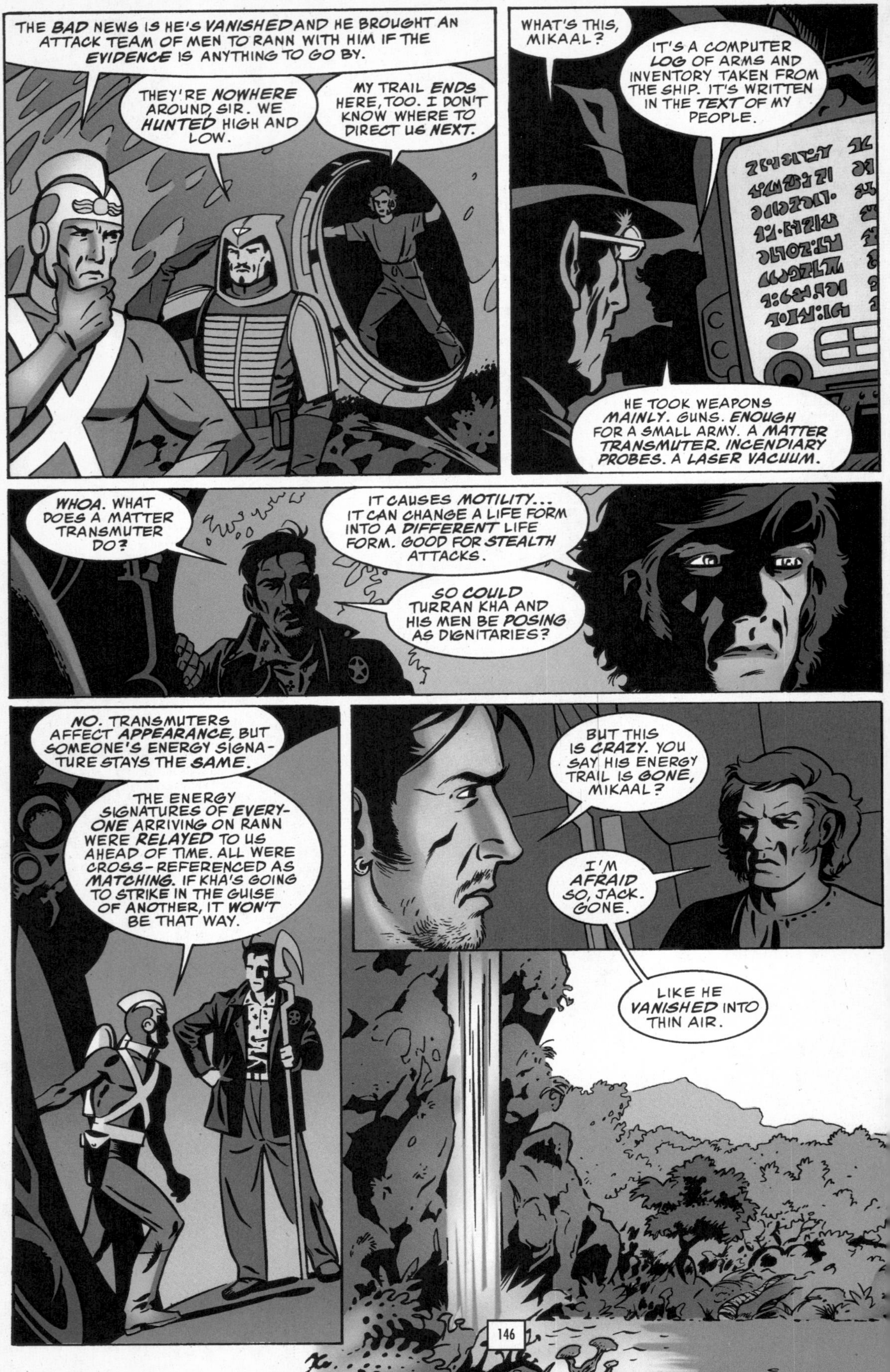
THE BAD NEWS IS HE'S VANISHED AND HE BROUGHT AN ATTACK TEAM OF MEN TO RANN WITH HIM IF THE EVIDENCE IS ANYTHING TO GO BY.
THEY'RE NOWHERE AROUND, SIR. WE HUNTED HIGH AND LOW.
MY TRAIL ENDS HERE, TOO. I DON'T KNOW WHERE TO DIRECT US NEXT.
WHAT'S THIS, MIKAAL?
IT'S A COMPUTER LOG OF ARMS AND INVENTORY TAKEN FROM THE SHIP. IT'S WRITTEN IN THE TEXT OF MY PEOPLE.
HE TOOK WEAPONS MAINLY. GUNS. ENOUGH FOR A SMALL ARMY. A MATTER TRANSMUTER. INCENDIARY PROBES. A LASER VACUUM.
WHOA. WHAT DOES A MATTER TRANSMUTER DO?
IT CAUSES MOTILITY... IT CAN CHANGE A LIFE FORM INTO A DIFFERENT LIFE FORM. GOOD FOR STEALTH ATTACKS.
SO COULD TURRAN KHA AND HIS MEN BE POSING AS DIGNITARIES?
NO. TRANSMUTERS AFFECT APPEARANCE, BUT SOMEONE'S ENERGY SIGNATURE STAYS THE SAME.
THE ENERGY SIGNATURES OF EVERYONE ARRIVING ON RANN WERE RELAYED TO US AHEAD OF TIME. ALL WERE CROSS-REFERENCED AS MATCHING. IF KHA'S GOING TO STRIKE IN THE GUISE OF ANOTHER, IT WON'T BE THAT WAY.
BUT THIS IS CRAZY. YOU SAY HIS ENERGY TRAIL IS GONE, MIKAAL?
I'M AFRAID SO, JACK. GONE.
LIKE HE VANISHED INTO THIN AIR.

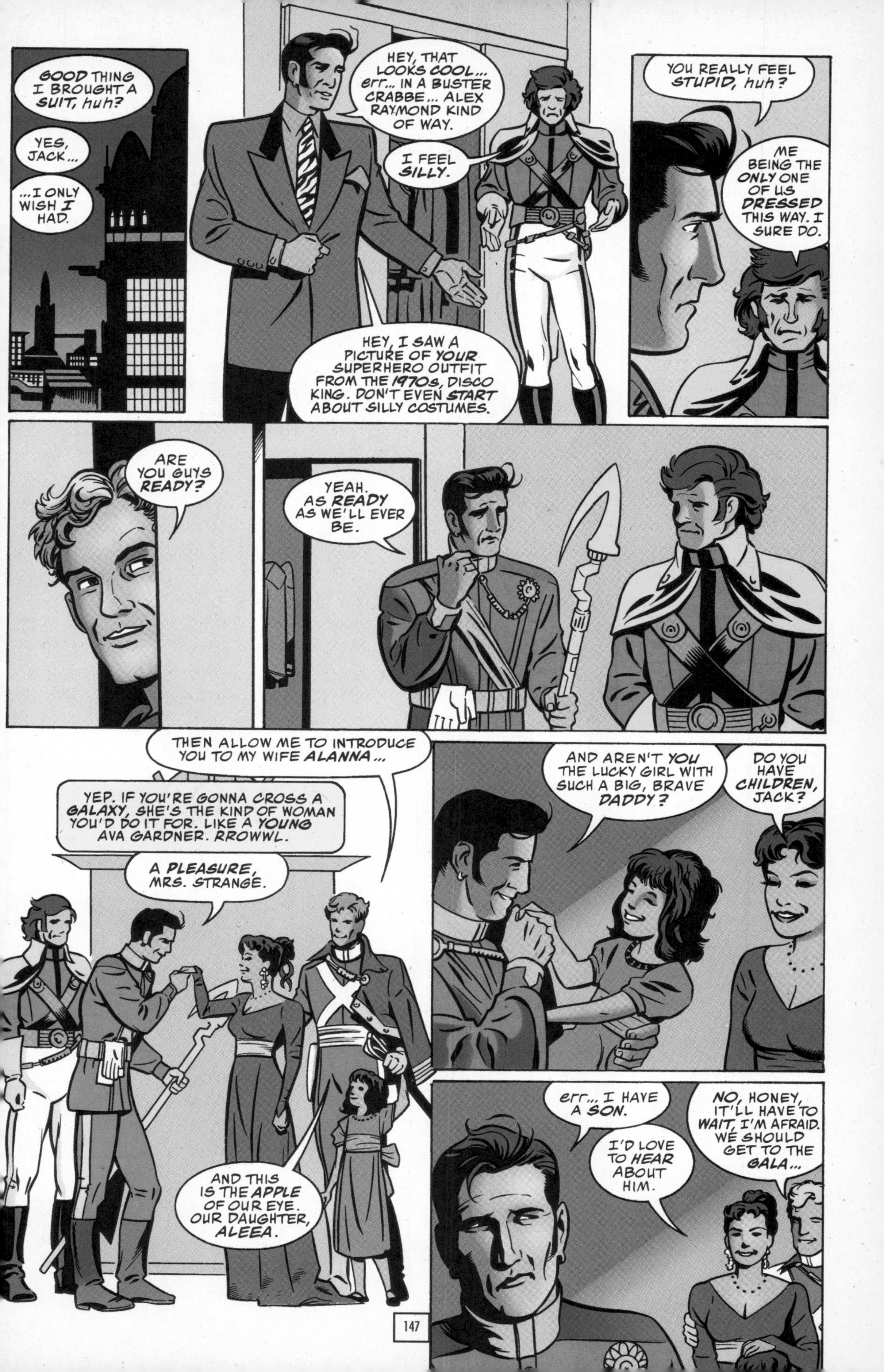
GOOD THING I BROUGHT A SUIT, huh?
YES, JACK...
...I ONLY WISH I HAD.
HEY, THAT LOOKS COOL... err... IN A BUSTER CRABBE... ALEX RAYMOND KIND OF WAY.
I FEEL SILLY.
HEY, I SAW A PICTURE OF YOUR SUPERHERO OUTFIT FROM THE 1970s, DISCO KING. DON'T EVEN START ABOUT SILLY COSTUMES.
YOU REALLY FEEL STUPID, huh?
ME BEING THE ONLY ONE OF US DRESSED THIS WAY. I SURE DO.
ARE YOU GUYS READY?
YEAH. AS READY AS WE'LL EVER BE.
THEN ALLOW ME TO INTRODUCE YOU TO MY WIFE ALANNA...
YEP. IF YOU'RE GONNA CROSS A GALAXY, SHE'S THE KIND OF WOMAN YOU'D DO IT FOR. LIKE A YOUNG AVA GARDNER. RROWWL.
A PLEASURE, MRS. STRANGE.
AND THIS IS THE APPLE OF OUR EYE. OUR DAUGHTER, ALEEA.
AND AREN'T YOU THE LUCKY GIRL WITH SUCH A BIG, BRAVE DADDY?
DO YOU HAVE CHILDREN, JACK?
err... I HAVE A SON.
I'D LOVE TO HEAR ABOUT HIM.
NO, HONEY, IT'LL HAVE TO WAIT, I'M AFRAID. WE SHOULD GET TO THE GALA...

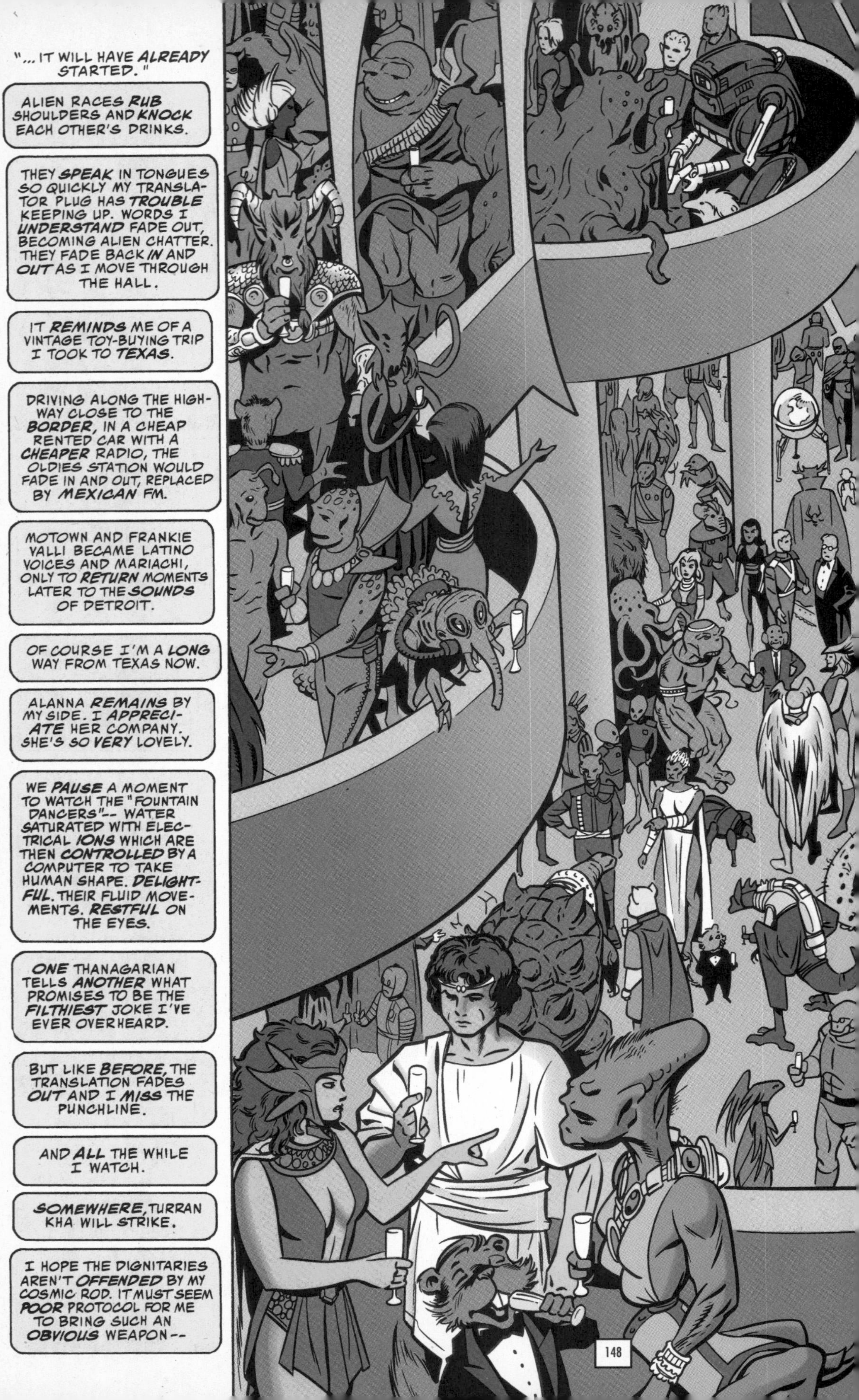
"... IT WILL HAVE ALREADY STARTED."
ALIEN RACES RUB SHOULDERS AND KNOCK EACH OTHER'S DRINKS.
THEY SPEAK IN TONGUES SO QUICKLY MY TRANSLATOR PLUG HAS TROUBLE KEEPING UP. WORDS I UNDERSTAND FADE OUT, BECOMING ALIEN CHATTER. THEY FADE BACK IN AND OUT AS I MOVE THROUGH THE HALL.
IT REMINDS ME OF A VINTAGE TOY-BUYING TRIP I TOOK TO TEXAS.
DRIVING ALONG THE HIGHWAY CLOSE TO THE BORDER, IN A CHEAP RENTED CAR WITH A CHEAPER RADIO, THE OLDIES STATION WOULD FADE IN AND OUT, REPLACED BY MEXICAN FM.
MOTOWN AND FRANKIE VALLI BECAME LATINO VOICES AND MARIACHI, ONLY TO RETURN MOMENTS LATER TO THE SOUNDS OF DETROIT.
OF COURSE I'M A LONG WAY FROM TEXAS NOW.
ALANNA REMAINS BY MY SIDE. I APPRECIATE HER COMPANY. SHE'S SO VERY LOVELY.
WE PAUSE A MOMENT TO WATCH THE "FOUNTAIN DANCERS"-- WATER SATURATED WITH ELECTRICAL IONS WHICH ARE THEN CONTROLLED BY A COMPUTER TO TAKE HUMAN SHAPE. DELIGHTFUL. THEIR FLUID MOVEMENTS. RESTFUL ON THE EYES.
ONE THANAGARIAN TELLS ANOTHER WHAT PROMISES TO BE THE FILTHIEST JOKE I'VE EVER OVERHEARD.
BUT LIKE BEFORE, THE TRANSLATION FADES OUT AND I MISS THE PUNCHLINE.
AND ALL THE WHILE I WATCH.
SOMEWHERE, TURRAN KHA WILL STRIKE.
I HOPE THE DIGNITARIES AREN'T OFFENDED BY MY COSMIC ROD. IT MUST SEEM POOR PROTOCOL FOR ME TO BRING SUCH AN OBVIOUS WEAPON--

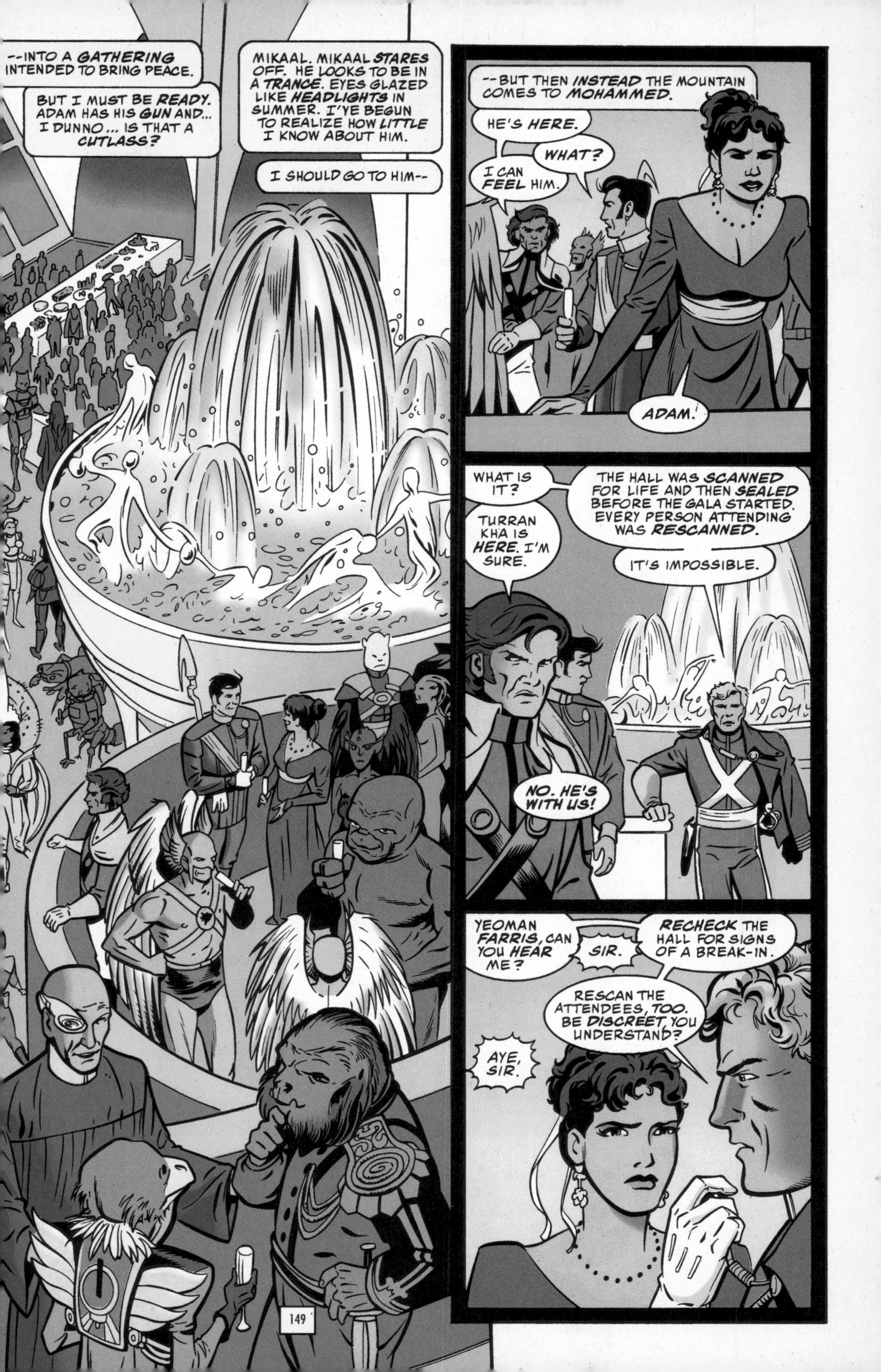
--INTO A GATHERING INTENDED TO BRING PEACE.
BUT I MUST BE READY. ADAM HAS HIS GUN AND... I DUNNO... IS THAT A CUTLASS?
MIKAAL. MIKAAL STARES OFF. HE LOOKS TO BE IN A TRANCE. EYES GLAZED LIKE HEADLIGHTS IN SUMMER. I'VE BEGUN TO REALIZE HOW LITTLE I KNOW ABOUT HIM.
I SHOULD GO TO HIM--
--BUT THEN INSTEAD THE MOUNTAIN COMES TO MOHAMMED.
HE'S HERE.
WHAT?
I CAN FEEL HIM.
ADAM!
WHAT IS IT?
THE HALL WAS SCANNED FOR LIFE AND THEN SEALED BEFORE THE GALA STARTED. EVERY PERSON ATTENDING WAS RESCANNED.
TURRAN KHA IS HERE. I'M SURE.
IT'S IMPOSSIBLE.
NO. HE'S WITH US!
YEOMAN FARRIS, CAN YOU HEAR ME?
SIR.
RECHECK THE HALL FOR SIGNS OF A BREAK-IN.
RESCAN THE ATTENDEES, TOO. BE DISCREET, YOU UNDERSTAND?
AYE, SIR.

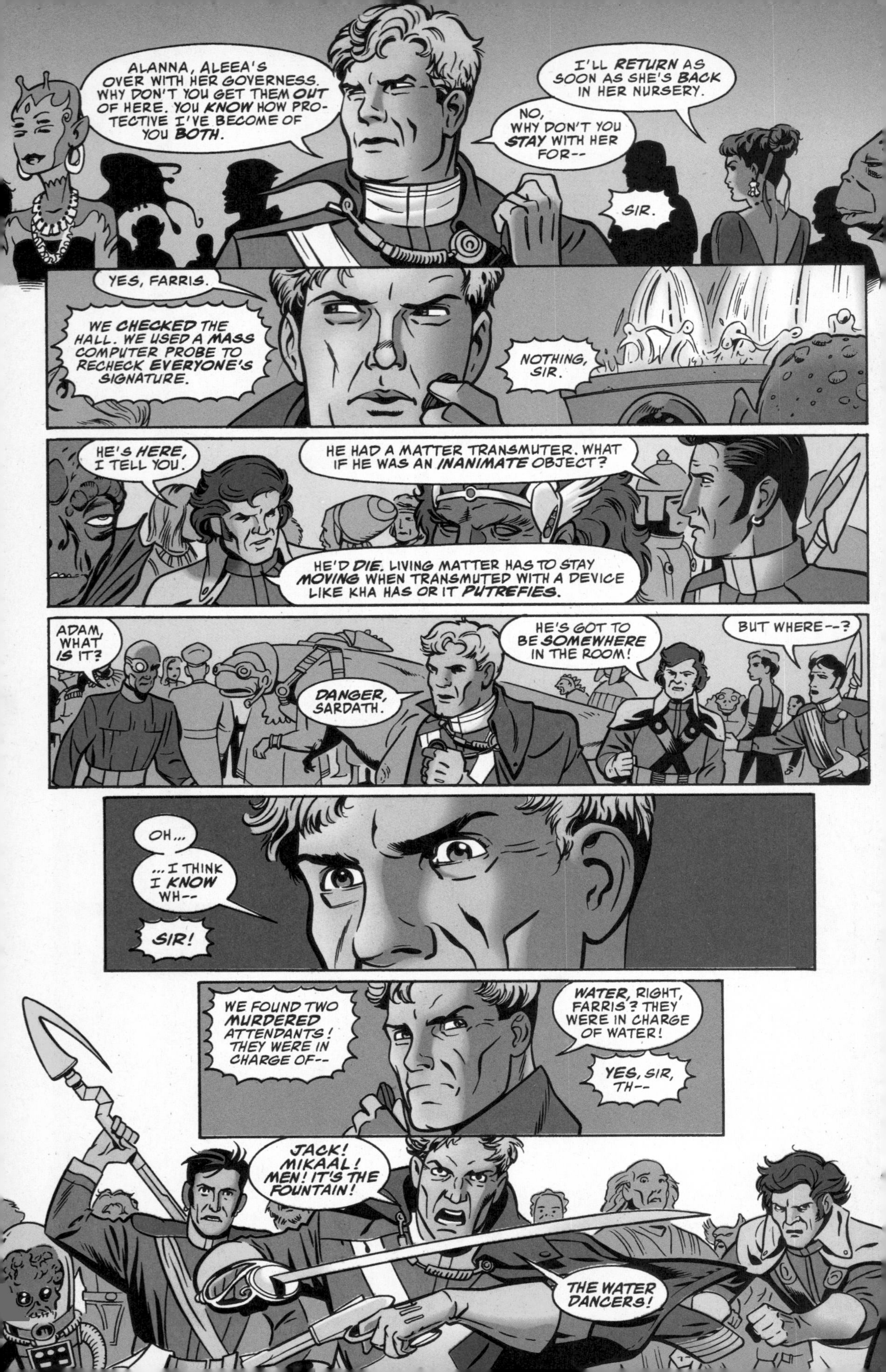
ALANNA, ALEEA'S OVER WITH HER GOVERNESS. WHY DON'T YOU GET THEM OUT OF HERE. YOU KNOW HOW PROTECTIVE I'VE BECOME OF YOU BOTH.
I'LL RETURN AS SOON AS SHE'S BACK IN HER NURSERY.
NO, WHY DON'T YOU STAY WITH HER FOR--
SIR.
YES, FARRIS.
WE CHECKED THE HALL. WE USED A MASS COMPUTER PROBE TO RECHECK EVERYONE'S SIGNATURE.
NOTHING, SIR.
HE'S HERE, I TELL YOU.
HE HAD A MATTER TRANSMUTER. WHAT IF HE WAS AN INANIMATE OBJECT?
HE'D DIE. LIVING MATTER HAS TO STAY MOVING WHEN TRANSMUTED WITH A DEVICE LIKE KHA HAS OR IT PUTREFIES.
ADAM, WHAT IS IT?
DANGER, SARDATH.
HE'S GOT TO BE SOMEWHERE IN THE ROOM!
BUT WHERE--?
OH...
...I THINK I KNOW WH--
SIR!
WE FOUND TWO MURDERED ATTENDANTS! THEY WERE IN CHARGE OF--
WATER, RIGHT, FARRIS? THEY WERE IN CHARGE OF WATER!
YES, SIR, TH--
JACK! MIKAAL! MEN! IT'S THE FOUNTAIN!
THE WATER DANCERS!

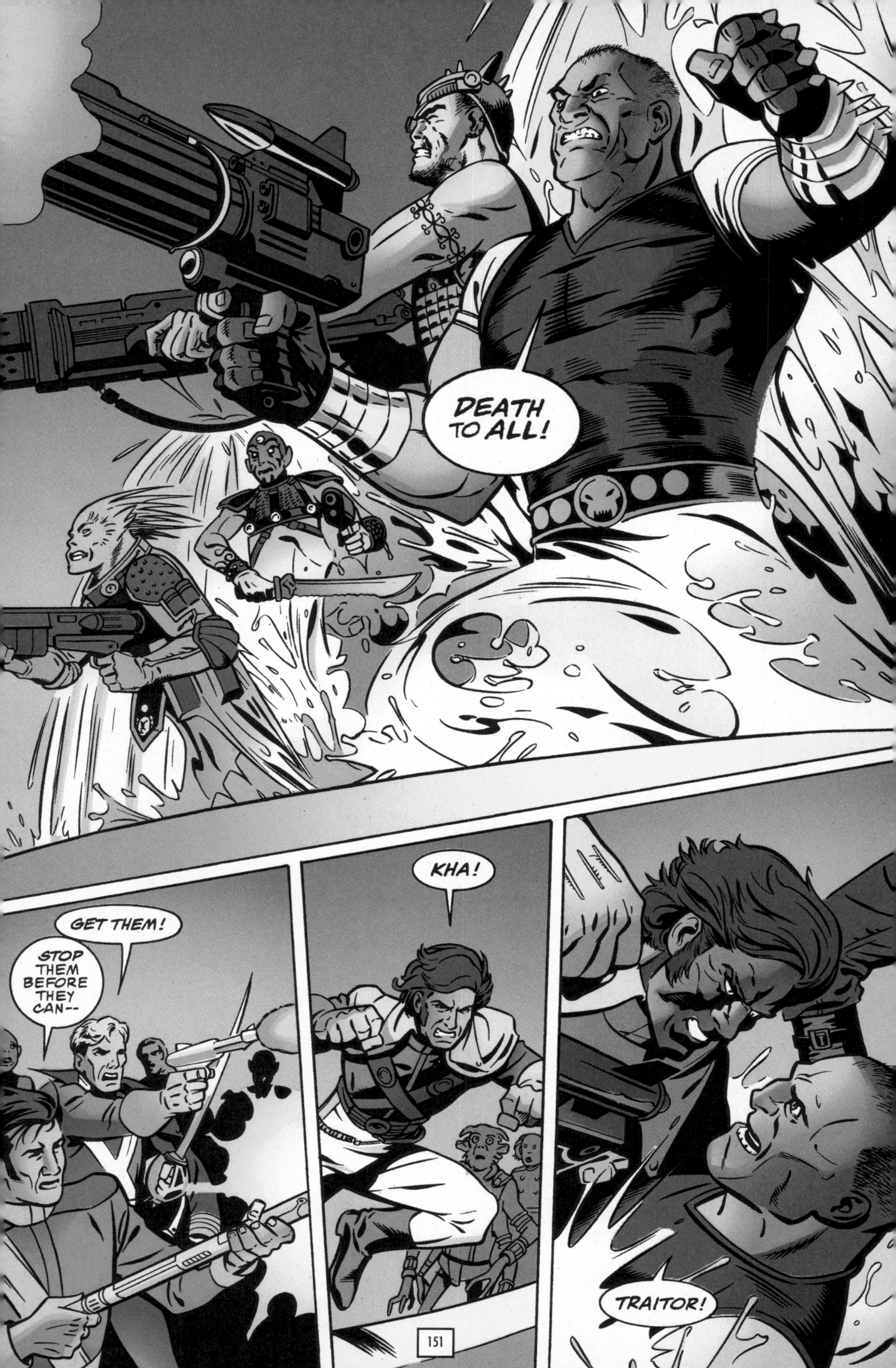

DEATH TO ALL!
GET THEM!
STOP THEM BEFORE THEY CAN--
KHA!
TRAITOR!

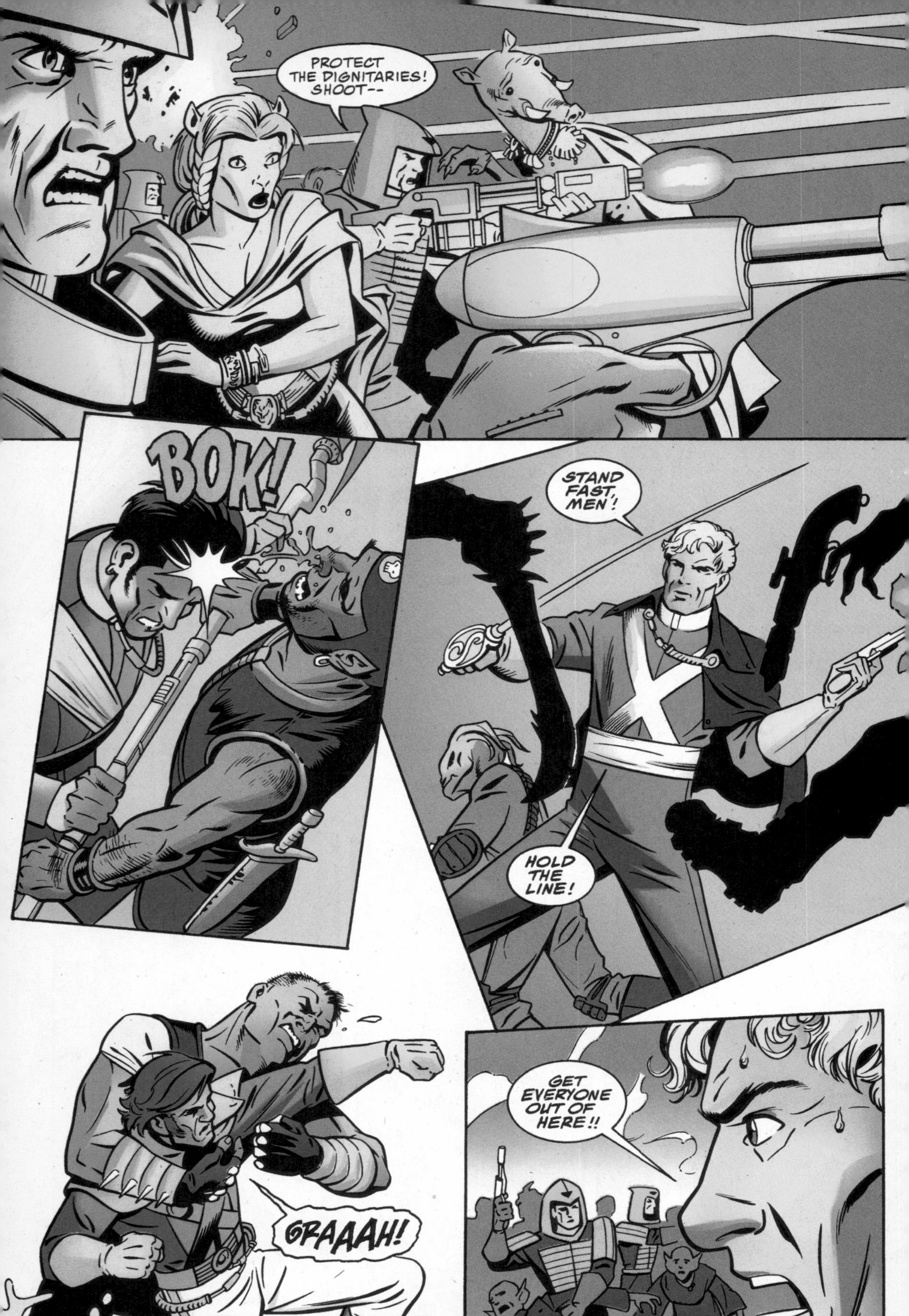

PROTECT THE DIGNITARIES! SHOOT--
BOK!
STAND FAST, MEN!
HOLD THE LINE!
GRAAAH!
GET EVERYONE OUT OF HERE!!

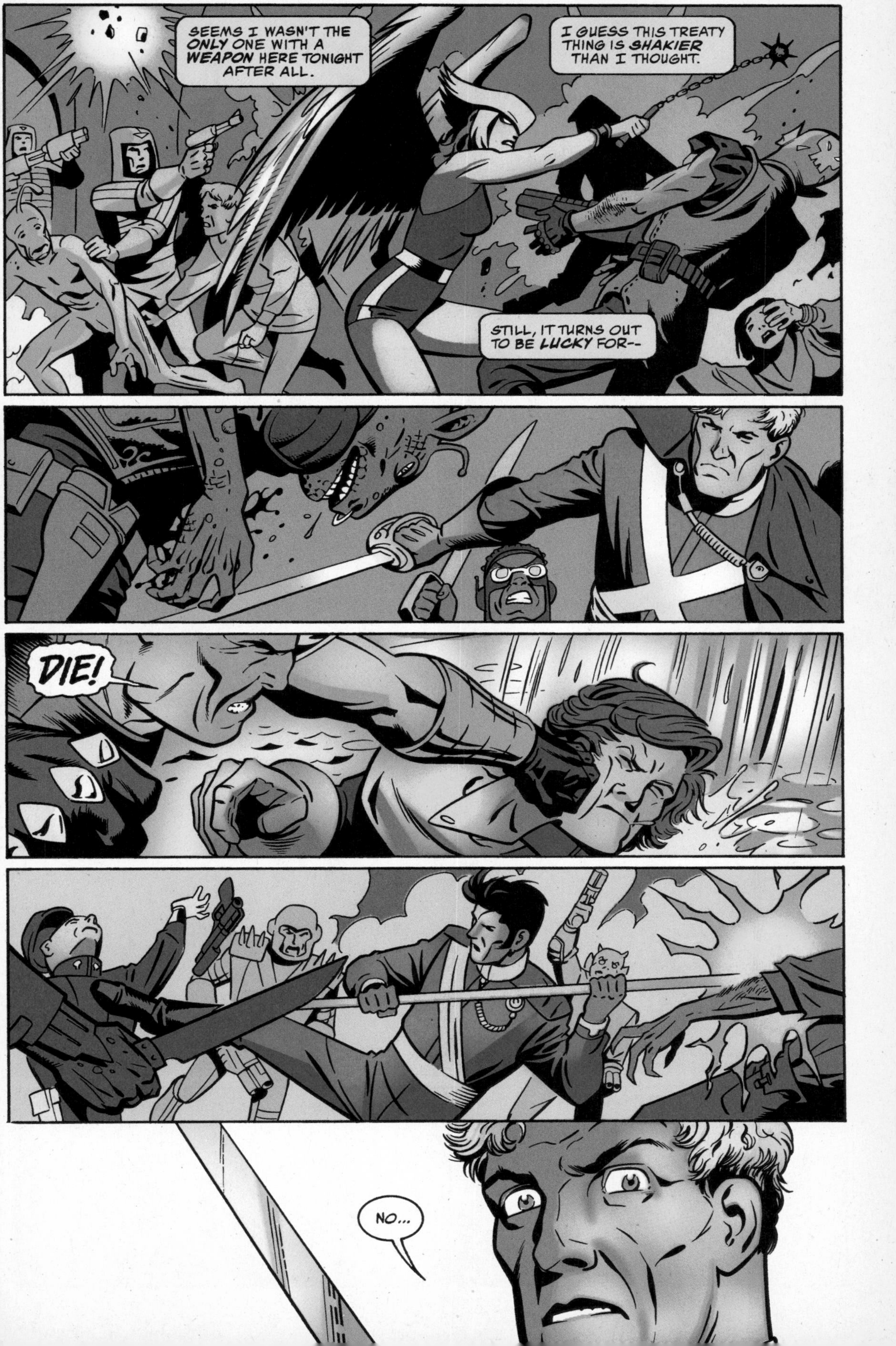
SEEMS I WASN'T THE ONLY ONE WITH A WEAPON HERE TONIGHT AFTER ALL.
I GUESS THIS TREATY THING IS SHAKIER THAN I THOUGHT.
STILL, IT TURNS OUT TO BE LUCKY FOR--
DIE!
NO...

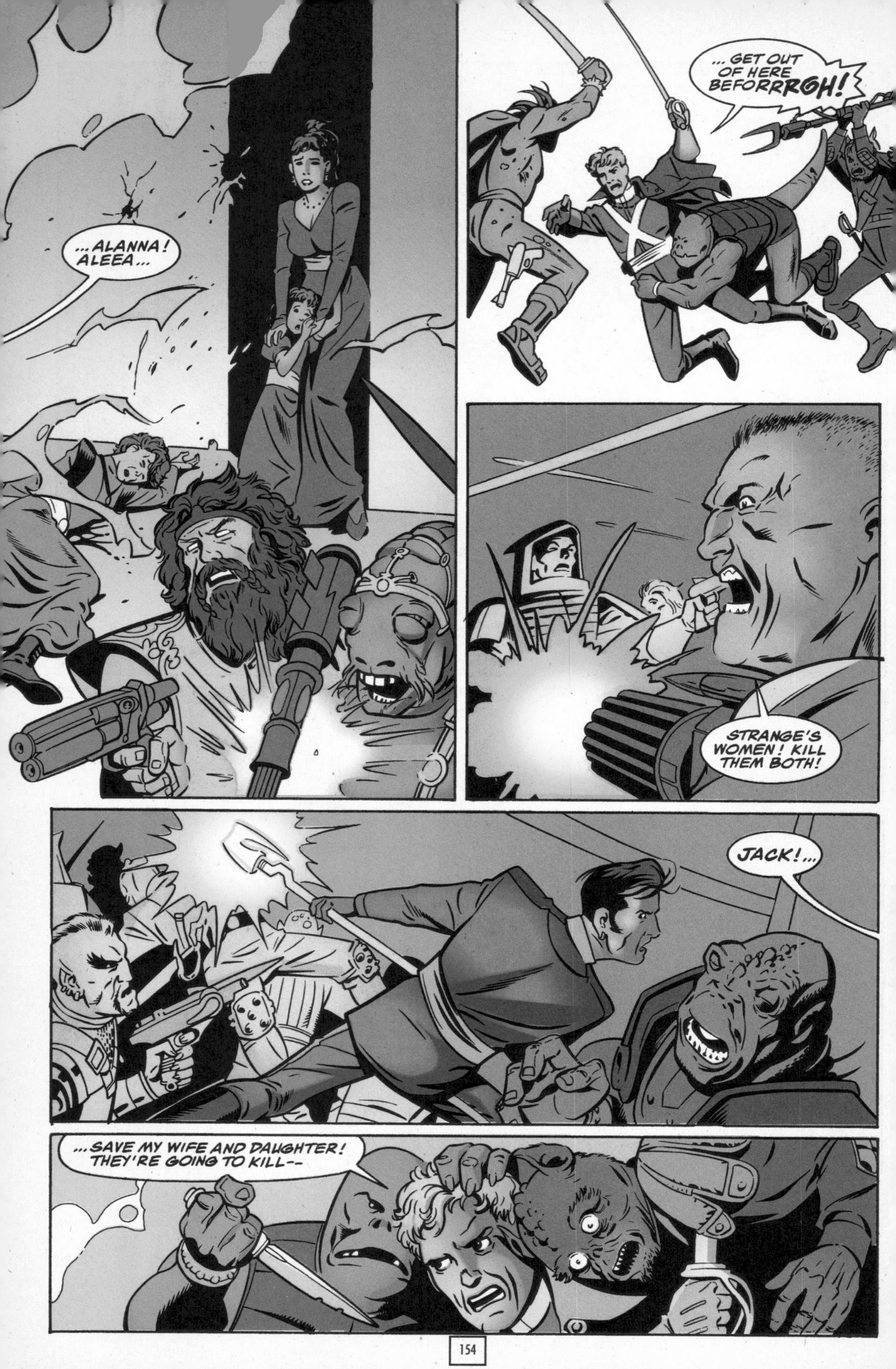
...ALANNA! ALEEA...
...GET OUT OF HERE BEFORRRGH!
STRANGE'S WOMEN! KILL THEM BOTH!
JACK!...
...SAVE MY WIFE AND DAUGHTER! THEY'RE GOING TO KILL--

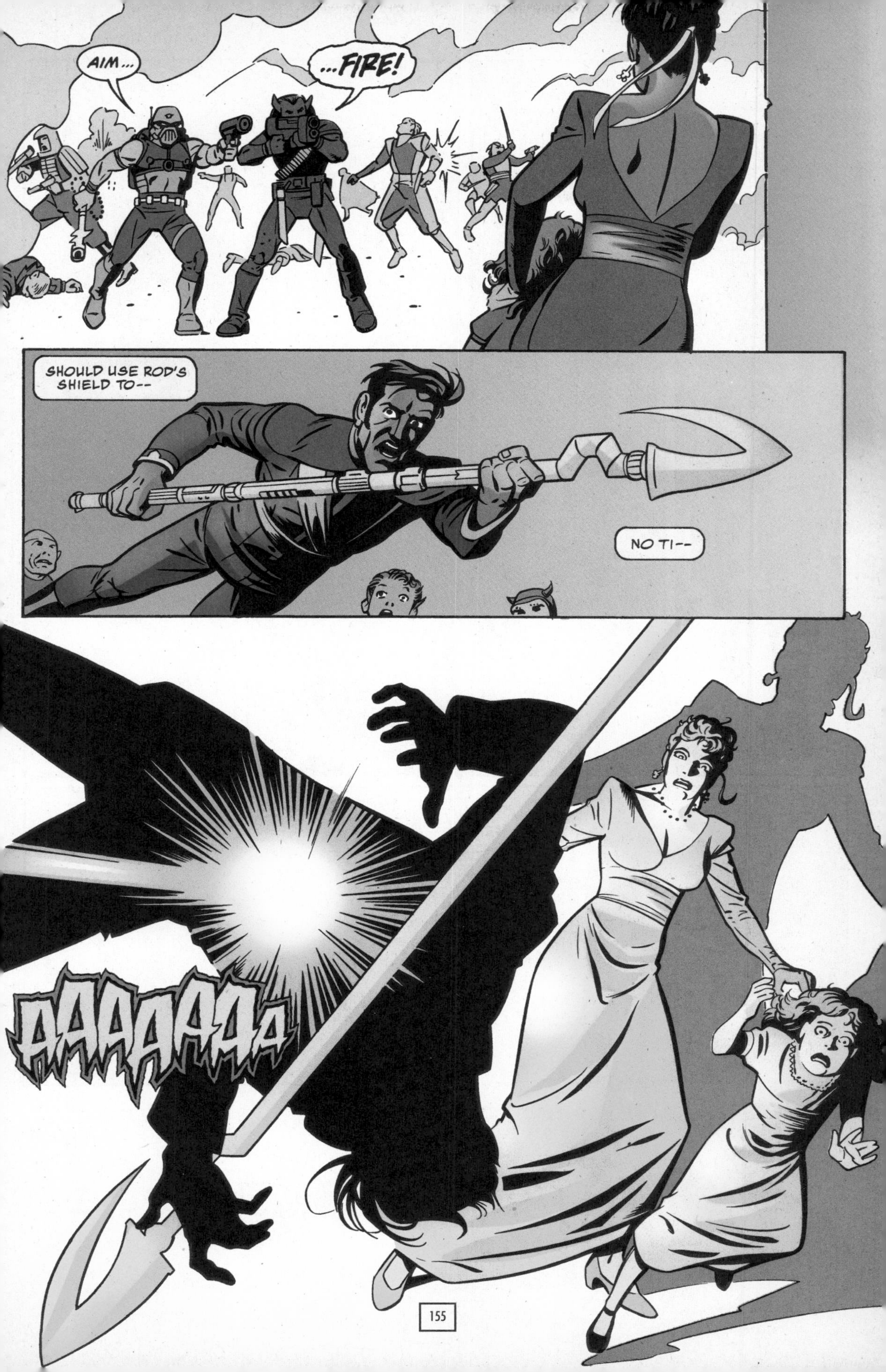
AIM...
...FIRE!
SHOULD USE ROD'S SHIELD TO--
NO TI--
AAAAAAA

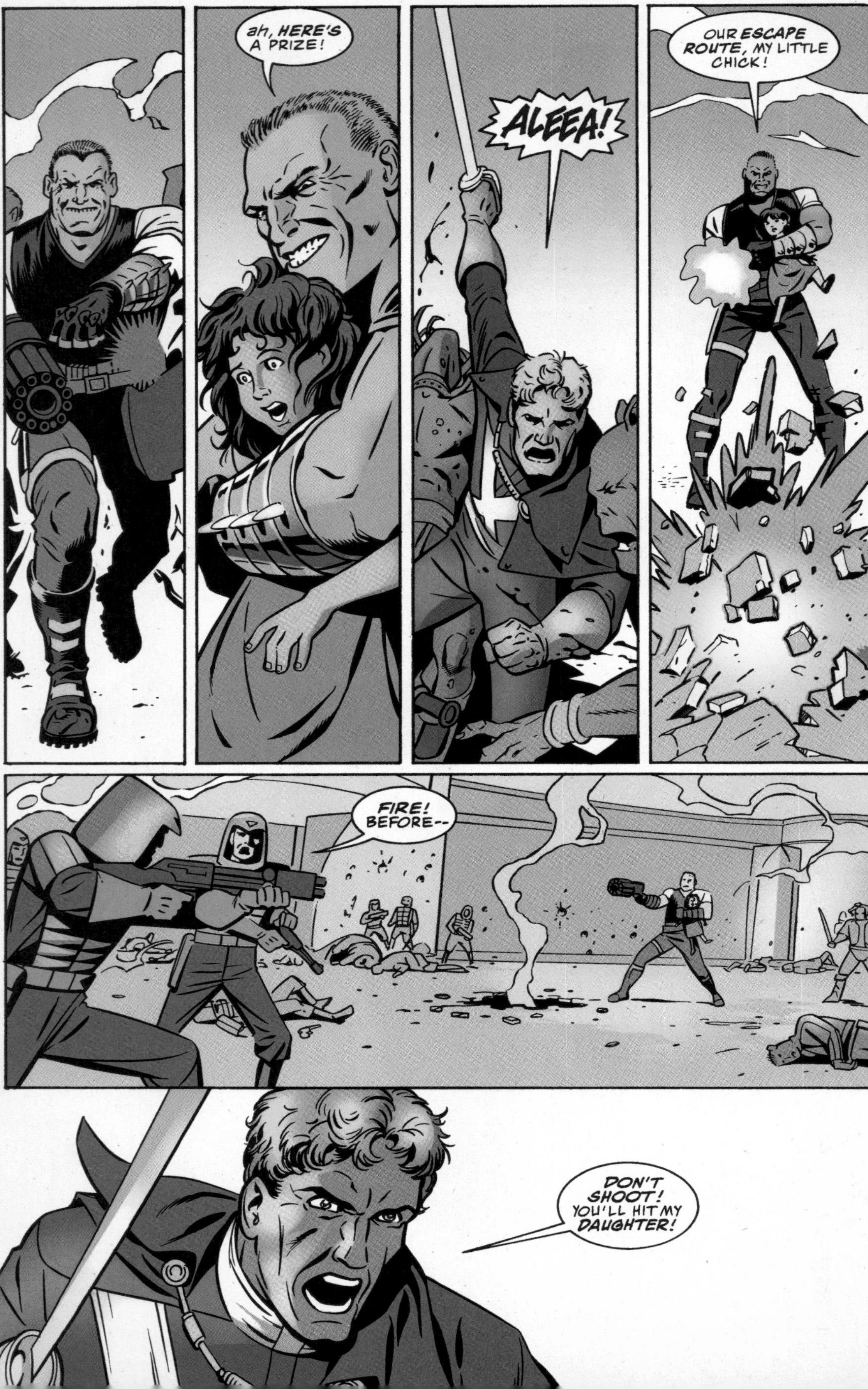
ah, HERE'S A PRIZE!
ALEEA!
OUR ESCAPE ROUTE, MY LITTLE CHICK!
FIRE! BEFORE--
DON'T SHOOT! YOU'LL HIT MY DAUGHTER!

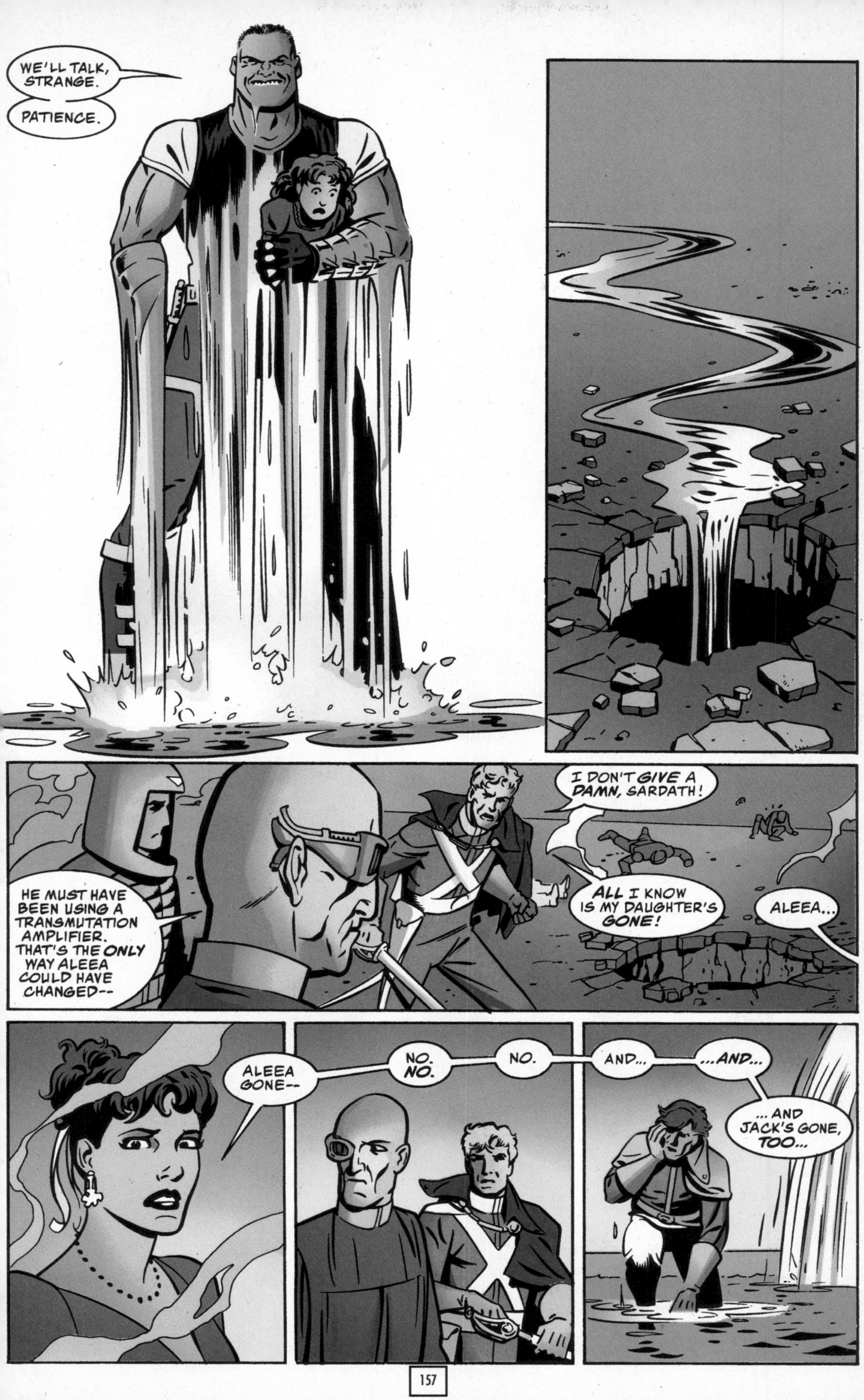
WE'LL TALK, STRANGE.
PATIENCE.
I DON'T GIVE A DAMN, SARDATH!
HE MUST HAVE BEEN USING A TRANSMUTATION AMPLIFIER. THAT'S THE ONLY WAY ALEEA COULD HAVE CHANGED--
ALL I KNOW IS MY DAUGHTER'S GONE!
ALEEA...
ALEEA GONE--
NO. NO.
NO.
AND...
...AND...
...AND JACK'S GONE, TOO...

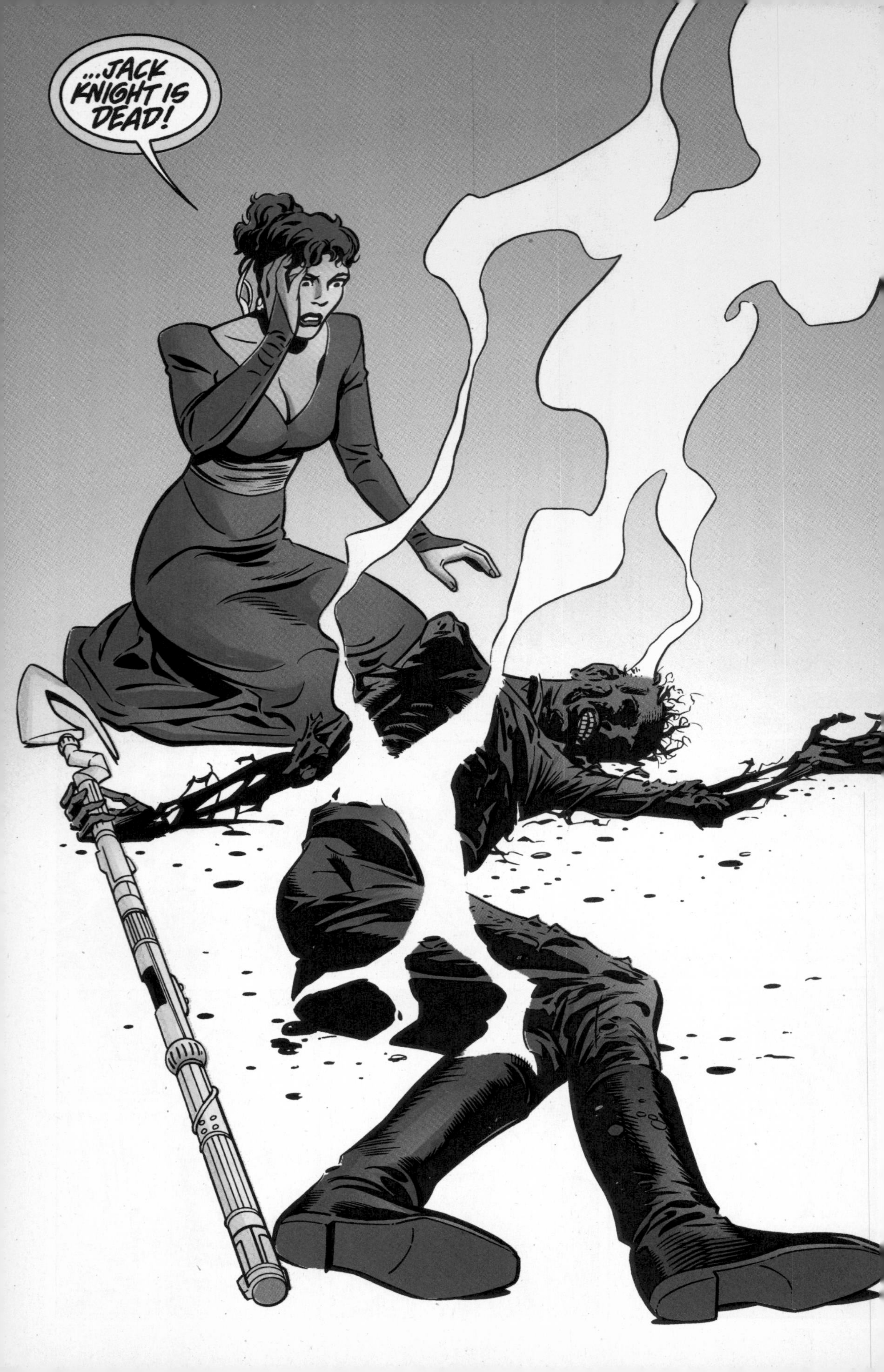
...JACK KNIGHT IS DEAD!

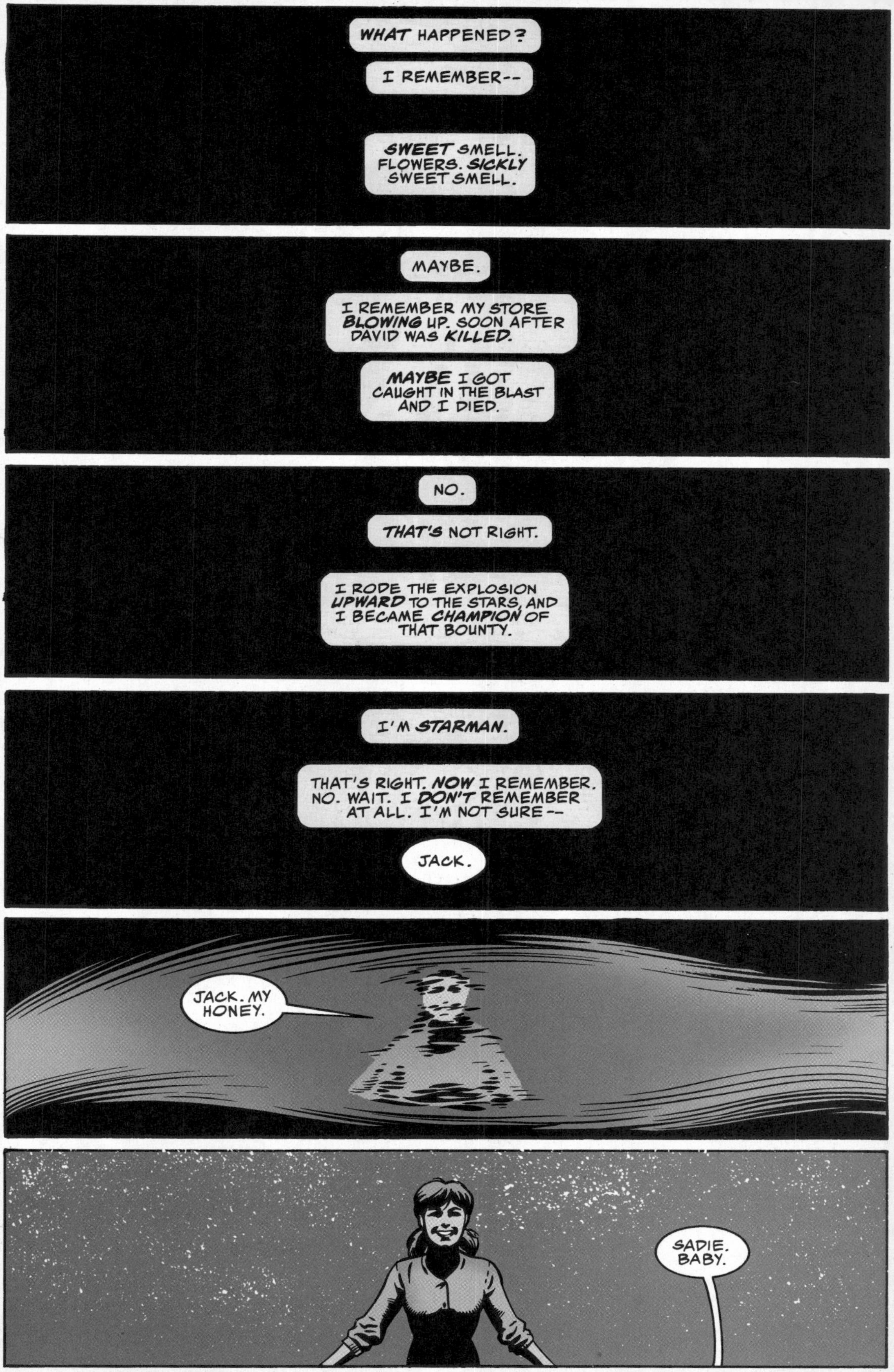
WHAT HAPPENED?
I REMEMBER--
SWEET SMELL. FLOWERS. SICKLY SWEET SMELL.
MAYBE.
I REMEMBER MY STORE BLOWING UP. SOON AFTER DAVID WAS KILLED.
MAYBE I GOT CAUGHT IN THE BLAST AND I DIED.
NO.
THAT'S NOT RIGHT.
I RODE THE EXPLOSION UPWARD TO THE STARS, AND I BECAME CHAMPION OF THAT BOUNTY.
I'M STARMAN.
THAT'S RIGHT. NOW I REMEMBER. NO. WAIT. I DON'T REMEMBER AT ALL. I'M NOT SURE--
JACK.
JACK. MY HONEY.
SADIE. BABY.

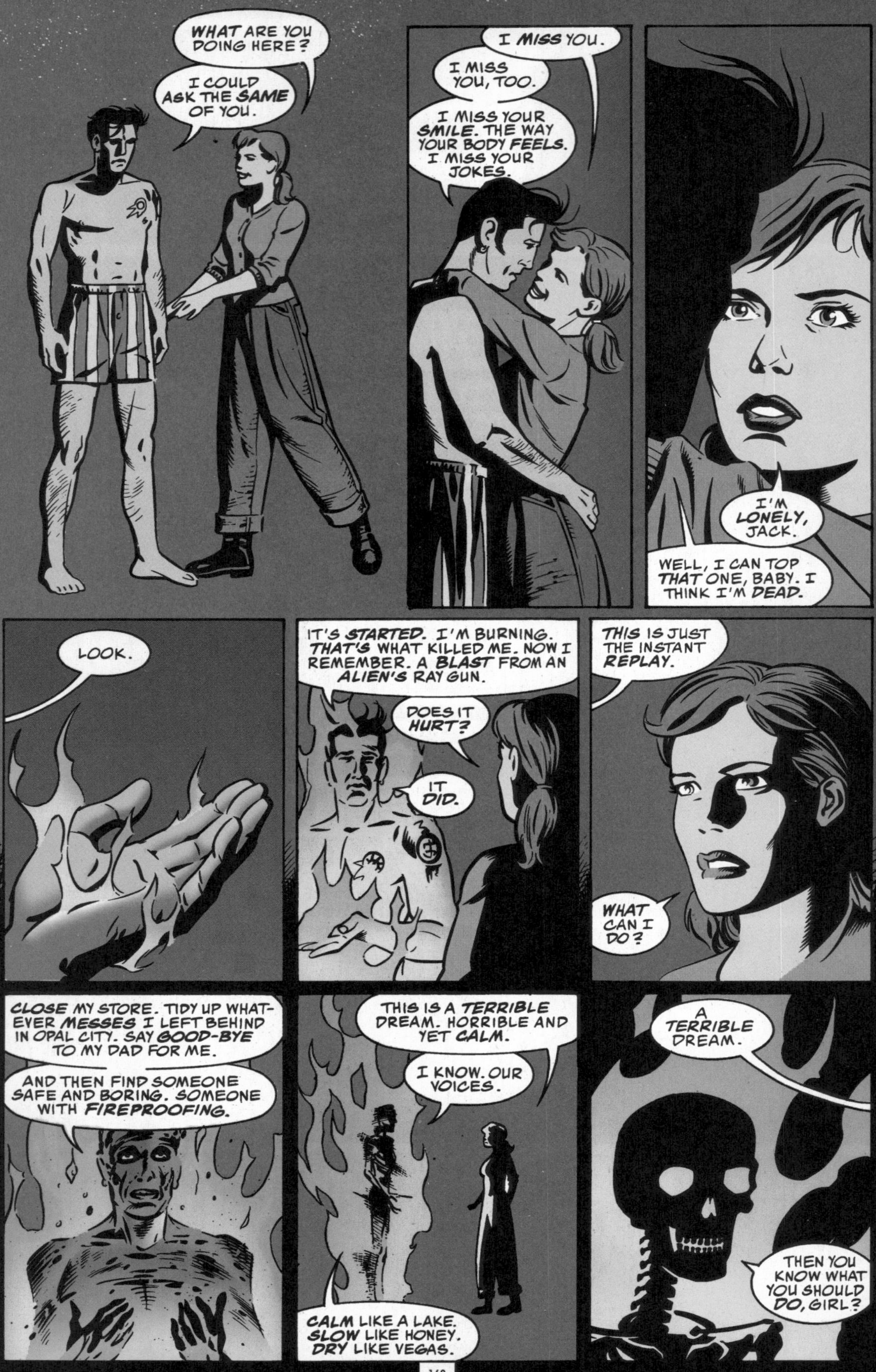
WHAT ARE YOU DOING HERE?
I COULD ASK THE SAME OF YOU.
I MISS YOU.
I MISS YOU, TOO.
I MISS YOUR SMILE. THE WAY YOUR BODY FEELS. I MISS YOUR JOKES.
I'M LONELY, JACK.
WELL, I CAN TOP THAT ONE, BABY. I THINK I'M DEAD.
LOOK.
IT'S STARTED. I'M BURNING. THAT'S WHAT KILLED ME. NOW I REMEMBER. A BLAST FROM AN ALIEN'S RAY GUN.
DOES IT HURT?
IT DID.
THIS IS JUST THE INSTANT REPLAY.
WHAT CAN I DO?
CLOSE MY STORE. TIDY UP WHATEVER MESSES I LEFT BEHIND IN OPAL CITY. SAY GOOD-BYE TO MY DAD FOR ME.
AND THEN FIND SOMEONE SAFE AND BORING. SOMEONE WITH FIREPROOFING.
THIS IS A TERRIBLE DREAM. HORRIBLE AND YET CALM.
I KNOW. OUR VOICES.
CALM LIKE A LAKE. SLOW LIKE HONEY. DRY LIKE VEGAS.
A TERRIBLE DREAM.
THEN YOU KNOW WHAT YOU SHOULD DO, GIRL?

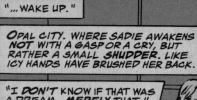

"...WAKE UP."

OPAL CITY. WHERE SADIE AWAKENS NOT WITH A GASP OR A CRY, BUT RATHER A SMALL *SHUDDER.* LIKE ICY HANDS HAVE BRUSHED HER BACK.

"I DON'T KNOW IF THAT WAS A DREAM. MERELY THAT," SHE THINKS. "OR DID I *JUST* LEARN THE MAN I LOVE IS *DEAD?*"

WHAT HAPPENED?

OH, YEAH. NOW I REMEMBER.

LIKE I TOLD SADIE.

ALIENS WITH RAY GUNS FIRED AT *ALANNA STRANGE.* I GOT IN THE WAY...

"NO," SHE THINKS THEN. "NO. I'D KNOW. JUST LIKE I KNOW MY BROTHER *WILL* IS STILL ALIVE. MY LOVE CAN'T BE DEAD. NOT HIM. NOT MY JACK.

"BUT SOMETHING HE SAID IN THE DREAM. HIS MESSES. I SHOULD TIDY UP HIS MESSES.

"I'VE BEEN DOING NOTHING THIS WHOLE TIME. ALL THIS TIME WHILE JACK... JACK..."

...AND I DIED.

FINITO.

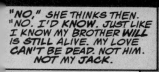

NERVOUS FINGERS DIAL...

CHARITY? HI.

YEAH, IT'S LATE. I'M *SORRY* TO WAKE YOU. I NEED YOUR HELP. I NEED YOU TO CONTACT SOME- ONE.

NO, I CAN'T USE THE YELLOW PAGES.

NOT UNLESS THE *DEAD* HAVE THEIR OWN EDITION.

END OF...

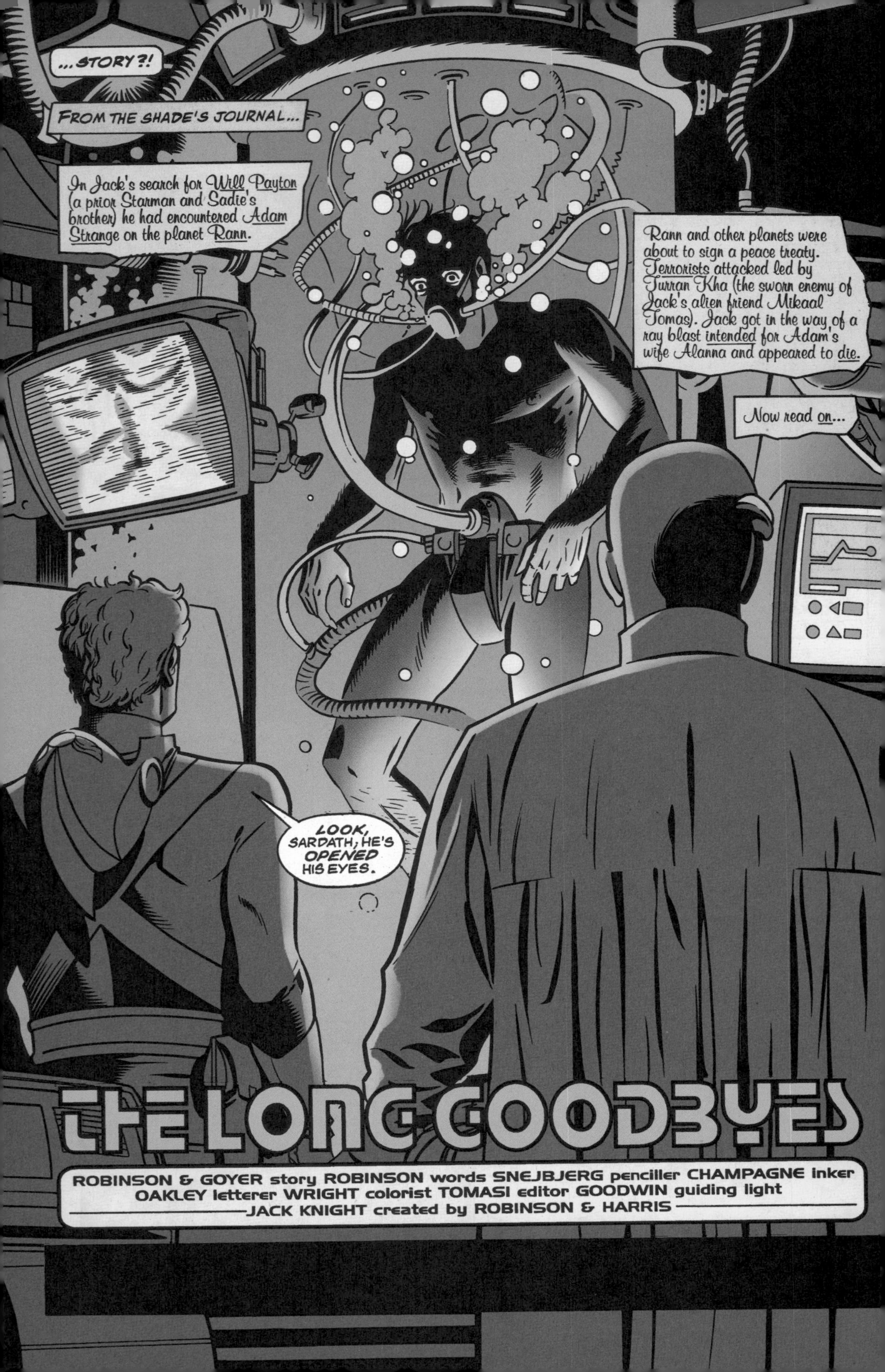
...STORY?!
FROM THE SHADE'S JOURNAL...
In Jack's search for Will Payton (a prior Starman and Sadie's brother) he had encountered Adam Strange on the planet Rann.
Rann and other planets were about to sign a peace treaty. Terrorists attacked led by Turran Kha (the sworn enemy of Jack's alien friend Mikaal Tomas). Jack got in the way of a ray blast intended for Adam's wife Alanna and appeared to die.
Now read on...
LOOK, SARDATH, HE'S OPENED HIS EYES.
THE LONG GOODBYES
ROBINSON & GOYER story ROBINSON words SNEJBJERG penciller CHAMPAGNE inker OAKLEY letterer WRIGHT colorist TOMASI editor GOODWIN guiding light
JACK KNIGHT created by ROBINSON & HARRIS

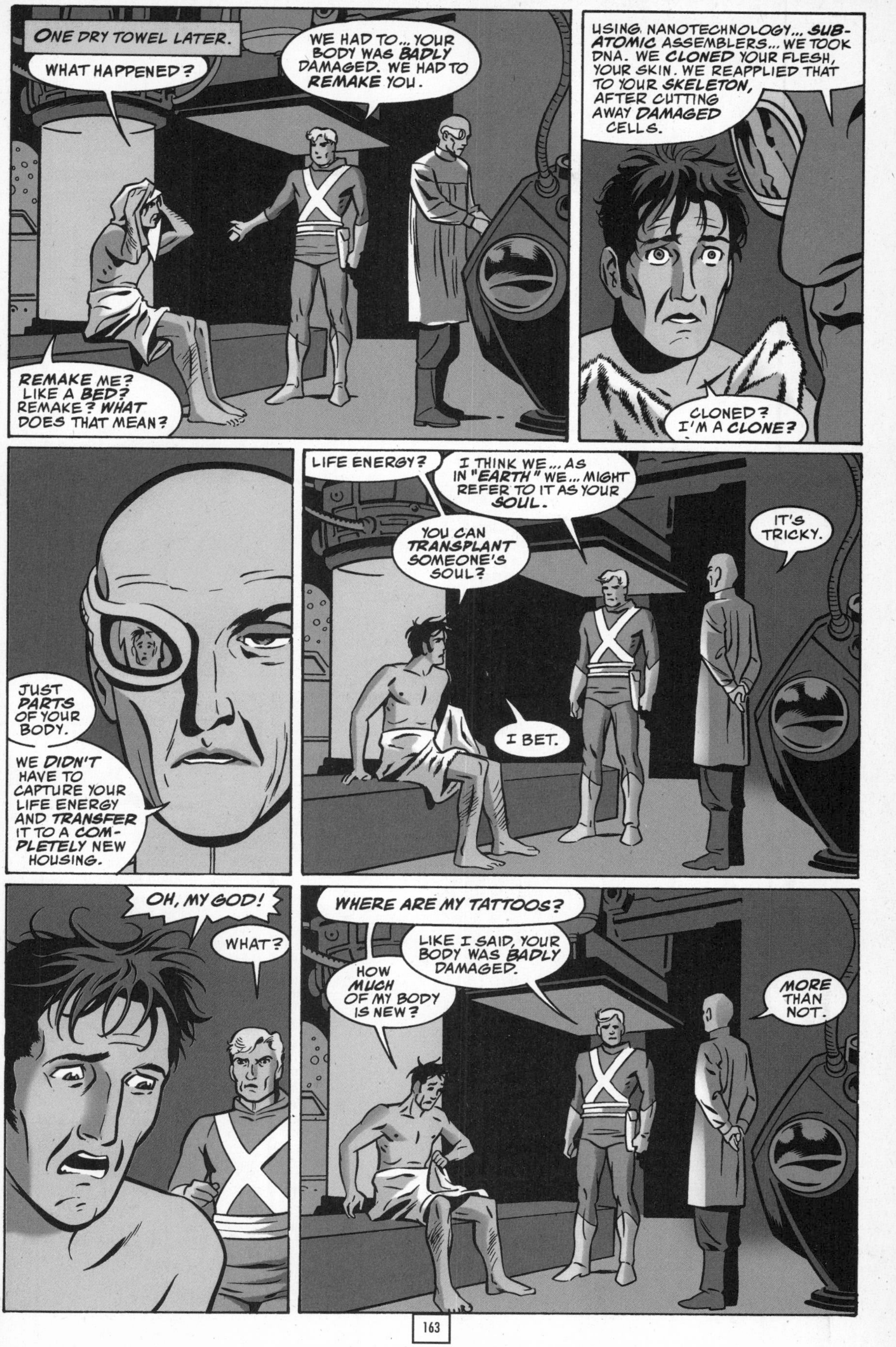
ONE DRY TOWEL LATER.
WHAT HAPPENED?
WE HAD TO... YOUR BODY WAS BADLY DAMAGED. WE HAD TO REMAKE YOU.
REMAKE ME? LIKE A BED? REMAKE? WHAT DOES THAT MEAN?
USING NANOTECHNOLOGY... SUB-ATOMIC ASSEMBLERS... WE TOOK DNA. WE CLONED YOUR FLESH, YOUR SKIN. WE REAPPLIED THAT TO YOUR SKELETON, AFTER CUTTING AWAY DAMAGED CELLS.
CLONED? I'M A CLONE?
JUST PARTS OF YOUR BODY.
WE DIDN'T HAVE TO CAPTURE YOUR LIFE ENERGY AND TRANSFER IT TO A COM-PLETELY NEW HOUSING.
LIFE ENERGY?
I THINK WE... AS IN "EARTH" WE... MIGHT REFER TO IT AS YOUR SOUL.
YOU CAN TRANSPLANT SOMEONE'S SOUL?
IT'S TRICKY.
I BET.
OH, MY GOD!
WHAT?
WHERE ARE MY TATTOOS?
LIKE I SAID, YOUR BODY WAS BADLY DAMAGED.
HOW MUCH OF MY BODY IS NEW?
MORE THAN NOT.

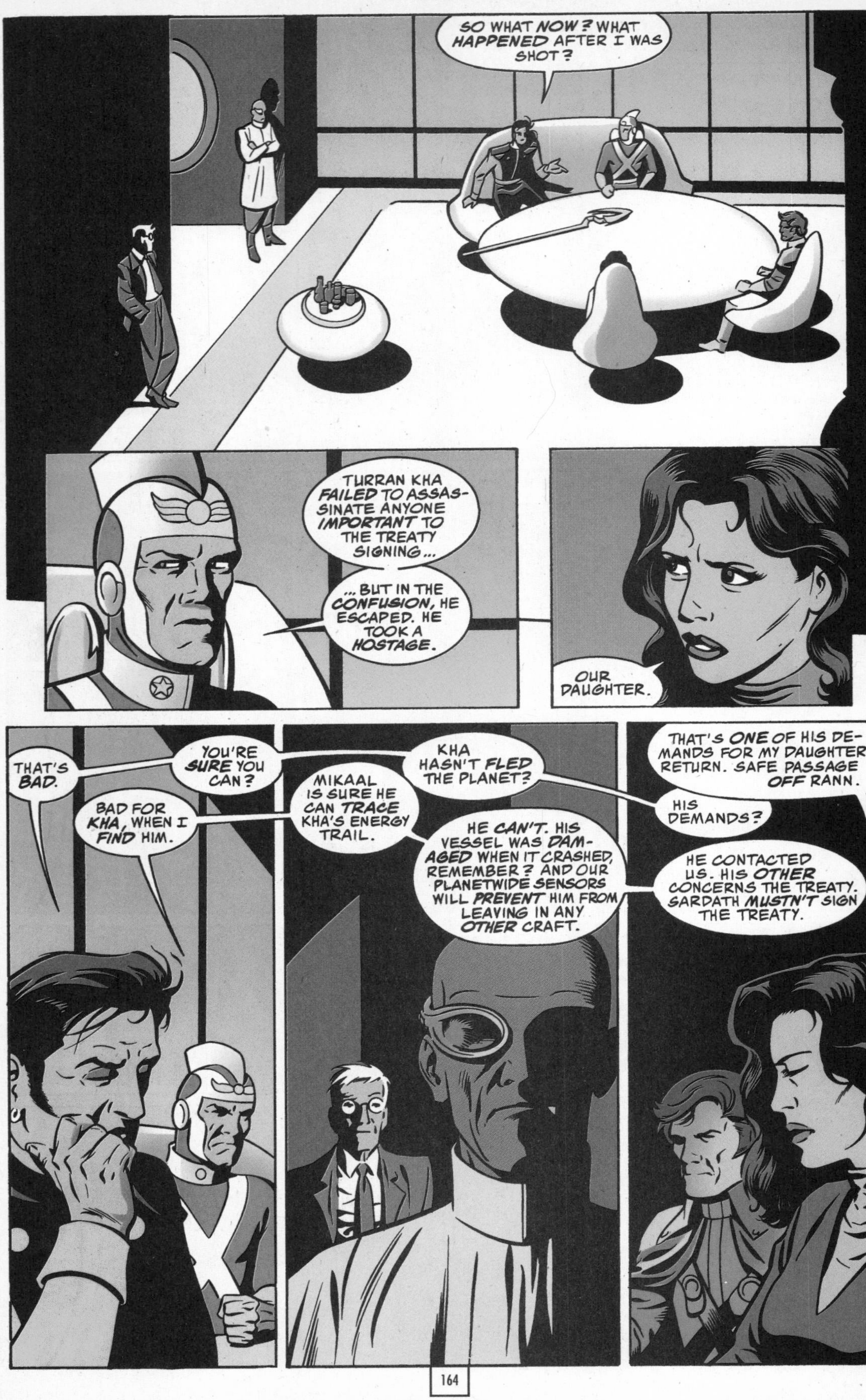
SO WHAT NOW? WHAT HAPPENED AFTER I WAS SHOT?
TURRAN KHA FAILED TO ASSASSINATE ANYONE IMPORTANT TO THE TREATY SIGNING...
...BUT IN THE CONFUSION, HE ESCAPED. HE TOOK A HOSTAGE.
OUR DAUGHTER.
THAT'S BAD.
YOU'RE SURE YOU CAN?
BAD FOR KHA, WHEN I FIND HIM.
MIKAAL IS SURE HE CAN TRACE KHA'S ENERGY TRAIL.
KHA HASN'T FLED THE PLANET?
HE CAN'T. HIS VESSEL WAS DAMAGED WHEN IT CRASHED, REMEMBER? AND OUR PLANETWIDE SENSORS WILL PREVENT HIM FROM LEAVING IN ANY OTHER CRAFT.
HIS DEMANDS?
THAT'S ONE OF HIS DEMANDS FOR MY DAUGHTER'S RETURN. SAFE PASSAGE OFF RANN.
HE CONTACTED US. HIS OTHER CONCERNS THE TREATY. SARDATH MUSTN'T SIGN THE TREATY.

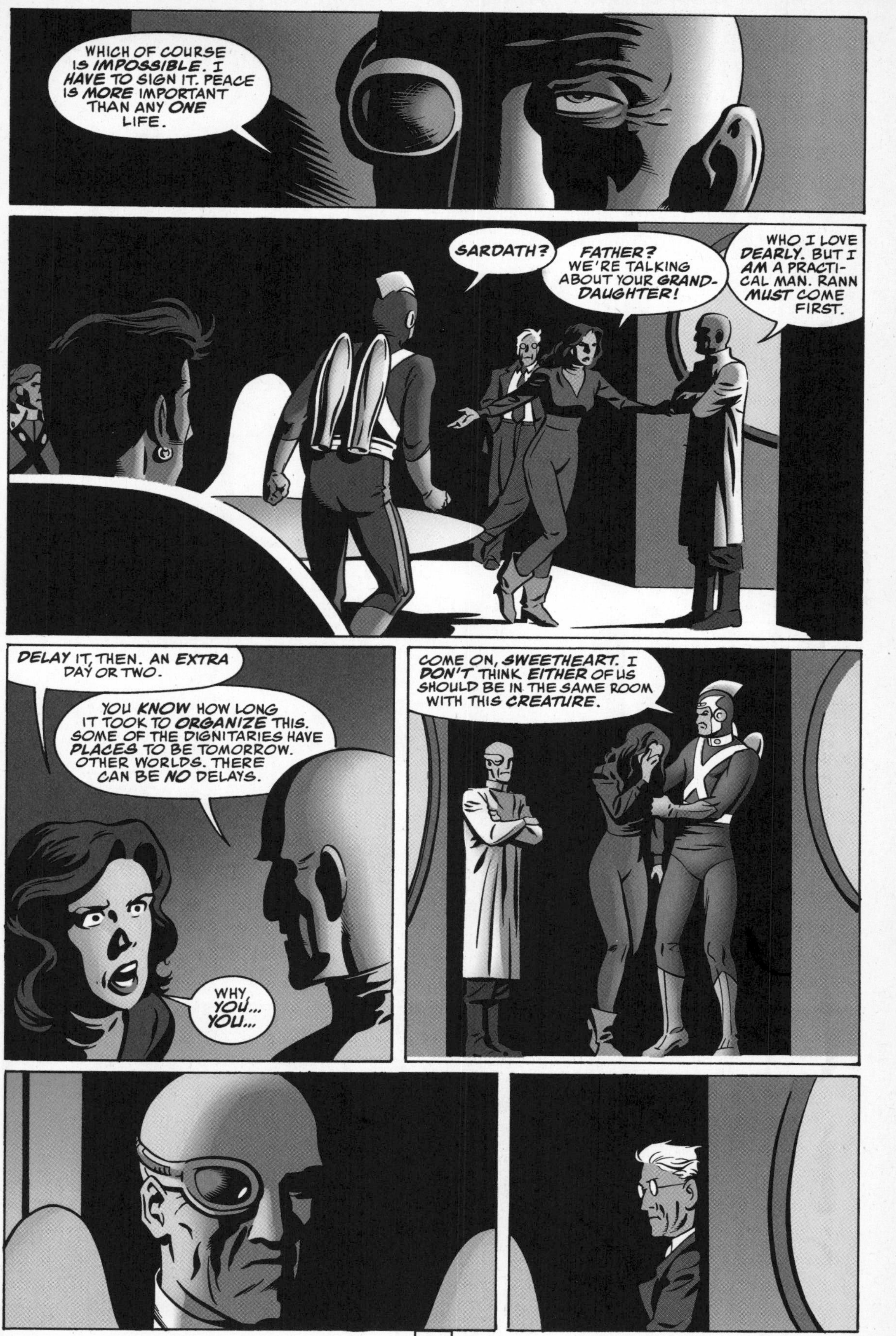
WHICH OF COURSE IS IMPOSSIBLE. I HAVE TO SIGN IT. PEACE IS MORE IMPORTANT THAN ANY ONE LIFE.
SARDATH?
FATHER? WE'RE TALKING ABOUT YOUR GRAND-DAUGHTER!
WHO I LOVE DEARLY. BUT I AM A PRACTI-CAL MAN. RANN MUST COME FIRST.
DELAY IT, THEN. AN EXTRA DAY OR TWO.
YOU KNOW HOW LONG IT TOOK TO ORGANIZE THIS. SOME OF THE DIGNITARIES HAVE PLACES TO BE TOMORROW. OTHER WORLDS. THERE CAN BE NO DELAYS.
WHY, YOU... YOU...
COME ON, SWEETHEART. I DON'T THINK EITHER OF US SHOULD BE IN THE SAME ROOM WITH THIS CREATURE.

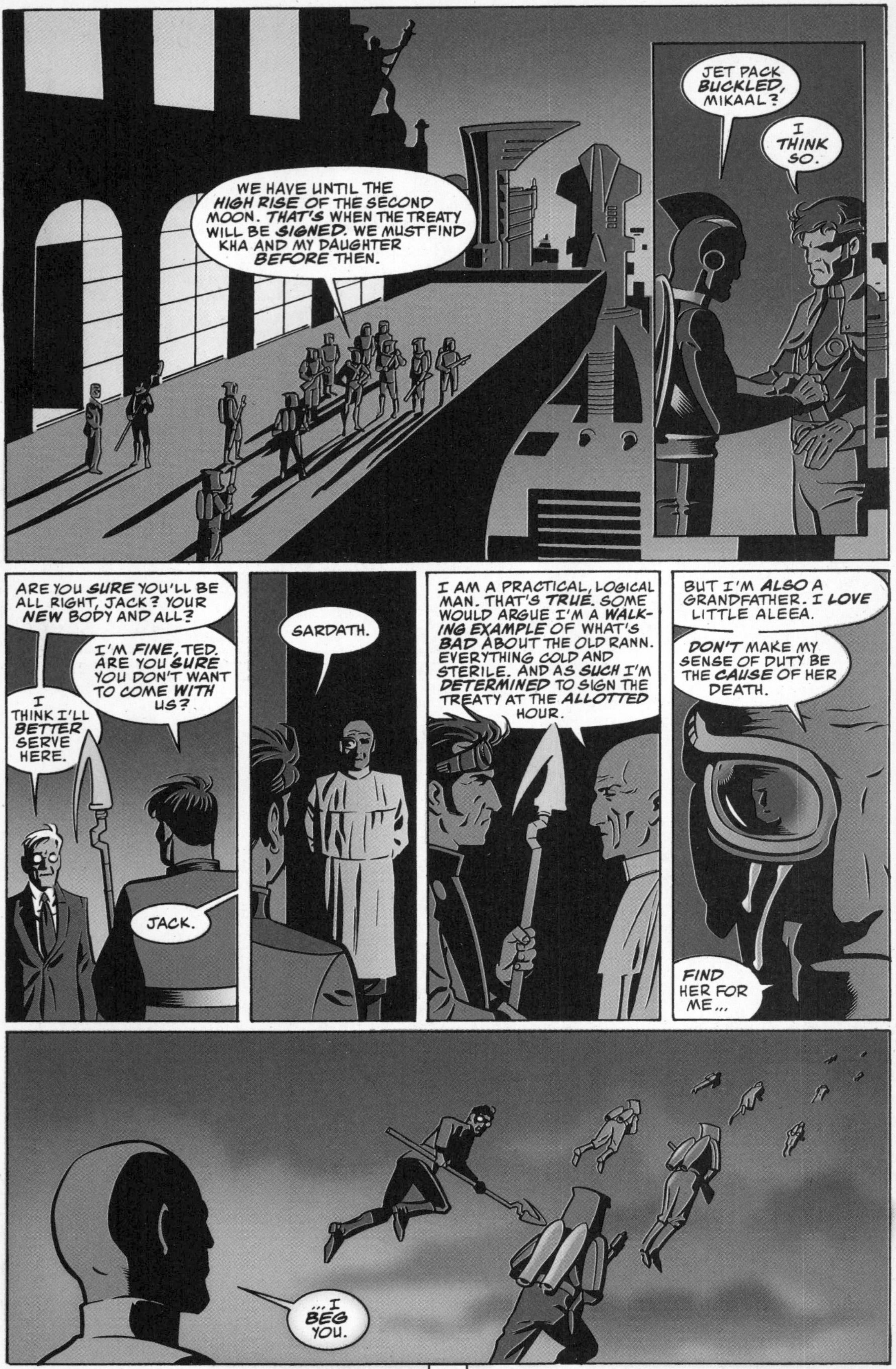
WE HAVE UNTIL THE HIGH RISE OF THE SECOND MOON. THAT'S WHEN THE TREATY WILL BE SIGNED. WE MUST FIND KHA AND MY DAUGHTER BEFORE THEN.
JET PACK BUCKLED, MIKAAL?
I THINK SO.
ARE YOU SURE YOU'LL BE ALL RIGHT, JACK? YOUR NEW BODY AND ALL?
I'M FINE, TED. ARE YOU SURE YOU DON'T WANT TO COME WITH US?
I THINK I'LL BETTER SERVE HERE.
JACK.
SARDATH.
I AM A PRACTICAL, LOGICAL MAN. THAT'S TRUE. SOME WOULD ARGUE I'M A WALKING EXAMPLE OF WHAT'S BAD ABOUT THE OLD RANN. EVERYTHING COLD AND STERILE. AND AS SUCH I'M DETERMINED TO SIGN THE TREATY AT THE ALLOTTED HOUR.
BUT I'M ALSO A GRANDFATHER. I LOVE LITTLE ALEEA.
DON'T MAKE MY SENSE OF DUTY BE THE CAUSE OF HER DEATH.
FIND HER FOR ME...
...I BEG YOU.

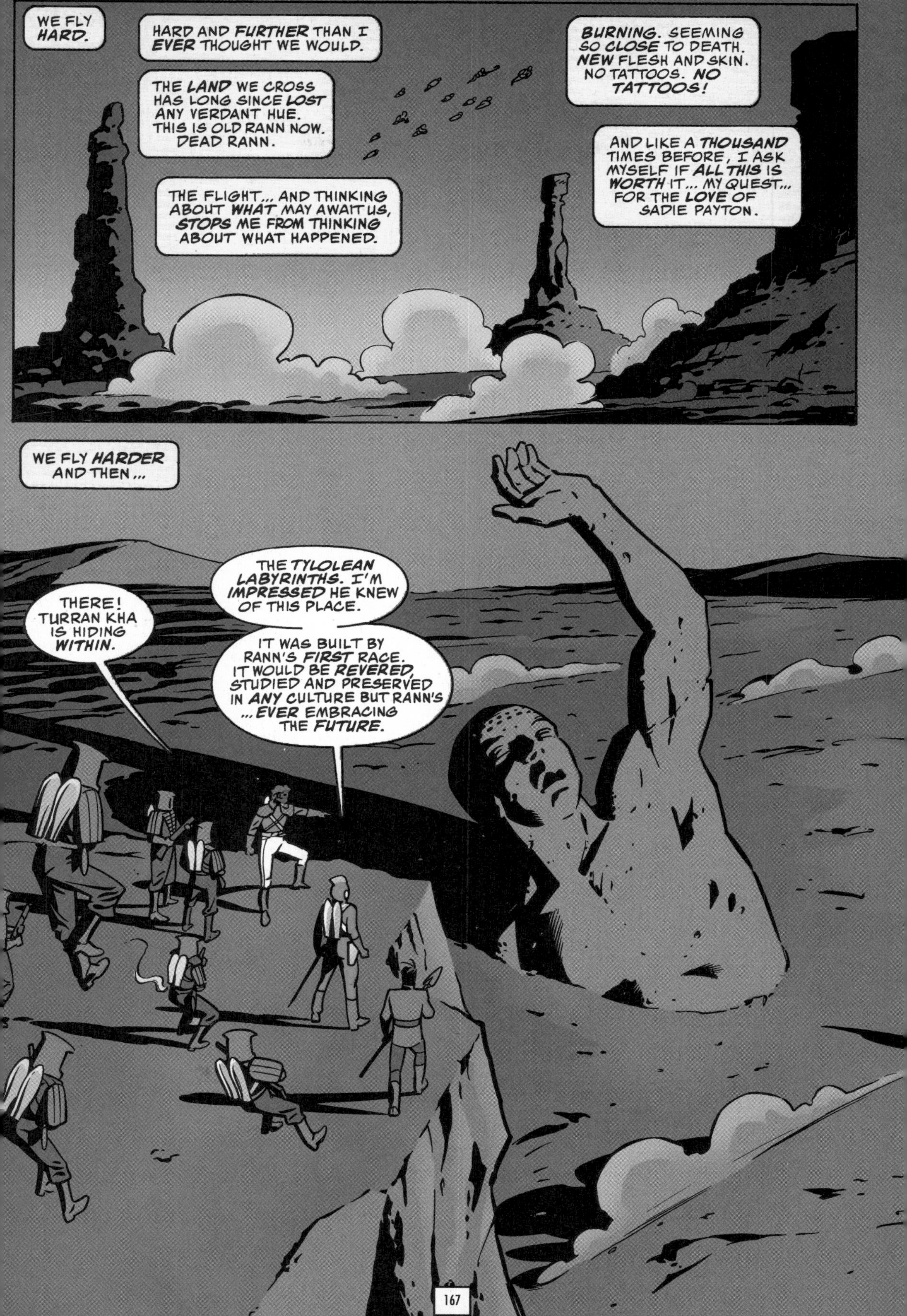
WE FLY HARD.
HARD AND FURTHER THAN I EVER THOUGHT WE WOULD.
THE LAND WE CROSS HAS LONG SINCE LOST ANY VERDANT HUE. THIS IS OLD RANN NOW. DEAD RANN.
THE FLIGHT... AND THINKING ABOUT WHAT MAY AWAIT US, STOPS ME FROM THINKING ABOUT WHAT HAPPENED.
BURNING. SEEMING SO CLOSE TO DEATH. NEW FLESH AND SKIN. NO TATTOOS. NO TATTOOS!
AND LIKE A THOUSAND TIMES BEFORE, I ASK MYSELF IF ALL THIS IS WORTH IT... MY QUEST... FOR THE LOVE OF SADIE PAYTON.
WE FLY HARDER AND THEN...
THERE! TURRAN KHA IS HIDING WITHIN.
THE TYLOLEAN LABYRINTHS. I'M IMPRESSED HE KNEW OF THIS PLACE.
IT WAS BUILT BY RANN'S FIRST RACE. IT WOULD BE REVERED, STUDIED AND PRESERVED IN ANY CULTURE BUT RANN'S ...EVER EMBRACING THE FUTURE.

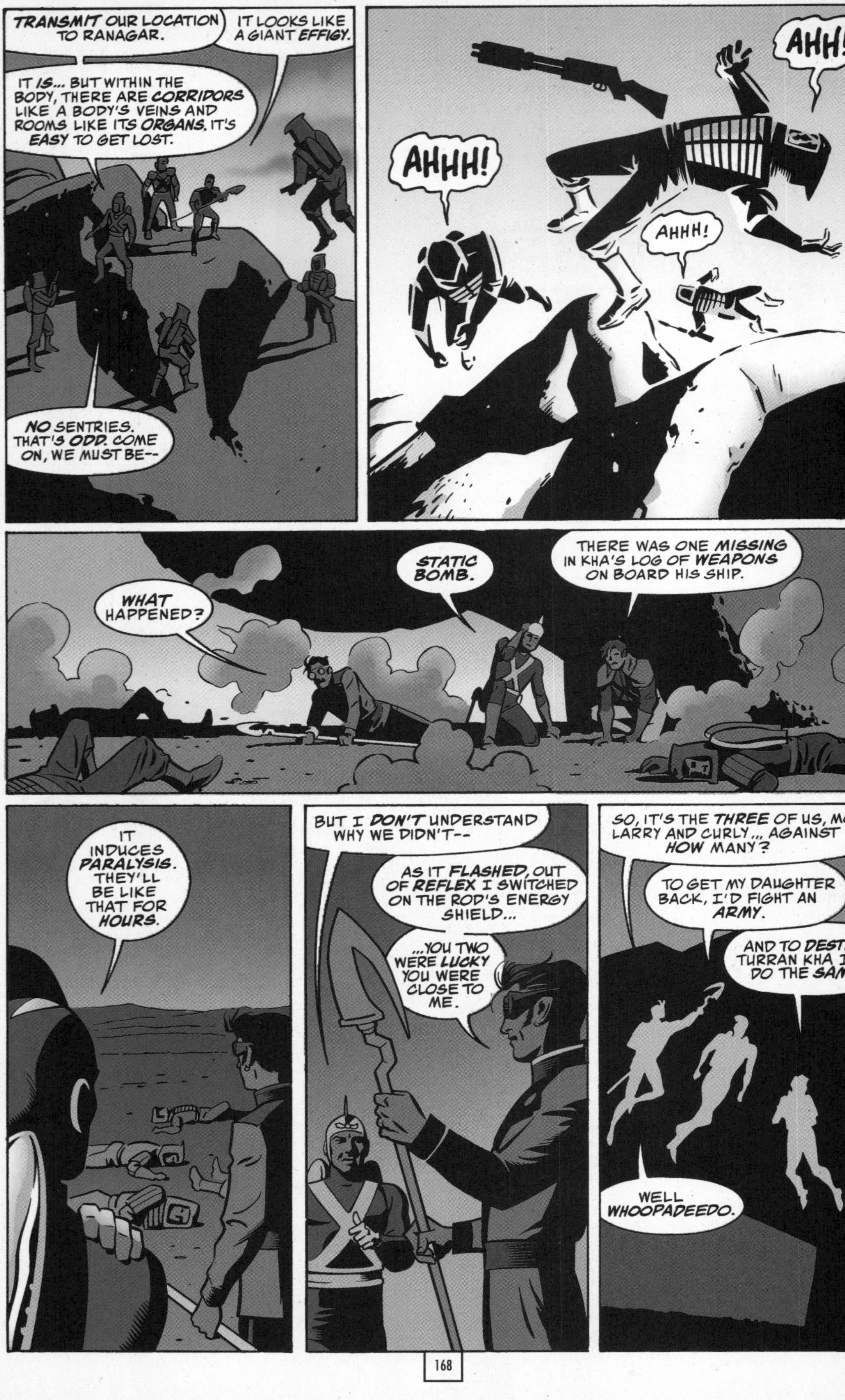

TRANSMIT OUR LOCATION TO RANAGAR.
IT LOOKS LIKE A GIANT EFFIGY.
IT IS... BUT WITHIN THE BODY, THERE ARE CORRIDORS LIKE A BODY'S VEINS AND ROOMS LIKE ITS ORGANS. IT'S EASY TO GET LOST.
NO SENTRIES. THAT'S ODD. COME ON, WE MUST BE--
AHH!
AHHH!
AHHH!
WHAT HAPPENED?
STATIC BOMB.
THERE WAS ONE MISSING IN KHA'S LOG OF WEAPONS ON BOARD HIS SHIP.
IT INDUCES PARALYSIS. THEY'LL BE LIKE THAT FOR HOURS.
BUT I DON'T UNDERSTAND WHY WE DIDN'T--
AS IT FLASHED, OUT OF REFLEX I SWITCHED ON THE ROD'S ENERGY SHIELD...
...YOU TWO WERE LUCKY YOU WERE CLOSE TO ME.
SO, IT'S THE THREE OF US, MOE, LARRY AND CURLY... AGAINST HOW MANY?
TO GET MY DAUGHTER BACK, I'D FIGHT AN ARMY.
AND TO DESTROY TURRAN KHA I'D DO THE SAME.
WELL WHOOPADEEDO.

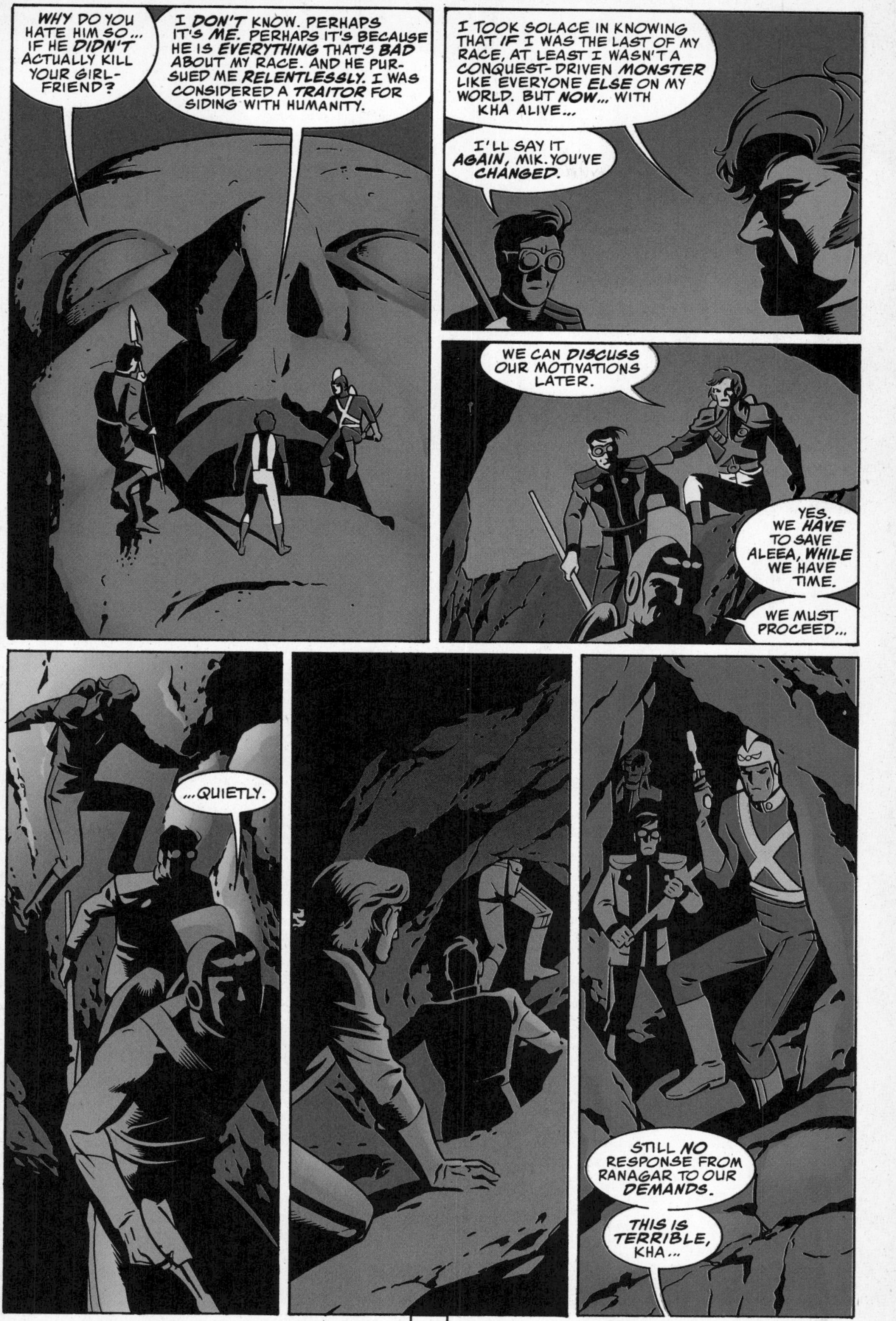
WHY DO YOU HATE HIM SO... IF HE DIDN'T ACTUALLY KILL YOUR GIRL-FRIEND?
I DON'T KNOW. PERHAPS IT'S ME. PERHAPS IT'S BECAUSE HE IS EVERYTHING THAT'S BAD ABOUT MY RACE. AND HE PURSUED ME RELENTLESSLY. I WAS CONSIDERED A TRAITOR FOR SIDING WITH HUMANITY.
I TOOK SOLACE IN KNOWING THAT IF I WAS THE LAST OF MY RACE, AT LEAST I WASN'T A CONQUEST-DRIVEN MONSTER LIKE EVERYONE ELSE ON MY WORLD. BUT NOW... WITH KHA ALIVE...
I'LL SAY IT AGAIN, MIK. YOU'VE CHANGED.
WE CAN DISCUSS OUR MOTIVATIONS LATER.
YES. WE HAVE TO SAVE ALEEA, WHILE WE HAVE TIME.
WE MUST PROCEED...
...QUIETLY.
STILL NO RESPONSE FROM RANAGAR TO OUR DEMANDS.
THIS IS TERRIBLE, KHA...

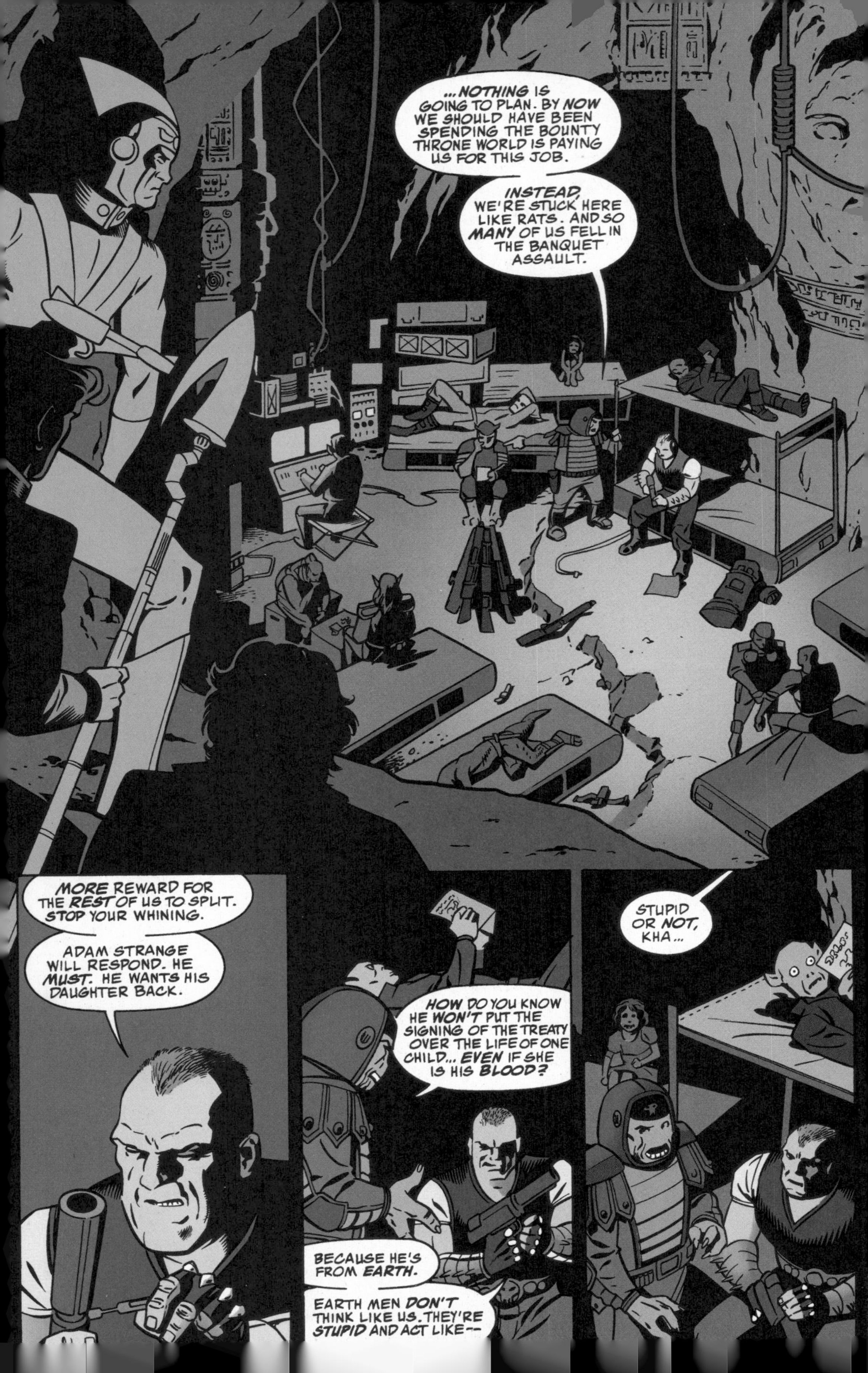
...NOTHING IS GOING TO PLAN. BY NOW WE SHOULD HAVE BEEN SPENDING THE BOUNTY THRONE WORLD IS PAYING US FOR THIS JOB.
INSTEAD, WE'RE STUCK HERE LIKE RATS. AND SO MANY OF US FELL IN THE BANQUET ASSAULT.
MORE REWARD FOR THE REST OF US TO SPLIT. STOP YOUR WHINING.
ADAM STRANGE WILL RESPOND. HE MUST. HE WANTS HIS DAUGHTER BACK.
HOW DO YOU KNOW HE WON'T PUT THE SIGNING OF THE TREATY OVER THE LIFE OF ONE CHILD... EVEN IF SHE IS HIS BLOOD?
BECAUSE HE'S FROM EARTH.
EARTH MEN DON'T THINK LIKE US. THEY'RE STUPID AND ACT LIKE--
STUPID OR NOT, KHA...

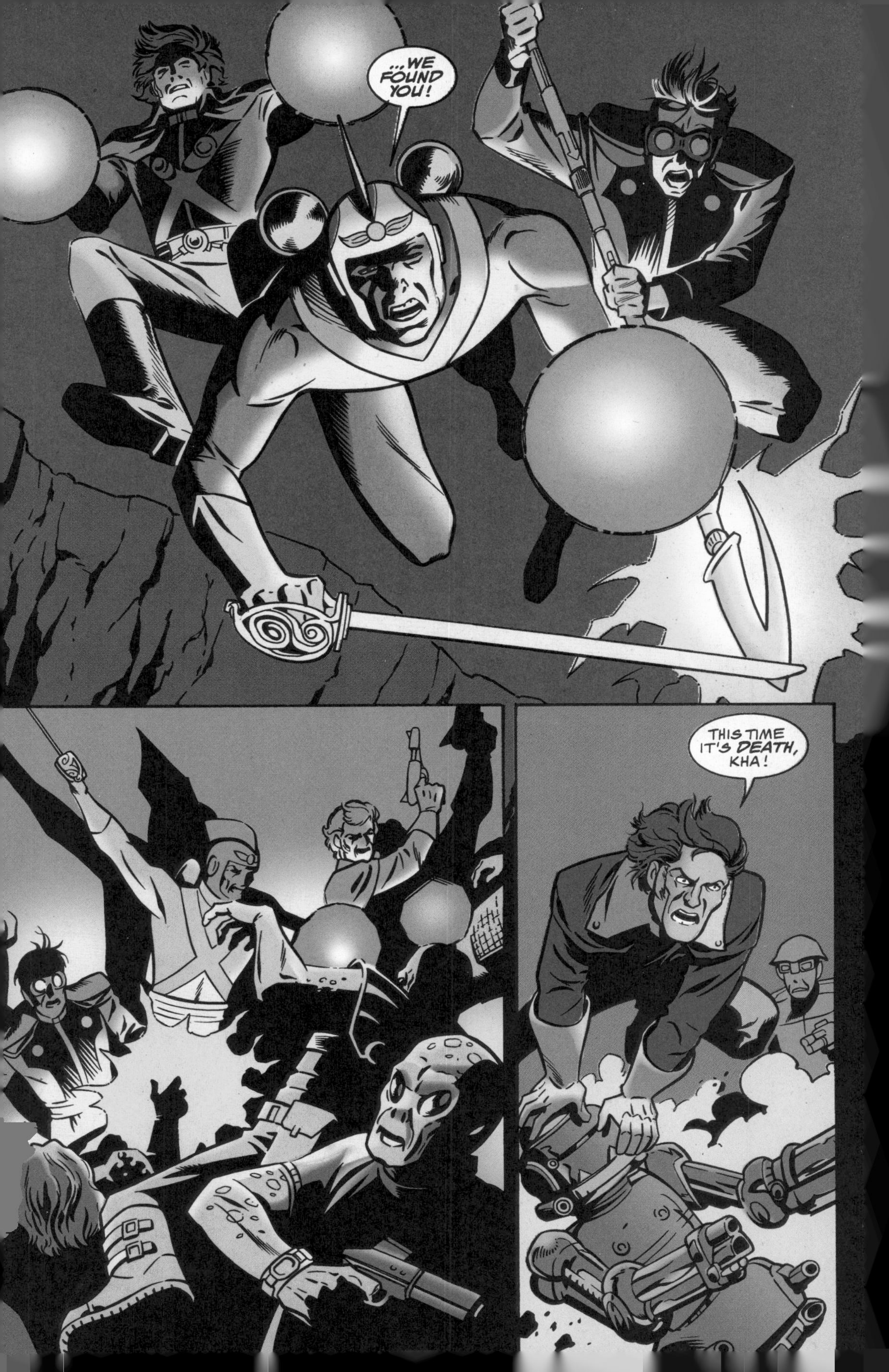
...WE FOUND YOU!
THIS TIME IT'S DEATH, KHA!

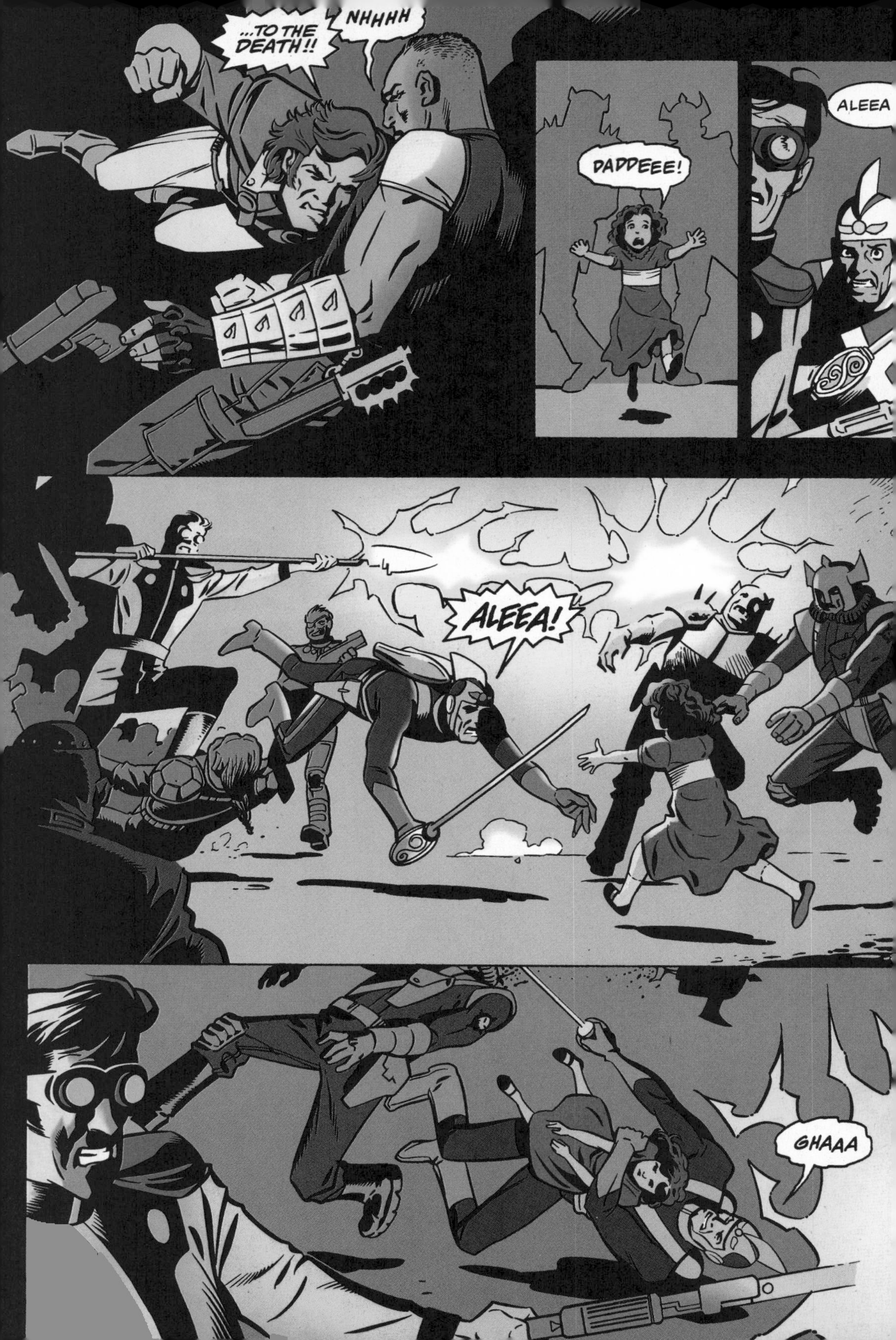
...TO THE DEATH!!
NHHHH
DADDEEE!
ALEEA
ALEEA!
GHAAA

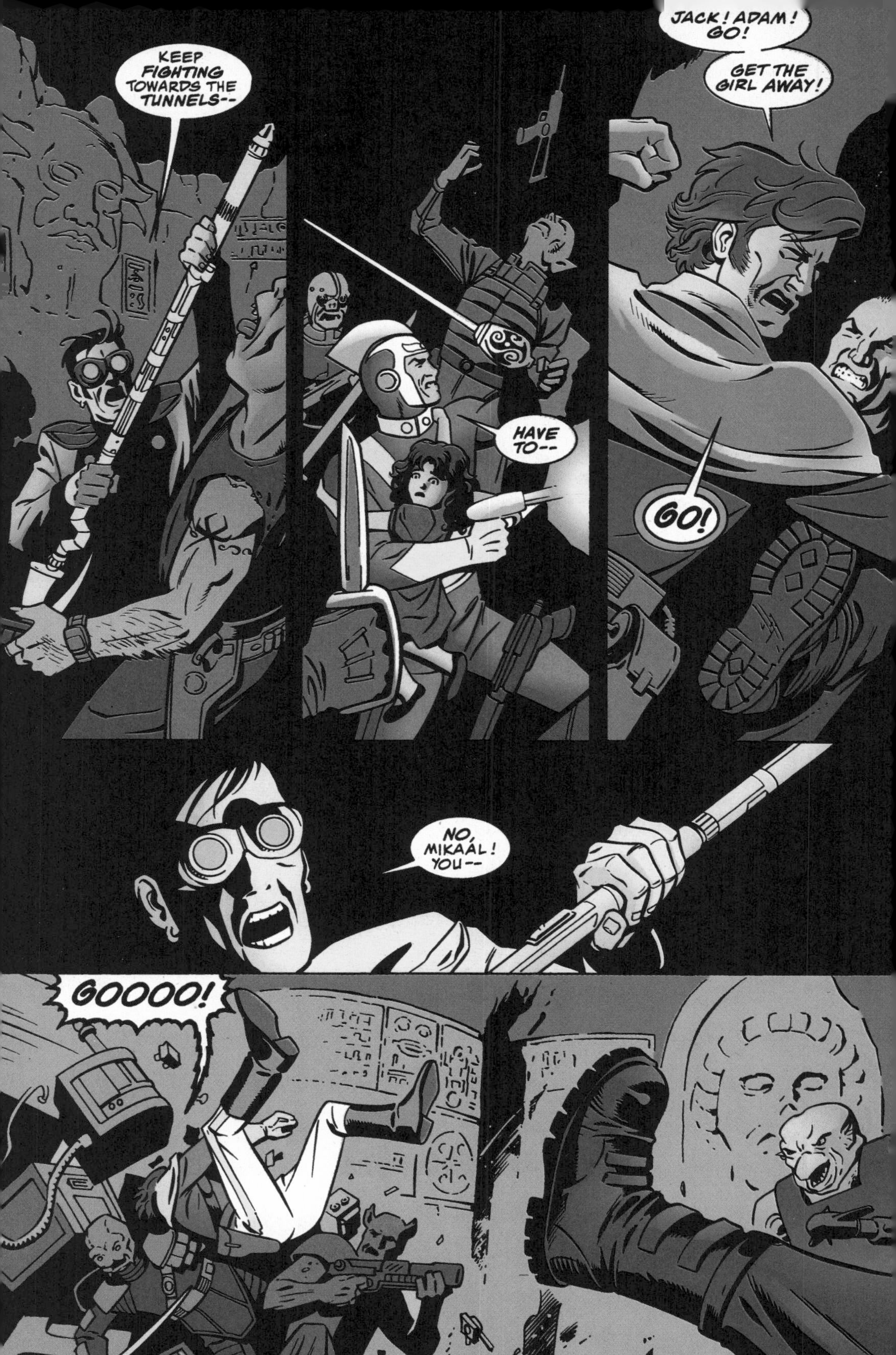
KEEP FIGHTING TOWARDS THE TUNNELS--
HAVE TO--
JACK! ADAM! GO!
GET THE GIRL AWAY!
GO!
NO, MIKAAL! YOU--
GOOOO!

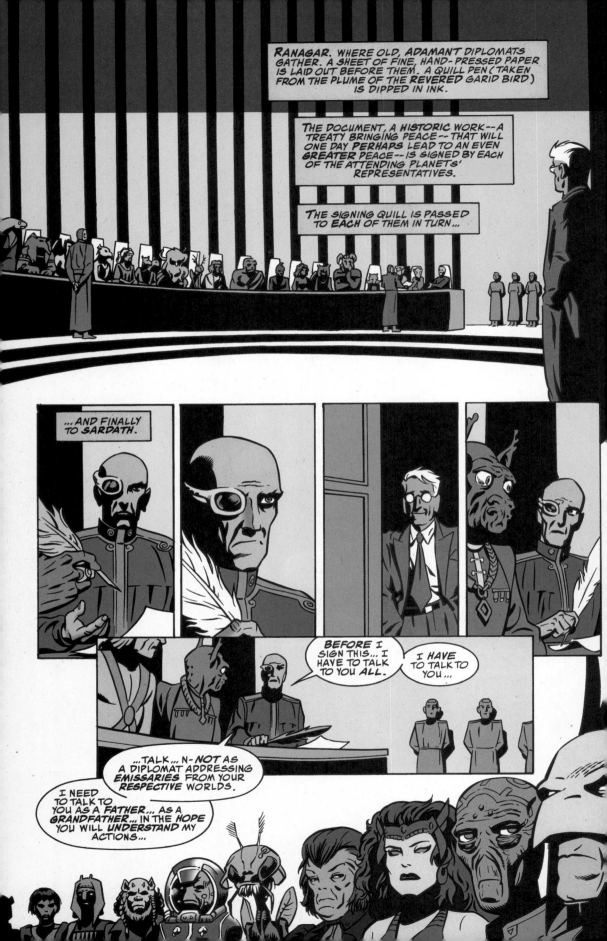

RANAGAR. WHERE OLD, ADAMANT DIPLOMATS GATHER. A SHEET OF FINE, HAND-PRESSED PAPER IS LAID OUT BEFORE THEM. A QUILL PEN (TAKEN FROM THE PLUME OF THE REVERED *GARID BIRD*) IS DIPPED IN INK.

THE DOCUMENT, A HISTORIC WORK--A TREATY BRINGING PEACE--THAT WILL ONE DAY *PERHAPS* LEAD TO AN EVEN *GREATER PEACE*--IS SIGNED BY EACH OF THE ATTENDING PLANETS' REPRESENTATIVES.

THE SIGNING QUILL IS PASSED TO *EACH* OF THEM IN TURN...

...AND FINALLY TO SARDATH.

BEFORE I SIGN THIS... I HAVE TO TALK TO YOU *ALL*.

I *HAVE* TO TALK TO YOU...

...TALK... N-NOT AS A DIPLOMAT ADDRESSING EMISSARIES FROM YOUR RESPECTIVE WORLDS.

I NEED TO TALK TO YOU AS A *FATHER*... AS A *GRANDFATHER*... IN THE HOPE YOU WILL *UNDERSTAND* MY ACTIONS...

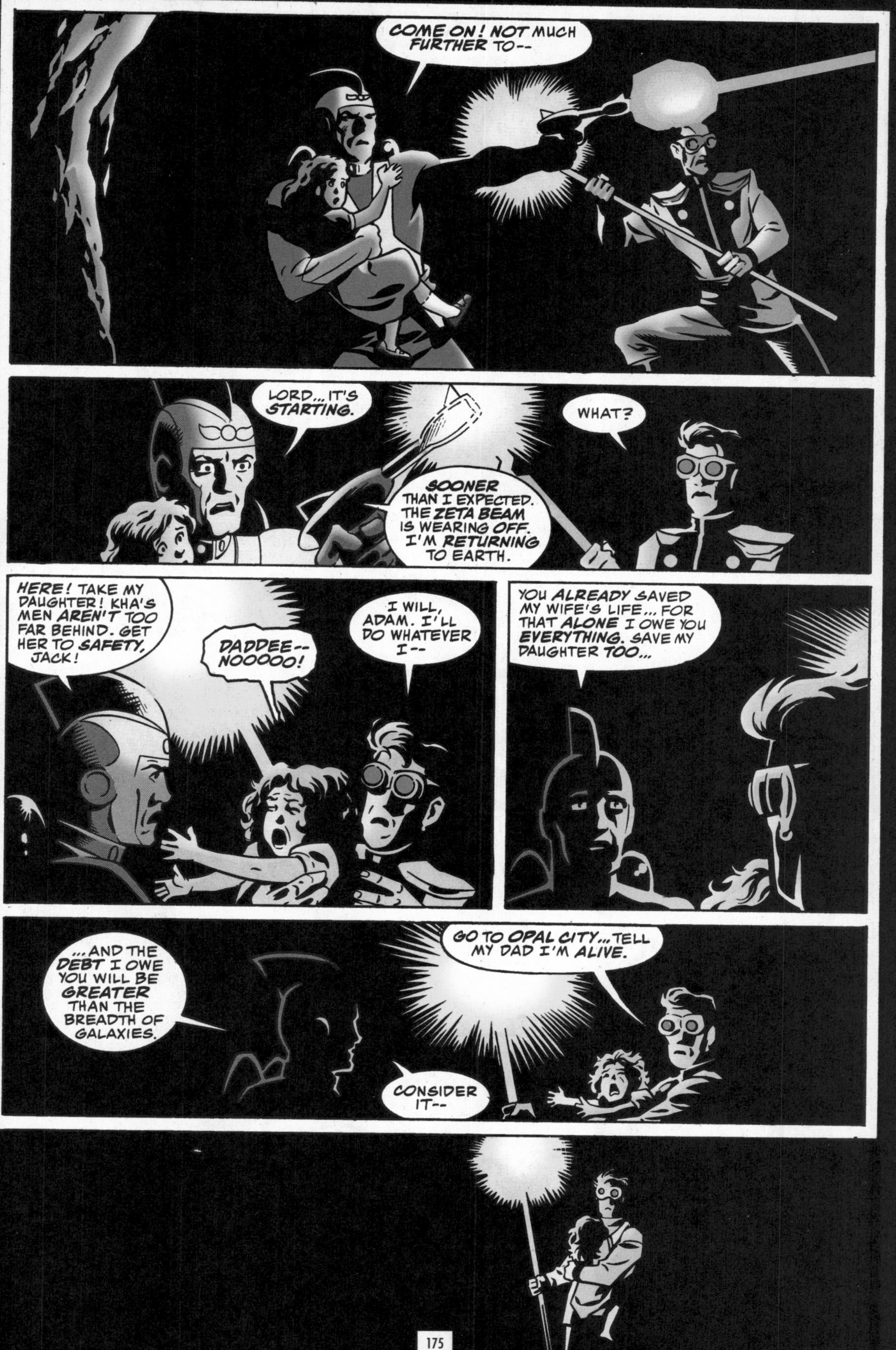
COME ON! NOT MUCH FURTHER TO--
LORD... IT'S STARTING.
WHAT?
SOONER THAN I EXPECTED. THE ZETA BEAM IS WEARING OFF. I'M RETURNING TO EARTH.
HERE! TAKE MY DAUGHTER! KHA'S MEN AREN'T TOO FAR BEHIND. GET HER TO SAFETY, JACK!
DADDEE-- NOOOOO!
I WILL, ADAM. I'LL DO WHATEVER I--
YOU ALREADY SAVED MY WIFE'S LIFE... FOR THAT ALONE I OWE YOU EVERYTHING. SAVE MY DAUGHTER TOO...
...AND THE DEBT I OWE YOU WILL BE GREATER THAN THE BREADTH OF GALAXIES.
GO TO OPAL CITY... TELL MY DAD I'M ALIVE.
CONSIDER IT--

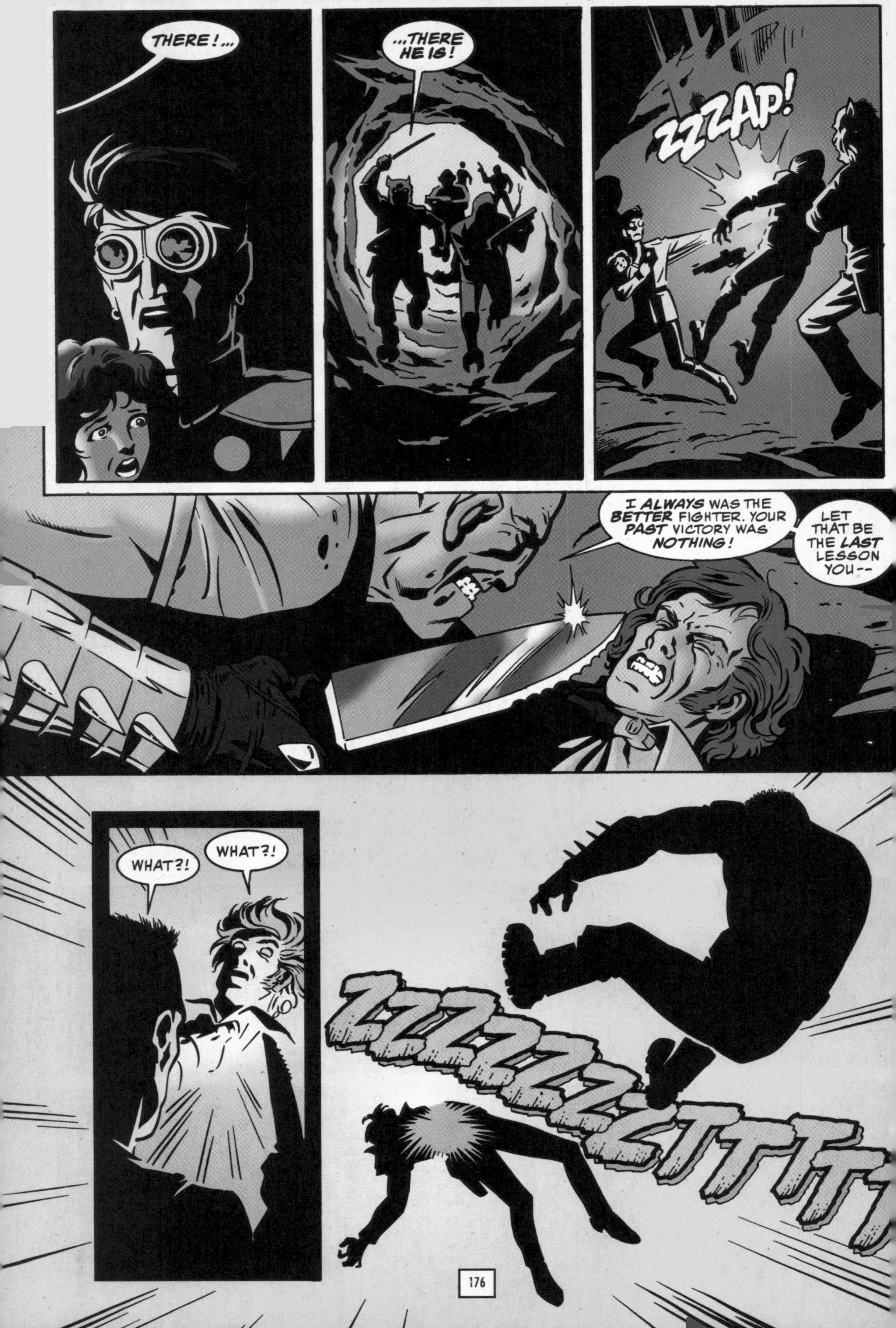

THERE!...
...THERE HE IS!
ZZZAP!
I ALWAYS WAS THE BETTER FIGHTER. YOUR PAST VICTORY WAS NOTHING!
LET THAT BE THE LAST LESSON YOU--
WHAT?!
WHAT?!
ZZZZZZZTTTTT

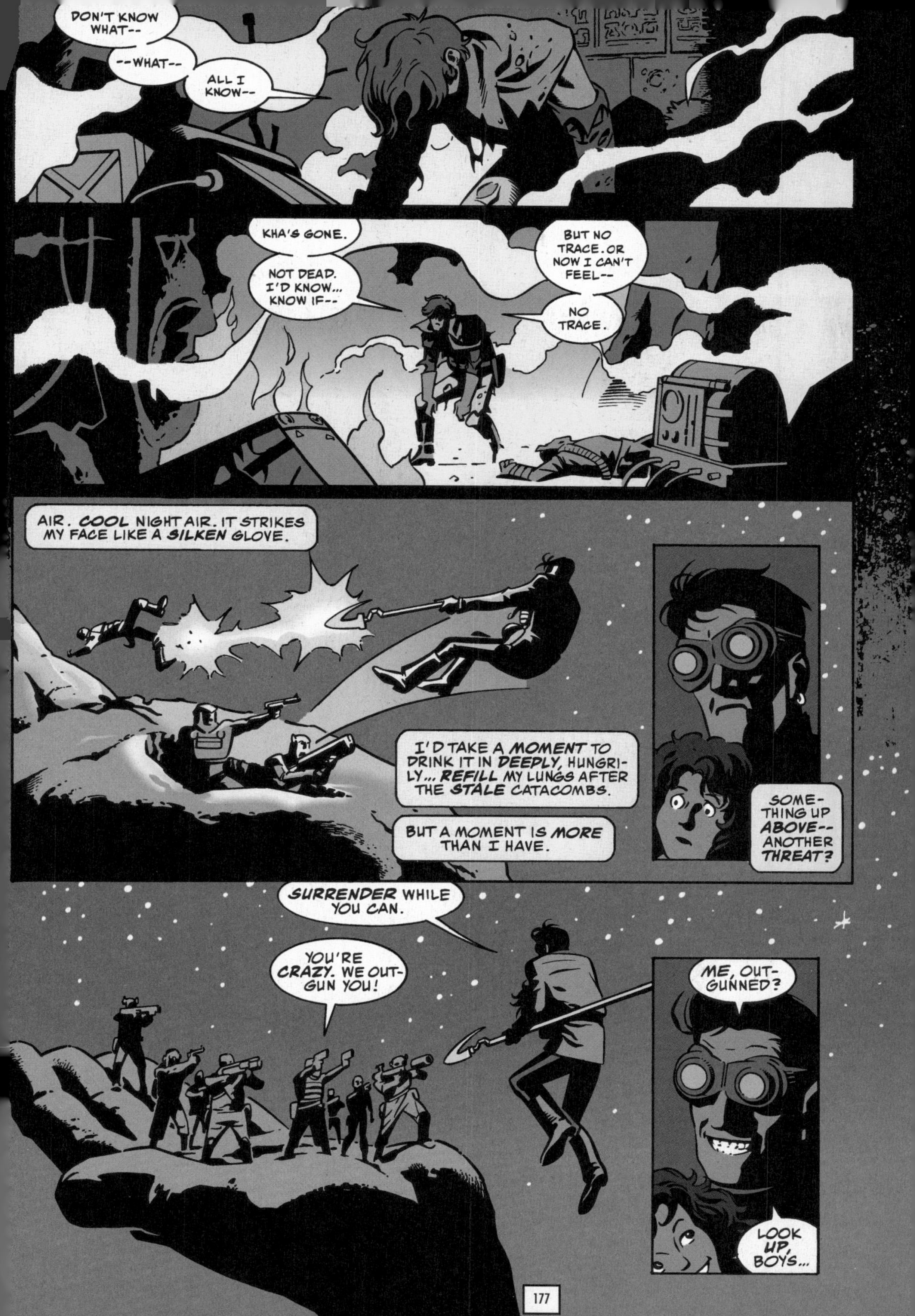
DON'T KNOW WHAT--
--WHAT--
ALL I KNOW--
KHA'S GONE.
NOT DEAD. I'D KNOW... KNOW IF--
BUT NO TRACE. OR NOW I CAN'T FEEL--
NO TRACE.
AIR. COOL NIGHT AIR. IT STRIKES MY FACE LIKE A SILKEN GLOVE.
I'D TAKE A MOMENT TO DRINK IT IN DEEPLY, HUNGRILY... REFILL MY LUNGS AFTER THE STALE CATACOMBS.
BUT A MOMENT IS MORE THAN I HAVE.
SOMETHING UP ABOVE--ANOTHER THREAT?
SURRENDER WHILE YOU CAN.
YOU'RE CRAZY. WE OUTGUN YOU!
ME, OUTGUNNED?
LOOK UP, BOYS...

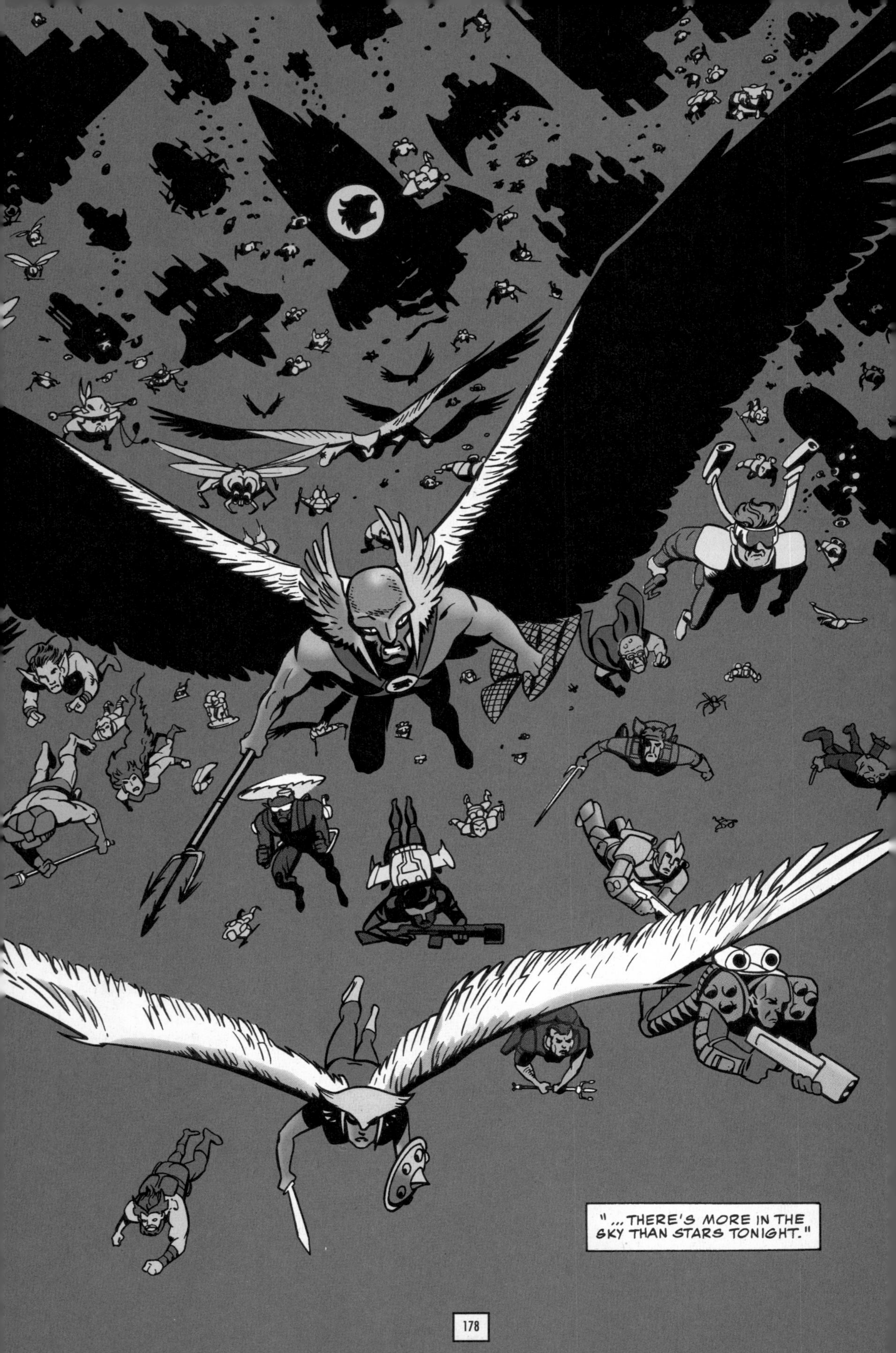
"...THERE'S MORE IN THE SKY THAN STARS TONIGHT."

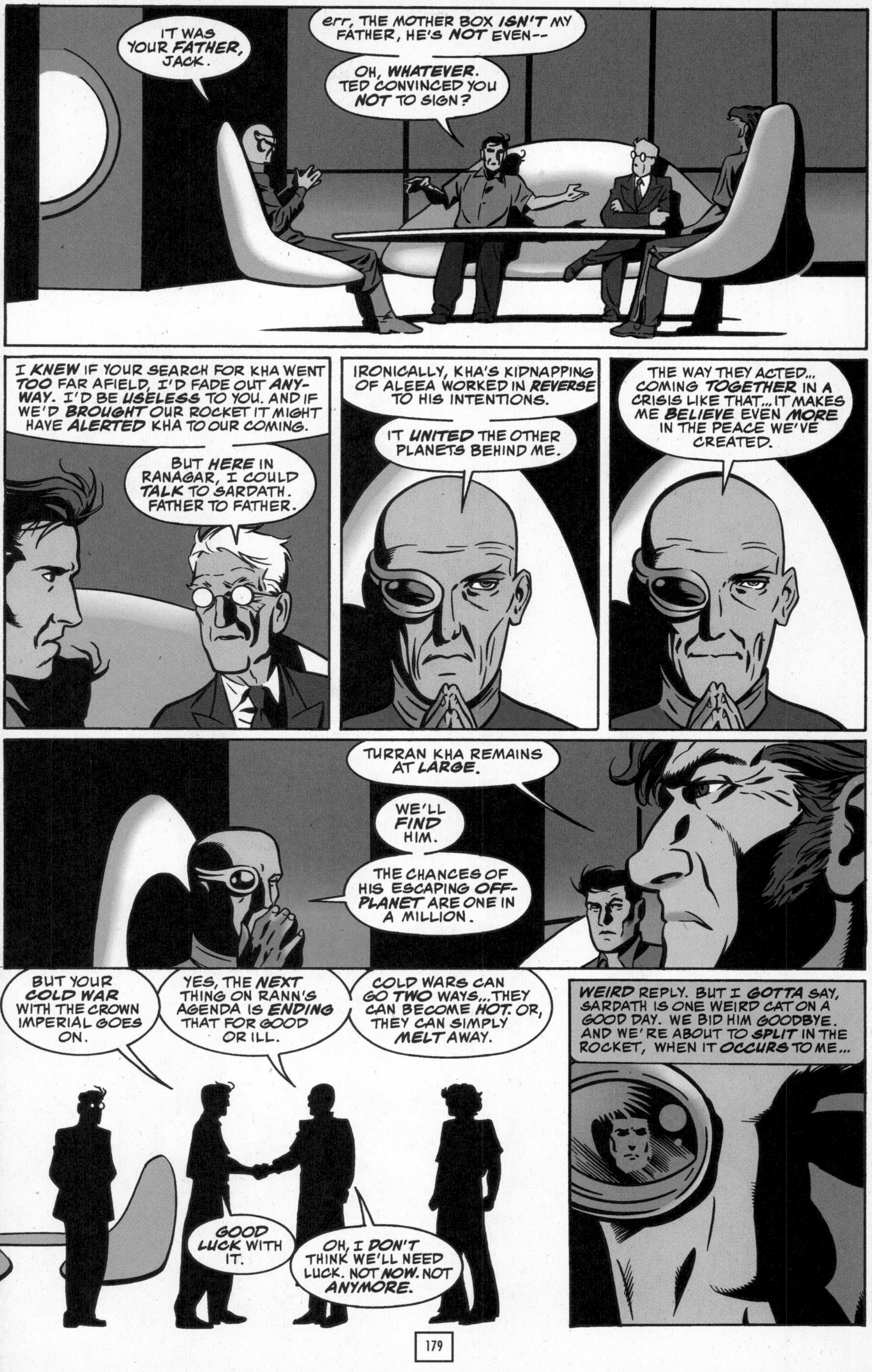
IT WAS YOUR FATHER, JACK.
err, THE MOTHER BOX ISN'T MY FATHER, HE'S NOT EVEN--
OH, WHATEVER. TED CONVINCED YOU NOT TO SIGN?
I KNEW IF YOUR SEARCH FOR KHA WENT TOO FAR AFIELD, I'D FADE OUT ANYWAY. I'D BE USELESS TO YOU. AND IF WE'D BROUGHT OUR ROCKET IT MIGHT HAVE ALERTED KHA TO OUR COMING.
BUT HERE IN RANAGAR, I COULD TALK TO SARDATH. FATHER TO FATHER.
IRONICALLY, KHA'S KIDNAPPING OF ALEEA WORKED IN REVERSE TO HIS INTENTIONS.
IT UNITED THE OTHER PLANETS BEHIND ME.
THE WAY THEY ACTED... COMING TOGETHER IN A CRISIS LIKE THAT... IT MAKES ME BELIEVE EVEN MORE IN THE PEACE WE'VE CREATED.
TURRAN KHA REMAINS AT LARGE.
WE'LL FIND HIM.
THE CHANCES OF HIS ESCAPING OFF-PLANET ARE ONE IN A MILLION.
BUT YOUR COLD WAR WITH THE CROWN IMPERIAL GOES ON.
YES, THE NEXT THING ON RANN'S AGENDA IS ENDING THAT FOR GOOD OR ILL.
COLD WARS CAN GO TWO WAYS... THEY CAN BECOME HOT. OR, THEY CAN SIMPLY MELT AWAY.
GOOD LUCK WITH IT.
OH, I DON'T THINK WE'LL NEED LUCK. NOT NOW. NOT ANYMORE.
WEIRD REPLY. BUT I GOTTA SAY, SARDATH IS ONE WEIRD CAT ON A GOOD DAY. WE BID HIM GOODBYE. AND WE'RE ABOUT TO SPLIT IN THE ROCKET, WHEN IT OCCURS TO ME...

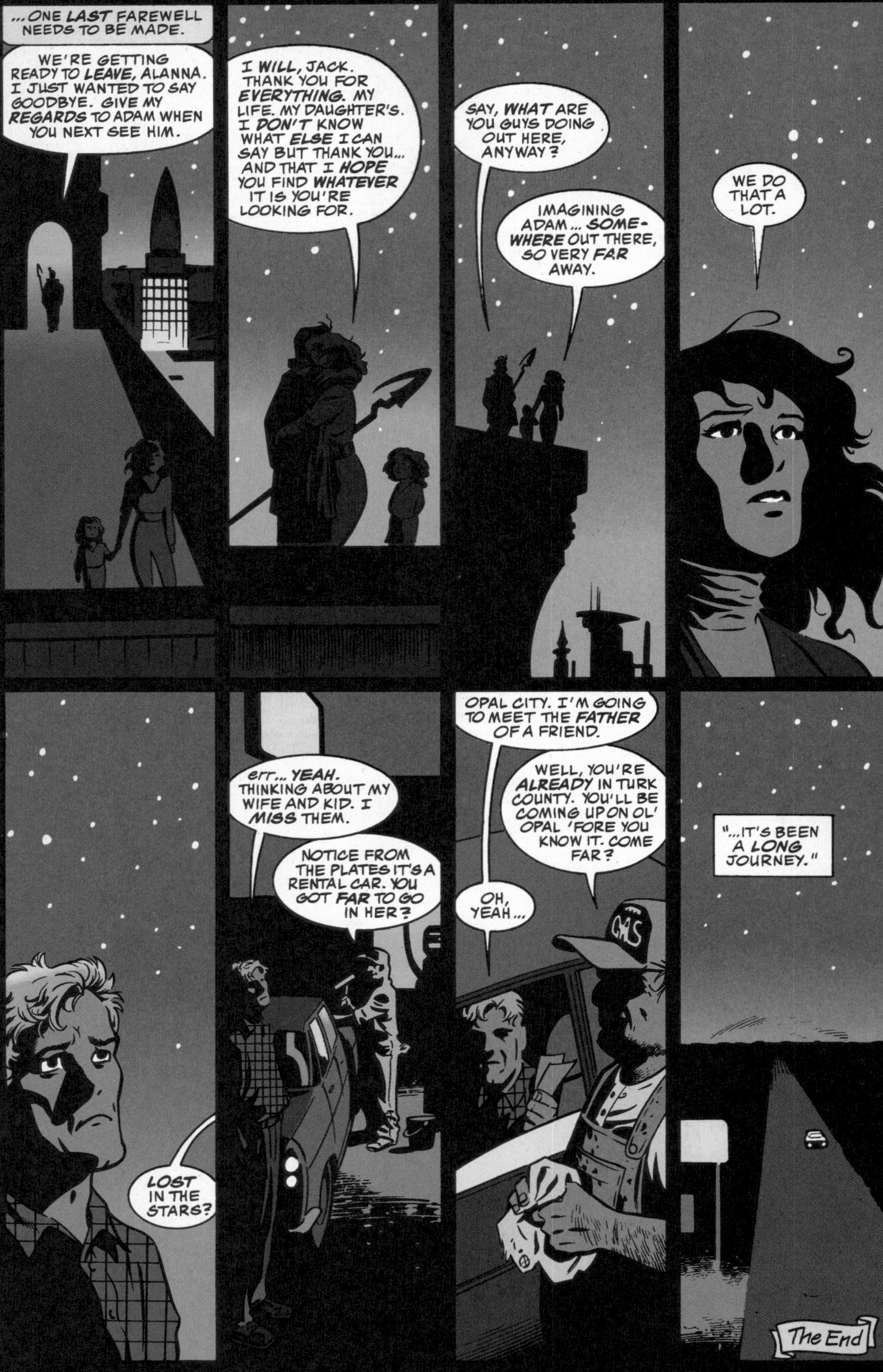
...ONE LAST FAREWELL NEEDS TO BE MADE.
WE'RE GETTING READY TO LEAVE, ALANNA. I JUST WANTED TO SAY GOODBYE. GIVE MY REGARDS TO ADAM WHEN YOU NEXT SEE HIM.
I WILL, JACK. THANK YOU FOR EVERYTHING. MY LIFE. MY DAUGHTER'S. I DON'T KNOW WHAT ELSE I CAN SAY BUT THANK YOU... AND THAT I HOPE YOU FIND WHATEVER IT IS YOU'RE LOOKING FOR.
SAY, WHAT ARE YOU GUYS DOING OUT HERE, ANYWAY?
IMAGINING ADAM... SOME-WHERE OUT THERE, SO VERY FAR AWAY.
WE DO THAT A LOT.
LOST IN THE STARS?
err... YEAH. THINKING ABOUT MY WIFE AND KID. I MISS THEM.
NOTICE FROM THE PLATES IT'S A RENTAL CAR. YOU GOT FAR TO GO IN HER?
OPAL CITY. I'M GOING TO MEET THE FATHER OF A FRIEND.
WELL, YOU'RE ALREADY IN TURK COUNTY. YOU'LL BE COMING UP ON OL' OPAL 'FORE YOU KNOW IT. COME FAR?
OH, YEAH...
"...IT'S BEEN A LONG JOURNEY."
The End